CHELMSFORD 2012

Many Hearts One Mind

By

Michael Haley

First Published in Great Britain 2014 by Mirador Publishing

Copyright © 2014 by Michael Haley

All rights reserved. No part of this publication may be reproduced or transmitted, in any form or by any means, without permission of the publishers or author. Excepting brief quotes used in reviews.

First edition: 2014

Any reference to real names and places are purely fictional and are constructs of the author. Any offence the references produce is unintentional and in no way reflects the reality of any locations or people involved.

A copy of this work is available through the British Library.

ISBN: 978-1-910104-76-7

Mirador Publishing
Mirador
Wearne Lane
Langport
Somerset
TA10 9HB

FOREWORD

Happy Accidents

This book is a happy accident. Perhaps, in Dickenspeak it is a fortuitous happenstance. In fact it is the result of a series of happy accidents.

Before this year I had never intended to write a novel, or imagined that I would be motivated to do so. Back in the late 90's I had written a book which I called "Taking Chances, Making Choices", which was a biographical account of my struggle with heart problems, and subsequent recovery. Apart from friends and relatives, few people have read it, and the British Heart Foundation was actively disinterested in even taking a look at it. Possibilities for writing anything substantial and having it published were minimal. So bearing that in mind, I feel an explanation may be necessary to illustrate how I came to a situation where this work was written.

Ever since I was a teenager I had been writing poems, and after taking up playing the guitar in 1967, I began writing songs. Writing had never been a raison d'être, and over the years has often not so much taken a back seat, but has been clinging on by a fingertip to the back bumper. In the late 90's I had retired from doing proper jobs for a living, and had more time on my hands, and the quality of my guitar playing and song-writing improved immensely. So much so, that I recorded many of my self-penned songs at a local studio called Amber Sound and Light, in Navigation Road in Chelmsford, now sadly long demised and sorely missed.

I busked in Chelmsford Town Centre in the much favoured spot of the Moulsham Street underpass before the street level crossing was constructed and ruined the potential. For a brief period in the year 2000 I ran the Evelyn Wood Folk Club in Widford Road. I've performed in the bands at the Church of the Holy Spirit in Forest Drive, and Holy Trinity Church in Springfield during a period from 2000 to 2007. Playing guitar in church bands helped me in honing my expertise, and enjoying the experience of working with other musicians. In 2003 I began teaching guitar, and eventually I and some of my pupils formed a band called Redberryash, and played regularly at local open mike sessions in various venues throughout Essex.

After more than 10 years of performing either solo or together with many different groups of friends, in 2008 Redberryash folded due to what's usually termed as musical differences, and my 7 year relationship with church bands also came to an end.

The world had moved on, and not only were my own songs seemingly stuck in a 70's time-warp, I was obviously too old to contemplate an appearance on the X-Factor, or a career in music. However, I was content with my creations and the very limited success that they brought me. I carried on with teaching guitar, and during the next year I wrote a guitar instruction manual. As the recession began to bite harder this work dried up, and ironically I lost my last customer just as I completed writing the manual.

This was a difficult time for me personally with relationship problems, depression, and counselling, and during this period I was hiding away like a hermit. I had to find a way out of the rut!

Through a referral from trusted friend, I began yet another counselling programme in June 2011, and from the skill and patience of someone I shall just call Jan, I began to climb out of my self imposed pit. During the six months of counselling I booked myself on an Adult Education Course called Creative Writing - Beginners and this became the launch pad for my renewed interest in writing.

Then came the first happy accident.

Due to other commitments I could not attend the Creative Writing Course in Chelmsford, and therefore came to the alternative option of attending the course at the Friary in Maldon. The first of 10 sessions started on 29th September, 2011. There were probably 20 people there, who all had different reasons for attending. When It came to my turn to introduce myself, I explained how I'd been writing poems and songs since the dinosaurs roamed the Earth, but that I'd recently dried up, and was on the course to try and spark my writing back into life. I quickly discovered what fine illustrious company I was in.

The course tutor was a lady called Maggie Freeman, and she was a patient, responsive and inventive tutor, and treated everyone with the same courtesy and respect. Gradually the process of reading my work out loud to the rest of the group became something that was exciting, rather than making me cringe with embarrassment.

On the 2nd week we were set a long term project to write something to be presented to the group after the half term break. For some reason which escapes me now, it was called the "Green project". Then there was happy accident number two.

A few weeks later I was getting off the Park and Ride bus at Sandon, when I bumped into Maggie Freeman and took the opportunity to ask permission to create my "Green project" as a song, and to bring my guitar along and perform it at the post half term session. She seemed delighted. So much so, that I recall her when next referring to the Green project, telling everyone about my forthcoming performance. Now I couldn't let them down.

A few weeks later, I nervously performed a song called "Last Song for You". It was the first time I'd performed in public for over 3 years. The song was well received, and it felt good to be back in the saddle. I listened to all the other stories penned by the project contributors, and marvelled at their superb wordsmith expertise. At that stage I was still writing poems and song lyrics and not stories. Over the next few weeks, other writers presented pieces that I had the privilege of putting to music for them, and then performing at the Friary sessions.

Soon we were set another project, to be presented at the last session on 8th December, and this was to have a Christmas theme with the working title of the "Walnut project". The outcome of this work for me was a song called "Talking Remember Road Blues" which I performed at the last session in December 2011.

The creative juices were really beginning to flow now, and in the meantime I had written and performed another song called "Wicked Angels, Luscious Demons". When the Creative Writing - Beginners was over it had achieved for me, exactly what I wanted. I was writing again, had fresh motivation, and had met some lovely inspirational people in the process. I had no hesitation in enrolling for the follow-up course.

Creative Writing - Improvers started on 12th January, 2012, again at the Friary in Maldon. Maggie had encouraged those who were intending to follow on as improvers to continue to write, with what was this time called he "Doors project". For me several pieces of writing developed from that, but the one I consider most worthy of note was a song called "Tricks with Time".

When we resumed with the Improvers Course and another 10 weeks of writing ahead, it was brilliant to see old friends, and to meet some new ones. We continued in the same vein, with a core of about 10 writers attending each week, every one with unique and personal talents for writing. Many of the lovely people on the course, who in the meantime have become good friends, were also interested in writing not only short stories and novels, but also poetry.

By the time this course was finishing my writing had become quite prolific. There were many pieces that stood out, all songs, but my choice as the best was "Departures".

Around the time that the course finished I had written a song called "Dangerous Curves". The inspiration for this song came initially while I was driving along the Baddow bypass into Chelmsford, and being tailgated by someone driving a Porsche. With a little invention and imagination, I drew a mental picture of the young man who was pushing me along. The title actually came from a book I had been reading at the time about dwindling global oil resources. When I googled the words "Dangerous Curves" some time later, I learned that there are Simpsons connections, and also some interesting websites glorifying large ladies like Mae West and Jayne Mansfield.

When the Improvers Course came to an end on 29th March, 2012, the group members resolved to carry on independently with our own writing group, and so now we meet every month in the White Horse in Mundon. This is a very informal group, but we have quickly evolved a format which works, so that everyone has a chance to present their work to the group for critique and encouragement.

After performing "Dangerous Curves" to the White Horse writing group, they decided to stick with this theme for the next piece of homework. And so we were asked to write a piece on why "Mr Porsche" behaved the way he did. At the next meeting this produced an enthralling variation of possibilities from all of the people attending the group. My response was to write a short story called "A few days in the life of a man with a Porsche." I had never written anything like it before. Perhaps this was the third happy accident?

When I read the story to the group I received an incredible amount of encouragement to turn the piece into a novel. I thought about it for few days, and then resolved to try and write something based upon my characters in the "Dangerous Curves" story, and to set the action in Chelmsford in the year 2012. So, with some amendments "A few days in the life of a man with a Porsche", became the first chapter of my novel, re-titled "A change from the Norm".

The original working title was "Chelmsford 2012 - Caesaromagus no more", but as I began to write, the content seemed to grow almost exponentially. Initially I worried about being able to cobble together the template norm of 100,000 words, but it wasn't long before my characters and plotlines expanded to over 200,000.

The writing process which began in May 2012 with the song "Dangerous Curves", was completed in October 2013 with the final chapter of 46 called "This time next year we'll be millionaires." (I wonder where that idea came from.)

Given the volume of the finished story I decided that it would be better to present the work as two separate novels. The first is titled "Chelmsford 2012 - Many Hearts One Mind", and the follow up will be called "First City of Essex - Many Diversions One Destination".

The lyrics for the songs "Last Song for You", "Talking Remember Road Blues", "Wicked Angels, Luscious Demons", "Tricks with Time", and "Departures", will be available at a later date, together with many of my other poems, song lyrics, and short stories which I am currently compiling into a collection called "Tall Words on a Wall."

DEDICATION

I have to mention a few names of lovely people I am indebted to, for listening to me and laughing with me, throughout and beyond the Creative Writing courses, and most of all, for encouraging me to attempt this work. Even if it means, as I have already discovered, that for long periods of time I have to revert to being a lonely hermit again, while I conjure up and record the exploits, rises and falls of my characters.

I give many thanks and wish good luck with their own writing to Estella Boxell-Hutson, Sheena Cundy, Gill Adams, Margaret King, Robert Chatterton, Christine McDonald, Victoria Rossiter, Jerry Beckett, Jack Dighton, Paul Ebbs, Peter Fox, Elaine Langford, Hazel Smith, Paul Brooks, Patricia Harris, Kerry Barr, Marion Lewis, Susan Cushway, Linda Ventris-Field, Alan Currie, Linda Dyer, Lorraine Rous, and Dennis Chinnery.

Most of all my biggest thanks must go to Maggie Freeman.

Dangerous Curves

Written by Michael Haley, 5th-10th April, 2012

I'm driving in my Porsche in the dead of night,
Roaring through the countryside, blazing headlights,
Pedal to the metal, squealing tyres and burning rubber,
Shifting through my gears beyond a hundred miles an hour,
I'm your tailgater and I'm bringing up your rear,
I don't want no motorways, no straight roads, or low gears,
Want to feel the G-force, the horsepower, and the swerve,
Man I'm just a petrol-head on dangerous curves,
Dangerous curves, dangerous curves,
Man I'm just a petrol-head on dangerous curves,
Running my wheels over dangerous curves,
Showing my skills on dangerous curves,
Moving in for the kill on dangerous curves,
Man I'm just a petrol-head on dangerous curves.

Dressed up in my finery for nightlife on the pull,
Wallet stuffed with ready cash, attitude full of bull (shit),
Not looking for that special someone, no just a one night stand,
No long term commitment babes, no-one ties my hands,
I'm God's gift to women, you know I'm the man,
Got the looks, got the dosh, ain't no also-ran,
No computer dating, can't get what I deserve,
Looking for a lady with dangerous curves,
Dangerous curves, dangerous curves,
Looking for a lady with dangerous curves,
Kissing and caressing those dangerous curves,
Counting my blessings for dangerous curves,
Ain't doing no confessing on dangerous curves,
Looking for a lady with dangerous curves.

I went to see the doctor, I was feeling below par,
Drove there at breakneck speed in my turbo charged car,
He fixed monitor wires to my body and my head,
He umm'd and ahh'd, and took some notes, and this is what he said,
I've been looking at your test results, so let's not pretend,

Someone here's been burning the candle at both ends,
You'd better slow down my friend, you been living on your nerves,
There's overwhelming evidence for dangerous curves,
Dangerous curves, dangerous curves,
There's overwhelming evidence for dangerous curves,
Live fast, die young, on dangerous curves,
Won't last too long on dangerous curves,
One day you'll die on dangerous curves,
There's overwhelming evidence for dangerous curves.

CREDITS

For song lyrics and quotations used

The Christian hymn, "Morning Has Broken" was first published in 1931. The words are by the English author Eleanor Farjeon, and the music is a traditional Scottish Gaelic tune known as "Bunessan". The folk singer Cat Stevens (now known as Yusuf Islam) included a version on his 1971 album Teaser and the Firecat.

The song, "My Way" was popularized by Frank Sinatra. The lyrics were written by Paul Anka and set to music based on the French song "Comme d'habitude" composed in 1967 by Claude François and Jacques Revaux. Anka's English lyrics are unrelated to the original French song.

The song, "Silver Machine" is by the UK space rock group Hawkwind, and was originally released as a single in June 1972. The music was composed by Dave Brock, and the lyrics were written by Robert Calvert, who sang the lead vocal on the original live recording.

The words, "The Lord's my Shepherd, I'll not want; He makes me down to lie. In pastures green; He leadeth me, the quiet waters by........" are from Psalm 23 and the Book of Common Prayer. Psalm 23 has become particularly associated with funeral liturgies in the English-speaking world.

The song, "All Things Bright and Beautiful" is an Anglican hymn. The words are by Cecil Frances Alexander and were first published in her Hymns for Little Children. It is usually sung to the 17th-century English melody "Royal Oak", adapted by Martin Shaw.

The words, "Man that is born of a woman hath but a short time to live ....." are from Job 14.1 and the Book of Common Prayer.

The words "Earth to earth, ashes to ashes, dust to dust ....." are from the Book of Common Prayer.

The words, "For when the One Great Scorer comes, to mark against your name, He writes - not that you won or lost - But how you played the Game." are accredited to the American sportswriter Grantland Rice.

The words, "She flies like bird..." are part of the song "I Can't Let Maggie Go" by the 1960's pop group Honeybus. The song was written Peter Dello and Ray Cane.

The song, "Snoopy vs. the Red Baron" was written by Phil Gernhard and Dick Holler and recorded in 1966 by the Florida-based pop group The Royal Guardsmen.

The song, "Those Magnificent Men in their Flying Machines" featured in the film of the same name starring Stuart Whitman, Sarah Miles, Robert Morley, Terry-Thomas and James Fox, directed and co-written by Ken Annakin. The lyrics were by Ron Goodwin, and the song was performed by Ron Goodwin's Orchestra.

INTRODUCTION

There's a Place

I heard the brilliant news on 14th March, 2012 that the Queen had granted city status to my home town of Chelmsford. So therefore what started out nearly 2000 years ago as a fort called Caesaromagus, possibly also a brothel, on the Roman Road midway between Londinium and Camulodunum, can in the year 2012, claim its rightful place as the premier location in Essex. I won't apologise that I have no sympathy for the claims of city status for Colchester (or Southend for that matter). To me there was never any doubt.

All I would say is that there is a comforting irony in the fact that if Boadicea hadn't destroyed the much bigger settlement of Camulodunum in AD 60, then Chelmsford might not exist as it does today. If you take into account that the status of Colchester had advantage over Chelmsford in nearly every way throughout history, then I have still less sympathy. Perhaps it looks very much like a case of tortoise and hare, especially when you consider that Caesaromagus ceased to exist after the Romans left Britain in AD 407. By that time Camulodunum had grown to a substantial town, and at the time of the Domesday Book in 1086, Colchester's population was estimated at 2,000.

Just for comparison Colchester was granted its market charter in 1189, and Chelmsford in 1199, and Colchester was greater population-wise until well into the 20th century. However, latest population figures for 2011 are quoted as Colchester 104,000, and Chelmsford 120,000. Colchester may not have become the first City of Essex, but it is the oldest recorded town in England (first recorded AD 77). Congratulations Colchester. You get the 2nd prize!

I have lived in Chelmsford since 15th February, 1980, and I'm proud to say that I've been an Essex boy all my life. I was born "down by the riverside" in a smelly village called Rainham, and through the years have migrated to Chelmsford via Elm Park in South Hornchurch, Hutton near Brentwood, Noak Hill near Romford, and East Tilbury in Thurrock. I could probably navigate my way by car or on foot, without the aid of a map, or a satellite navigation system, to almost anywhere in the county of Essex. I regard myself as a fully accredited Essex boy.

To be precise I've lived most of the time since 1980 in North Springfield, and then for a short while close to the town centre in Springfield Road, before ending up at the largely unspoilt village of Sandon. During the last 32 years I've seen Chelmsford grow from a market town and industrial base, to a much larger and more diverse urban sprawl, and to a large part principally a dormitory town. Chelmsford is my adopted home, but it doesn't make me any less proud that in 2012 the place that has been the County Town of Essex since 1218 became the first City of Essex, even if it has taken nearly 800 years.

I love this county and its wide, tall skies, and anybody who says Essex is all flat and featureless probably never got any further than the first roundabout after the Dartford Tunnel. Essex has a lovely countryside and coastline, it's got character, and it's got history.

As for Chelmsford itself, I love this place, and I hate it, as it has grown and developed around me. It's been good to me, and it's been bad to me. But it's still the best place in Essex bar none. In a contest with any other Essex town it is game, set, and match to Chelmsford.

Despite the conspicuous lack of Roman ruins, there is history to be found here.

My home City is recognised as the birthplace of radio, after Marconi set up the world's first wireless factory there in 1899. On 15th June, 1920 came the first official radio broadcast in the UK, which featured Dame Nellie Melba, and in 1922 the world's first regular wireless broadcasts began from a wooden hut in nearby Writtle.

Chelmsford Cathedral is dedicated to St Mary the Virgin, St Peter and St Cedd, and it became a Cathedral when the Anglican Diocese of Chelmsford was created in 1914, and is the seat of the Bishop of Chelmsford. Therein lays another tale.

Strangely despite the recent transition from town to city there is one enterprise in Chelmsford that won't need to change its signboards or letterheads. The story may or may not be true, that when the original amateur Chelmsford Football Club was reconstituted as a professional outfit in 1938, they met to discuss their future in the Golden Fleece Inn in Duke Street. The founding committee, no doubt fortified by several pints of the best Essex ale, finished their business, and noticed on leaving that Chelmsford Cathedral was in view. Making the assumption that any place with a cathedral must therefore be designated as a City, they named the club Chelmsford City Football Club.

The club itself has a fairly illustrious history, and was often considered the finest and best supported non-league club in the country. But it's been a rollercoaster ride in the last 20 years, first losing the New Writtle Street ground in the 90's, and almost disappearing altogether from the football map, and then ground sharing with Maldon and then Billericay in exile for 9 years.

In January 2006 with assistance from the Chelmsford Borough Council, the club moved back to the town sharing the Melbourne Athletics facility.

Some 6 years later by 2012 the club have been promoted from the Ryman Isthmian Premier League, and have established themselves as a major player in the Blue Square Bet South League. They have a fine record of playoff qualification in 4 out of the last 5 seasons, and a major achievement in the F.A. Cup of reaching the 2nd round proper in each of the last 3 seasons. I'd like to think that the football club played a small but significant part in strengthening the campaign for City status. Needless to say, I am a proud supporter and season ticket holder for my beloved Clarets. "Wheel 'em in!" as the Claret Army would say.

In 2012, Chelmsford like the rest of the country was "enjoying" the 6th year of recession, with record petrol prices between £1.30 and £1.40 per litre in and around the City all year long.

The High Street was changing and evolving just as the world around us was changing economically, politically, and socially. But Chelmsford was and still is a vibrant, busy, and thriving city, brimming with positivity and optimism and I hope that I reflect that in this book.

The story centres around two principle characters, Norman Noble, a reluctant immigrant from Yorkshire turned Essexboy, and Hugh Ramsbottom, his uncle, a born and bred Essexman, and the progress of the computer games company that they both work for. They have a small tight-knit group of work colleagues and drinking friends, and some strong family ties. Throughout the interweaving of these characters everyday lives, their ups and downs, their triumphs and failures, their strengths and frailties, there is a strong theme of positivity and progress. There are no car chases, catastrophes of biblical proportions, or massive impenetrable super-plots. The backdrop to the story is Chelmsford and Britain in the great and unforgettable year 2012, and the actions and interactions are a soap opera about people, good or bad, cheerful or sad, going about their lives the best way they can, and making their way through. It is undoubtedly a tale about real hopes and dreams, social and personal issues in the 21st century, and things that we all care about.

With the exception of real characters mentioned by name, all of the characters you will meet in here are figments of my imagination. Any similarity to real people, living or dead is purely and unintentionally coincidental. They don't exist, and they don't live in my city, they only live in my imagination. But the reality is I do live here.

All of the places mentioned in Chelmsford itself are real, and most of the places outside Chelmsford are also real. Norman's flat and Hugh's grand house are both real, but I only imagine them living there. A great deal of the dialogue takes place in a public house in Springfield Road called the Two Brewers which does exist.

There are a only a few exceptions to the reality, such as the Skinny Pig restaurant in Great Baddow does not, as far as I know, exist.

All opinions expressed are those of my characters and do not in any way represent my personal views. Where political incorrectness is displayed it is theirs not mine, so I don't consider that I need to make an apology if you become offended in any way.

You may have noticed that I have amended the Chelmsford City motto "Many Minds One Heart". This isn't a mistake! I have intentionally titled the novel "Chelmsford 2012 - Many Hearts One Mind".

Read on, and be proud of the City of Chelmsford, the County of Essex, and the nation of Great Britain!

CHAPTER 1

A Change from the Norm

(Friday 24th to Monday 27th February 2012)

The clock radio alarm burst into life and the familiar voices of Martin and Sue on Heart FM introduced another play of the Black-eyed Peas singing "Tonight's gonna be a good, good night". It was a frosty February 24th, a Friday at 8 am, and the usual buzz of activity was starting to well up around the town centre of Chelmsford. In a posh apartment in the Hub, all was as neat and tidy as Norman Noble liked it. Beginning to stir awake, he looked very briefly at the red digits on the face of the alarm. "Hmm 7.59." he muttered. He was never at his best first thing in the morning. Through bleary eyes he noticed there was someone lying next to him in the bed, and propped up on one arm dared to take a peep. His gaze panned slowly from the shapely bosom heaving suggestively with each heavy breath under the expensive duck-down duvet, to a mass of dyed blonde hair and smudged make up. She was still asleep, but only just, and oh that awful garish red lipstick, reminded him of his mum. He rubbed the sleep from his eyes, and focussed a little more bravely. Closer inspection revealed hair greying at the temples, 3 chins, and a slightly wrinkly neck.

"Oh my God!" he recoiled" It's what's-her-name? No! Not Caroline, from the Two Brewers, Shit! I've been cougared. Oh, how will I live this down?"

Then, she trembled and blinked awake, and looked at him with some surprise. As she moved there was the faint stale whiffy mixture of Malibu and pineapple and Impulse body spray. He smiled a thin nervous smile, and struggled for something to say, thinking in this situation he'd better be polite.

He quietly slurred, "Um! Hi, sweetie, how was it for you?"

She tried to answer as honestly as she could with a curt, slightly sarcastic, "Wonderful", but what she really thought was, "Only 6 hours too late for it to matter at all."

"Good!" he replied, quickly turning, and sitting up on the side of the bed, and then getting up, ready to go for a quick shower. He had a boyish, inane smile on his face, as he was thinking, "Hung like a horse, that's me."

If he'd said it rather than thought it, she would probably have replied, "Yes you are. Like a sea horse!"

The man in the Hub was a man of taste, especially in women, and he was embarrassed at the way his standards appeared to have suddenly plummeted to the barmaid from the local in his bed. That wasn't him at all. He was attracted to smart, well-dressed girls who could make intelligent conversation and shared the same interests as him. It wasn't that he was looking for Miss Right, at 26 he was enjoying playing the field, and he seldom took any girl on a second date. He knew he was good looking, a fine catch, neatly turned out, and financially magnetic, but he was also nobody's easy touch.

After Susie his first girlfriend, had dumped him for a bloke with Arnold Swarzenegger muscles, and an intellect which would only just rival a goldfish on tranquilisers, he resolved never to fall for anyone ever again. That had happened when he was 17 and still at school. Susie was a year older than him, working at Debenhams in the High Street, and they were together for 4 months. He loved her in the way that only a teenager with a first experience can. So when it was over, he was cut to very small pieces, blown to mangled molecules, devastated beyond any possible redemption. It took him 6 months of heartache and melancholy to dig his way out of the crevasse that he had fallen into. That was when he had decided to never be taken on that painful, excruciating, undermining ride again. Since then, he had never weakened or wavered towards even liking someone. His women were the proverbial notches on the bedpost, temporarily interesting conquests, disposables, and he liked it that way.

After a while he reappeared in the bedroom saying, "I've got to go off to work. Why don't you have a little doze? I'll bring you a coffee before I go, and then you can leave when you're ready. Just let yourself out."

"OK", she replied snuggling back into the bed, thinking "How sweet", not realising in her early morning doziness that all he was doing was making sure they didn't leave his apartment in the Hub together, and have any of his neighbours, or worse still his friends, bump into them,. He cringed at the thought that they might see him and desperate Caroline Bangs in close proximity.

At 8.45 am precisely the Porsche Carrera 911 engine roared, and slid out onto Springfield Road, making for the A12 and Colchester. The driver gunned it on the slip-road at the Cramphorn flyover, looked at his watch, and gave it the turbo large.

"18 minutes, to the office, easy."

He popped out a Coldplay CD, and pushed it into the player.

"Para, para, paradise", sang Chris Martin, and the Porscheman joined in as best he could.

"Barret, barret, barret eyes."

He wasn't in his best singing mode due the fat lip Caroline had inflicted on him just before he left. Perhaps, he shouldn't have stopped and asked "Can you please make sure you leave quietly?"

At least he'd managed to calm her down before he left for work. Well, she seemed calm enough, and he had let her stay in his apartment and get showered and dressed.

The office of NerdiSoft, on the outskirts of Colchester, soon came into view, and he glanced at his watch. It was 9:10 am. He smiled "Right on time, Yeah!"

He leaned over and picked up his leather briefcase, containing all his important papers, and his laptop, and gave himself a congratulatory splash of Erection aftershave. That morning there would be a board meeting. He expected that it would be the usual crew, and that it would follow a standard route.

Company Chairman Tim (Tiny) Balls, the boss, smart, good dark blue suit, silk tie, patent leather shoes, would give his best "We're a big company, in a little office, running on a shoestring, must grow and prosper." speech.

Hugh Ramsbottom the incredibly obese Marketing Director, Norman's uncle, scruffy, old grey suit, no tie, brown shoes, would puff his way through a rain forest of reports justifying the same marketing strategy he'd trumpeted for a least 5 years.

Gordon Bullock (affectionately known as Golden Bollocks) the worst nightmare, the very gay company accountant, dapper, prematurely grey silver hair, 3 piece pin-striped suit, Gucci loafers, would produce graphs, pie-charts and spreadsheets showing the company was still making a healthy profit, and briefly discuss projections for the next financial year.

And then it was him, Norman Noble, the Development Director, tainted with the boardroom in-joke of being addressed by his uncle Hugh as Mr Nobless. But he knew he was the best dressed bloke by far and modern man about town. It was always his bit of the board meeting that mattered most. He was proud of his position, and the way he had acquired it.

Not academically brilliant, but nevertheless shrewd, he had spent all his teenage years, and a few of his twenties, studying the only thing he had ever been good at. He was a self-confessed computer games supernerd. He had dissected every game and sussed out the way to write the software for all of them. He knew every line of code for the programs for Super Mario, Sonic the Hedgehog, Modern Warfare 1, 2 and 3, Grand Theft Auto, Assassins, all of them. He had reached top level on every game he'd ever played, bar none. Nearly four years ago at the age of 23 he had written a game called Viking Ninja Holocaust 9, perfected it, meticulously prepared the artwork etc., and marched up to NerdiSoft chairman Tim Balls at a Computer Exhibition in the Brentwood Centre, and challenged him to beat him at the game. Tiny's computer game skills were legendary, and he had never been beaten, but after 30 minutes of VNH9 (as the creator called it) he was hooked and baffled, and offered the young man a job on the spot.

Now the continued success of the company hung on the young genius' fevered brain, and his next computer game creation, like a spider on a damp autumn morning web. None of the lads had grown fat and lazy on his account. Although it's true that the incredibly obese Marketing Director had certainly grown fat. That was mostly due to his lifestyle. Norman certainly wouldn't want to become fat and lazy. He had looked after himself. Sure he was top nerd, but he was well-groomed, fairly slim, not unfit, and liked to think of himself as someone waiting for a call (any day now!) from the production team of the next series of The Only Way is Essex. He idolised Mark Bright, he loved every series of Big Brother, and he hid his Yorkshire upbringing and particularly his northern accent under a veil of acquired Essex boy.

At 9:15 am the TOWIE fan grabbed a frothy coffee and sat down next to his chairman's empty seat. Hugh and Gordon didn't acknowledge his arrival, as they were entrenched in an argument about a rumour that was beginning to circulate, that Mo Farah had beaten The Cube and won £250,000 for his foundation. The accountant didn't believe it was possible, but the marketing director was confident that the rumours had been substantiated. They negotiated a £60 bet to be honoured as and when the relevant episode of The Cube was televised. As they argued the young man's mind wandered while the irritation of another delayed start to a board meeting began to bite, and numb his brain into unconnected thinking. He would much rather have been getting on with something useful, but instead his thoughts swirled around the name NerdiSoft, as he attempted to amuse himself with what he might make it stand for.

"Nutcases in Essex really daft software? No that might be NerdaSoft. What about, nobody expects radically different software?"

The truth was it was something far more mundane. NerdiSoft stood for North Essex Research and Distribution Software. Tiny had only recently moved to Chelmsford from East Bergholt, and when he and Hugh first started the company in Colchester they were mainly a software distribution company with aspirations to start writing their own products.

He came back from his distraction, shuffled in his seat and coughed nervously not to draw too much attention, and hoped that nobody had seen him leave their favourite watering hole, the Two Brewers in Springfield Road, the previous evening with desperate Caroline Bangs. It had been unusual for them to assemble at the Brewers on a Thursday anyway. Fridays were the night they habitually met. He wondered how he'd managed to find himself waking up in the morning with the barmaid beside him. He hadn't been drunk and incapable, so it wasn't a loss of memory problem. Nowadays he only drank Evian water, and isotonic sports drinks. His colleagues ribbed him about it, especially his uncle, who saw bottled water as a huge marketing con, and only drank draft Guinness and real ale. Hugh reminded everybody as often as he could that Evian spelt backwards was "naive", and claimed that only boys drank Lucozade look-alikes. According to him, real men drank real beer; Guinness, bitter, and certainly not what he would describe as "that piss-water called lager".

Norman had only been drunk once in his life. After his very boozy vodka drenched 18th birthday party, he had woken up the next morning stark bollock naked and shackled by hand and foot with chains and padlocks to the top of a bus shelter in Danbury. He couldn't remember a single thing about how he got there till this day, and had vowed never to get in that state again.

The Cube argument began to fizzle out, and Hugh looked up for the first time, and noticed his nephew's swollen lip. "Christ, Nobless! What have you done? "Did you trip over your wallet?"

"No!" he insisted, and wanting to cover his tracks." Remember when we left the Brewers last night?"

There was a pause before the answer came.

"Can't remember a thing, far too pissed to care." said Hugh, as Gordon grinned in agreement.

"No change there then." thought a relieved and embarrassed young man.

Then he explained," When I walked back to the Hub some brainless oik was puking in the doorway, so I picked him up and gave him a right pasting. He got a lucky slap on me once, bumped my lip, but now he's probably in intensive care, having breakfast through a straw."

They didn't believe him, but both responded with "Nice one Norm!"

Despite his apparent bravado, he began to feel a bit uncomfortable again about having spent the night with Caroline. She wasn't that old, only 34, and she certainly wasn't old enough to be his mother. So why did he feel that he'd been cougared? His mind wandered again to thoughts of how that had happened, and how best to avoid feeling quite this uncomfortable in future.

Just as the chairman came into the room, and silence fell before the meeting began, he settled back on the conclusion that he had let standards slip, and that he should be a bit more selective in future.

The meeting droned on, taking the predictable route through the set pecking order. Although his was always the penultimate report, when it was Norman's turn he was well aware there were only two things keeping the company going. First was the money that his uncle put up for new projects. But foremost were his ideas for new computer games.

The supernerd presented early versions of 2 new games he was working on. Everybody loved the ideas he presented for R. McGeddon's Nerd World Apocalypse, and it was gone 11 before they'd all finished playing an embryonic version of Beer Festival Bastards Final Frontier.

The chairman liked to be very matter-of-fact about his business, and had a habit of leaving the most important items till last. As the meeting was about to break up he spoke.

"I'm in the process of tying up a big new deal at the moment, which will put the company on a global footing" he said.

"OK, so we're taking over the world, are we?" Hugh joked, putting his left index finger to his top lip, and raising his right arm in a Hitler salute. The others looked at each other and laughed.

"No, listen boys," interrupted Tiny, also amused by the flippancy, "This is important. In the next few weeks I plan to fly to China for a meeting with Wang Wu Hoo Du Production."

The marketing director couldn't help but chuckle under his hand, which he'd brought down from the Nazi stance, as he carried on listening.

"And then, I'm going straight on to Columbus in the U.S.A. to meet the guys from Softly Softly Catchee Monkey Distribution." he continued.

Hugh never missed an opportunity to illustrate his knowledge of history, so he piped up with a grin, "I'm sorry to have to tell you that Columbus died in 1506, 20th of May I think it was."

The chairman ignored him and said, "I will call another meeting when I've finalised everything, and before I go I'll fill you all in on the details. Needless to say, this is a bit hush, hush at the moment, but it's going to be massive. I don't want the workforce to get wind of this plan yet, because I think we're going to have to leave this little shack, and move to bigger premises."

He took a deep breath and then added, "Oh, and by the way we'll need to re-brand the company. We won't be going global under the NerdiSoft label. I'll explain more about that later."

The chairman left the room with a dramatic wave, and Hugh burst out laughing.

"What a crafty bugger!" he chuckled, "He flies round the world in 8 days at company expense. Who does he think he is, some modern day Phileas Fogg?"

The others knew that was just their fat colleague being himself. The board members also knew that the marketing director was totally aware of what was going on. The meeting broke up, and they all went to attend to their work.

At 4:30 pm Norman left and drove his favourite route back home through the country lanes, listening to Coldplay again. He purred the Porsche on its way through Stanway, Tiptree, Maldon, and Hatfield Peveril, before smashing through the gears onto the last bit of the A12. Soon he was back in his pad in the Hub.

Desperate Caroline had gone, but not before she'd trashed the bathroom, smudged "ARSEHOLES" in very red lipstick on all the wardrobes, and thrown all 15 pairs of her one night stand's Calvin Klein boxer shorts over the balcony into the River Chelmer. He could see them floating in a line in the reeds, all the way up to the Tesco store.

"Hmm! Might have to collect them up later, when it's dark?" he thought.

After a quick run out along the Bunny Walk as far as Fifth Avenue and back, he showered, made a healthy quorn bolognaise for his meal, and was ready to go out to the Two Brewers. He was just about to finish another session of Viking Ninja Holocaust 9 when just as expected the phone rang. It was the familiar voice of his father Stanley.

"Ey Oop, son, 'ow yer diddlin'?"

"Alright, Dad, how are you?"

"Mustn't grumble, nobody listens anyway."

"Mum alright, is she?"

"Aye, son, same as ever."

"What can I do for you, Dad?"

"Well, I'm just phonin' oop to remind thee 'bout t' game tomorrow. You know t' 'ockey match yer sister's playin' in. Oh, and yer mum says if yer stayin' for lunch after she'll do yer fav'rit."

"OK, Dad, I hadn't forgotten, I'll be there about 10, see you then, love to Mum."

"Bye son, drive carefully."

"Oh, horror of horrors." thought the man in the Hub as he put the phone down, "Not again."

Every couple of weeks his sister, the unfortunately named Cher Noble, played hockey for a local team. She was built like her mother; like Geoff Capes on steroids. In fact she looked a bit like Geoff Capes without the beard. Her hockey team were called the Norfolk Enchants, they always lost, it was always a family affair, and Norman always hated it, but felt obliged to go along. The team's home ground was near Beccles in Suffolk on a paddock near the Gillingham Dam. Cher liked it because it was handy for the Swan Inn, a hotel, pub and restaurant offering South African cuisine. The owners prided themselves on their game steaks of springbok, ostrich, eland and crocodile as well as other South African specialities like Bobotie, Koeksisters and Chakalaka. The hockey girl sometimes indulged in a game steak or two after the match. To say the pitch was out in the open was pure understatement, and sometimes all the families stood there in the freezing cold, trying to drum up some enthusiasm, chanting away. It sounded really encouraging in Stanley's Yorkshire accent "Norfolk Enchants, Norfolk Enchants."

Ms Noble would play her socks off to no avail, come off with badly bruised legs, covered in mud and cowpats in various states of fermentation, and give her brother a big sisterly hug. "Yuk!" It was dire, and it got worse. Whenever he attended a match she always insisted on coming back in his Porsche, to the bungalow near Leiston, on the accurately named New Clear View Estate. She was always covered in excrement, and he would fret about yet another expensive valet for his pride and joy, and wonder how quickly he could get rid of the stink. Mum and Dad Noble usually returned sometime later in their clapped out Mondeo.

Norman loved his parents, but they were the oddest couple on the planet, Stanley, in his heavy tweed suit, thick set, bushy moustache, yellow, fag-stained teeth, unmistakable Yorkshire clichés, and Lisalotte, of German stock, posh frock, too much very red lipstick, pigeon English at best. They had met at the Munich Beer Festival, when he and a group of master butchers, for that was his trade, had gone on his once in a lifetime trip abroad. She was one of those strappingly built serving wenches, a great bustling clod-hopper of a girl, who could carry 8 huge steins of beer without spilling a drop. Having never been abroad before, he mistook her beery bonhomie for some kind of mutual attraction, and had invited her to a bockwurst eating contest. Surprisingly, she had obliged, only to eat him under the table. Sausages were his life's work, and he was gutted when she beat him. But it was the start of a beautiful relationship, and within a month she had moved to Yorkshire, and they had married by special license. Life was kind to both of them, and the butchery business thrived. Then a celebrity chef called Chester Gannet came on the scene. They held him responsible for screwing it up for them, and forcing them to sell up, and retire to Suffolk.

Every year in mid-June Stanley's business had made a fortune after he had perfected what he called the Seasonal Burgundian, a sausage with an unusual, but very popular twang. He guarded a secret recipe, created something with true rarity value, and managed to sell his goods to some very posh shops and restaurants. Even the Queen ordered them from Fortnum & Mason. Only one man in the whole Universe apart from the butcher himself knew the real secret of his success, which had come about through a stroke of good fortune.

Several years back, the authorities had been forced to reroute the storm water drainage system around the village of Ainderby Steeple, where the Nobles lived and ran their business. This had forced the local frog population to find a new migration route to the River Swale not far away from the butcher's premises.

Stanley came home one night quite late from his favourite pub, The Wellington Heifer, which he had affectionately renamed t' Effin Boot, and ran over and squashed thousands of migrating frogs on the road outside. Never one to miss an opportunity for free meat, he wheel-barrowed them all into his shop, and invented a recipe to use them in an exotic foreign sausage. The migration always took place for 10 nights on the trot, and so eventually he had absolutely thousands and thousands of squashed frogs to process. He reasoned that the French ate frogs' legs, and what was the harm in using the whole frog, beautifully tenderised by the tyres of his van, and then made fresh into the finest bangers he could imagine.

The River Swale frog squash became Stanley Noble's annual windfall.

But after 5 successful years, and local fame and some small fortune, there was an unfortunate slip-up, which quickly developed into a full-blown scandal. The celebrity chef Chester Gannet was appearing on a TV series highlighting regional food throughout Britain, and had come to Yorkshire. He had already acquired notoriety for offering what many considered to be odd choices and combinations of food. He'd suggested that all meat whatever source, as long as it was tasty and non-toxic was up for grabs, including dogs, cats, rodents, birds, reptiles and even goldfish. He appeared on a news programme talking to Stanley and Lisalotte about Yorkshire butchers, and in particular the Seasonal Burgundian sausage.

Lisalotte, never the brightest button in the box, innocently made a reference to "zoze froggy bangers". Pretty soon a grossly exaggerated magnification of the interview got to the front page of the Northallerton Echo, and that was the end. She had a nervous breakdown, and shortly after that the family felt obliged to sell up, and move, and become anonymous. The Nobles only son Norman had to go down south and stay with his uncle Hugh in Chelmsford to finish his schooling. From that day on the family had held the TV chef responsible for their demise. Stanley said at the time "Bloody Gannet 'im of all people, with 'is pretentious crap infested concoctions. Eeee I'm sure 'e was just jealous. 'E wouldn't know a good sausage if one fell on 'is 'ead."

On Saturday at 1 pm, the Porsche screeched to a halt outside the bungalow. The driver was relieved that yet another awful hockey match was over, but annoyed about the state that his sister had put his treasured car in yet again. He persuaded her to get out and have a bath, as the smell of sweat and cowpat was overpowering, and 10 minutes later the oldies arrived in their old Mondeo backfiring onto the drive.

"Come in, sohn," said Lisalotte, "Take your shoes off, and pur uz all a drink."

"Zere's some Blue Nun for ous, some Perry wasser for you my dearest boy, and an Adam's beer for you farzer."

"She always gets it wrong." thought Norman, because she never could say Adnam's, but he never corrected her. Far too many Munich October fests having her ears assaulted by very loud oompah bands had taken their toll, and she had developed a slight deafness problem. Nobody referred to this problem, but everybody enjoyed the frequent misunderstandings that occurred as a result. Soon the German feast was ready. The young man hated bockwurst, and he loathed sauerkraut, but scoffed with pretend enthusiasm to please his mum, even though to him the combination tasted like globules of plastic and flakes of disinfectant. Soon after they'd finished the meal mum and sister had quaffed 3 bottles of Blue Nun between them, and were both snoring contentedly, legs akimbo on the sofa. Father and son made for the garden, where usually Stanley would show off his roses and his prize rhubarb, but it was too early in the season, and there wasn't a lot of promise for either roses or rhubarb. In the previous few days the government had declared a drought in the Southeast of England after an almost rainless 6 months. The Yorkshireman loved his garden, and his son appeased him by showing a bit of interest.

"Come and 'ave a butcher's at this." said Stanley, strolling towards his greenhouse and lighting another cigarette. The persistent use of his favourite phrase, "To 'ave a butcher's", was just another cross to bear in the father and son relationship.

"I'm growin' this funny plant for Sid up t' road, you know 'im what lives in t' flats, 'e sez it's 'erbal; 'elps 'im wi' 'is arthritis."

They entered the greenhouse, damp and humid, and filled floor to ceiling with a prolific green mass of foliage. Norman didn't have the heart to tell his dad what it was. During his teens he had once smoked some wacky baccy, but to him it did the same things as booze, and so it was struck off the list along with alcohol.

The ex-butcher explained further, "Sid dried these leaves and made us some cakes wi' this once, ah tell thee lad, they didn't taste of booze, but I think 'e laced them wi' it. Me and yer mum, both felt like we'd 'ad 10 pints down t' Effin Boot. It took us 5 days t' get back t' feelin' reet again."

The son grinned, and longed for the open road, Coldplay, and a turbo fix. Soon after the greenhouse visit he said his goodbyes and jumped into the car, breathed a big sigh of relief, and burnt some rubber.

"Sixty-two minutes dead on!" he chuckled, pulling into his parking space at the Hub in Chelmsford. A while later, on that Saturday evening he was showered, shaved, preened, moisturised and ready. He had to go commando due to a sudden shortage of boxer shorts. After another generous splash of Erection aftershave he was on his way, down to Brentwood, to Sugar Hut, to try and be spotted by the scouts for The Only Way is Essex.

The next morning the clock radio alarm burst into life, and the familiar voices of somebody other than Martin and Sue of Heart FM introduced another play of "Tonight's gonna be a good, good night". It was Sunday at 8am and the man in the Hub opened one eye and looked very briefly at the red digits on the face of the alarm. "Hmm 7.59." he muttered. Then he realised there was someone lying next to him in the bed, and propped up on one arm dared to take a peep. His gaze panned slowly from the fine bronzed leg sticking out the side of the expensive duvet, to a neat head of dark hair tinted red and the perfect make up. She was still asleep, but only just, and breathed gently through her understated light pink lipstick. He rubbed the sleep from his eyes, and focussed, with a wry smile, a little more keenly. "Blimey! Not bad!" he thought, "Must have been a lucky night."

"Hang on, think quick, what is her name? I've got it, Clarisa. Phew!"

She turned towards him, blinked awake, focussed, and smiled back. As she moved he caught the expensive fragrance of Hugo Boss Deep Red. He maintained a big toothy grin, and quietly whispered "Hi sweetie! How was it for you?"

"It's a bit late to ask now." she thought but answered convincingly, "You were wonderful, big boy."

"Good!" he replied, and quickly turned full towards her, kissed her on the mouth, forgetting all about his sore lip, and enfolded her in his arms.

"Do you fancy a quick replay then?"

"Oooooohhh! Yeeees!" she enthused.

At about 8:30 am she reappeared, "I've finished in the bathroom now." she grinned, "Sorry, but I've got to nip back home, and then get to Trinity by 9:30. I'm singing in the choir this morning. Will I see you again?"

Norman got up, grinned at her and made his way to the bathroom saying but only half meaning it, "I do hope so."

The luscious feel of the warm water was running all over him from head to foot as she opened the shower door. He leaned forward out of the spray, and she gave him a quick peck on the lips, followed by an affectionate tug on his willy, smiled, turned and went. He didn't quite catch what she said as she left due to the noise of the running water in his ears, but it sounded like "I must go now, (pause) I've got to feed Phyllis."

"Never mind, whatever it was it can wait." he mused, contented. When he thought about it, he was quite pleased with himself. In the space of 2 days, he'd gone from feeling very uncomfortable about bedding Caroline, to feeling very happy waking up next to somebody as classy as Clarisa. Yes! He was back in a familiar saddle.

"More of the same please." he told himself.

On Monday morning 27th February at 10:30 am, the computer games supernerd was back at work. He visited the gents' urinals and was trying to squeeze in alongside his bulky uncle.

"Were you at the Sugar Hut again on Saturday, Nobless? We missed you down the Brewers, no one to take the piss out of."

The young man was puzzled, and replied, "Saturday? Are you going to the Brewers on Saturdays as well? That's three nights on the trot."

"Yeah, I needed a drink, I was pissed off after the City boys had lost 1 - 0 away at bloody Bromley, and dropped to 4th in the table. That's their 19 game run of away wins come to an end as well. They are so frustrating to watch this year. They've been winning away, but can't string a bunch of wins together and do the business at home. If they're not careful they'll be out of the playoffs."

Norman wasn't that interested in football, but humoured his uncle by offering "I don't suppose this cold weather helps; some matches were called off due to frozen pitches; weren't they?"

"Yes. That's right," replied Hugh, "Anyway, answer the question, Nobless, where were you?"

"I went to Sugar Hut, picked up this lovely bit of stuff, Clarisa's her name."

The fatman laughed," Good looking bird, dark red tinted hair, nice make up, good perfume, sings in the church choir at Trinity."

"Yeah, that's her, do you know her?" the young man said with a hint of surprise.

"Yes mate, that's Clarisa Hinton, and there's something you should know."

"What's that?"

The fat one stepped back from the urinal, didn't wash his hands, farted enthusiastically, and before he turned and left the room, he raised his hands above his head, and clapped just once, and let out a strange cry like he was a demented seal at a marine park. The fit one looked down, now in panic, and still peeing shrieked, "Oh My God!"

CHAPTER 2

Clap, Whistle, and Cheer

(Thursday 1st to Friday 2nd March 2012)

A few days later, just another day at NerdiSoft, and Norman was finishing his rather late lunch as he had been working on the details of Beer Festival Bastards Final Frontier. He switched off his PC and emptied his coffee cup, grabbed his jacket, and made for the door. Hugh's Land Rover was missing from his parking space, as he had complained of a toothache and left early to go to the emergency dentist. Tiny's Lexus was still there, as he was still working on the new deal he'd mentioned at the last board meeting, and Gordon's brand new Galaxy stood in its usual spot.

"Nobody will miss me for a few hours." thought the games genius.

He climbed into the Porsche, started her up with a quiet purr, primed a Coldplay fix, and slipped ever so quietly out of the car park. It was 3:00 pm, and he had an appointment at the Sexual Health Clinic in New London Road, Chelmsford at 4.00 o'clock which he didn't want anyone to know about. His uncle's jokey suggestion a few days earlier had set him into panic mode, and although he understood the risks of his promiscuous lifestyle, he had never been in this situation before. He had covered his tracks at work by remaining as calm and professional as possible in the intervening period, but at the bottom of his heart he felt both frightened and nervous. Clarisa was such a lovely girl, she seemed different to all his other brief encounters, and he found it hard to believe that she could be the cause of his distress, but he had to be sure.

He drove back through the country lanes, listening to Chris Martin and Co, whistling through Stanway, Tiptree, Maldon, and Hatfield Peveril, before crashing through the gears onto the last bit of the A12. Soon he was back in his safe haven at the Hub.

He quickly changed into his oldest and for him oddest clothes. He was usually smartly dressed, but he decided to go to his appointment as incognito as possible. He donned a dark blue overall that he wore for polishing the Porsche, it was still immaculate, but to a man of his calibre it spelt scruffy. Then he put on a pair of sunglasses, and wore a blue baseball cap with the peak turned backwards, and in his mind's eye he imagined that he looked like a Kwikfit mechanic on a lunch break. Carefully he skulked out of Bond

Street and up Waterloo Lane, and sneaked across the churchyard at the Cathedral. Then keeping his head down and avoiding the town centre he negotiated Market Street There was a momentary panic blip, when he had to take a quick diversion into the foyer of the library, as he thought he saw someone he knew crossing the road from the market. Then he turned right, up towards the station. Like a cat stealthily stalking his prey he carefully made his way along Duke Street, past the station, under the railway bridge, and left into Viaduct Street. With this huge diversion, and his not-too-clever disguise he certainly wasn't risking anybody knowing who he was, or where he was heading. His walk continued back under the viaduct at the end of the street, and quickly along the subway into Central Park. Once across the park and over the hump-backed River Can Bridge he made his way along New Writtle Street, thereby able to approach the Sexual Health Clinic in New London Road from the opposite direction.

He felt relieved that he had reached his destination, and pleased with the subterfuge he had employed in getting there unnoticed. He quickly removed his sunglasses, and removed his cap, and took a quick look behind him satisfied to have reached the clinic without a hitch. But as he turned and entered the building he heard a voice over his shoulder.

"Oy, Norm is it you?" he heard someone behind him say. He squirmed. "Disaster!"

"Yes, I thought it was you, remember me? Terry! Terry Smith! We were at Boswells together. Haven't seen you in a few years."

He turned around to see a familiar face, slightly older, and sporting a moustache but still familiar, and whispered "Oh shit! It's Smithy!" under his breath.

Unlike him, his school chum was fairly respectably turned out in a shirt and tie, and grey suit, and smart black shoes, and he was sporting a really healthy tan.

"You look well, been abroad recently have you?" he made polite conversation.

"Yeah, me and Sharon have just had two weeks in the Dominican Republic. It was fantastic."

There was a groan "Please don't tell me all about your holiday." he thought.

"Anyway, What are you doing here, you dirty dog?" said Terry with a grin and a nudge, nudge, wink, wink attitude.

"Oh possibly a little accident," answered Norman quickly, "How about you?"

"Well the missus sent me to be checked for chlamydia, but it's just her being stupid. I haven't been unfaithful or anything. Honestly! No, she saw this poster in the doctor's surgery, and we're supposed to be trying for a baby at the moment."

"You not being unfaithful, I don't believe it, you always were a randy sod.

You'd roger anything with a pulse, and probably most things without one."

They went through the entrance together, where the male and female waiting areas were segregated. "Good thinking, don't want to bump into an old flame in here?" he thought.

After reporting, and being handed a clipboard with a not too complicated form on it, he sat down. He completed the form, including the question "Do you consider yourself heterosexual, bisexual, homosexual, don't know, or don't want to say?" handed it in, and waited.

There were three other gentlemen in the room. In the far corner was a spotty, scruffy teenager reading the Sun, who sniffed incessantly and looked terrified. At the front was a middle aged bloke in a well worn pin-striped suit. He was immersed in his laptop, his face expressionless and relaxed. And then there was an old fellow in a light green track suit, with thinning grey hair covering the slightly bald bits of his profusely sweating head, who scratched his groin every few seconds.

"We all know what he's got," smirked Terry, "Now tell me the truth. Why are you here, Norm?"

Reluctantly Norman whispered, "Well, I had a one night stand with a girl I met at Sugar Hut. That was no problem! But my workmate reckons she's got the clap."

Smithy chuckled, "Is that your uncle Hugh?" with a knowing smile.

"Yeah! Of course, you know him don't you?"

He laughed again," It was your uncle who we phoned to say which bus shelter in Danbury we'd left you on top of after your 18th birthday party. God! Mate! You were well pissed that night. But for most of the night you thought you were drinking orange juice, and we laced all your drinks with vodka. We had a bit of a job heaving you up on top of the bus shelter, but it was worth it."

"My uncle wasn't very pleased. He had to pay a locksmith over £100 to undo all the padlocks."

"I know. We were all watching from behind the bushes across the road."

Just then a nurse in a white outfit appeared, and quietly took Mr Scratchy away much to everybody's relief.

"Where do you go drinking nowadays?" asked Terry.

"Well, I'm teetotal since that night, but I still go to the pub. The Two Brewers is my local, and I'm usually there on a Friday evening and so is my uncle."

And as he immediately regretted offering that information, another nurse appeared and took his old chum away.

Smithy left with a quick "See you around mate. Nice to meet you again after all this time."

When Norman's turn came he was re-questioned about his sex life, had his naughty bits examined, and gave a urine sample. Then there were blood-tests, and swabs, and he was relaxed to find it was all so matter-of-fact and professional. He was informed that the outcome of his tests would be emailed to him in a few days, and then he departed, pleased that the ordeal was over.

After a furtive glance out of the exit, he dispensed with wearing the cap and sunglasses, and strode confidently home. "No need to hide myself now." he thought, crossing under Parkway, and then quickly along New London Road, and through Marks and Spencers and the town centre, and back to the Hub. He flung himself down on the couch and took a deep breath, and closed his eyes. It wasn't quite a power nap, as within a minute or two he had decided the best way to relieve the recent stress was to change quickly, and head for the Excel gym just around the corner for a quick workout.

During the week at NerdiSoft everybody seemed to be very busy with their own projects, particularly Hugh who was being very secretive. The computer games genius still had plenty of work to do finishing off his two new games; Beer Festival Bastards Final Frontier, and R. McGeddon's Nerd World Apocalypse. He was also working on a rough schematic for a another new game with the working title of Interstellar Paranoid Overdrive involving driving as badly and dangerously as possible in order to win an interplanetary spaceship marathon. Visiting the clinic recently was still playing on his mind, but he was a creature of habit, and went about most of his activities just as he normally would. He always arrived at work on time. He was reliable and conscientious, and loved his work and the freedom of creativity it gave him. He was a bit of a loner, but he was quiet and confident, and a perfectionist. Even though he had now adopted an Essex boy persona, he had inherited a healthy and positive cocktail of characteristics from his parent's mixed marriage. He considered himself to be single-minded and tenacious, some very German traits inherited from his mum. Whilst his dad was Yorkshire born and bred, giving him honesty, loyalty, and a solid work ethic.

During the week he concentrated on his work, but also enjoyed his leisure time, going to the gym and jogging. He kept himself in good shape. He played computer games, mostly on his own, and bought and tested every new game, if possible to destruction or failure, but at least to the very top level attainable. Religiously teetotal, he had no interest in alcohol, and was fussy with his diet, except when appeasing his mum. His weekends fell into a familiar pattern. Friday nights he would usually spend in the Two Brewers with workmates. Saturday he would be with the family up in Leiston, and watching his sister Cher play hockey. Visits to Sugar Hut, or time with a girlfriend were his Saturday evening pursuits. When Sunday came round he would relax at home, or go driving around in the Porsche. But frequently on a Sunday afternoon he followed a tradition, going back to when he had first come to live with his uncle as a teenager. Sunday roast at the Ramsbottom's was always on the menu, and that gave him an opportunity to test his computer games skills against Hugh's three sons, Tom, Dick and Harry. He had never lost a game to any of them.

The one exception now to his usual routines was that he had suddenly developed a total disinterest in pulling any more women. It wasn't that he was turning gay. God! No! Perhaps he thought it was just that the clinic business had temporarily put him in limbo, or was it something about Clarisa?

When Friday late afternoon at NerdiSoft arrived the man in the Porsche stormed back to the Hub, through the country lanes, listening to Coldplay again, burning rubber through Stanway, Tiptree, Maldon, and Hatfield Peveril, and then onto the last bit of the A12. He changed, and went jogging out along the Bunny Walk for half an hour, before fixing himself a healthy tuna salad for his evening meal. Despite the continuing shortage of boxer shorts, he prepared himself for the usual end of the week meet in the Two Brewers for the customary drinking session with all the usual crew. As he was about to leave the phone rang. It was the familiar voice of his dad Stanley.

"Ey Oop, son, 'ow yer diddlin'?"

"Alright, Dad, how are you?"

"Mustn't grumble, nobody listens anyway."

"Mum alright, is she?"

"Aye, son, same as ever."

"What can I do for you, Dad?"

"Well, I'm just phoning up to tell thee 'bout there bein' no game tomorrow. Yer sister's not playing, it's bin postponed due to a stomach bug decimating t' team. They've all got t' shits. Shame!" he laughed." Nobody would notice on their pitch would they?"

"That's a shame, Dad," replied Norman, as convincingly as he could, "But I'll come up and see you anyway."

"Reet lad, see thee 'bout 10, and yer'll be there for lunch, and I'll do me best t' persuade yer mum not to do yer fav'rit again."

"OK, Dad, Thanks, I'll be there about 10, see you tomorrow, love to Mum."

"Bye son, drive carefully."

Once the phone call was over the young man left his flat and walked across the car park between Bond Street and the Chelmer River at the back of Debenhams on his way to the pub. He hated this bit of the town because he thought it was scruffy and semi-derelict, and not at all in keeping with the poshness of his apartment. He looked forward to the prospect of it soon being turned into the planned John Lewis complex. It was only a 5 minute walk and soon he opened the door at the Brewers.

Hugh and Tiny were there; having made the customary walk with the necessary stops all the way down the hill along Springfield Road, and they were already on their 4th pint. The jolly fatman looked up from reading the jokes page of March issue of The Edge.

"Hello, Nobless" he said," Usual poison?"

He proceeded to order a round of drinks, and when a minute later, Gordon arrived with his gay entourage of Spike, Ike and Mike in tow, Hugh blurted out "Hey, you lot, this isn't a Gay Pride event you know?", and then he started singing out of tune," We're gonna stay at the YMCA, we're gonna stay at the YMCA."

They were used to the derisory greetings, and incessant jibes that only their fat friend could make without too much offence, and made their usual gesture raising their middle fingers in unison. The joker continued, "Oh look! It is the Village People, isn't it?" He was as mocking and mischievous as always, but applied his habitual generosity with, "What are you bunch of poofs drinking then?"

Despite the jibes, and his constant leg-pulling antics, none of them refused a drink. Even Spike, who shared an intense mutual dislike with the Hugh, would nevertheless not refuse a free drink.

"Better a poof, than a fatboy." he sneered as he took his Bacardi and Coke from the bar.

The fatman smiled. He could take it, as well as dish it out.

The scruffy decorator continued, "Oy! Fatboy! You should go to the gym like Norm does; you could do with losing a few pounds. Oh did I say pounds? I meant stone."

"The last time you were in a gym, Scruffbag, he had a moustache and tattoos." Hugh smirked.

"And your idea of exercise is eating with your fingers."

Hugh just smiled, and Spike glared at him saying, "That really is the face that munched a thousand chips."

Everybody laughed. It was just the standard Friday evening banter.

"There's a rumour that Caroline was seen leaving your flat recently?" said the joker turning back towards his nephew.

"Shit!" he thought, but knew he couldn't deny it. He suspected that she might be a kiss and tell kind of girl anyway.

"Haven't seen here recently though." continued the fatman, "What did you do with her, Nobless?"

"She's on holiday in Thailand with her mates." interrupted Gordon.

"Thailand?" replied the laughing comedian, "No chance that they're going to ban cock, while she's there then."

They all giggled again, at yet another witty riposte from their resident comedian.

He proceeded with, "Come on Nobless, spill the beans then. What happened with Caroline?"

Norman felt compelled to own up, before the barmaid had an opportunity to tell all and sundry. So he bent the truth a little and related a tale of how she'd stayed the night on his sofa. Nobody believed him, mostly because she only lived round the corner in Navigation Road. And then he explained how he'd left her asleep in the morning and gone into work, only to find on his return, that she'd trashed the bathroom, smudged "ARSEHOLES" in red lipstick on all the wardrobes, and thrown all his Calvin Klein boxer shorts over the balcony into the River Chelmer.

"You must have upset her, Nobless, didn't you rise to her expectations?" grinned the fatman. His nephew didn't feel there was a need to reply.

"I bet you're glad she's away?" he concluded.

The young man just quietly smiled, and wandered over to play darts with the gay Gordon's. But his fat uncle had fixed this episode firmly in his memory bank. He was like the proverbial elephant. He never forgot.

The evening eventually developed into the Ramsbottom Olympics, starting with a darts match which Spike and Gordon won. This was followed by an incredibly messy lemonade drinking contest, which the organiser was convinced he would win, until he showered everybody when a lemonade stream shot out of his nose. He wasn't very pleased to have to concede defeat to his archrival gay accountant. As was usual the night finished with an arm wrestling contest. The fatman never lost, mostly due to his enormous bulk, and his habit of farting very loud and disgustingly whenever he got bored. Everybody was aware that when he was on form, just one of his farts would have the potential to clear the Albert Hall.

Not too soon for some, the end of the evening's boozing was fast approaching, and a stranger entered the bar and quietly sidled up to several jolly boozers saying "I look for Ramsbottom" sounding very comical in his Polish accent. The stranger was Pavel, a cabbie for the local taxi firm PAMTAX, that NerdiSoft had a long running contract with. The firm took their name from the 3 Indian partners Dilip Pandya, Ahmad Alahan and Devindra Mukerjee.

The response to the cabbies introduction as he drifted around the bar was mostly of the sort "Whatever rattles your cage my friend." or "That's funny you don't sound Welsh." This was usually followed by derisive laughter and no helpful response. Eventually the greenhorn cabbie gave up confused, and left the bar totally oblivious to the fact that he had been set up by Ahmad his boss. He contacted base from the radio in his cab for clarification.

Laughter continued in the bar, until Pavel re-entered with a new instruction, and then the bar fell totally silent as everybody turned towards him.

It was all too soon for some, but the end of the evening's boozing had arrived, and as the cabbie entered the doorway of the Brewers for a second time, and shouted, "Cab for Mr Ramsbottom!" the whole place erupted in a noisy round of applause. Pavel began to think that he would never understand the English and their strange way of doing things.

"I am Mr Ramsbottom, it is me," Hugh smirked in his best foreign accent, "And these gentlemen are Mr Balls and Mr Bollocks.", he added pointing to Tiny and then Gordon.

"OK, I am Pavel; Ahmad is on airport duty." said the taxi driver, "Are you ready Zir?"

Messrs Ramsbottom and Balls downed the rest of their pints in one and both wiped their mouths with their sleeves.

"Where are you from?" the joker enquired.

"I am from Krakow in Poland, but I live in Colchester now."

"Beautiful country, lovely people. I am referring to Poland of course, not Colchester!"

"But Colchester will be a City next week." offered Pavel intelligently without any reply forthcoming, and then added, "You want to go to Tyrell's Close? Yes?"

"Yes, if you please." answered Hugh as he and Tiny climbed into the taxi, "But don't hold your breath my friend about your chances of living in a City next week."

Pavel began to think what a nice man Mr Ramsbottom was as the taxi headed up Springfield Road. Before they reached Tyrell's Close, the joker looked at his colleague and said, "Watch this." and brought his finger up to his lips to signal keep quiet.

"OK, my friend, see that bus shelter on the right; pull up there, and we'll walk the rest of the way." he instructed as they neared Oaklea Avenue. The taxi made the requested diversion, and then the fatman popped out of the back as the car pulled up, and went over to a tramp sitting in the bus shelter. With a grand flourish, making sure that he could be clearly seen, he put an arm over the tramp's shoulder, and gave him a £10 note, saying "Get yourself a bed in the hostel mate, it looks like it's going to be cold tonight."

By this time the cabbie's heart was warmed by the generosity this English gentlemen could show when jollied up by plenty of the Mr Happy juice. It reminded him of how people looked out for each other in the village outside Krakow where he had grown up, and how uninhibited things would be when his countrymen had indulged in their vodka swilling celebrations. As Tiny got out of the taxi, the joker leaned over to the cabbie with a grin saying, "By the way, as this is on account to NerdiSoft, you will understand that I gave your tip to our vagrant friend there?"

Pavel managed a thin smile at the loss of his tip, but uttered a fairly convincing "Of course!"

"Have a very successful night, Pavel." offered Tiny in parting, and the two friends both waved with false enthusiasm as the taxi drove away. They looked at each other; giggled, and walked on the few remaining few yards before they went their separate ways.

CHAPTER 3

Brewers Droop

(Early March 2012)

On the following Wednesday afternoon Norman arrived home, and upon checking his email, found that his inbox had a message from the Sexual Health Clinic. For some time he avoided opening it fearing the worst, but eventually he steeled himself, hit the button, and there it was, a positive all-clear.

"What a relief!" he thought. To celebrate, he quickly got changed and popped over to the Excel gym at Riverside Ice and Leisure. Going through his workout routines, he gravitated towards a running machine, and proceeded to burn some trainer rubber. After a while he began to slow down, and it was then he noticed a familiar female figure at the other end of the row on another running machine. But she wasn't running very fast as she seemed to be smiling a lot, and it looked as if she was being chatted up by a member of the gym staff. He was one of those I-don't-half-fancy-myself clean cut fellows with muscles on his muscles, and he wafted around the gym in a haze of Lynx Africa, looking like he might have been a personal trainer for Action Man.

Norman wasn't sure whether he was glad that Clarisa was distracted, and didn't seem to notice him, but he quickly finished his workout, and slipped out for a shower. But 20 minutes later he was passing through the refreshments area of the leisure complex on his way out, when they just happened to bump into each other.

"Hello, Normie, nice to see you." she smiled at him sweetly. He noticed how cutely her mouth turned up at the corners making two little dimples in her soft cheeks.

"Er, Yes! You too." he replied as coolly as possible.

"Buy me a cuppa then, and tell me what you've been up to." she smiled again.

He thought that would be a bit awkward; as his immediate thoughts were focussed on the experience of visiting the Sexual Health Clinic, but he bought them both a coffee and sat down to have a chat.

"Why didn't you say hello in the gym?" she enquired.

"Oh, I thought you were with the gorilla, you looked as if you were having a good time."

"What, Ryan?" she frowned, "No, he's definitely not my type, I don't like Michelin men, they're all muscle and no brains."

That was a thought that the young man immediately related to. It made him hurt a little inside as he thought of the teenage angst he'd endured when losing his very first girlfriend Susie to a muscle-bound knucklehead. The conversation continued. It was easy, and they got on really well. He felt rather guilty that he had taken his uncle's word for granted, and been convinced that he should seek medical advice. Hugh was always winding him up and playing practical jokes. It was unlike Norman to want to take a relationship any further than one night, but after spending some time with Clarisa, he warmed to the idea of trying to make another date with her. But he didn't have to try very hard. She finished her coffee, looked at him and asked "Do you fancy going out for a meal on Friday evening?"

"Why not? Let's go to Prezzo downstairs from me." he replied without hesitation.

"Yes, that'll be nice, I like Italian food," she continued, "And then afterwards you can take me to the Two Brewers, I've heard its good fun in there on a Friday night."

He was a little unsure that going to the Brewers would be the best idea, but replied after a brief while thinking, "Yes, OK. It's my local watering hole, but you'd better be prepared for a large dose of political incorrectness."

"Sounds good to me." she said. And with that she kissed him on the cheek and waved a quick farewell, and there were those cute dimples again.

The computer games genius who drove a Porsche floated on air as he strolled back to the Hub, it had been a good news day. Not only did he have the all-clear from the clinic, but one woman was now back on the agenda. He had an unusual feeling about how the date had come about. He was used to being the one pulling the strings where ladies were concerned, but he liked the idea she seemed to have made all the running. It made him smile inside, even though he also was a little apprehensive about going to the Brewers.

On Thursday morning Norman arrived at NerdiSoft determined that he'd collar his uncle and have a serious discussion with him. He wanted to tell him that he'd been to the Sexual Health Clinic and had been given the all clear, and he also wanted to make sure that when he brought Clarisa along to the Brewers, that things would not be screwed up for him. During the previous few days the marketing director had seemed to be busy, and he had been very secretive about what he was doing, and so getting hold of him was likely to be quite difficult. Norman worked through the morning on his latest batch of new games software, and then poured two cups of coffee and strolled along to Hugh's office. Usually he would just knock casually and stroll in, but this time when he pushed the door it wouldn't give. It appeared to be locked from the inside, so he knocked again more forcibly.

"Yes!" came a shout from behind the door, "Who is it?"

"Er, It's me, uncle."

"Just a minute, Nobless." The reply was accompanied by a sound of papers being gathered up, and filing cabinets sliding closed. Then the office door was opened by a very shifty looking fatman. He accepted the cup of coffee that was passed to him, and asked, "What can I do for you?"

"Well! You know what you said about that Clarisa?" he asked as casually as possible.

There was a smile and the same seal impression was repeated.

"Yes, that!" he said, "Well, I went to be checked out at the Sexual Health Clinic, and I've got the all clear, no problems."

Hugh spluttered on his coffee, and when he regained his senses, said, "It was a windup you stupid boy, just a windup, and blimey you're so gullible, it seems you fell for it hook, line, and sinker. Clarisa Hinton, she's a nice girl, sings in the church choir at Trinity. Oh, Nobless, you are a prize berk."

Norman wasn't pleased with this prank, and went to walk away. When he got to the door, he turned, pointed, and answered emphatically, "Really! You've overstepped the mark, Uncle, and I don't think that's very funny."

The joker just looked at him grinning, and wickedly repeated the seal impression. The frustrated nephew continued, "I like her! And I'm bringing her along to the Brewers tomorrow night. I need you to assure me that you won't screw things up for me. I don't want to fall out with you over this. Can you make me a promise?"

The fat one carried on with a donkey smile, going," Eeh Aww Eeh Aww." The young one put his hands on his hips and stood still indignantly in the doorway.

Then the jester stopped and said, "Oh, alright then, Nobless, don't lose your rag over it."

Norman knew that his practical joking relative may have been a well-heeled and privileged person, but he also knew that he wore no airs and graces. He had a common touch, and did not consider himself above anybody. He accepted everyone at face value whatever their status in life, and because of his openness and matter of fact way of expressing himself he had made many friends. Even though he was inclined to be excessive in his leg-pulling, his practical jokes, and his passion for just plain taking the piss, he was still always the life and soul of every party. Whatever he said or did, he genuinely meant no harm, and everybody knew it was just his way. He would be the first to admit to a mischievous need to wind people up. Norman left the room not convinced that his uncle would behave himself. The practical joker carried on drinking his coffee and planning his latest very elaborate windup, which had taken him some time and effort to prepare. He now knew that he needed to tread carefully with the prank, and think of a way to accommodate his nephew.

On Friday evening the man in the Hub was fully equipped with a brand new pair of Jeff Banks boxers, and a major splash of Erection aftershave, and had just finished getting ready when the doorbell rang. It was Clarisa, looking gorgeous, wafting Hugo Boss Deep Red through the flat. Just as she came in the phone rang, as it did at the same time every Friday evening. It was the familiar voice of Stanley.

"Ey Oop, son, 'ow yer diddlin'?"

"Alright, Dad, how are you?"

"Mustn't grumble, nobody listens anyway."

"Mum alright, is she?"

"Aye, son, same as ever."

"What can I do for you, Dad?"

The phone call was as quick and precise as ever. Stanley wasn't one for long chats on the phone. He was old school, and to him telephones were still new fangled nonsense. He would be the last person in England to have a mobile phone. The Friday evening call was predictable, and as usual it was just a reminder about Cher's hockey match at their home ground up at Gillingham Dam near Beccles.

The young couple were both ready to go out, and soon they were sitting down for a meal in the Prezzo Restaurant downstairs. She had Pinot Grigio, and he sipped fizzy mineral water, and they chatted their way through a healthy and tasty vegetarian meal. He was pleased that she was so easy to talk to, and they found a lot of common interests in keeping fit, eating sensibly, and enjoying the music of Coldplay and Stereophonics. They were both avid watchers of The Only Way is Essex, or TOWIE as devoted followers of the programme had relabelled the enigmatic view of young people's lives and relationships in middle Essex. Neither of them regarded it with any seriousness. To them it was a comedy programme, and just another reality television exercise. Clarisa revealed that she had once had a date with Mark Wright, and that she loved going to the Sugar Hut nightclub in Brentwood where she and Norman had first met. They talked about their jobs. She couldn't believe that he created computer games for a living, and she revealed that she worked as a legal secretary for the Chelmsford partnership of Crooks, Watt, Sawyer, Cumming. When they compared the places they lived, he was surprised to find that she lived in a small flat in Sandon, and commuted to work on the Park and Ride.

He had always been nervous about taking any relationship beyond a one night stand in the past. He had enjoyed playing the field, and he somehow thought that the game he played with women would go on and on. His mum was always nagging at him to find a nice girl, and settle down, and make her a grandmother, but in truth he didn't really know how to take a relationship any further. Now he was with someone who was doing the leading for him, who wanted him. He found himself strangely attracted to Clarisa in a way he had never felt before. When they left Prezzo they made the short walk to the

Brewers holding hands, and they both laughed all the way there. Outside the door of the pub it was eerily quiet. Normally the jolly fatman would be in full swing, and the laughter and joviality would be audible from the outside. They entered the bar, but it was in darkness and complete silence.

Then suddenly, the lights came on and pandemonium broke out. All the usual crew were there, but the whole bar was decorated to celebrate somebody's recent visit to the Sexual Health Clinic. There were balloons and party poppers, whoopee cushions, and all the other party paraphernalia. There was a whole wall plastered with General Kitchener style posters, superimposed with Norman's face, with the finger pointing, but instead of "Your country needs you!" they all said "Hey you, fancy a shag!"

Everyone in the pub, punters and bar staff were all wearing t-shirts picturing someone outside the Sexual Health Clinic, not looking much like a Kwikfit mechanic on a lunch break, and with the legend "CLAP FOR ME!" underneath. There was so much whooping and cheering, and piss-taking the victim was slightly dumbstruck, and most of all he felt embarrassed for Clarisa. But she instantly got the joke, and was laughing along with everybody else.

"Phew! What a relief." thought Norman, and then Hugh came over, put an arm over his shoulder, and asked, "And who's this lucky lady, Norm?" That was unusual, because he never referred to him as Norman or Norm, it was always Nobless.

"Er, this is Clarisa," he replied, relieved that his uncle seemed to be on good behaviour. The prankster kissed her hand very graciously and looking her straight in the eyes said "You're lovely sweetheart; I hope you look after my little Norm."

The evening continued in the usual vein, and despite being on his best behaviour Hugh was in fine form, living up to his reputation as resident comedian. Now it was clear why he had been so busy and so secretive recently. All these posters and t-shirts had taken a lot of time to prepare, and it was now obvious that when he had claimed he had a toothache, he had really been staking out the clinic so that he could take all his photographs

Later on, Clarisa took Norman aside and asked "Why did you go to the clinic then?" But he couldn't tell her the truth about the windup, so thinking quickly, he remembered what Terry had said to him, and replied, "I saw this poster in the doctor's surgery about chlamydia, so I decided to get checked out." She thought that was a sensible thing to do, and just kissed him on the cheek, and smiled. The jolly fatman had heard the conversation, and chimed in with,

"Isn't he a good little boy, he's like a son to me, and one day I want to be a granddad."

Throughout the evening the joker buttoned his lip to any jibes in the young couple's direction. He seemed to be getting on really well with his nephew's new girlfriend, and once he had found out she was a legal secretary, they even had a long chat about solicitors. Hugh's parents had made their first fortune working in the Chelmsford based legal practice of Large, Ramsbottom, Torso, and Smallpiece. Later in the evening when Clarisa went to the ladies, Hugh took his nephew aside, and said quietly," Hey Norm, I'm on my best behaviour, just as you asked, and everything's going fine isn't it?" Then he winked at a nervous Nobless.

"I suppose so," was the reply, "But this is a very elaborate prank, and I'm still worried that something might go wrong."

"You worry too much Norm." the fatman reassured quickly just before Clarisa returned to the bar. He then flitted away, and went to take the piss out of gay Gordon and his entourage who as usual were playing darts in the opposite corner. After the darts, the Friday night arm wrestling championships were started up, and were won by the organiser with the standard and all too obvious disgusting finale.

Just as the evening was beginning to wind down, three very drunk revellers fell through the door, and went to the bar to order some drinks. Norman recognised one of them as an old school chum. Suddenly he was struck with a blind panic, just as he was being pushed into another game of darts. He didn't want the whole circus to start up again, and so he attempted to attract Clarisa's attention to leave. But she was still talking to Hugh, who had also noticed Terry's arrival, and was equally agitated by the potential for a disastrous end to the evening. Smithy couldn't help but notice all the posters and t-shirts around the bar, and drunkenly barged his way over to his old Boswells schoolmate, intercepting him on his way over to Clarisa, shouting and grinning "Hey, Norm, what a great ruse. I bet your uncle's at the bottom of this."

The reply came with an irritated sigh, "What are you doing here?"

"You invited me, mate, don't you remember when we were at the clinic last week."

"You're pissed, Smithy! Why don't you just go home?"

It was a desperate plea to divert the situation, and it failed. Norman was wishing that his unwanted guest would just disappear, or better still that the ground would swallow him up, chew him into tiny bits, and puke him up again 10,000 miles away.

"No, Norm, I'll have a drink with you and your mates, and a game of darts," answered the slightly annoyed drunkard.

Meanwhile, after trying to no avail to persuade the barman to call time early, the fatman attempted to break the fire alarm with his elbow, so that everybody would leave the bar in panic. He had several stabs at it, much to Clarisa's amusement, missing his target due to a few too many pints of Fuller's Pride, before the barman shouted at him to stop. And then all attempts to avoid a catastrophe came to an abrupt halt. It was too late.

Terry spotted someone he definitely wanted to talk to, and nearly tripping over himself made his way over to him.

"Hi, Mr Ramsbottom, all this is down to you is it?"

"Er no, not really." squirmed Hugh, knowing that now the evening had full potential to fall over the edge of a cliff.

"No! Don't be silly, you done it, didn't you?" he continued, "Norm told me that he shagged this bird he met at Sugar Hut, and you told him he should go and be checked out at the clap clinic. But I didn't know you were setting him up with all these posters. What a brilliant ruse!"

For once in his long life the joker was silenced, and felt very, very uncomfortable. He looked at Clarisa and she was boiling with anger. For her things had just clicked into place.

"Oh really, is that so?" she fumed, and grabbed Terry's drink and splashed it into his face. Then just as quickly she snatched Tiny's pint, and poured it over the crotch of the interloper's trousers, before inflicting the coupe-de-grace and kneeing him in the nuts. He doubled over and began writhing about on the floor. Then she turned to a frowning fatman and snarled,

"You think that what you've done is funny? It's not; it was a disgusting thing to do!" Then she jumped on to a chair and punched him in the nose, and then leapt back down and kicked him smartly on both shins. Like a whirlwind, she grabbed her coat, and ran swiftly out of the door in tears, knocking over tables, drinks, and fellow revellers in the process.

Norman stood frozen to the spot, and stared in despair at what was occurring. It was over very quickly, but he was helpless to do anything about it. He rushed outside to try and catch Clarisa, but she had disappeared. The evening had ended in disaster, and it was all down to somebody's stupid prank. The butt of the joke went back into the Brewers, walked straight up to his uncle, who was still nursing his bruised shins, and said quietly, "Are you happy now?"

Then he left and walked in much distress back to the Hub alone.

Meanwhile back in the Brewers, normal service was not quickly restored. Tiny walked over to pick Terry up very roughly, and then suggested diplomatically, "I think you and your friends had better leave now, don't you?" Without protest the drunkard and his friends beat a hasty exit. There was a strange gloom hanging over proceedings, particularly where the resident comedian was concerned. He had thought for so long that his charm offensive had smoothed things over for the target of his joke. He had sensed first of all the tension, and then relief that things went so well, but now Hugh was so bloody annoyed that stupid Smithy had spoiled it all with his insensitive drunken ramblings. Try as he might, in the end he had been unable to avert disaster.

The taxi driver Ahmad appeared at the end of the evening, ready to take his usual passengers home. As the Village People climbed into Gordon's

Galaxy with Ike in the driver's seat, the joker couldn't resist one last jibe, and shouted "Hey Bean Counter! Your turn in the barrel tonight is it then?" The car moved off with four men inside, and four middle fingers pointing in the air.

The taxi proceeded to make the journey with complete silence in the cab, and shortly after arrived at Tyrell's Close. Without a word the two friends left the taxi, and then the two passengers looked at each other with thin smiles. They walked on the remaining few yards, and then before they went their separate ways Tiny turned to his colleague and quietly affirmed, " We've known each other a long time mate, and I know better than anyone about your windups. But I think that this time perhaps you went too far. You took too big a risk with that lovely girl being there with Norman, and I don't know how you can put it right."

"I know, I know." replied a distinctly unjolly fatman as he trudged off home.

Norman didn't sleep much that night. He had never been so annoyed before. His uncle's stream of pranks and ever more elaborate practical jokes had often got him into trouble, but this time, having Clarisa disappear on him after what had been up to then an enjoyable evening was just too much. He was at home alone in his apartment, instead of being tucked up cosily with her. Up to about 2am he tried to concentrate on playing Beer Festival Bastards Final Frontier, but whereas previously he had easily worked his way through all the levels, this time he found his mind wandering, and kept crashing out early. He went to bed but slept fitfully, and woke about 7am without feeling refreshed, but still found it impossible to get back to sleep. He decided to get up, get showered and dressed, have breakfast, and take his frustrations out on the Porsche by driving up to Suffolk early, whilst there was still very little traffic on the roads. Cher's hockey match would be starting at 10.30am, but by 8am her brother was burning rubber, and listening to Coldplay. His mood was forcing bursts of acceleration putting the car through its paces. By the time he reached Gillingham Dam he was an hour early, but by then felt exhausted, so he set an alarm on his mobile phone, and enjoyed a long nap. He was woken at about 10.15 with his hockey playing sister tapping on his windscreen.

Hugh by contrast, despite being at the root of the trouble, slept like a baby, but then he had drunk about 8 pints. He woke up on Saturday morning, and in the cold and sober light of day began to think about what had happened the previous evening. His wife Millicent found him pensive and quiet, which wasn't like him at all. By the time early afternoon arrived he had decided that he must get in touch with his nephew, and attempt to resolve the situation. But he knew he would be up in Leiston with his family at least until late afternoon. At 4.30pm he sent a text message.

"I'm so sorry, mate! Please call me when you get back to Chelmsford. Uncle H."

The text was received but there was a decision to ignore it.

Saturday followed the standard course. Cher's team lost the hockey match by a magnificent margin, she returned in the Porsche to Leiston covered in mud and cowpats. Norman's mum cooked something German; this time it was Goulash. Lisalotte and Cher fell asleep pissed again, and father and son had a butcher's at the greenhouse and garden.

"I don't know why she can't do it!" said Stanley exasperated.

"What's that, Dad?" said son to father confused; his mind drifting to somewhere else.

"Just make a beef stew, or a hotpot, or a nice steak and ale pie," he continued, "But no! She 'as to ruin it by puttin' bloody ladles of bloody paprika in it. I 'ate that bloody foreign muck!"

His mother's son allowed himself a little chuckle. Goulash was one of the German dishes he didn't mind too much.

"Yes, Dad." he replied. But he was elsewhere, miles away back in Chelmsford.

Late in the afternoon he said his goodbyes and jumped into the Porsche, breathed a big sigh of relief, and burnt some more rubber. Another hockey match, another family meal, another Saturday routine was thankfully over. "61 minutes dead on" he murmured to himself unjoyfully, as he pulled into his parking space back at the Hub in Chelmsford.

By Saturday evening he was showered, shaved, preened, moisturised and ready. Right at that time he considered that the best way to get over a crashed relationship was to start another one. "Get back on the horse after a fall." he told himself. Although he didn't want to let the recent events upset his routine, it was with something of a heavy heart that he was about to set off for his visit to the Sugar Hut nightclub. A generous splash of Erection aftershave, and he was on his way again to present himself for the scouts for The Only Way is Essex. But as he walked to his car, there was his uncle looking very sheepish.

"We need to talk," he said quietly, "I'm so sorry, Nobless. It shouldn't have turned out that way. I know it's entirely my fault for playing the prank in the first place, but I did my best not to screw things up, didn't I? I'd put so much effort into setting the prank up, I had to carry it through, and I was very careful where you and Clarisa were concerned last night. In the end, it would have been fine, if that drunken prat Terry Smith hadn't turned up, and opened his big ugly gob."

"You finished?" answered Norman, "Is that all you can say? I told you I liked her. She's different, and YOU did screw it up for me, uncle. Am I supposed to forgive you that easily?"

Hugh was almost in tears, in fact they both were. They had never before been so far from being the best of mates. The fatman shuddered a deep breath, and then pleaded, "Norm, you are like son to me, I love you like one of my own. Don't let's fall out; I'll do whatever I need to do to repair the damage. Please!"

The young man was surprised. He knew how hard it was for the insatiable practical joker, to say something like that. They looked at each other very intensely, and then anger turned to wet eyes, and they spontaneously hugged. After a few seconds they moved apart, and then the fat one grinned and mockingly exclaimed, "Pack it in mate, anyone watching would think we were a couple of poofs. We'll be joining Gordon's clan for a quick bum job." And then they fell about laughing, both relieved that they had broken the ice. Without the practical jokes, and the quick-fire humour, Hugh wasn't the man that Norman knew at all, so he just uttered, "OK! Let's forget it, but in future please just try to be a bit more sensitive when it involves my relationships, will you?"

"OK mate, thanks!" replied the joker, and then Norman got into the Porsche, and was quickly gone.

The prankster celebrated with a couple of pints of Fuller's Pride in the Brewers.

The man in the Porsche only drove as far as the Widford roundabout, and then turned back and went home. He didn't feel like any kind of making jolly. He had great sense of losing something very important to him, and learning a big lesson about relationships at the same time, and he didn't know why he'd never felt quite like that before.

CHAPTER 4

Caesaromagus no More

(mid March 2012 up to 17th)

It was 5.30 pm and the end of another week at NerdiSoft, and the "Gotta-get-home-get-outa-my-way" traffic was building up all along the A12. The marketing director of NerdiSoft was returning from work, and had just turned off at the Boreham Interchange. When he was in Springfield Road, and just opposite the Endeavour he pressed the remote control device fitted in his Land Rover, to open the automatic gates to enter his property. The gates closed behind him, he switched off the engine, and when the front door to the house opened, there stood his little darling wife Millicent, being pushed out of the way by Bimbo, the maddest, craziest labradoodle that ever was interbred. It came bounding towards him as he got out of the car, and with a long, loping stride that seemed to take no time at all, and only 3 steps to cover the distance, jumped all over him, howling, and licking, and wagging his happy tail.

"Hello, Bimbo" Hugh responded stroking the hound's teddy bear coat, "Down now, you mad dog."

Then he walked over and greeted his wife with a big hug and a sloppy kiss, as he entered the house and carried on walking towards the kitchen.

"Where are the boys?" he asked, adding "Silly question!"

"Yes!" she replied looking up at him, "In their playroom, on the Xboxes."

There was a pause before she continued, looking at him with a concerned expression on her face, "But we had a bit of a problem earlier on, which I think I'd like you to sort out."

"What's up then, sweetheart?" he said recognising the expression as something he couldn't avoid.

"Well, earlier on, I went into the playroom with some drinks, and found Thomas had tuned into Babestation on the TV. He was a bit embarrassed when I saw him, and I didn't say anything. As far as I could make out the other 2 were well distracted in NerdiSoft's latest game, and I don't think they saw what he was doing. Can you deal with it please, darling?"

He looked at her, and burst out laughing, and hardly able to contain his mirth, he blurted out "Well at least we know he's not a poof then. OK, leave it with me."

She looked at him with a fleeting smile, but was still concerned that her husband would not take this little matter seriously enough.

"Naughty boy." she answered pretending to slap his wrist.

Quickly he turned and headed for their swimming pool saying, "Has the maintenance man been? I'm going for a quick dip."

"Yes, darling, it's nice and warm in there now." she replied.

He stripped off completely, shouted "Geronimo!" and jumped into the water with a theatrical bomb, which because of his size caused a tidal wave, and washed a substantial amount of water out of the pool. He lay there on his back, blanking his mind, relaxed and contented, looking like a giant hairy pink lilo.

Hugh Ramsbottom had never known what it's like to be poor, and that was unlikely to ever change. He lived with his pretty, petite wife Millicent and their three boys, Thomas (Tom) who was 16, Richard (Dick) who was 15, and Harold (Harry) who was 14. The names he'd given to his offspring warmly amused him. Tom, Dick and Harry had probably been an adaptation from Pop, Dick and Harry in the Beezer comic. It was just one of the jolly fatman's childhood obsessions that he had been fascinated by comics and comic book characters, and was an avid reader of the Beano, Dandy, Beezer and Topper.

Their home was a magnificent mansion along Springfield Road which they had named Avalon House after the mythical kingdom of King Arthur. It had automatic gates, flanked by a high brick wall, a huge paved drive, with 3 good sized garages, and a substantial well established un-overlooked garden. It was well built from fine red brick, with 6 bedrooms, 3 bathrooms, a massive fitted kitchen, two lounges, a dining room, a conservatory, 2 playrooms, a Victorian style study room, a balcony, and a small swimming pool.

After the evening meal Hugh was lolling lazily in his recliner chair in his study. He had finished reading the March copy of The Edge, and was attending to his mail. Millicent came in and put down a cup of black coffee, two sugars; the way he liked it, kissed him on the cheek, smiled and went back to the kitchen. There were some letters from Brentwood School referring to his support for their fundraising efforts for the Burkina Faso paralympians, an electricity bill from EON, and the usual small pile of dividend notices from his Stock Exchange investment portfolio. Whenever he received dividend notices it made him think of his mum and dad. He knew how hard they had worked to give their only child the best, and how clever, and lucky, they had been with their financial investments. He knew that he owed his charmed life to them. Born of wealthy parents, he had been educated at Brentwood School as a boarder. He didn't like being away from home, but he appreciated now that it had taught him to be self-reliant and outgoing. His parents were both legal eagles, and were partners in a practice called Large, Ramsbottom, Torso, and Smallpiece in Chelmsford. That made them fairly comfortably off, but they became super-rich overnight, after some American friends of theirs invested 10,000 dollars for them in the early 80's, in a small software company called Microsoft. When Microsoft was floated on the New York Stock Exchange they became millionaires overnight, and after a few years retired fairly young, and lived for 5 months of every year in the Channel Island of Jersey. So at the age of 26 Hugh was living alone in the big house in Springfield Road. By that time he had gained his BA (Honours) History degree from the OU, and had met Tiny again, after they had first run into each other at Brentwood School. They were both working in I.T. and never dreamed that one day they would go into business together. Sadly, in 1995 the Ramsbottom seniors were both killed in a skiing accident in Val d'Isère, and their only son, who had just been married to Millicent a month before, inherited the house and all their investments, and thus became a very rich man indeed.

He browsed quickly through the paperwork, because he was looking forward to his Friday night drink with the usual crew down at the Two Brewers. When he'd finished he ambled slowly out of his study and along the hall to the boy's playroom. This was fully equipped with three Xboxes, three 32 inch plasma screens, and a vast assortment of computer, Internet and games equipment, plus a huge bookcase full of computer games and other software. He grinned as he tumbled clumsily through the door.
"Get that homework finished, you techno-brats." he shouted as the playroom door fell open, and he landed on the floor, "And don't spend too long on those Xboxes." He patted each one of his sons softly on top of the head, as they carried on playing an early version of R. McGeddon's Nerd World Apocalypse, each of them entranced by Norman's latest marvellous creation, and not averting their gaze for one second from their screens to their dad.
"My three boys," he thought, "What a great test bed for NerdiSoft games." as he continued his amble down the stairs.
He went to the kitchen with his empty coffee cup, "Hello, Minnie Mouse," he said, and gave his wife a soft bear hug and a slushy coffee flavoured kiss on the lips. They looked at each other fondly, eye to eye, beautiful green to soft brown, and as he enfolded her in his arms, she knew he was like her big cuddly teddy bear.
"I'm off, down the pub, see you later, Reepicheep" he smiled.
"Have a good time, sweetie-pie." she replied.
Millicent had many pet names from her husband, Minnie Mouse was her favourite, and she also loved being called Reepicheep after the brave little mouse in the Chronicles of Narnia. They were an affectionate couple, and he would describe her to his friends as "My wife Millicent, cute, tiny, petite, and as sweet and curvy as a cashew nut."
She loved him intensely even though he was now almost twice the man she had married seventeen years ago. He had been a sturdy 12 stone then, but

now at 48 he had ballooned to nearly 20 stone. She tolerated her "lovely man"; all the massive bulk of him, because she loved him, even though she knew all the bad habits that he had that were making him obese.

Every evening she prepared and cooked a lovely meal, all healthy, lean and good for you. That night it had been fresh salmon with new potatoes, chantenay carrots and broccoli, followed by freshly made fruit salad and low fat yogurt. The Ramsbottoms always ate as a family at their antique oak kitchen table, and the boys had been brought up to appreciate good food. But Millicent knew about her man's extra curricular eating habits; that he always cleaned his plate, and that he would eat anything. Hugh's 3 boys loved their occasional secret junk food binges with their dad at McDonald's or Pizza Hut.

At 8 pm it was time for a ritual Hugh had observed for over 20 years. The Friday evening ritual had changed only a little as he had grown older and larger. He remembered how, on his 25th birthday he had indulged in the ultimate Chelmsford pub crawl. From his house he had walked to the Endeavour, 200 yards up Springfield Road in the wrong direction, and started with a pint of Guinness. He had then crossed the road to the Plough, sunk a quick one, and then changed direction and headed down to the Red Lion. This was followed by a small diversion to the Alma, and then a return to the Red Lion, before another stop off in the Oddfellows Arms, topping up with a pint of the black stuff in each watering hole. Only 50 yards away across the Trinity garage forecourt in those days was the Squirrels, which now appealed to him on a different basis, as it had become a Tandoori restaurant called the Sitar. A few more strides away he entered the Three Cups, which at one time had a snooker room upstairs, but was now another Indian restaurant called Chadni. Continuing the pub crawl with another diversion he included the Riverside Inn, before returning to the Three Cups, and then completing his crawl in the Two Brewers. He was very proud that he'd managed a pint in each pub, which totted up to 11 pints in all. No mean feat, especially 11 pints of Guinness, even though the crawl had taken several hours.

Just as every Friday night, he left his car on the drive. He wasn't ever going to risk driving over the limit. He loved driving, and the Land Rover Discovery LR4 with the personalised number plate P155 ORF although not exactly in pristine condition, was one of his many pride and joys. He was always chuckling at how massive it looked parked alongside Millicent's purple Ka convertible. It looked to him as if you could stuff the Ka into the Land Rover's tailgate.

The Friday night walk to the pub was now the jolly fatman's solitary form of exercise, or rather his concession towards it. He pushed the button which automatically closed the huge wrought iron gate with a pleasing clang, tested to make sure it had caught by shaking it, and set off walking. After all the predictions of a drought due to 6 months of no rain, there was no need for a raincoat or a brolly. It was one of those evenings when it wasn't cold, and it wasn't warm, it was just right.

"Good drinking weather." he mused as he turned away from the gate and crossed the road moving slightly downhill, and turned into Tyrell's Close to collect his mate Tiny who had recently moved there from East Bergholt.

The NerdiSoft chairman was a dependable bloke, 49 years young, similar age to his colleague, and a very stable character. His Christian name was really Timothy, but he had acquired his alternative moniker while at Brentwood School. Hugh had heard Tiny Tim singing "Tiptoe through the tulips" which he thought was hilariously funny, and named his friend after the ukulele playing crooner. Mr Balls had no kids, and was married to Tina, 36 years young, a posh spoken ex-model, a former Miss Iberia, professional name Tina Bonita, whom he had met on a flight back from Madrid.

The door bell rang, and Tina came to the door dressed as she always was, like some gorgeous celebrity. She was a honey blonde, with dark hazel eyes, perfect dazzling white teeth, and a wonderful, curvy figure. She was tall, and confident, with an ever so slight air of superiority, and she oozed charisma. If ever Hugh had been tempted to covet his neighbour's wife, then the object of his coveting would definitely have been her.

"Hola, hombre," she grinned, and added "Where do you go, Hugo?" with a huge smarmy smile.

"Don't smile at me, Argentina." he replied, kissing her outstretched hand.

She turned her back towards him and wiggled her arse, and then looked provocatively over her shoulder with a smile saying, "Does my boom look big in this?"

"Sure thing, sister!" he answered, giving her a playful slap, and they both fell about laughing, just as Tiny came to the door. He'd heard it a 100 times before. It was their personal in-joke.

"Hello mate", said his drinking buddy as he kissed his wife goodbye on both cheeks Mediterranean style.

"Hasta la vista, Chica, don't wait up" he said, as she closed the door behind them still smiling.

"Getting sorted are you?" enquired Hugh, as they made their way past the other big houses, the traffic lights at Stump Lane, and along the pavement opposite the new estate where until recently there had been allotments. The chairman offered an update on how the unpacking and refitting work had been getting on since they had moved in, and then tailed off with, "I think my wife spends all her time flirting with the delivery men and the builders, and making cups of tea, but they've made a bit of progress in the lounge and kitchen. We should be ready to start on the interior decoration soon, and Spike's firm comes with a good reputation, and I know she's safe there with him. After all, he's one of Gordon's boyfriends."

"And they're all queers together." sang the joker derisorily.

That night there was a special reason for a celebration, not that the boys needed an excuse for a piss-up. On the previous Wednesday 14th March the Queen had granted City status to Chelmsford as part of her Diamond Jubilee celebrations. Hugh was a proud, born and bred Chelmsfordian, despite his boyhood exile in the boarding school at Brentwood. As a scholar of history he knew more than most about the illustrious past of the town, and the contention between Chelmsford's claim to City status, and the rival claims of Colchester and Southend.

The friends were making for the Two Brewers, but there was no set plan. Of all the public houses that the Old Chelmsfordian had frequented, and the list was longer than War and Peace, this was easily his favourite. He had done some local research on public houses, and the Brewers appealed very strongly to his sense of history. He had discovered that it had originally been a farmhouse built circa 1680, but was known to have been an alehouse called The Crown and Shears by 1765. By 1802 it was known as the Jolly Brewers, serving the workers from the foundries and engineering works along the Chelmer and Blackwater canal terminating nearby. At one time it had been used as a Coroner's Court.

The pace of their arrival at the destination pub depended mostly on how thirsty they were on the way down. A few minutes later, they had crossed Springfield Road and turned into the first port of call, the Red Lion. Everybody in the Red Lion knew the jolly fatman, it wasn't that he had presence, it was more that when he entered a room he took up three times as much space as anybody else, so people tended to notice when he was around. Pubs were places where he felt comfortable and at home. Nods were exchanged, but privacy was respected.

"What'll it be?" enquired the landlord.

"Two pints of draft Guinness, please." answered Tiny.

The drinks were poured and quaffing began. It was just a taster, and Hugh wasn't that keen on what he called football pubs. He always thought there were a time and a place for football, and as an ardent Clarets supporter he loved his footie as much as the next man. In truth he preferred non-league honesty, sweat and endeavour much more than the overpaid prima donna circus of the Premier League, and had frequently cultivated the idea that he'd like to be more involved with his City heroes. After all, he was a relatively rich man, and in his view a directorship would be most appropriate. The duo ignored the football on the large screen, but began to discuss the latest situation concerning the Clarets.

"I don't suppose you've had any time to keep up with City recently, what with your move to Chelmsford, and the plans you've got in hand for the company going global?"

"No mate. How are they getting on?"

"Well, since the turn of the year, they were OK in 2nd or 3rd place, looking good, but realistically they have no chance of catching Woking. But after losing to bloody Bromley they've become very inconsistent. They won against Hampton and Richmond 1 - 0 at home, but then lost two games on the trot, against Dover away 3 - 1, and then Welling at home 2 - 1. City are away at Sutton tomorrow, and I'm worried were going to blow it. But there is talk of us signing a new striker called Jamie Slabber."

"It'll be a shame if they don't at least make the playoffs again this year. But that's the way that football goes, mate."

"Yeah, sometimes it's hard work watching them. Never mind!"

Gulps of ale followed and then the subject quickly changed to the chairman's forthcoming trip to America and China.

"When are you off then?"

"Where?" answered Tiny, playing a game he'd played hundreds of times before, as he knew exactly what his colleague was asking.

"On your round the world in 8 days jolly jaunt pretending to be Phileas Fogg."

The chairman smiled, he knew how his mate's humour worked, and he wasn't rising to the altogether too obvious bait.

"Oh that," he replied keeping to the subject, and not acknowledging the jibe, "In a couple of week's time. It's going to be big you know. If the deals come off, we'll have to put the company on a whole new footing. We'll need a re-branding, a change of direction, and we'd better think about relocating to Chelmsford."

"I'm sure you know what you're doing. And in the meantime we'll keep the detail, or most of it, under our hats. Don't want to confuse the workers, do we?"

"Too right, mate."

They both finished their pints simultaneously.

"Onwards and upwards?"

"Off we go then."

A few minutes later they entered the Oddfellows Arms. Everybody in there knew the jolly fatman, it wasn't so much his presence, it was more that when he entered a room he occupied three times as much space as anybody else, so people tended to notice when he was around. Pubs were always places where he felt comfortable and at home. Many nods were exchanged, and much privacy was respected.

"Two pints of Black Sheep, please," requested Tiny of Sarah, the landlady," And how are you today, sweetheart?"

"I'm OK thanks." she answered pouring the required nectar, and then added," Your pies are ready if you want them now?"

"What's that?" he replied.

"Oh, I pre-ordered us a couple of the hand-crafted steak, stilton and mushroom pies" interrupted Hugh.

"Blimey mate, I'm sorry but I've only just finished one of Tina's chicken and chorizo specials, and I couldn't possibly eat anything else at the moment." said Tiny.

"Never mind!" smiled the joker, "I'll eat both of them."

He tucked into his delicious pies, liberally interspersed with gulps of Black Sheep, and his fellow drinker waited patiently making small talk not to interrupt the fat one's ravenous appetite too much. When his friend was nearing the end of the second pie, he ordered up some more drinks, calling to Sarah over his shoulder.

"A couple of pints of Doombar, please."

"Coming up." she replied.

"Bloody good idea." agreed the pieman, licking his knife and fork.

When the pies had been polished off Hugh started to relate the tale regarding Thomas's interest in Babestation to his mate, who listened intently, then grinned, and only offered the advice to tread carefully. He knew that it would be dealt with in a light-hearted and overtly fatherly way.

It didn't take long for them to finish their Doombars, and soon they continued down Springfield Road. Sometimes in the past they had stopped off for a quick one, at either the Squirrels/Sitar or the Three Cups/Chadni, or sometimes both, but tonight they agreed to bypass the bars in these two restaurants and head straight on down to the Two Brewers.

In a short while they reached their destination. Everybody in the Brewers knew the jolly fatman, in there he had presence. When he entered there he still took up three times as much space as anybody else, and people knew that this was where he felt most comfortable and at home. Handshakes and backslaps and high-fives were exchanged, and no privacy was respected.

Norman was already there on his second J2O.

"Good Evening, Nobless," said Hugh, and turning away towards Gordon and Spike who were playing darts added," Hang on! I'll just give the two poofs a wave."

He flapped a limp wrist in their direction, and as was their custom they both saluted him with their middle fingers and carried on playing darts.

"Bit quiet in here tonight," grinned the resident comedian," Nobody been to the clap clinic this week?"

That was an unfortunate slight reprise for his nephew, and he reacted by giving his uncle a rather scornful look. He understood immediately and bit his lip in recognition of his slip-up.

"I don't think Clarisa was all that amused." Norman complained.

"Yeah! Wow! She has a kick like a mule, my shins are still bruised." winced Hugh, "But I've tried to smooth things over."

"Oh really? What have you done?"

"Well, I found out where she lives, and sent her a huge bunch of flowers, and a megasize box of Thornton's chocolates. Oh! And a card of course saying how sorry I am."

Then he added, "If that doesn't do the trick, nothing will."

Norman wasn't sure, but he hoped his uncle was right.

The evening continued with pints of Fuller's Pride, darts, and mostly good-natured banter, and a full and frank discussion upon the merits or otherwise of the town being granted City status ahead of other Essex contenders Colchester and Southend. The Chelmsford born and bred enthusiast was pleased with the news, and proceeded to lecture informatively about the full legitimacy of the claim, whilst everyone else delighted in winding him up about it.

"OK, where was it then, this Roman town?" asked Spike

"There wasn't one, it was just a fort called Caesaromagus, meaning Caesar's market or Caesar's field, and it was just west of the bridge on the old A12."

"Near the Moulsham Mill then?"

"Possibly, But if you think about it carefully and logically, then as a stopping off point between Londinium and Camulodunum, and as somewhere they'd want to easily defend, it was probably on that strip of land between the two rivers that today we call the Chelmer and the Can. I think it was known at one time as Mesopotamia Island, and It's just east of the Meadows shopping Mall."

"Why there? Did the Romans want to go shopping then?"

"No you silly git! If you camp between two rivers it's easy to defend yourself, and you have the advantage of fresh water in one river, while you can look after the horses and piss in the other one."

"I heard that Caesaromagus was just a Roman brothel."

"OK then, so it was handy to wash your bits in the river afterwards."

Hugh was getting exasperated with the obvious ignorance of the windup merchants and so he attempted to embrace the discussion with a statement.

"The Romans would have invaded from the South. So they came through here first and maybe bypassed the place, before they got to Colchester, that's an indisputable fact. The Romans initiated a settlement at Camulodunum in AD44, but when Boadicea destroyed it in AD60 they set up a fort at Caesaromagus. When the Romans left Britain in AD407 the settlement at Caesaromagus disappeared, while Camulodunum was by that time an established town. Yes! Colchester has a legitimate claim to the oldest recorded town in England in AD77, but I know it's always been the arsehole of Essex. So there!" he asserted ordering another pint of Fuller's Pride for everyone.

"I always thought that the arsehole of Essex was Tilbury." Gordon offered.

"Well, there are a few alternative claims to that title, including of course the impossible to find Shellow Bowells near Willingale." Hugh answered, "Although I don't suppose any of you poofs would have any trouble finding a place with a name like that."

The gay contingent didn't rise to the bait, as that was just so typical of the joker's humour.

"But the consensus of opinion leans heavily towards Colchester having that dubious honour." the fatman continued.

"The consensus among who?" asked the accountant.

The resident comedian had exhausted his argument, and in another effort to end the subject said with a smirk, "Among learned professors of history like me of course. And what, pray tell, do bean counters know about anything except numbers?"

Gordon just smiled back without a word, and the subject was finalised.

The end of the evening's boozing was fast approaching and soon a stranger stood in the doorway of the Brewers and shouted "Cab for Mr Sheep's bottom!"

"OK, here we go." thought the prankster out loud with a mischievous grin. He was going to pretend that he'd not seen Pavel before.

"It's Ramsbottom! And I'm no Welsh sheep shagger," he snarled, "Or is that too difficult for you to understand?"

The taxi driver was shaken, "Zorry Zir." he squirmed in false reverence.

"Who are you?" Hugh sneered, "Where's Ahmad, my usual taxi driver?"

"You must remember me zir. I am Pavel," replied a now slightly confused cabbie, "And Ahmad's on another airport run."

They downed the rest of their pints in one and in unison wiped their mouths with their sleeves.

"You want your usual destination?"

"Too right! And please don't talk to me about Colchester."

"Why not? That's where I live."

Hugh pretended he had had enough, "You know Colchester had an earthquake in 1884?"

He didn't wait for a reply.

"Well it's a crying shame, it didn't tip the festering ugly blister of a place into a massive crater, and kill the whole effin' population."

He then added, "And don't tell me you've got a better football team, they're a bunch of second-rate selfish no-hopers!"

By this time Pavel feared for his life, and wasn't about to argue with a man of Mr Ramsbottom's considerable bulk, fired up by plenty of the Mr Angry juice, so he just drove quietly and was glad when his short journey to Tyrell's Close was completed.

The two friends extricated themselves from the taxi, and the fat one leaned over to the cabbie with a smirk saying, "By the way, as this is on account to NerdiSoft make sure you add a big tip my friend."

The cabbie smiled a worried man smile, and as a parting shot the joker added. "You know what, Pav? Have you heard the expression that there's no "I" in team?"

That resulted in shrugged shoulders indicating a lack of understanding.

"Well!" the joker continued, "Here's another expression. As sure as mud is mud, there is a you in fuck off!"

Then he grinned again, and shut the cab door ever so gently waving goodbye to the nervous cabbie. The boozing buddies looked at each other, laughed and went their separate ways.

Hugh Ramsbottom loved his Friday evening boozing sessions; all his closest friends and business buddies, loads of banter, and him being the centre of attention, but just lately Saturdays had not always pressed his jolly buttons, and the next day was exactly one of those days. He didn't habitually go to City's away matches, so when he found out late Saturday afternoon that City had lost yet again, this time 3 - 2 away at Sutton United he was definitely not in a jovial frame of mind. The following Tuesday, just to show how fickle football can be, he was Mr Jolly-bones again, when City managed to win 2 - 1 away at Dorchester, and the new striker Jamie Slabber scored on his debut.

"One day I'll be on the board of directors at City." confirmed City's number one fan to himself, "And then the Clarets WILL be the best team in Essex."

CHAPTER 5

Something in the Air

(Friday 23rd March to Saturday 7th April 2012)

Norman was waiting for the usual Friday evening telephone call from the Noble homestead, but he was secretly hoping that Cher's hockey match would be postponed so that he could have a decent excuse not to drive up to Leiston. He had good reason because during the week he'd received a short text from Clarisa. All it said was "Hello Normie, Miss you! Call me Friday evening. xxx"

He was pleased, and he hoped that he could persuade her to spend some time with him on Saturday as he'd managed to acquire 2 tickets for a concert to see Coldplace, a highly regarded Coldplay tribute band.

The phone rang. It was the familiar voice of Stanley.

"Ey Oop, son, 'ow yer diddlin'?"

"Alright, Dad, how are you?"

"Mustn't grumble, nobody listens anyway."

"Mum alright, is she?"

"Aye, son, same as ever."

"What can I do for you, Dad?"

"Well, You know t' 'ockey match yer sister's supposed t' be playin' in tomorrow at Gillingham Dam?"

"Yes, Dad, What about it?" answered the young man with a sense of dread.

"Yer sister, won't be playin', she's got a nasty dose of t' flu, and so's yer mum, so it's up t' you if you still want t' come oop."

Norman was elated, but pretended to be a bit upset, "Oh, Shame, hope they get better soon."

"It's their own bloody fault, shouldn't 'ave 'ad t' flu jab, bloody doctors don't know what they're doin'."

"I think if you don't mind, I'll give it a miss, Dad." he replied punching the air with delight.

"That's OK son, I'll probably tuck 'em both oop in bed wi' 'ot lemon drinks, and toddle off t' pub. Best get out of t' way when they're both feelin' sorry for 'emselves."

"OK, Dad, see you next weekend then, love to Mum."

"Bye, son, 'ave a nice weekend."

He couldn't believe his luck, not only would he escape the Norfolk Enchants ritual, but he wouldn't have to eat another Teutonic feast and pretend that he enjoyed it. On top of that, fingers crossed, he and Clarisa would be going to the Coldplace concert. He hadn't put the phone down for more than a minute, when it rang again. It was her.

"Wow!" He thought, "She's phoned me.", and that positive start continued through the conversation. She made it quite clear that she liked Normie, and she wanted to see him again. But even though she wanted him to say thanks to Hugh for the chocs, flowers, and apology, she also made it clear that she wanted to steer clear of the jolly fatman for the time being.

Normie was on a roll.

"How about tomorrow tonight then, doing anything?"

"No, what do you have in mind?"

"I've got tickets for Coldplace, and I'd like you to come with me."

"Mmm, well they won't be quite as good as the real thing, but it could be fun. Thank you, that'll do nicely."

An ecstatic Norman punched the air again; for the second time in a few minutes.

A little later down at the Two Brewers, Norman made his way across the bar armed with his highly alcoholic J2O. "Hey! Uncle, "he began," I've heard from Clarisa, and she said thanks for the chocs, flowers, and the apology. She still hates you, but she wants to see me again, so that's sorted out now."

"So, you're on a promise then are you?"

"Don't take it the wrong way, but she won't be going anywhere near you for the time being, and I intend to see to that." he answered very assertively.

The only response was a mock sad face, but it didn't last for long. There was leg-pulling, piss-taking and education to administer. When he wasn't winding up the gay Gordon's, the joker usually had something to say about either history, or his beloved Clarets.

"Hey, Rambo, you're quiet, no history lecture tonight?" began Spike.

"Pearls before swine," the fatman responded, "Pearls before swine."

"No, you haven't been doing your homework. Have you? What's on the next page of Ramsbottom's History of the World?" asked Gordon.

"Gay Boys of the Roman Empire. But I'm saving my lecture on that for Julian Clary's birthday."

The gay entourage all laughed, and then Mike changed the subject, though still in wind up mode.

"What chances have your Carrots got of making the playoffs this season then, fatboy?"

"Clarets! You deaf bastard! Clarets!"

"Got a new striker called Slobber, haven't they?"

"That's Slabber, Jamie Slabber, and he scored on his debut at Dorchester last Tuesday."

"Are you going to Melbourne tomorrow for some more torture then?"

"You got it, and yes, it's crunch time, we have to beat Basingstoke tomorrow or we are truly in the shit."

Suddenly in unison the Village People all piped up with a quick rendition of "Things, can only get better, can only get, can only get."

Hugh went back to the bar for another pint of Fuller's Pride trying not to show that he was worried.

The Brewers session went on till 11 pm, and then the two mates took the usual taxi home.

It had been an unusually quiet night for the regulars. There was no Ramsbottom Olympics, and the resident comedian seemed to be in a peculiar fractious mood. The NerdiSoft team had been working very hard on their global project over the previous week, and possibly they were all a bit tired.

Sure enough when late Saturday afternoon rolled round at Melbourne, Claret fan number one was having his miserable buttons firmly pressed as City managed to lose at home 1 - 0 to Basingstoke, and thereby slipped to 5th in the table. The only saving grace was that at the same time Welling and Sutton turned out as a draw, and both Dartford and Dover had lost. The ardent fan afforded himself a little chuckle at the Dover result as they had lost 4 - 0, but City's precarious situation wasn't getting any better. The misery was compounded when at the next game on the following Saturday, City only scraped a 0 - 0 draw away at Tonbridge Angels.

Two weeks later it was Good Friday, and on a Bank Holiday, while everyone else was enjoying a day off work, the NerdiSoft crew had been called in for a special meeting. There had been a concession to the Bank Holiday for all the other staff when the office had been shut early at 4 pm on Thursday, but the boardroom members had been advised to turn up for 10:30 on Friday. This was to be no ordinary progress meeting like all the others. The expectation was that after the usual updates the chairman was about to reveal his ambitious plans for the future of the company.

Norman arrived at 10:10, glanced at his watch and assured himself smiling, "Right on time, yeah!"

He leaned over and opened his leather briefcase, retrieved some papers, and gave himself a congratulatory splash of Erection aftershave before exiting the Porsche. He surveyed the car park, and the predictable parking disciplines of his boardroom colleagues, and found everybody else had already arrived

Company Chairman Tim Balls, the Boss had neatly parked his highly polished silver grey Lexus GS250 in his reserved space.

The increasingly obese Marketing Director, Hugh Ramsbottom had applied his random approach, and his slightly careworn black Land Rover

Discovery LR4 sporting the personalised number plate P155 ORF was untidily parked wherever he had randomly dumped it that day.

Company Accountant, Gordon Bullock, had recently purchased his brand new Ford Galaxy Titanium X, which now had Gay Pride stickers in the back window, and it was parked safely against a wall in a corner so no possible damage could come to it.

And so it was obvious that "Norman Nobless", Development Director, modern man about town arriving in his Porsche Carrera, best motor by far, would park close to Tiny's Lexus, as it was the only other vehicle in the car park with any class or charisma.

The computer games genius went into the office, it was another dry day, good for driving, and he was looking forward to going up to Leiston for the Easter break visiting his family. He poured himself a frothy coffee and sat down in the boardroom. But the only other person there was Gordon.

"Morning!" he greeted the accountant cursorily," Where are they, then?"

There was an answer while the accountant carried on reading the Financial Times.

"Your uncle's been in Tim's office for a while. (He always called him Tim for reasons that nobody was interested in.) I expect they'll be poring over the plans before they let us know what's happening."

The two of them never had a lot to say to each other, they were the proverbial chalk and cheese. The accountant continued to read the F.T. and the man in the Porsche continued with some programming work on Interstellar Paranoid Overdrive.

Meanwhile, in the Chairman's office Hugh and Tiny were deep in discussion. They were very old friends, and regarding their business affairs they always confided in each other.

The boss began. "So, first of all, mate, I want to talk about Norman. He is very important to the future success of the company, and we don't want to have him upset, to be disgruntled, and leave us. Some dubious chancer might come along and headhunt him, and then it'll be curtains for our company. I know we've got him tied up on copyright for all the current games, but he is the inspiration man, and we can't afford to lose him. So, the first question is; have you sorted things out with him now?"

"Yes! We are back on an even keel, and I've promised to show more discretion where his love life is concerned. We had a man to man after one of our Sunday roast dinners, and a reconciliation with a new understanding about my behaviour. But there's something about him and the lovely Clarisa, which I've not seen before. I know him very well, and he hasn't ever behaved like this towards any of his women in the past. He's normally a find 'em, fu---."

"Er Yes, OK!" Tiny interrupted, "Right that's out of the way then."

They grinned, and enjoyed gulps of coffee. "Now!" he continued, "Apart from that, the other thing this company has heavily depended on is you."

The joker knew exactly what his friend was getting at, but he couldn't resist a bit of winding up, so he looked quizzically at him and responded, "How's that, mate? What do you mean?"

The chairman leaned back in his chair, took a deep breath, and another slurp of coffee. He was well aware that he was the driving force behind the company, but that the company was set up with Ramsbottom money. He proceeded," Listen mate, you are my oldest friend and confidante. I remember when we were at Brentwood School together you were the rich kid, and had everything you ever wanted, and I came from the other side of the tracks. My parents sweated blood to get me properly educated. We really didn't have a pot to piss in."

Hugh stifled a grin, but he knew where this was going, and he wasn't going to pass up the opportunity for his friend to grovel and then praise him a bit, so he just tried to appear nonchalant with a fixed furrowed brow. He was well aware that Tiny was the driving force behind the company, but that the company was set up with his money.

"This company only came about because you put the money up for it, and have continued to do so, and you've got to admit we haven't done too badly?"

"No," was the interruption, "What is it, do you want to borrow a fiver?"

The comment was ignored and they sat there for a moment, until they both broke into grins. A very comfortable silence fell over them, and then the chairman added "Neither of us is getting any younger, and I think it's about time we took a big chance."

The joker couldn't resist it, "Do you want me to hire you a mobility scooter, or will a Zimmer frame do for now?"

The comment was ignored again, and Tiny sat there with a mock stony-face, as his friend's grin widened. Another comfortable silence fell.

Then the discussion continued, "It's time to put this company on a different footing. We are small beer while we stay as we are, and as you know I have been working on a plan to go global. This will involve upheaval and big changes, not all of which will be universally appreciated. But if; or shall we say when it comes off, we'll make a big killing, and then in the not too distant future we can consider retiring."

"And this time next year, Rodney, we'll be millionaires." chuckled the joker still playing games, and then he went all serious and added, "Listen mate, you're right! And I trust your business instincts, we've already thrashed out all the details, and I'm sure you'll be giving 200% to make it work. No need for any more confidential chat between me and thee. Let's you go tell the others what's on the table."

Now it was grinning time again, and they knew as friends they would be on the same wavelength. Then the fatman added," I assume that you've got it all planned in detail and you know where you're going then, not only on the forthcoming trip to China and the U.S.A., but with the 5 year plan?"

The chairman nodded, and then the marketing director joked again, "As long as it's not a Columbus expedition."

There was a pause as the boss considered what was coming next, knowing that his colleague would never resist the temptation to illustrate his knowledge of history.

"Well, he set off not knowing where he was going, arrived not knowing where he was, and returned not knowing where he'd been, and who knows, maybe he then sat at home for a while wondering why the fuck he'd bothered to go in the first place."

Tiny laughed, "No, it's certainly not like that, although as you know I am going to Columbus, Ohio. But I can't promise to bring you back any potatoes or tobacco."

"That was Sir Francis Drake." corrected Hugh, "Let's go, and talk to the others."

They shook hands spontaneously, and the Boss knew he had never needed to doubt that his oldest friend would be up for whatever he suggested. Together they came into the boardroom where Gordon and Norman had been waiting.

"Right, thanks for your patience," began the chairman," As its Good Friday, I have some good news, and I'll keep it short, so that when we've finished here, we can all pack up and go home. What I want to do is dispense with all the usual reporting we do at these meetings, and go quickly to the crunch. Besides which, I don't think you'll want to listen to our marketing director's ancient strategy once again."

They all chuckled, and shifted in their seats.

"So this is the plan that we have been working on and discussing for quite a while now. You know that I'm always saying that we're a big company, in a little office, running on a shoestring, and that we must grow and prosper? Well, we think it's time to set up the company in a different direction. We will remain small-time if we stay as we are. So we plan to go global."

The Chairman paused and looked at his three colleagues in turn, and they all appeared to be listening intently. He continued "The plan will involve rethinking our direction and our major business strategy, and some things will have to change. Inevitably you may not like everything that we have planned. But when it comes off, we'll make a big killing, and then we'll all be better off. Any questions so far?"

Norman seemed delighted, but Gordon shifted again in his seat again, this time noticeably a little more uneasily than the last.

"I've mentioned before that I'm flying to Wuxi in China for a meeting with Wang Wu Hoo Du Production. If we're going global, we need to produce our software on a massive basis. The Chinese have that capability at a competitive price. But if we seal the deal there, we'll need a much better distribution strategy, and that's why I'm going straight on to the U.S.A. to meet the guys from Softly Softly Catchee Monkey Distribution, because I think they'll be able to deal with our projected global volumes. They're based in Columbus, Ohio, which it is claimed is going to be the next Silicone Valley." continued Tiny.

The dapper, grey-suited one remained silent, and he looked almost frightened.

"Sounds good." said the young man delighted, "But I've never heard of Wuxi, where is it, and why are you going there in particular?"

"I'm glad you asked that. It's not well known that Wuxi is twinned with Chelmsford, just as Backnang and Annonay are. It's a real enterprise town, big on I.T. about 100 miles from Shanghai in the Jiangsu province."

He paused for a moment looking at the accountant, and then said, "Are there any more questions? No? OK then, that's what I'm doing in the next week. I fly to Shanghai tomorrow, and by the time I've got back, got over the jetlag, and sorted out the details, it'll probably be the middle of the week after next. And while I'm away there are some things that I want you to do for me."

First he turned to Hugh and said, "These offices are too small, and I think they're in the wrong place for our plans. We need to relocate. So find us new premises in Chelmsford, on the Dukes Park Estate or somewhere like that. Then establish a plan for moving our existing operation and staff there."

"Yessum, Masser!" was the mocking reply.

Then the chairman said, "Norman, you're the ideas man, we need to re-brand the company. We have a recognisable brand in the UK with NerdiSoft, and with that name we are renowned for a quality product. But what I would like to do is go global with a different label that fits an International image better. In time we will develop into a group of companies under the new umbrella label, and the current NerdiSoft will just be one of those companies. So I want you come up with a new company name, logo, and artwork, with an International emphasis. Also can you devise a new game based around 2012 and Chelmsford's City status? That'll be brilliant."

"OK, Boss, that's as good as done."

That was the answer the chairman expected.

And finally, Tiny indicated "Gordon, what I want you to do is----."

"Er! Are you absolutely sure you know what you're doing, Tim?" queried the accountant interrupting the flow, "Have you done a business cost analysis on your proposals?"

"Look, Gordon we don't need any doubting Thomas to enter the argument at this stage. What I want you to do is a full accounting revue, auditor's reports, and make sure all our paperwork is fully up to date."

There was a worried look, but the accountant offered, "OK, if you're sure, Tim."

The chairman didn't answer. He just concluded with, "Right! Now! All go home. Have a happy Easter, don't grind the company into the ground while

I'm away, and I'll see you all in the Brewers tonight for a drink anyway." Then he left the boardroom and went back to his office.

"If I ruled the world, every day would be the first day of Spring, every heart would have a new song to sing, and we'd sing of the joy every morning would bring." warbled Hugh out of tune expressly for his gay friend's benefit as the meeting ended.

"Awesome!" smiled Norman.

The accountant was very quiet, and he muttered "Shit! Shit! Shit!" under his breath.

Later on in the Two Brewers, the Friday night booze up was under way, but as it was Ike's birthday he had hired the function room and set it up for karaoke. When Hugh and Tiny arrived the party was already in full swing, and Gordon and Spike were on stage singing the Elton John and Kiki Dee duet "Don't go breaking my heart". They weren't much like Elton and Kiki, but they sure did camp it up, much to everybody's amusement. The joker had got himself and his mate a couple of pints of Fuller's Pride by the time the song finished, and couldn't help shouting out "Get a room you two, get a room!"

They responded in the middle finger way.

It was time to watch the next X-factor reject. Caroline was back working behind the bar having returned from Thailand a few days before. She had just started singing "Lady Marmalade" not quite as well as Labelle, but just as good as Christina Aguilera. She finished with whoops of delight and approval, and went straight into the Beyonce song "Single Ladies". Norman watched, entertained and amused, but as soon as she'd finished, he sneaked into the gents' to avoid her. He had no idea how she would choose to react to their recent bedroom encounter, but he knew it wouldn't be long before he had to face her, and sure enough when he returned to the bar, there she was.

"Hi, Norm, Alright?" she began.

"Er, Yes! Are you?" he replied nervously.

"I'm fine, what can I get you?"

"Get them in, usual round, and a double Bacardi and Coke for the birthday boy."

"OK, I'll bring them over." She said smiling as he gave her a £50 note.

And much to his surprise that was it. He breathed a quizzical sigh of relief and thought" She's had more fellas than Hugh's had chips, she probably doesn't even remember being with me, especially after 6 weeks in Thailand."

There was a break in the karaoke, and so the jolly fatman was making sure that his knowledge of history wasn't going to waste, and while he was spouting forth his Village People were winding him up, as only they knew how.

"Enjoying your last ever birthday?" he offered.

"How's that then? You're more likely to pop your clogs than me, fatboy." Ike responded.

"Don't you know, you silly wooftah? The world will end on 21st December, 2012, that's this year, mate."

"Who says?"

"It is written in the Mayan calendar."

"Aren't the Mayans the blokes who invented Mayonnaise?"

"No, stupid, the Mayan civilisation existed from 250 to 900 AD in Mexico and Guatemala."

"They all wore huge sombreros, played outsize guitars, and formed Mariachi bands then did they, and I suppose they would have called us all gringos?"

"God you lot are ignorant, it's a good job I'm here to educate you." scoffed Hugh in his usual mocking tone.

"So how will it end then? Will the world run out of food for you to eat so that you'll starve if you don't turn into a cannibal?"

"Ho, bloody Ho! No! It's possible that the Earth is going to collide with a planet called Nibiru, or fall into a Black Hole at the centre of our galaxy."

"Or the Brewers will run out of booze, and you'll die of thirst."

They all laughed, and then their lecturer continued, "But don't worry, most of these predictions are proven untrue in the end."

"Except for Nicodemus." said Spike.

"That's Nostradamus, you Ignoramus," corrected the fatman," And he predicted that the world would end in 2242. But I don't think I'm going to worry about that."

He took a large swig of his beer and then continued, "Some of his prophecies which were published in 1555 seemed to be accurate though. Do you know he predicted the rise of Adolf Hitler, and the 911 tragedy?"

"So what you're saying is that nearly 500 years ago some Dutch bloke, probably high on medieval smack or wacky baccy made from Edam cheese and herrings, wrote down a load of old shite and we're supposed to believe it? You'll tell me next that he predicted England would win the World Cup in 1966, or maybe that the 2012 Olympics would be a fantastic triumph for Great Britain."

They all broke up into collective laughter again, and soon the karaoke recommenced. Ike got up and did some very bad Tina Turner impressions with "What's love got to do with it" followed by "Nutbush City Limits", and the jolly obese one delighted in taking the piss out of Ike's beard by shouting "Bush mush city limits" over the chorus.

The resident comedian was pleased with his end of the world discussion, and that he had educated his great unwashed again, and now it was his turn to hog the mike. Everybody knew that he could play a stonking boogie piano, but his breathless singing was mediocre to say the least. Nevertheless, he rattled his way energetically through a medley of Status Quo standards including "Paper Plane", "Whatever You Want", and "Rockin' All Over the World", by which time the party was really banging. He then finished with a hilariously drunken version of Fats Domino's "Blueberry Hill" adding an utterly filthy impromptu verse and chorus about "Sailor Boys". Then flushed with enthusiasm he tried his best to persuade his other friends to stretch their vocal chords. He knew Tiny was a lost cause, and that it would never happen, but he managed to get Norman to reluctantly have a go. To much expectation that he would fall flat on his face, he made a surprisingly excellent job of singing the Stereophonics song "Dakota". Then despite the efforts of all present to get him to sing a Coldplay number he stepped down. He knew that you had to go out on a high, and he wasn't risking any crash-landing with something not perfect.

Soon, it was back to Gordon, who sang 2 appropriate duets with Spike after an unfortunate introduction. They began with the Sonny and Cher's "I Got You Babe", or as Hugh comically introduced them, Scummy and Queer, and then topped that with their version of the Grease song sung by Olivia Newton John, "Hopelessly Devoted to You". The fatman couldn't stand it when just for his benefit; they sang looking deep into each other's eyes like Kathy and Heathcliff from Wuthering Heights. He wandered off saying "Help! I'm going to be sick!"

By this time all were wondering what had happened to Mike, but they weren't kept waiting long, for suddenly he reappeared in full drag. The joker goosed him as he went up on stage, and blew a kiss pleading "Oooohh! Give us a snog, Blondie!", and Mike told him to "Bugger Off!" before he put on a convincing performance of Gloria Gaynor's "I Will Survive".

It had been a more than brilliant evening at the Brewers, and everybody left in high spirits.

The usual taxi arrived driven by Ahmad, and they quickly mulled over the evening somewhat philosophically.

"It's funny how what people sing at a karaoke reflects their personality, isn't it?" asked the chairman.

"Too right!" his mate said, "The poofs were all top notch, Nobless was brilliant, and I think he was singing about Clarisa, and Scummy and Queer were top dogs."

They rolled about the taxi laughing, and when it stopped at Tyrell's Close, and they got out Ahmad spoke. "You're so right about that my friends. Everyone always wants me to sing that football song."

"Which one is that?" enquired Hugh not expecting it to be "I'm Forever Blowing Bubbles".

"Oh I think it's called Vindaloo.", and with that he began to sing very humorously in his Asian accent "Me and me mum, and me dad and me gran, we're going to Waterloo...."

Saturday morning began with more than the expected hangover chaos in the Bullock household. Gordon was up and about fairly early, showered and impeccably dressed as ever, but looking a little pale. He had told the others that he would be busy in the morning, but wouldn't let on what he was up to. He busied himself making the expected tea and toast for his harem. He was a typical accountant, frugal, crafty and secretive, or as Hugh would have said, stingy, underhand, and sneaky. He was queer and proud of it, went to Gay Pride events, to Figueretas in Ibiza for his holidays, and was singularly obsessed with Julian Clary. He had spent 10 years working in local government, where the biggest lesson he'd learned was to play his cards close to his chest and to trust no-one. He owned the house, and everybody else paid exorbitant rent to live there. That was convenient for him because that meant that the mortgage was paid from the three rents he collected. Therefore he was fairly well off, and the joker would have said that was always a bit of a waste for an accountant.

Tea and toast made, he stood at the bottom of the stairs and called his troops to order, and got no response. The house in Vicarage Road which he shared with Spike, Ike and Mike was fairly large and rambling, so at first his hangover prompted a reluctance to go wandering. He sat in the kitchen reading, or to be truthful trying to focus on the Daily Telegraph, but after some while he decided to go and wake up his partner Spike. They had met ten years ago in Figueretas, and they shared the master bedroom. The master of the house took a tray of lukewarm tea and cold toast up to Spike, who was in an awful state, looking even more dishevelled than usual. His face was as white as the duvet, and his eyes looked as if he'd gone a few rounds with David Hay. Gordon left the tea-tray and retreated swiftly while softly saying "Time to get up!"

Scruffbag as he was known by his drinking colleagues was the mirror image of his partner, quite literally one of the great unwashed and unkempt. His encounters with bars of soap were rare, and owing to his decorating profession, he was habitually flecked with paint of many colours, which blended in an interesting way with his many tattoos, He cut his own hair badly, but then he was almost bald, and his idea of smart was black or brown leather jacket, trousers and captain's cap. None of that mattered to Gordon, because Spike MCormack was the 32 year old man that he was very fond of. He didn't love him in a romantic sense, but he did admire his Bohemian existence and his soft Scottish accent. It was definitely a case of "Vive la difference!"

Along the corridor the landlord tapped quietly on Ike and Mike's bedroom door, and reminded them that they had work to do at Tyrell's Close. Ike Jobson and Mike Blofeld were the 2 lodgers. They were in a civil partnership, and were faithful to each other. The jolly fatman did not accept this, because he considered that all gay men were promiscuous, and to him the whole bunch of them were rogering each other senseless, swapping partners at will.

Ike and Mike were both in the gardening business, albeit in different aspects. They were a perfect couple. Ike was an ancient 27 year old, black, muscle-bound, bearded, and outspoken, and had worked in the Wyevales Garden Centre for 5 years. Mike was a young 40 year old, white, slim, effeminate and soft spoken, with a dyed blonde ponytail. He had studied and qualified at Writtle Agricultural College and now ran his own gardening and landscaping business.

Suddenly, before their host could knock on the door a second time, it burst open and Ike came rushing across the landing making for the bathroom like Linford Christie including the lunch-pack. Gordon beat a retreat downstairs as he couldn't stand the sound of anyone retching up, and soon after he jumped into his car and left.

The scruffy decorator ate the cold toast, drank the lukewarm tea, and snorted his way back under the duvet like a hedgehog hiding under a pile of leaves. Mike struggled to bring Ike to his senses with gallons of black coffee, but eventually they both left in their tatty old van, and headed for work.

Hugh was ringing the doorbell at Tiny's house, and Tina came to the door dressed, or to be more precise scantily clad in her underwear and a dressing gown like some expensive call girl. Even though it was only 8:30 am, she was still gorgeous, with perfect makeup and hair.

While the boss planned to be away on his U.S.A. and China trip there was going to be a lot of activity at his house, and that was why he'd asked his friend to turn up.

"Buenos Dias, hombre," she grinned, adding "How do you go, Hugo?" with the usual smarmy false smile.

"Barcelona! Barcelona!" he replied in his best Freddy Mercury, and kissed her outstretched hand.

Tina waved him into the house with a flourish, wiggling her arse as she made her way to the garden, and looking provocatively over her shoulder with a smile asking, "Does my boom look big in this?"

"Sure thing, sister!" he answered, giving her a playful slap, and as they fell about laughing Tiny appeared saying, "When you two have quite finished, we have work to do."

Spike and his decorating company were going to continue with their work, with the expectation that they would finish painting and wallpapering the complete interior of the house by the time Tiny got back. Meanwhile, Ike and Mike were contracted to completely remodel the garden.

Within minutes Ike and Mike arrived at the house, both bleary-eyed and hang-dog, in contrast to Hugh, who was bright eyed and bushytailed. Tina now wanted the already impressive garden remodelled on a grand scale, and so the two gardeners had been enlisted to carry out her gardening desires. She took them aside and began issuing instructions. Starting that Saturday they were to lay a huge patio, with a pergola overhead, install a substantial water feature including a large fishpond complete with a massive shoal of goldfish, and 2 waterfalls, and build a fully populated Alpine rockery. The Ramsbottom's garden was pretty amazing, but Tina wanted something even better, and Hugh was quick to compare the planned project as close to the neatly sculptured landscape of Disneyworld.

"Blimey boys, where are you going to put Minnie and Mickey Mouse?" he asked. They ignored him, and they were quite happy to have a very lucrative piece of work to do in the next few days. After all the instructions had been issued and understood, Tiny called his best mate to follow him to the bottom of their garden. "While I'm away I want you to keep an eye on all this work; decorating, gardening, and not least of all what goes on at work." he asked.

"I'm worried mate, there's something not right with our bean counter." said Hugh, "Did you see how strangely he reacted yesterday when we talked about the global project?"

"Yeah, I agree he was a bit odd, but keep an eye on it all for me will you?"

"OK, mate, I'll do my best. But I might need to grow two heads to do it all. Don't worry, it'll turn out alright."

Then he added with a wry smile, "Although I don't know why you're bothering, it's going be the end of the world on 21st December this year."

"It's going to be the end of your world a lot sooner if you mention that again." replied Tiny turning away. He had more important things than the end of the world on his mind.

They ambled back up the garden where Tina was still adding details, and then Mike said to his fat tormentor, "I don't understand it, Hugo. You drink twice as much as anybody I know, but the next morning you're still like an enthusiastic 18 year old. How do you do it?"

There was too much temptation to resist, and so he replied, "It's just a simple case of heterosexual abandon, but you two wouldn't understand."

Ike and Mike both knew that they wouldn't get any sense out of him, especially when he quickly added, "Hey, you don't usually work together, but just think what a great name your company could have?"

They looked at each other, confused, and brains still temporarily erased by alcohol, "What do you mean?" drawled Mike.

"Well its Blofeld and Jobson, isn't it? You could call yourselves Blojob Enterprises." Hugh replied corpsing with laughter.

They both groaned and turned away, and began discussing the garden work again.

While all this was going on, somewhere not far away a Porsche Carrera 911 engine roared, and slid out onto Springfield Road, making for the A12 and Colchester and then beyond, up to Leiston for the weekend. Norman intended to pull into the office briefly to download some stuff onto his laptop. Although he would enjoy being with his family for a few days, he knew there would be times when he'd have to seek refuge in his work, or to play his latest creation. He gave the Porsche some welly on the slip-road at the Cramphorn flyover, looked at his watch, and gave the turbo some work to do.

"15 minutes, to the office, easy". It was Saturday, and the journey was expected to be quicker than usual. He popped the Coldplay CD out of the player, pushed in a Stereophonics CD, and skipped to his favourite track.

"You made me feel like the one, made me feel like the one"; he and the Stereos sang "Dakota", as he recalled his previous night's karaoke performance with a satisfied grin thinking about Clarisa. She had been the first thing on his mind more and more as the days had been passing, and he saw her in his daydreams, imagined being with her at home listening to their favourite tunes, smelt her perfume wherever he went, and always, always couldn't wait to see her again.

Traffic was indeed light, and sure enough almost exactly 15 minutes later he arrived at NerdiSoft. He found it strange that Gordon's car was in the car park, and curious as to why he was there, he entered the building quietly, and sneaked up to his office. Then as he burst in the door, the accountant was so surprised he looked as if he'd been hit by a ten ton truck. "W... w... what are you doing here?" he spluttered.

"I might ask you the same question." replied Norman unflustered.

"I...I... I am starting on that work that Tim asked me to do, you know, the accounts review."

"What on a Saturday? And on Easter Saturday at that?"

"Y... Yeah! No time like the present, Eh?"

"But you never work on a Saturday. Accountants only do what they get paid for."

The young man grinned, and the gay one sat stock still like a rabbit caught in the headlights. There was a heavy uncomfortable silence.

Then the bean counter squirmed in his seat, and asked "Why are you here then?"

"Oh, I just popped in to download a new game on my laptop. I'm going to see the oldies in Leiston, and need something to do when I get bored with the small-talk. And I just noticed your car was here."

"Well, I've got lots to do, see you Tuesday then." concluded Gordon still looking nervous and twitchy, and then he turned back to his screen.

"OK, see you."

Within a few minutes Norman had downloaded his games, and set off again. But the unexpected meeting he had just experienced with his work colleague left him with an uneasy feeling. Although he never did have much to say to Gordon, he was worried that he seemed more on edge than usual, and appeared to be behaving furtively.

Work began at the Ball's household. The gardeners started digging huge holes for the patio and fishpond, and piling up the removed earth for the rockery. At about 11:30 Spike turned up with his decorating team and a van full of paint and wallpaper. He looked even more dirty and smelly than usual. In fact, he looked like a refugee from Albania, and Tina wasn't all that sure she wanted him in the house in his present state.

Hugh waddled back to his palatial pad just over the road, and prepared for the short drive to Dartford that afternoon. He felt it was necessary for him to support City away for a change, because their position was increasingly worse after a 0 - 0 draw against Tonbridge Angels the previous Saturday. Dartford was a relatively easy drive, and their ground was a superb new edifice that had been built for them by the local Conservative Council. How he wished the newly invested City of Chelmsford Council would grace his fair city with a purpose built football stadium of the same impressive stature.

Tiny began packing for the forthcoming trip, while in the middle of all this upheaval Tina held sway, entertaining, flirting to no apparent avail, making cups of tea and coffee, and sandwiches, and enjoying every minute of the attention she was receiving from her servants.

Ahmad pulled up in his special airport taxi at 12:30 ready for the journey to Heathrow. Stansted and Heathrow International Taxis Executive Service was his new project. He thought it would create a better image with the name he'd devised. Trouble was a taxi with S.H.I.T.E.S. written on the doors didn't give off quite the image he wanted.

The chairman wasn't good at farewells, so he just kissed his wife on both cheeks, asked if she would be OK, and then just said "Hasta la vista, Chica, see you next week." In a flash he was gone. She closed the door behind him still smiling, and resumed her Queen of all she surveyed role with her workmen. Tiny wasn't worried much about that, after all they were all friends, and they were all gay anyway. But he didn't like flying much, and London to Shanghai, Pudong was an 11 hour flight. The flight left on time, and his adventure was beginning. He felt a strange mixture of apprehension and excitement, a bit like a naughty child running away, feeling very grownup and a bit scared at the same time. He knew that China was likely to be a culture shock, but he was well prepared for the business end of things, and was confident he could swing the right deal. So he resolved to spend his travelling time vegetating, reading, sleeping, watching in-flight movies, and drinking only soft drinks. The intrepid traveller's relaxation was contrasted by Hugh's frustration on his away day at Dartford as City only managed another 0 - 0 draw against them.

CHAPTER 6

A Tale of Three Cities

(Saturday 6th April to Monday 16th April 2012)

During the weekend most things back home were very relaxed and in some cases following standard patterns. Mike and Ike had made excellent progress with the gardening work. Spike had moved from downstairs to upstairs with the preparation for decorating at Tyrell's Close. Norman hadn't enjoyed another round of bockwurst and sauerkraut, and went to have another butcher's at the garden and greenhouse up at the bungalow in Leiston. The Ramsbottom family had enjoyed another Sunday roast.

On Monday afternoon, things hadn't gone smoothly for the Claret's number one fan. He spent the time at Melbourne Park where Chelmsford City were playing at home to Eastbourne Borough. In the end City managed to win 1- 0, but that was after their winger Ricky Modeste was punched by the Eastbourne goalkeeper, and then they were both sent off. City's position at 5th in the league was still precarious, and a playoff place was now becoming less certain.

The combination of an 11 hour non-stop flight, and an 8 hour time difference meant that Tiny arrived in Shanghai at 3 am local time on Monday 8th April. He was so knackered he hardly noticed the changes in his surroundings, and made straight for his thankfully much westernised hotel. Effectively he had lost nearly a complete day in the process of flying to China. At about 11 am a large Mercedes limousine came to pick him up and take him to his hotel in Wuxi, and that was when he realised he was on a very different and very crowded planet. The 100 or so mile drive took under 2 hours to cover in comfort with a smiling Chinaman who didn't speak much English. The most intriguing bits of the journey were at the beginning, while making the way out of Shanghai, and the end, entering into Wuxi itself, also known as Little Shanghai. At the start of the journey, perhaps it was the time zone difference, the excessively long flight, or the lack of proper sleep in his bed at home next to Tina, but everything seemed to be happening at top speed, maximum noise level, and with a relentless and at times unstoppable drive. The Jiangsu province was very flat, low-lying, and not very interesting. Most of it was plains and small settlements with frequent interruptions for rivers, canals and small lakes. As the drive continued the traveller began to relax a little more, and enjoy the experience.

While Tiny's limousine was taking him to the meeting at Wang Wu Hoo Du Production in Jiangsu Province in China, on the Bank Holiday Monday in England work continued in Tyrell's Close. The intrepid traveller had done his homework, and found out that since 1992 the Wuxi New District had developed into one of the major industrial parks in China. The City was the solar technology hub of China where two major photovoltaic companies were based.

He was very impressed with the high-tech setup at Wang Wu Hoo Do, and Mr Wang and Mr Woo were charm personified. Negotiations went well, and the chairman of NerdiSoft negotiated the deal he wanted, and was then feted at a 4 hour, 28 course Chinese banquet in the best restaurant in town. He finished the day at 11 pm, retiring for a very welcome sleep in the best hotel in Wuxi after his exhausting technology tour.

By the time the Earth's rotation had brought 7 pm Monday evening from China to England, work had come to halt at Tyrell's Close and Ike and Mike had returned to Vicarage Road. But Gordon was a little worried because his scruffy partner didn't return home from his decorating mission until about 8 pm.

Tuesday in China went well, and after their final meeting Messrs Wang and Wu were keen to show their guest around. So during the early afternoon they took him on a short flight over Lake Tai, where a local English speaking guide pointed out the Islet of Turtlehead and the Islands of the Deities. They then landed for a late lunch, and another magnificent Chinese banquet followed. The icing on the cake was a trip on a 377 foot tall Ferris wheel, the Wuxi version of the London Eye as the sun was going down. In honour of his visit his hosts presented him with a pair of A Fu, Huishan clay figurines, one of the local handicraft specialties. He was delighted, and he knew that Tina would love the figurines, which consisted of two figures, a boy with a red carp representing prosperity, and a girl with a chicken representing success. Later, the NerdiSoft Chairman was transported to the main railway station and waved off on the Shanghai-Nanjing Intercity High-Speed-Railway, which whizzed him back to Shanghai in less than 45 minutes. It had been a very exciting, but also very tiring 3 days and the elated businessman was soon fast asleep in his hotel room.

The rest of the team had returned to work at NerdiSoft, and yet again the accountant remained detached and secretive. Norman took the opportunity to advise his uncle what had happened when he'd bumped into him at work on the previous Saturday morning.

"He's behaving strangely," advised the young man, "I don't know what he's up to, but at our last meeting you'll have noticed he didn't seem too keen to carry out the work he was asked to do for the global project. But the very next day he turned up at work and told me he was starting to do the accounts review."

"OK, leave it with me." The stand-in boss replied.

The games genius returned to his work on Interstellar Paranoid Overdrive, and Hugh went straight off to find Gordon. As he entered his office the accountant quickly blanked his screen, and shuffled some papers under his Daily Telegraph.

"What can I do for you?" he asked.

"Not much, sweetie pie, but is there anything up with you at the moment?"

"No! And even if there was, it wouldn't be any of your business."

"OK, I'm only asking. No need to bite my head off, you old batty man."

"Sorry, fatboy, but I'm a bit worried."

"I know! You're going to have to part with hard cash over that bet on Mo Farah beating The Cube. Would you like to pay me the £60 now?"

"No! It's not that you daft bat, it's Spike. He's gone all cold on me."

Hugh laughed. "Never mind, you've still got the other two, you randy old bum-boy."

The accountant turned away, and the conversation was over. They both got back to work. The quick chat had served no purpose other than to antagonise the accountant, but the fatman was convinced that he was up to something.

That evening Gordon sat in his lounge in Vicarage Road even more worried, when again Scruffbag was late back from his work. This time it was 9 pm, and he couldn't let it go without comment.

"Hello, Soldierboy, what time do you call this?" he asked.

"Oh, I didn't realise how late it was, and we're a bit behind with the painting on the bedroom ceilings."

"But it's dark. How can you do a proper professional job in the dark?"

"Yeah, I know, but Tina is so demanding. She won't let us waste any time. It's all about getting what SHE wants."

"Well I expected you home ages ago. Don't let it happen again, please." concluded Gordon, not really knowing in what way every word the decorator had said was true.

While the scruffy decorator had been employed satisfying Tina's insatiable demands, Hugh had popped round to see how things were going, just as his friend had asked him to do. But although he rang the doorbell several times, and could see a light on upstairs, nobody came to the door, and all the curtains were pulled together. He wandered back home puzzled, and later he phoned, and a sleepy Tina told him she had gone to bed early with a throbbing head.

In China on Wednesday morning Tiny was waiting at Shanghai Pudong airport for his 11 and a half hour flight to Los Angeles. Once again the time difference would turn the journey into another nearly a full day lost. Tired but very pleased with his progress so far, he looked forward to another bout of travelling time vegetating, reading, sleeping, watching in-flight movies, and drinking only soft drinks. Then he anticipated a good old American steak and fries, and some relief from Chinese cuisine.

Wednesday in England saw the completion of all the gardening work at Chateau Balls by lunchtime, and Mike left satisfied with his 5 days work in the early afternoon, while Ike returned to his job at Wyevales. Spike turned up at lunchtime to carry on decorating alone, sending his 2 assistants off to another job in Witham.

Norman had been hard at work at NerdiSoft and had come up with a new name for the company, which he was adamant that he wouldn't reveal to anybody just yet. He had also invented the required logo, and developed the necessary artwork ready for the global re-launch, and he had the germ of an idea for a Chelmsford based computer game. Hugh had been busy visiting a few suitable premises in Chelmsford ready for the relocation, and the company's typical accountant was still tucked away being frugal, crafty and secretive, or was it really stingy, underhand, and sneaky?

By the time late evening arrived Gordon was again waiting for his partner to come home, and Hugh was on stakeout duty, hiding in the bushes opposite the Ball's household. Luckily it was a quite pleasant evening weather-wise, so the lengthy observations were not uncomfortable. The decorator's van was still on the drive, all the curtains were drawn, and there were lights on upstairs. What was uncomfortable was that at about 10.30 pm Tiny's minder saw 2 people apparently naked wander across the landing, which didn't have curtains, from the bedroom towards the bathroom. He went home shortly afterwards not quite believing his own eyes, and wondering how he would deal with that discovery. Whereas Hugh's vigil had uncovered an interesting and unexpected outcome, Gordon's vigil was fruitless, because Scruffbag failed to come home at all.

More than half way round the world on Thursday, Tiny woke up in his hotel in Los Angeles, and prepared for his next flight. He knew he could never get used to a jet-set lifestyle. By now, if he was honest with himself, he longed to put his feet up at home, and to sleep in his own bed, but he still had work to do, and people to see. He was incredibly lucky that all his flights had taken off and arrived more or less on time, and this continued with his 8.5 hour flight from L. A. to Columbus via Philadelphia where there was a 1.5 hour layover. During the layover he was able to enjoy a good old American burger and fries which he had looked forward to while in the land of fast food.

Back in Chelmsford Spike now pushed his luck, and spent another night away from Vicarage Road. The fat minder popped round to Tyrell's Close at just before midnight, and as expected the scruffy van was stuck like glue to the drive again.

Nearly a week flying across the world and on Friday the NerdiSoft chairman was in a taxi taking him to the meeting at Softly Softly Catchee Monkey Distribution. He was convinced about the suitability of Columbus as his ideal distribution centre, and equally impressed with the location's potential to become the next Silicone Valley. The tremendously affable Americans, Carlton Schumann, and Bates Masters, were very accommodating. Negotiations went well again, and the required deal was sealed. The NerdiSoft chairman then celebrated with his new business acquaintances over a good old American steak and fries at the best fast food diner in town. Unfortunately that was the best that his new American friends could manage. Columbus wasn't a particularly interesting place other than in the business sense that it had been chosen for. However, the traveller was grateful to be in bed in his very posh hotel nice and early.

Quite some time later, but still on Friday in England, Scruffbag suddenly turned up at Vicarage Road after going missing for 3 days. He steamed straight up the stairs and into the bathroom, and then his absolutely incensed partner could hear him running a bath, a very rare event for the decorator. After some time sat in the lounge watching TV, desperately trying to contain his anger and exasperation, Gordon pretended not to notice when his partner finally put in an appearance. After a heavy pause he spoke.

"So what have you been up to?"

"Decorating!" the reply was spat.

"Day and night for 3 days solid. You expect me to believe that?"

"Believe what you want, it's the truth."

"You could have called me. No phone, no text, and no message. I was worried about you."

"Who are you kidding, all you're worried about is your effin' job. You've been impossible since last Friday; I just thought I'd stay away and avoid all the shit you're flinging around."

The accountant deflated like a party balloon, and the scruffy decorator just stared at him.

"I'm sorry," he said, "You're right I have been a bit on edge, but where have you been?"

Spike calmed down as well, and offered an explanation.

"You were being difficult, and I had a job to do. At first we fell behind with the work when the bloody paint wouldn't take on the ceilings. It needed 3 coats in some of the bedrooms, and then while I was working late on Wednesday Tina was sure there was someone hanging about in the back garden, and she was scared. She begged me to stay, and made me up a bed in lounge. All the other bedrooms were in a state from the decorating. Then on Thursday night the same thing happened again about 10:00 pm. I had no choice. But the job's all but done now, just a few finishing touches and it's complete. I'm sorry; I should have let you know what was happening."

And just at that moment the telephone rang, and when Gordon picked it up he couldn't believe his ears when it was Tina, who said "The police had just been, and caught someone in my back garden trying to steal all my magnificent new goldfish from my lovely fishpond."

Then she ended by saying," I am sorry I detained Spike at my house for the last few days, but I feel safe again now, and will you please say a big thank you to him for being such a brave little boy?"

Gordon couldn't help but burst out laughing with the sudden relief that the man in his life was back home, and what he had said appeared to be all true. He put the phone down after thanking Tina, and felt the tension drain from him.

"Come here, Soldierboy." he smiled giving his partner a huge hug.

Perhaps this issue had been resolved, and perhaps it hadn't, but the worried man's mental state as this time wanted a quick resolution, and on the basis of "least said, soonest mended" it would do for him for now. He was well aware that Spike ploughed his own furrow, and was only semi-domesticated, and that was exactly what he found so appealing about him. The relationship between the smartly dressed, finely groomed, always well turned out, logically thinking accountant, and the scruffy, dirty, unkempt, Bohemian attitude decorator was living proof that opposites do attract. But there was a delicate balancing act going on between them, an acceptance of the difference in lifestyle and outlook by both the men, and sometimes the strange incongruity of it all became too obvious on both sides.

As Saturday midday came around in the U.S.A. Tiny was boarding his flight from Columbus, Ohio to New York JFK, and the only things that kept him going were the success of his weeklong business trek, and the thought of being home soon with his wife. He was looking forward to seeing his little Spanish Chica, and the outcome of all the decorating and gardening endeavours that she had been presiding over while he was away. This flight was only 80 minutes duration and there was only a slight delay in takeoff.

He was mighty glad to arrive in the Big Apple at last, primed for the final flight home to Heathrow. The possible thrills of New York in the evening were of no interest. He was too tired to care and went to bed early in his very plush, but due to his tiredness, totally unnoticed hotel.

Waking mid-morning he had time to kill before his flight from JFK, and so he called a yellow cab, and took a tour with a cab driver from Queens who had the New York knowledge, and showed him lots of bridges, and tall buildings including the Empire State Building. He cruised down Broadway, walked around Time Square, rode the Statten Island ferry, took a stroll in Central Park, and saw the Statue of Liberty. But it was a mega-fast, whistle-stop tour, and he finished at JFK wishing he hadn't bothered, because by then he was totally exhausted again.

So, on Sunday evening he settled back in his seat on his final 7 hour flight to Heathrow relishing the idea of a nice long sleep. But it was not to be that easy. Unfortunately, he had the middle seat in a row of three, just in front of Mr and Mrs Moron from Hell, and their 6 year old spoilt brat, who hated flying. The child screamed incessantly and then proceeded to kick the back of the seat, like he was a prize fighter punching his practice ball. Every time the latter day Phileas Fogg tried to drop off to sleep, little brat features would shout, scream and kick again, and after several attempts at pleading with his parents to keep their budding Osama bin Laden under control, a very irritated Tiny was obliged to complain to a stewardess.

He was lucky. Realising the lack of intelligence and courtesy, displayed for all to see by Mr and Mrs Moron and their awful protégé, the stewardess promptly moved the brat's victim to an empty seat in Club Class. With an immense sense of relief, he found himself very quickly beginning to think those disconnected thoughts that precede dropping off. Gradually a comfortable, warm sense of wellbeing pervaded his brain, and he was somewhere else.

The modern day Phileas Fogg was smiling to himself as he thought back to his school days, when he and Hugh had invented their classic windup routines, and when a teenage joker put itching powder in the P.E teacher's jockstrap, and they both watched Jones the Phys Ed jump around in a frenzy like a victim of St Vitus' dance. Then, the intrepid traveller fell into a beautiful, sunny, lazy, July day on the playing fields at Brentwood School. He could see himself, a young, slim, man again, full of promise and ambition playing cricket Now he was the demon bowler sending a succession of googlies and china-men down to a lean, good-looking young Ramsbottom, who was fooling around, hitting shots off the edge of the bat, and smashing sixes into the trees way beyond the boundary. At the end of a maiden over, when his deliveries had stopped the other unidentified batsman scoring any runs at all, he had switched to wicket keeper. As a ball tipped the edge of Hugh's bat, Tiny dived athletically to his left and caught the ball, jumped in the air, and jubilantly shouted "Howzat!" The scene repeated itself, as if in a continuous tight loop, or a video-bite action replay on TV, and he could hear himself repeating "Howzat! Howzat! Howzat!" Each time he said it with decreasing volume. Then it seemed he fell over, and everything around him was sucked out of the scene, like it was being removed by a giant vacuum cleaner.

That's when he woke up, and a smiling stewardess was nudging him gently, and softly requesting him "Please sir, could you keep the noise down?"

She then added with a wink, "Or I'll have to move you back to Economy."

After a few more hours of dozing, Tiny had a coffee, and then began to notice people around him. The gentleman next to him looked familiar, but in his current exhausted state he couldn't place him. Then the passenger put his magazine down and spoke.

"Like cricket then do you?"

"What! Oh Yes! Sorry about that, I've been on a business trip for a week, and my brain's starting to play tricks on me."

"Yes, flying is potentially worse than night work for turning your brain cells to mush."

"Tim Balls, pleased to meet you." said the sleepy passenger offering a handshake.

"Chester Gannet, likewise." his companion answered returning the gesture.

"I thought I recognised you; you're a TV chef aren't you? I've been to your restaurant in Great Baddow, the Skinny Pig, isn't it?"

"Yes, right on both counts. Did you enjoy the meal?"

"Can't remember what it was now."

"That's disappointing for me. We always try to make memorable dishes that will excite and amuse, and possibly challenge our guests."

"I'm sorry, but let me blame it on the jetlag again."

"Apology accepted. Do come and see us again at the Skinny Pig, we're changing the menu all the time, and we're working on some innovative dishes at the moment."

"Thank you for the invitation. What have you got planned then?"

"Oh, loads of new ideas, like a three course menu of Cockroach Pate, Cow and Eel Pie, and Kangaroo Barb Crumble."

Tiny chuckled, and said, "You're pulling my leg."

Chester smiled back at him, and then rolled his eyes while putting his tongue in his cheek, before responding with "You'll have to book a table, and find out."

"What else have you got to tempt my taste-buds then?"

"Well, we have main courses like Snake and Kidney Pie, Real Toad in the Hole, Bohemian Ratstudy, and Cock au vin which is a kangaroo's penis slow stewed in Jacob's Creek Chardonnay."

Tiny chuckled again, and Chester realising he was on a roll added," Our premier menu is very special. We have a starter of Sparrow's Arse Soup, a main course of venison in a special marinade called Stag Night in Hamster Jam, and a dessert of Pommes de Pear Frites with Strawberry Ketchup which is presented to look like bowl of chips with tomato sauce."

"OK you've convinced me. I'll pay you a visit at the Skinny Pig as soon as I can."

During the long conversation, skimming the tops of the North Atlantic clouds, the chairman remembered how Norman had family issues with Chester Gannet. But he didn't raise the subject. He was far too tired. He just felt satisfied that a chain of events starting with the annual migration of frogs in North Yorkshire, had resulted in the creative abilities of a very talented computer nerd bringing his company close to global status. The fellow travellers swapped business cards before they landed at Heathrow.

After what seemed like hours in Passport Control, Baggage Reclaim and Customs, the intrepid traveller emerged into the cold London air, and was picked up by the Stansted and Heathrow International Taxis Executive Service. The 7 hour flight and 5 hour time difference meant that by the time he was back in Merrie England he'd been occupied for another half a day. The week's travelling exertions had surely taken their toll, and by this time he really didn't know what day it was, or what time of day it was. The S.H.I.T.E.S. airport taxi negotiated the way back to Chelmsford, skilfully driven by Ahmad in almost complete silence apart from the passenger's snoring. The chairman was severely jetlagged, and when he arrived home it was mid-morning in Chelmsford. He wouldn't have noticed the decorating was all but finished, and he certainly wasn't going to look at the garden. All he wanted was a quick greeting from Tina, and a long, lazy, uninterrupted sleep until the next day in his own bed.

CHAPTER 7

The Shape of Things to Come

(Friday 13th to Thursday 19th April 2012)

On Friday 13th April superstition demands that the wise man stays in bed, thereby avoiding danger, accidents, and bad fortune. But that wouldn't normally stop the Friday night session in the Two Brewers for the boys from NerdiSoft and their drinking buddies.

Well, things were not exactly normal.

Tiny was still circum-navigating the globe, and bearing in mind the time difference between Chelmsford and Columbus, at about 8pm when the boys and their buddies would have been assembling in the pub, he was in Columbus, meeting his business associates at Softly Softly Catchee Monkey Distribution. By all accounts it had been a week of unusual activity not just for him, but for all of them. Somebody had perhaps had the worst burden of all to bear.

Norman had unloaded his concerns about what Gordon was up to, and they were now Hugh's problem, He then proceeded to get on with what he was good at. So for him, things were close to normal, but he gave the Brewers a miss, and spent Friday evening with Clarisa.

Gordon had concerns about his partner's overnight absences, but at least they were partially allayed by the confirmation that a prowler had been arrested in Tina's garden trying to steal her brand new shoal of fish. Waiting in for his partner, he hadn't gone to the Brewers.

Spike had claimed that he was still playing brave boy at Tyrell's Close, and then went home to Vicarage Road, so he hadn't gone to the Friday night session.

While the latter day Phileas Fogg had been on the final legs of his journey flying from Columbus to JFK, taking a whistle-stop tour of the New York sights, and then travelling back to England, his best mate had been grappling with a number of weighty problems. What is more, none of them could be sorted out before the NerdiSoft boss had returned and recovered from his jetlag.

The fatman was deliberating about how to handle the suspicions over Gordon's behaviour. His natural outspoken way of dealing with things would have had him confront his colleague in the manner of, "What are you up to, you cheating gay bastard? Are you cooking the books, or working some kind of fiddle?" But this was a critical time for NerdiSoft, and rocking the boat wouldn't go down well, and might undermine the global project.

Then there was the issue of whether the part-time minder's eyes had deceived him a few nights before. He did see the decorator's van still parked outside the Ball's house at 10.30 pm, but who did he see wandering apparently naked across the landing? And if his worst fears were realised, how was he going to deal with that?

So on Friday 13th April a man without superstitions was sat in the Two Brewers alone nursing a pint of Fuller's Pride, and deprived of his usual audience he was a bit like a fish out of water. When Ike and Mike arrived they came with a revelation that added fuel to flame.

"Hey, you'll never guess what happened earlier?" said Mike

"Your landlord has enrolled in the British National Party, and issued an edict against Gay Pride." Hugh jested, "Or perhaps he's joined Al Qaeda and issued a fatwa against those that approve of gay marriage."

"No, seriously," Mike interrupted, "Just before we left for the pub, Spike was having a row with Gordon because he's been staying over at Tyrell's Close."

The joker, played his cards close to his chest, and remained quietly interested, only saying "And....?"

"Well, apparently Tina's been frightened because she thought she saw an intruder in the garden, and that's why she asked Scruffbag to stay over."

"I don't know why she didn't tell me; after all I only live across the road?"

"Probably because by the time you'd have walked over there, fatboy, the intruder would have heard you coming like the tyrannosaurus rex in Jurassic Park, and would have scarpered." Ike joked.

"Ho! Bloody Ho!" was the reply.

"Well, like I said, just before we left it happened. There was a phone call from Tina saying the police had arrested somebody in her garden trying to steal her new goldfish."

The joker just smiled. Now he doubted even more what he thought he had seen from across the road. "Bastard!" he said," I hope they lock him up."

Mike and Ike soon left, and so did the resident comedian. No audience, no fun!

After Friday 13th had passed without disaster, City's number one fan woke Saturday morning looking forward to his beloved Clarets playing a home match at Melbourne Park against Salisbury City. Due to a number of inconsistent results amongst the other contenders, qualification for the Blue Square Bet South playoffs was still in the Claret's hands.

With 3 matches to play, 3 wins would definitely see them at least into 5th place, but 2 wins and a draw might be enough. Hugh turned up at the ground about 2 pm ready for a beer and a bit of banter with the Claret

Army. As a season ticket holder for the main stand, he would normally take his seat in the first half, and then providing things were going well, swap to behind the goal for the second half. The match began with a promising outlook. The Clarets were playing extremely well, and the full-timers of Salisbury looked lacklustre, being outrun, outplayed, and outclassed throughout the first half. New striker Jamie Slabber was putting in a superb performance, and scored in the 6th minute. The brilliant Cliff Akurang added a second in the 45th minute. Craig Parker was having his best game of the season, and City were cruising to an easy win. After the half time whistle blew, the jolly fatman moved confidently to behind the goal at the Cro-ro end, ready for the second half, and expecting to see more City dominance and more goals. The second half continued in the same vein as the first, and Salisbury failed to impress.

Hugh described what happened next to his three boys later.

"Then manager Pennyfather dropped an almighty clanger. He made all 3 substitutions, based on who knows what? Maybe it was some churlish whims rather than injuries or tiring players. He substituted Jamie Slabber, taking off a proven goal-scorer, and putting on Kezie Ibe, a player I thought was long past his best before date. I know Ibe's fans think he's an Alan Shearer type player, a hold-up man, playing with his back to goal, and at times in the past he had scored and assisted with some great goals. But recently I thought he had been playing more like Alan Sugar. Then strangely our muddled manager decided to replace Parker, who had been impressive throughout the game, with Corcoran, someone I'd always thought was erratic and unpredictable."

In the 85th minute Salisbury had one of their few, and up to that point ineffective, attacks. City fullback Ben Nunn committed a foul in the penalty area, and having prevented an obvious goal-scoring opportunity, was red-carded and sent off. Salisbury scored the subsequent penalty kick, and it was 2 - 1, with City down to 10 men.

Hugh and the Claret Army now assumed that the boys could see out the last few minutes, and keep the 3 points with an all hands to the pump defensive attitude. Sadly, in the 88th minute, as Salisbury suddenly found new resolve to attack, there was a defensive mix up between Mark Haines and Aiden Palmer, resulting in a clash of heads and a facial injury to Mark Haines, and worse still a giveaway 2nd goal for Salisbury. To make matters even more desperate Haines had to go off for treatment.

The fatman was no longer jolly, because in the space of less than 5 minutes, the Clarets had gone from 2 - 0 up and cruising to an easy and well-deserved victory, to 2 - 2, and down to 9 men, and struggling to stay on top. Salisbury tasted blood and came alive, as the referee exasperatingly added 4 minutes injury time, and the City faithful now fretted at possibly having to settle for a point. But even that was not to be.

In the 96th minute a Salisbury forward called Abdulai Bell-Baggie scored a wonder goal. It was the sort of goal that you might see once in season, that would have easily made goal of the month on a Match of the Day programme. If he played for another 10 years as a striker, he would never score another goal quite like it. Shortly after that the whistle blew, and City had lost 3 - 2 and the City faithful knew they had been drinking in the last chance saloon.

Along with the rest of the fans, a disgruntled Hugh left the ground in disgust, not staying for his customary after the game bottle of Old Speckled Hen.

Forty minutes later the Player of the Season presentation took place in the clubhouse, and Kenny Clark deservedly received this accolade, but tragically for him in an almost empty bar. By that time one very sad supporter was floating like giant whale in the middle of his swimming pool. It was a good way to hide his tears. City's tenuous hold on a play off place had now all but evaporated in an unbelievable sequence of events occurring in something close to 12 minutes.

When Sunday morning arrived Hugh decided to pay a visit to Tyrell's Close just to see how the land lay. It was an easy pretext; he was just making a friendly call to see how the garden projects and the interior decorating had turned out. He ambled out of his mansion, and was soon ringing the bell at the Ball's household. Three rings later a sleepy Tina arrived at the door looking gorgeous as she always did, dressed in her underwear with a big white fluffy dressing gown on top, and silver slippers, not a hair out of place, and perfect makeup.

"Hola, hombre," she grinned, and added "Where do you go, Hugo?" with a huge smarmy smile.

"Don't smile at me, Argentina." he replied, kissing her outstretched hand.

"Hugo, my dahling," she crooned, "To what do I owe this pleasure?"

He was calmness itself, despite his worries about what might have been going on in Tyrell's Close whilst his friend had been away. He smiled and replied," Buenos Diaz senora. I just thought I'd pop in and see how the decorating is coming along. Just being el nosy gringo really."

"Oh come in, mi amigo, and I will show you around. Coffee?"

"Yes, that would be nice, two sugars."

She turned her back towards him and wiggled her arse, and then looked provocatively over her shoulder with a smile.

"Does my boom look big in this?"

"Sure thing, sister!" he answered, giving her a playful slap

She breezed through to the kitchen like she was gliding on little wheels, and poured two coffees from the percolator.

"Do you like the colour?" she enquired, waving her hand at the kitchen walls. "It's called dormouse."

"Yes, it's quite neutral and understated." he said sipping his coffee.

"I'm glad you approve dahling, come into the lounge, the wallpaper is superb and very expensive."

"It's a bit too floral and fancy for my liking," he said, as they moved into the next room, "Looks like one of them Lawrence Llewelyn Bowen designs. Not my taste, but if that's what you like...."

The former Miss Iberia was in her element, showing off, and there was no stopping her now. She slid the patio door aside with a theatrical sweep, and offered," Come and look at the garden. I am so pleased with it. I have bought new patio furniture and a parasol, a chiminea, and some lovely standard roses. I do hope that my darling Tim will love it all when he comes home tomorrow."

The garden was indeed impressive, and the boys had done a first class job. No expense had been spared. Tiny always just wanted to keep his little Spanish senorita happy, and Hugh knew he wouldn't bat an eyelid at the extravagance of it all.

"I like your fishpond and rockery, and it does look like something out of the Ideal Home Exhibition. It is beautiful." he enthused. They stood next to the fishpond, complete with lily pads, little waterfalls, and at least 50 goldfish of different sizes.

"Estupendo!" Tina gushed, "I have always dreamed of having a garden like this."

"I hope you'll be able to maintain it, sweetie. I'd recommend my gardener, Clive, if you need one. But, it's a worrying time with the drought, and the pathetic nonsense of a hosepipe ban if you're with the wrong water company."

"Oh, Hugo." she reassured," Really, there is no need to worry. In Spain where I come from, we have droughts all the time, and we don't run out of water."

They moved around the garden sipping coffee, with the glamour puss pointing out all her new highlights.

"I heard the police came and arrested someone trying to steal the goldfish?"

"Yes, the thief must have been watching the work going on. I thought I saw someone a few nights ago in the garden, but when Spike went out to have a look, they must have run away, or been hiding. Hugo, I was so frightened, and as he was working here quite late, I asked him to stay over and protect me."

"But I'm only round the corner. Why didn't you just come and stay over at our place? We've got plenty of room."

"Don't you see, dahling? I couldn't leave the house in turmoil, everything was upside down, and I didn't feel safe here on my own. Asking Spike to stay was the easiest choice. Anyway if the man was watching, they would have seen me leave, and that would have been like an invitation to come in and take what he wanted."

The fatman just smiled "Yes, I suppose so." he replied, and then thought, "Anyway, Scruffbag is supposed to be gay, isn't he?"

They moved through the garden, and back into the house, with Tina enthusiastically describing every detail, and the team had indeed completed a superb job decorating throughout the house. Hugh felt a bit uncomfortable as they walked across the landing, as his mind played a flashback of what he thought he had seen from across the road a few nights ago, but even more now he began to doubt his own recollection of events.

"Thank you for popping in, Hugo." she smiled, kissing him on both cheeks as he left the house.

"Hasta la vista, baby." Hugo chuckled in his best Arnold Swarzenegger accent as he left and went back to the Ramsbottom mansion.

From 16th April and during the next few days, news items featured worries about the continuing dry weather. Drought restrictions were already in place in South-East England, East Anglia, and parts of the South and Yorkshire. Now official drought zones were declared in a further 17 English counties, in the South West and the Midlands. The Environment Agency said dry weather over the past few months had left some rivers in England exceptionally low, and that after two dry winters rivers and ground waters were becoming depleted. Officials said that the hosepipe ban would ensure that public water supplies were unlikely to be affected by the continuing drought, and then reiterated calls for water to be used wisely. Newspapers carried headlines that the drought and water shortages could last until Christmas.

Following his hectic business trip the chairman had been sleeping off his jetlag at home until Wednesday, and the marketing director had been holding the reigns at the office. Tiny had noticed that his lovely wife was strangely aloof. There was something peculiar about her attitude, but he put it down to over-excitement for her new home, and being frightened by the thought of prowlers in her garden. He returned to work on Wednesday morning full of enthusiasm for the global project, and eager to tell all about his travels and meetings. Despite having separate informal chats with all the boys throughout the day, during which he repeated all the details of his recent business trip, he decided to call a board meeting at 10 am the next morning.

On Thursday 19th April in Chelmsford it rained all day, and it didn't stop. At 9 am precisely in Colchester there was an unusual traffic jam at the entrance to the NerdiSoft car-park, as all of the board members arrived together. The chairman was very pleased with this simultaneous turnout, and saw it as a keenness to hear formally what he had to say, and for each to present an update on their expected contribution to the global project.

If they had sorted out the traffic jam in order of car quality it would have been Porsche, Lexus, Land Rover, Ford Galaxy, but the pecking order and age difference protocol was preserved. So, the NerdiSoft supremo parked his highly polished silver grey Lexus GS250 in his reserved space first. He was followed in by the marketing director in the slightly careworn black Land Rover Discovery LR4, parked wherever he dumped it. Next was the company accountant in his nearly new Ford Galaxy Titanium X, parking safely against a wall in a corner. Finally the development director parked his Porsche Carrera close to the chairman's Lexus.

Unusually the board meeting started dead on time at 10 am.

The boss began, very focussed and businesslike.

"We'll dispense with all the usual reporting again, and just discuss the one item on the agenda, which is the outcome of my trip, and your progress in meeting my requests. I don't want to give you chapter and verse for every detail of the trip, as I've probably already bored you individually with my travel overview. There's a lot of work to do, and not a lot of time, so we'll forego all the usual banter as well if you don't mind."

The others had really never experienced their boss being quite for forthright and purposeful before, and they all instinctively moved from their relaxed postures in their chairs into a more upright position. Even the marketing director managed to bite his lip, and respond positively to the "no banter" request. This was indeed a very different atmosphere to the casual approach they'd all enjoyed at the many previous board meetings.

Tiny looked at everyone, one at a time, and they all nodded in agreement. Then he continued.

"Let me discuss production with you first. The draft contracts have been drawn up and agreed in principle with Wang Wu Hoo Du Production. They have agreed to our production volumes, and as soon as we have formulated our advertising campaign, and are ready to go, they will tool-up and manufacture our products. We have developed a business plan that projects our volume growth for all the games in our current product range that have global potential. We looked at the figures for our UK sales, and projected from there on."

Hugh had never heard his colleague act like this before, and he didn't dare to crack a joke, or make any asides, so he just looked straight at him and said "Right, Boss."

"OK then," he went on, "Next is distribution. The United States is obviously our biggest target market, and I consider it strategically important that our distribution centre will be somewhere totally relevant to that fact. That's why we're going to use Softly Softly Catchee Monkey Distribution. They're well-placed geographically, and Columbus as you probably know is the upcoming Silicone Valley. Again, the draft contracts have been drawn up and agreed, and our deal with them will be based on our projected increase in volumes over the first year of production. They already have some links with Wang Wu Hoo Du Production for other manufacturer's products."

Gordon decided to interrupt, "Can I ask a question? While all this global market invasion is going on, if we begin by concentrating on the U.S.A., then what will we do about the UK market and Europe?"

"I'm glad you asked that question," answered a confident Tiny, "Like I said we've got a lot of work to do, and not a lot of time. We can't stay here in this tin-pot little place. I plan to move us to new, bigger premises in Chelmsford, and we'll manage the UK and European operations from there initially under our NerdiSoft label. I've said already that this plan will involve upheaval and big changes, and we'll be working hard to keep the current workforce informed and batting on our side."

The accountant was almost deflated with the positivity of the answer, and replied, "I see Tim. You seem to have covered all the angles."

The chairman then turned to his marketing director and said, "Have you found us any possible new premises in the Chelmsford area?"

He already knew the answer to that question, but his mate answered," Yes! I've arranged for us to view 2 possibilities next week. One of them is on the Dukes Park Estate, and the other is on the Hedgerows Business Park. I've had a preliminary look at both of them, and I think you'll agree that the potential is there."

Next, it was the development director's turn. "Bring us up to date on your work Norman." requested Tiny.

The company's ideas man had been working really hard in the previous 2 weeks, and he knew the chairman would be absolutely over the moon with his progress.

"Well, first of all, "Beer Festival Bastards Final Frontier" is finished and ready to go. All the software, artwork, and advertising preparations are complete. I can hand it over this afternoon. Also, "R. McGeddon's Nerd World Apocalypse" is about a week away from completion. I've just a few loose ends to tie up, and that also will be ready to go. I'm confident it'll be ready by the end of the month."

"Brilliant, well done," said the ecstatic boss, "We'll release those two games together with your new version of "Viking Ninja Holocaust 9" as our first global games under our new label. I think that will start us off on solid ground. Do continue."

The young man beamed an enormous smile around the room, as he knew he was definitely on a winner with his next offering. "Well, as you requested." he said, "In order to re-launch the company we needed to come up with a new internationally suitable name. What you asked me for was a new name and logo, and artwork, and to dream up a game based around 2012 and Chelmsford's City status."

The Chairman was beginning to relax, and replied, "Your memory is impeccable as usual."

"Well here it all is," continued Norman, handing round some paperwork, "The new name I suggest is 1stCitySoft, and here's a first stab at a logo and some artwork. Plus, I've got a game on the drawing board called "Secrets of the First City."

Just for a moment, the room fell silent, as they all perused the paperwork, and then they all broke into smiles. Even Gordon seemed happy.

"Fantastic, Norman, That's all brilliant. I like the sound of that. 1stCitySoft. Yeah! That's just the job." Tiny was gushing enthusiasm," Oh, and the logo and artwork are just unbelievable."

Hugh slapped his nephew on the back, and now that the atmosphere was more relaxed chuckled, "That's my boy!"

At this point in the proceedings everybody's expectations were that the meeting could be quickly wound up with a declaration that the accounts review was ready to go. There was a cheery, confident, very professional feel about this moment, and things had become far less formal since the beginning of the meeting. When the enthusiasm for the excellent progress thus far had subsided a little, the boss referred directly to his accountant friend and asked, "Right, Gordon, are the accounts ready to go?"

He shuffled uncomfortably in his seat, cleared his throat twice, looked downwards, and replied nervously, "Er! Well! No! I'm sorry but I've been snowed under with other work, and I think I've suggested before that it would be best to synchronise this review with our end of year returns to Companies House. I'll get it done as soon as I can."

There was a massive pregnant silence, as the atmosphere in the room plummeted into a bottomless abyss. It was like everybody was waiting for a bomb to go off. And then the short fuse hit the accurately positioned detonator.

With a tone of voice that none of the board members had ever heard before the chairman exploded. "What exactly have you been snowed under with? Is it not absolutely clear to you how important this project is? If we can't provide evidence of our financial stability, why would the Chinese and the Americans want to do business with us? Have I not made it clear what I want and expect from you? Why do you keep stalling? What the fuck are you up to? If you delay this anymore I'll have your bollocks on a plate?

This was a torrent of questions delivered machinegun style, for all of which the interrogator had no intention of waiting for answers, or excuses. His face was crimson, screwed up in frustration. He was completely beside himself with anger. He got up, his chair clattering to the ground behind him. He seemed to be much bigger than his name would suggest.

"Meeting concluded," he shouted, adding in no uncertain terms, and pointing his finger at the accountant, "My office. NOW!" and then he turned and left the room.

A doomy stillness hung over the room, like a giant rain-cloud blocking the sun. You could hear only breathing. Gordon looked like a first-former who just been told to report to the headmaster's office. He shuffled his papers together shaking, and skulked his way out of the room not daring to look up.

Hugh looked at Norman and they shared a moment's worried silence, and then he broke into a grin saying," Gordon Bullock's golden bollocks on a plate. By the time the Boss finishes with that shyster he'll be like Goebbels.", and then he sang, out of tune as usual, "And poor old Goebbels had no balls at all."

It broke the ice, but only slightly, and as they both went off to their work, they could hear the unmistakeable rumble of a very heated argument going on in the chairman's office.

Whilst one of them ear-wigged at the wall that divided the offices from each other, the other donned headphones to drown out the noise, while he played an embryonic version of Interstellar Paranoid Overdrive. The argument went on for 20 minutes or so, and then the slam of a door seemed to signify the end of the hostilities. Shortly after that both Hugh and Norman simultaneously made for the coffee machine. Then without saying anything or giving them the slightest glance, Gordon quickly ghosted past, face as grey as his suit, Seconds later there was the sound of his car starting up and then leaving the car park.

If they had sorted out a pecking order at that particular moment, in terms of their status within the company, it would have been Lexus, Porsche, Land Rover, and no Ford Galaxy at all, The chairman had asserted himself unequivocally as boss, while the development director had excelled with his contribution to the project, and the marketing director had done exactly what was asked of him. But the company accountant was the bad apple in the barrel. He had not performed to expectations.

It was after midday when Hugh and Norman were called into the office, expecting to hear why their work colleague had left, and what was going to happen. Tiny had calmed down a little, but there was still a tense rhythm in the way he spoke.

"Our colleague's been in here shouting and screaming at me, and suddenly he burst into tears. There's no excuse for his delays in producing the accounts review, but he's got other problems. It appears that what's at the bottom of this is.... is that he and Spike have fallen out in some way. He thinks Scruffbag doesn't love him. He's gone off him. Heaven knows why. Strikes me gay relationships are even more complicated than those between a man and a woman, and God knows they can be complicated enough."

This wasn't the boardroom chairman they'd seen a few hours ago; it was the all-mates Tiny down the Brewers. But both of the boys knew that there was more to this dilemma than their colleague was aware of. Neither could gauge whether this was the right time to reveal what they suspected about their accountant colleague. The question in both their minds was whether it would do any good to raise what may still be unfounded suspicions about him and the accounts. They were aware that this could jeopardise the global project.

In addition, Hugh had still said nothing about what he thought he had seen while his long term friend was on his recent business trip. He was absolutely certain that if he implicated Spike in something dodgy with Tina, then there would probably be three relationships in tatters. There would be serious, possibly unresolvable issues raised between Tiny and Tina, which he may have been held responsible for bringing to the surface. He and his best mate would almost inevitably find their friendship stretched at a critical time for the company they had built together. And Gordon and Spike would both blame him for stirring up a hornet's nest for them which would jeopardise their partnership. The fatman certainly didn't want all of that on his conscience. He attempted to make light of the situation, saying "Bloody pooftahs! I can't understand it. More trouble than they're worth. Always so sensitive about their status" It wasn't by any means the right thing to say, but it did the trick to ease the tension.

"Anyway, "continued Tiny," I've sent him home to try and sort himself out. We don't want him having a nervous breakdown, do we? And he's going to talk to his Soldierboy, and get them back to luvvy-duvvy."

"Yuk! Too much information! Stop him before he turns into Jeremy Kyle." The joker replied.

The frivolity of the remark was ignored, and then the boss added," I probably went over the top being angry today. I'm sorry fellas. The accounts are crucial, but not yet. They'll get done eventually. It's just, I'm so wired up with this global project, and I don't want anything to stop it happening."

There was no need to respond.

Although they all went about their work diligently, there was an overriding gloom about the place for the next few hours, and the end of the working day couldn't come too soon. Unfortunately on a day of crises there was more to come.

CHAPTER 8

All Hands to the Pump

(Thursday 19th to Saturday 21st April, 2012)

While the dramas at NerdiSoft had been going on, there were far more major events occurring all over the country. It seemed that perfectly synchronized with official announcements about the drought across the UK; the heavens had opened with true and unprecedented vengeance. A few days after predictions had been made to assert that the drought would last until Christmas, the fickle hand of fate had thrown weather patterns into complete confusion. It started raining, and it didn't look as if it would stop till Christmas. Within a few days rivers all over the country went from dried up and only a trickle, to burst banks and flood alerts. Despite this, the water companies in their infinite wisdom maintained their hosepipe bans.

It was just a matter of luck, but it was nearly the end of the working day in the office in Colchester when Tiny received a phone call from Tina. She was distressed, crying, and almost hysterical as she blurted out a cry for help. The newly installed fishpond in her pride and joy of a garden was overflowing, and the poor goldfish, having only just survived the recent kidnap attempt, were now gasping for breath as they were in danger of being washed out of the pond, and along a newly created stream running down the garden. She issued a tear-stained, all points bulletin, requesting immediate emergency assistance to save the goldfish, and prevent the pond and the garden from being obliterated in the sudden deluge. The chairman advised his wife to contact Ike and Mike right away, as they were likely to be closest to the disaster zone, and therefore quickest on the scene, and then to see if she could get hold of Spike. He decided not to bother Gordon in his current mental state.

Within minutes 3 cars were speeding along the A12 towards Chelmsford. It was still lashing down, and driving conditions were dangerous to say the least. Porscheman was first in the emergency convoy to leave, executing a perfect handbrake turn out of the car park, and very quickly storming ahead of the others. He was back at Tyrell's Close in just over 20 minutes, but both the others in the rescue party became embroiled in a traffic jam trailing from Hatfield Peveril to the Boreham Interchange, resulting from a minor accident at Sandon. Mike had picked up Ike at Wyevales Garden Centre, and they arrived at Tyrell's Close at the same time as Norman. Tina answered the door; tears rolling down her cheeks indistinguishable from the torrent of rain that had drenched her as she held back the flood alone. Her beautiful designer clothes and boots were plastered with mud, and her honey blonde hair and perfect makeup were in such a mess she was barely recognisable.

"Oh thank you, my brave boys. Come quickly, and save my poor goldfish. Please!" she cried.

Nobody replied. There was no need to. The two gardeners armed themselves with shovels, and Norman grabbed two buckets from Mike's van, and they went swiftly to work. Mike and Ike began digging a trench to act as a soak away, and Norman did his best to remove water from the overflowed pond, and to transfer it into the kitchen sink. From here the lady of the house took a small bowl and removed the larger fish into the bath in the downstairs bathroom. This process went on for over half an hour as the rain continued to hammer down. Eventually the smaller fish had to be transferred by a similar method. Nobody really knew how many fish there were, so the job carried on until it seemed to have been done. By this time the trench that the boys had dug was taking most of the water away, and Tina had calmed down a little.

Hugh and Tiny turned up after about 45 minutes just in time to see the kettle go on for a job well done, or at least done as well as could be expected in the circumstances. The Spanish beauty fell into her husband's arms uttering, "Oh darling, it has been a nightmare." and spreading mud all over his expensive suit. Mike and Ike were totally drenched and looked like two refugees from a "When the levee breaks" disaster movie, and Norman's best grey designer suit was ruined.

The garden would need a complete rebuild, but at least the continuously falling rain was now being effectively channelled away. There were trails of dirty water and mud, and a few dead squashed goldfish, trodden into the carpet along a trail from the kitchen door, through the hall, and into the downstairs bathroom. In the bath, which was filled nearly to the brim, was what remained of the precious goldfish collection.

"Never mind, sweetheart," soothed Tiny to his Chica, "It can all be cleaned up and fixed, and be good as new."

The distinctly unglamorous former Miss Iberia merged herself into him like a tired baby girl snuggles up to her daddy for warmth and protection. She didn't look or sound anything like the gorgeous, expensively dressed, confident woman they all knew. It was the first time in her life that she had cried buckets, and nobody would have noticed because of the downpour. Only Hugh was totally unscathed by the afternoon's drama. "Can I borrow a brolly?" he asked, as he left the scene of the devastation.

Just over 24 hours later, another working week came to an end, and the NerdiSoft crew all left Colchester bound for home in not so much frenzy as on the previous day. It was still raining, and there was a spate of minor accidents on the A12 heading south, delaying Tiny and Hugh's respective arrivals in Chelmsford. But the man in the Porsche took his favourite route home back through the country lanes, listening to Bruno Mars, as the car was purring its way through Stanway, Tiptree, Maldon, and Hatfield Peveril. He avoided the last bit of the A12, which he could see was stationary as he passed beyond the William Boosey public house, and continued through Boreham instead. Soon he was back in the dry in his pad in The Hub.

A while later he was scooting round the edge of the building. He passed the Loch Fyne and Prezzo restaurants and then went across to the Excel Gym for a quick workout. Ryan, the personal trainer for Action Man, moving in his cloud of Lynx Africa fumes was there chatting up another gullible lady, but apart from that the gym was nearly empty. After a few minutes, Clarisa arrived and she and her Normie enjoyed working out together on the running and rowing machines. After a homemade pizza of goat's cheese, kalamata olives, and vine-ripened tomatoes back at the Hub apartment, they prepared to go over to the Two Brewers for the Friday evening entertainment. Then just as it did at the same time every Friday, the phone rang, and it was the familiar voice of Stanley.

"Ey Oop, son, 'ow yer diddlin'?"

"Alright, Dad, how are you?"

"Mustn't grumble, nobody listens anyway."

"Mum alright, is she?"

"Aye, son, same as ever."

"What can I do for you, Dad?"

"Well, I'm just phoning up to tell thee 'bout t' ockey match yer sister's playing in tomorrow. Heh! Heh! They're playing away at St Margaret's FC along the Abbey Road in Leiston which is reet 'andy 'int it?" It was his idea of a joke.

"Oh, and yer mum wants yer to stay for lunch after, she's thinking about doin' Eisbein and Rotkohl."

"OK, Dad, I'll be there about 10, see you then, love to Mum."

"Bye, son, drive carefully."

The young man put the phone down showing a pained expression.

"Oh Dear!" He thought out loud.

"What's the matter, Normie?" enquired Clarisa.

"Oh, nothing, Sweet Thing!", he paused," After watching Cher play hockey again tomorrow, there'll be a fabulous lunch where I've got to fight my way through a massive ham hock with an inch thick layer of fat, and that awful red cabbage, served with 4 ton of potatoes."

"Can't wait to meet your mum and dad, and enjoy one of their tasty meals." she teased, as he faked a smile. She was a vegetarian of sorts, but she did eat fish occasionally, and wouldn't have touched any meat with a bargepole.

The young couple walked arm in arm across the car park between Bond

Street and the Chelmer River at the back of Debenhams on their way to the pub, partly shielded from the rain by a massive Dunlop golf umbrella. This hated bit of the town was still scruffy and semi-derelict and the prospect of it soon being turned into the planned John Lewis complex pleased them both. They made the 5 minute walk to the Brewers, skipping through the puddles, and scurrying out of the way of cars on Springfield Road going too fast and spraying pedestrians with rainwater.

If Hugh and Tiny had been hardened boatmen, they could have paddled a canoe down the rapids that flowed from where they lived in Springfield Road, down to the lake that was quickly forming around the Bond Street roundabout just past the Two Brewers. But their days of donning Davy Crockett hats and paddling canoes weren't long over; they had never begun, so they called PAMTAX to take them down instead. They would definitely miss the opportunity to have a quick pint or two on the way down at the Red Lion and the Oddfellows, but upon arrival at the Two Brewers the jolly fatman was sure as hell going to make up for it. Immediately on arrival he ordered 3 pints of Fuller's Pride, one for his mate, and 2 for himself. The first pint didn't touch the sides, and was finished before the second one was poured. Then a nervous looking Gordon arrived with Ike and Mike in tow.

"Are you OK then, gayboy?" asked the fatman, "Or are rumours of your death greatly exaggerated?"

"Very funny, fatso, your sense of humour never improves, does it?" was the retort.

What the joker would have loved to say was, "OK, Bean Counter, tell us all what you're up to with the accounting business."

But instead of that he politely enquired," When are you coming back to work, we need you to pull your weight, and do what's been asked of you." Then he added with a whining hint of sarcasm," We can't do it without you, lovely boy. We all miss you."

The accountant just said," My G.P.'s signed me off for 2 weeks because I'm suffering from stress."

He then turned away and made for the dartboard together with Ike and Mike. Strangely, up to that point Scruffbag was nowhere to be seen. There was no way Gordon would manage to allay anybody's fears about the accounts right then and there, so the fatman changed the subject and decided to inflict his worries about the Clarets on his best mate.

"It was a bloody disgrace on Saturday against Salisbury," he began, "City were cruising 2 nil up after 80 minutes, and then it all went tits up. Bloody Pennyfather subbed the two best players, and then we gave them a penalty, and Ben Nunn was red-carded. A few minutes later we give them another goal and are down to 9 men, with Haines going off with a head injury. The Jodrell Banker of a ref plays 4 minutes injury time, and they score a wonder goal in the 96th minute. How is that possible? We lose 3 - 2 and our place in playoffs is in serious doubt."

"That's a very critical summary, even for you." replied Tiny, "Was is really the manager's fault, or the player's or the referee's? You seem to be blaming everyone."

"No, mate! At the bottom of it all, it's bloody Funnyfarter. Right at the moment he's the man who puts the turd in my Saturday. After this demise, I'm worried, very worried."

Just as that subject fizzled out, Spike arrived looking even dirtier and more dishevelled than usual. He still had flecks of black and orange paint all over his hands and face, and on his nearly bald head. Hugh wanted to spill the beans about the scruffy decorator being bisexual and bonking Tina, and then he wanted to watch Gordon's reaction to the awful truth that his partner was a love rat. But he didn't. He just greeted him cursorily, and offered a drink, and then passed it to him with a comment, "There you are, Scruffbag."

He didn't reply, or even say "Thank you". He went over to join the others playing darts, and watching from a distance at the bar, it didn't look to the fatman like there was any difference in the way Gordon and his partner were behaving towards each other.

"I don't think I've told you this before," said the chairman," but, it slipped my mind for a while due to the jetlag I think. Most of my trip back from JFK, I was in Club Class, and I just happened to sit next to Chester Gannet, you know that oddball TV chef. He owns that pub and restaurant in Great Baddow, the Skinny Pig I think it's called."

"He's the thundering berk who ruined my dad's business, "interjected Norman," According to my parents Chester bloody Gannet's the reason I didn't finish my schooling at Northallerton College. I had to come south, and finish my schooling at Boswell's 'cause of him. My mum had a nervous breakdown over those froggy sausages, and my dad had to retire. That's why he was forced to leave his beloved Yorkshire, and went to live in Leiston. If I ever got my hands on that bloody chef, I'd kill him."

Tiny knew he didn't mean it, the young man couldn't kill anyone, but it appeared that he felt very strongly about the repercussions of the great sausage debacle, and he obviously was disgusted with Chester Gannet's apparent part in the situation.

The chairman asked, "Are you absolutely sure that this Chester bloke is to blame? He seemed like a charming fellow to me."

"Well, I was only a kid at the time, but my mum and dad seem pretty sure that he's behind their problem."

"Look on the bright side, Nobless."(His uncle had reverted to calling him that again, even in front of Clarisa.)" You've adapted very well to being an Essex boy. There's not even the hint of a Yorkshire accent in the way you speak, and I know you're a big fan of Mark Wright, and TOWIE. Tell me honestly that you don't like it here is Essex?"

"I don't know anything about that Chester Gannet business, or froggy sausages Normie." Clarisa said to her man, a little worried about how strongly he felt about the famous chef. Before he could reply to his uncle she added, "Why haven't you told me about it?"

"I will, Sweet Thing when I get the opportunity," he replied, "But not right now."

She looked concerned, and hugged her man's arm saying," I can tell that whatever happened still hurts, but OK, tell me about it later, please."

"Anyway," Tiny continued, "Getting back to the subject of my meeting with him, Chester probably now regrets any part he might have played in your family's exile. Who knows, maybe he wishes he could somehow make amends."

"I think my dad would probably take out his 12-bore shotgun, and shoot that man's legs off if he came anywhere near him again." Norman said, "He threw my family into turmoil. I wouldn't hold out much hope for a reconciliation of any kind. And if my dad didn't shoot him, then my mum would cheerfully strangle him."

"I went to the Skinny Pig once." Hugh smiled, "Didn't like the food much, although there's plenty of it. It's all very pretty, and presented with a lot of pomp and circumstance, but it's a load of pretentious crap really. Give me one of the Oddfellows steak and stilton and mushroom pies any day."

"Or two?" concluded Tiny with a grin, moving over to the bar to get in another round, just as the boys from Vicarage Road were finished with their games of darts.

"Let me get you all another drink, to say thanks for your efforts with the great flood yesterday. If it carries on like this, I'm thinking of either moving to higher ground in Danbury, or perhaps building an Ark."

Mike and Ike accepted gracefully, and although the other two gay men had not been involved in saving the garden from the deluge, they were included in the generous round.

"I'm sorry that this has happened, "said Mike, "The sudden rainfall we're suffering is unprecedented, and we couldn't have designed and built the garden any better to cater for it. The work we did yesterday won't prevent the problem occurring again, if it keeps raining like this. The pond is supposed to be ornamental and that works OK in normal weather conditions."

"I know you've done the best you can, and anyway my little senorita's decided that now she wants her fishy friends protected from any future potential trauma, so she's ordered a massive aquarium to be installed in the living room on Monday. Then I'll need to transfer all the fish from the bathroom to the aquarium to keep her happy."

"What do you want to do with the pond then?" Mike asked, "Do you want it filled in?"

"No, we're going to keep it, purely ornamental you understand. When this bloody rain stops, you can come round and pretty it all up again. Tina has the idea that we can transfer the fish to the pond a few times a year for a sort of holiday."

"Bloody hell," interjected Hugh, "That sounds like more trouble than keeping a dog. They're going to be the most pampered goldfish in Britain, whoever heard of it? Holidays for fish! Whatever next? Are you going to set up a telly for them to watch, and send out for a takeaway?"

Tiny was serious about what his wife wanted, but they all saw the funny side of her plans. The joker couldn't resist it while he was on a roll, and pointing to Mike and Ike added," Still time for you to consider setting up Blojob Enterprises. Besides the gardening, you could specialise in handling holidays for goldfish, that's carassius auratus auratus to you. Why not call it Carassius Vacations?"

They did not disappoint as they raised their middle fingers in the air in the expected response.

The evening's boozing was drawing swiftly to a close, and soon the usual taxi arrived. After a few skirmishes with Hugh, Pavel was now a little wary upon arrival at the Brewers, and in an attempt not to cause further confusion for himself he entered the bar, and asked Caroline to announce a "Taxi for Mr Ramsbottom.", and then went and waited outside. He didn't have to wait long before his fare spilled out of the door. As they waddled towards the taxi, the joker turned to the Village People and shouted out, "Hey, you lot remind me of that famous old rugby song."

"Which one's that?" pleaded Gordon with resignation knowing another jibe was on its way.

"Can't remember it all, but the chorus goes "One black one, one white one, and one with a bit of shite on..." (He sang it out of tune.) Can you guess who's who? It's got to be Ike, Mike and Spike in that order. No place for you in that song, Gord."

Seconds later the car with Gay Pride stickers in the rear window drove out on to Springfield Road carrying four gay men all with their middle fingers in the air.

The taxi made the short trip up the hill to Avalon House. It stopped on the corner of Springfield Road and Tyrell's Close, and Hugh was about to make his last quip of the night at the cabbie's expense, but before he could speak, Pavel surprised the passengers by breaking into song. "One black one, one white one, and one with a bit of shite on, and the hairs on her dickydido hang down to her knees." he sang, then stopped, smiled, and looked at the fatman expecting some recognition of this titbit of knowledge.

But Hugh just stared back incredulously, and paused for what seemed like an age, during which time the Polish cabbie's face grew visibly redder. When he knew that enough seconds had passed for embarrassment, the joker imitated a very stern expression and said "Pavel! That's disgusting! You could get deported back to Poland for saying things like that."

As he sat there disappointed his passengers laughed and departed.

Meanwhile back in his flat, Norman was making coffee and telling Clarisa all about the froggy sausages affair. She listened intently, and when he had finished with the story, she looked at him watery-eyed and said, "But I'm so glad that you're now an Essex boy, Normie. If all that business had not happened, you wouldn't be living in Chelmsford now, and we would very likely have never met." He just smiled back, and replied," Yes! That's true. Chester may have split my family up, and forced my parents to move, but I'm glad that I'm now living in Chelmsford, and that I've met you."

Clarisa embraced him, and looked deep into his eyes, and said, "I understand how all this has affected you and your family, Normie, but excuse me for asking...."

"Asking what, Sweet Thing?"

"I'm sorry, but are you absolutely certain that this Chester Gannet fellow is the cause of your exile in Essex? It sounds a bit circumstantial to me."

He paused and thought for a few moments mulling over the past, and then said, "Well, I was only 16 when it happened, so I suppose I have taken my parent's view of the situation. They don't get everything right all of the time. My mum's a bit headstrong, but my dad's a very steady sort of character. I guess it would be true to say that I don't have any reason to doubt their suspicions."

She looked at him with an expression that said, "Think about it!"

Then she said, "Things are not always quite as they appear, Normie. In any case after all this time, whatever happened you have to move on. You can't harbour grudges for 10 years. It's necessary to forgive and forget. It's the only way, Normie."

He did think about it. For the first time in his life he found himself sewing seeds of doubt about something that he had previously regarded as a certainty.

The next morning, when the clock radio alarm burst into life at 8 am, the man in the Hub woke up and propped up on one arm took a peep at Clarisa, still dozing peacefully next to him. He grinned, as his eyes panned slowly from the fine bronzed leg sticking out the side of the expensive duvet, to the neat head of dark hair tinted red, the perfect make up, the smooth, pretty little face, and understated light pink lipstick. He rubbed the sleep from his eyes still grinning, breathing in the fragrance of Hugo Boss Deep Red, and thinking how lucky he was to be with this lovely lady. He remembered their first night, and how he'd only expected it to be a one night stand like so many before. He squirmed a little, feeling slightly uncomfortable when thinking about his reaction when he'd woken up that first morning. How he had thought to himself, "Blimey! Not bad! Must have been a lucky night." and then how he had to think very fast to remember her name. Only a few months had passed since then, and things were very different. He was no longer a promiscuous bed-hopper. He was a one gal guy, and that girl was Clarisa

Hinton. He loved everything about her, from her cute little childlike hands and feet, to her lovely wide, sparkling green eyes, and those cute little dimples in her cheeks when she smiled. She wasn't just a body with bumps in all the right places, and buttons to trigger the required sensations 'like all the others, she was special, she was precious, she was perfect, she was God's own child. She was intelligent, clever, good fun, liked the same things as he did, and had a parallel sense of values about all those worldly things that would be so important in a long term relationship. Seeing her, being near her, just filled him with a sense of complete euphoria. The contented man was drifting back to sleep again while he thought about how she had completely changed his life. Then she stirred and blinked awake, and looked at her man, stroking his cheek, and kissing him gently on the lips. As she moved closer to him he smiled a big toothy smile, and quietly whispered "Hi sweetie, how are you today?"

"Happy to be here with you," she answered dreamily.

It was a little later than anticipated when the Porsche was fired up for the Saturday morning drive to Suffolk. But the A12 was remarkably free of traffic, and the journey to Leiston was an easy routine accompanied by the sounds of Stereophonics. Norman put the CD player on a short loop to repeat his favourite track, "Dakota", to which he sang along "You made me feel like the one. You made me feel like the one, the one." thinking again about how Clarisa had changed his life.

Just before the start of the hockey match between the Norfolk Enchants and the Leiston Lionesses, Norman pulled into the car park at the St Margaret's FC football ground, and parked in the available space alongside his father's clapped out red Mondeo. This ground was so much better than the Norfolk Enchants home-ground. There were real facilities for spectators, somewhere to buy drinks and food, proper changing rooms, and best of all, no cowpats. Unfortunately, there had been so much rain recently that the pitch wasn't in the best condition, but nevertheless it was playable. He greeted his father with a handshake and his mother with a kiss on the cheek, waved to Cher and then the game bullied-off. Stanley joined in when the few spectators and supporters repeated "Norfolk Enchants, Norfolk Enchants.", and these were prophetic words as usual. Lisalotte was in a bad mood, and didn't say very much, other than to complain bitterly that the halftime coffee was weak and cold. Nobody batted an eyelid when she swore emphatically as the wind blew her umbrella inside out several times during a squally shower towards the end of the match. Sister played her socks off, bruised her shins, and proceeded to get covered in mud, and her team predictably lost by a wide margin, but she seemed to enjoy it. They all waited at the end of the match for her to reappear, as she enjoyed the luxury of a proper shower and changing rooms in the excellent Leiston Lionesses facilities. When she finally emerged she was accompanied by a butch, large, quite bulky lady, and casually introduced her.

"Listen everybody, this is Helen, and she's the captain of the Lionesses." Cher said, "We're going for lunch together, so I'll leave you to enjoy your meal back home without me."

Lisalotte swore under her breath.

And then they wandered off together. As they strolled across the car park, from the rear they looked like two oversized rejects from Les Dawson's Roly Polys. The young man's immediate thoughts turned to the massive meal that had been suggested he might have inflicted on him at lunchtime. He imagined that the motherly instinct would force the extra Eisbein ham hock on him, together with an extra large portion of potatoes. It made him feel sick even to just think about it.

Lisalotte spoke, "Well, Never mind, sohn, zer vill be more for ous. I have done some luffley Kohlrouladen mit Knodel for our mittagessen."

"Champion!" uttered the Yorkshireman looking at his son. He grinned at him as if prompting him to say something encouraging. "That's lovely Mum." He felt forced to answer, relieved that the prediction of Eisbein and Rotkohl had been superseded by something a little less gigantic. But he was still dreading having to fight his way through another gut-busting German dish. As his sister would not be there to enjoy the meal, he imagined he would be obliged to eat at least two huge Kohlrouladen that would be stuffed with very fatty ground beef. Worse still, there would undoubtedly be at least three possibly indigestible Knodel, the size of cricket balls on his plate.

An hour later his fears were realised, as he did his best to tackle the huge meal, washed down by "Perry wasser", while his father enjoyed an "Adam's beer", and his mother worked her way through a bottle of her favourite Blue Nun. Her bad mood was even more evident than previously at the hockey match, and whilst preparing and serving the meal she swore repeatedly.

"Poor old cow," whispered Stanley, as his wife momentarily left the room to get the salt and pepper, "Her gout's playin' her oop again. She's got it in both feet at t' moment, and sometimes it's like living wi' a Gestapo interrogator."

"Vot are you saying about me, Stanley?" she asked curtly as she re-entered the room.

"Oh nothing', dear, I was just sayin' about 'ow yer suff'rin' from t' gout again, yer poor thing."

"Yes, it's very painful, I can hardly vucking stand up, and valking is so schwer. Und ze doctor says stupid sings like I must give oop eating all ze rich food, and change my diet to hellsier sings. Vot does he know, ze silly vanker?"

Then she sat down and blitzed her way through the huge meal like it was a light snack. Norman was a little concerned that her gout attack had brought on an episode of Tourette's syndrome, and he and his dad tried to humour her by talking about their "good old days" back in Ainderby Steeple. But as soon as Stanley mentioned the business, she interrupted and went on a tirade about sausages and bloody Chester Gannet. The men were batting on a sticky wicket, and they knew this was a no win situation, and so as soon as possible they beat a hasty retreat to "ave a butcher's" at the garden and the greenhouse, even though it had started to rain again. There was still no hope for the roses, as the weather had switched dramatically from drought to continuous rain, but Sid's therapeutic plants were thriving where they hid away in the greenhouse.

The rose grower lit a cigarette, and stared into space before saying, "I don't know lad, but when yer mother is grouchy wi' t' gout, life is bloody 'ard. If it ent that, it's 'er deafness, and 'er uncanny ability t' misunderstand everythin'. Sometimes she drives me round t' twist."

He paused briefly for another long draw on the cigarette.

Then he continued, "Eee lad, sometimes I wish I was still oop north in God's own country, goin' about me butcher's business, and keepin' out from underneath 'er feet. But it's not all goin' too well oop there either. We 'ad a letter from me old friend Arthur Fartworthy last week, and 'e's not bin well. 'E's 82 now, and bin in t' butchery business all 'is life. Now t' cancer's got 'im, and 'e ent got long t' go. Eee, it's true what tha says, life is 'ard, then yer die."

Norman didn't know what to say.

Nearly 30 miles away, two lady hockey players were enjoying a meal in the Swan Inn at Gillingham Dam near Beccles. Helen had decided that when she invited Cher out for lunch, they should go somewhere she would feel comfortable. She knew there was nowhere better than the place she had first set eyes on her, at the game where the Norfolk Enchants were at home to Leiston Lionesses earlier in the season. To say that she had designs on her lunch guest would be an understatement. She hadn't done any clever research to bag her victim. Just by sheer luck a while ago she had bumped into Stanley in his favourite pub, the Mill Inn in Aldeburgh, and as a result of the chance meeting, during which they had both enjoyed several pints of Adnam's ales, she had discovered that he was Cher's father. So, Helen had just waited until the return match at Leiston, so she could get to talk to the fellow hockeyist. Now they were sitting in the restaurant tucking into the Southern African Menu.

Cher had a starter of Safari style Zambesi Croc-tail, a sauteed crocodile tail fillet, served with slices of mango on a bed of leaves, with tomato and basil. Helen had Bafana Bafana, a traditional South African farmer's beef sausage, served with Chakalaka, a vegetable relish. Any subtlety in the dishes was lost on both of them, as they were two large, ravenous ladies, with heightened appetites from the morning's strenuous hockey pursuits.

Cher followed with her favourite main course, a huge Springbok steak, while Helen had the Bobotie, a sort of South African Shepherd's pie, topped with a light egg custard, served with yellow rice, and Mr Ball's chutney. After an indecently short break, they went for the desserts, and unable to make the choice between Koeksisters and Melktert, they both decided that they would order one of each. Helen was keen to make sure they both got their just desserts.

Throughout the meal, the main subject of conversation between them was hockey, plus some personal information about schools, families, interests and other leisure pursuits, and they seemed to hit it off right away. As they were finishing their meal, Helen had a proposition to put to new friend.

She explained, "One of our forwards, Maggie, has to give up playing in the next few weeks, as she is retiring from hockey after 20 years. She says she's getting too old to play, and get's too knackered. So we have to keep substituting her more and more. Would you be interested in a transfer to the Lionesses?"

Cher was shocked, and delighted at the same time, and simply sat there with her mouth agape. Helen continued, "I've watched you play, and I think you could do a good job for us. Anyway why would you want to stay with a team like the Enchants that's loses all the time, and is habitually bottom of the league? And why would you want to play all your home matches on that awful ploughed field getting covered in mud and cow shit when you could be playing at the St Margaret's FC Ground? "

Miss Noble was still catching flies as Miss Highwater went on," They're a really friendly bunch of girls in the Lionesses team, I'm sure you'd fit in right away. Go on, please say yes."

Cher took a deep breath, looked her new friend straight in the eye, and laughed, "Are you serious?"

"Of course I am, I wouldn't joke about hockey, it's my first hobby. Yes! I am serious. What do you say?"

She got up from her seat, raised her arms in the air, and shrieked at the top of her voice," Yeeeeeeees!" causing a lot of turning of heads in the packed restaurant.

"Good, I'm so pleased," smiled Helen, diving into her second dessert.

With their business concluded, they quietly finished their meals; one of them a little embarrassed at her reaction to the offer, and the other content with her afternoon's work.

Pretty soon they asked for the bill, and prepared to leave, and it was then that a slightly familiar figure came over to talk to them. He was a tall well-dressed man, tanned and completely bald, with a ginger moustache and beard, and thick-rimmed designer glasses. Both of them were sure that they had seen him on television. He sat down at an adjacent table, and began to speak, "Hi ladies, I was just wondering if you enjoyed your meal, and I'd like to know what you thought was the best part of it?"

"Do you work here then, "answered Helen, "I'm sure I've seen you somewhere before. Have you been on TV?"

"Nothing gets past you does it?" said the mystery man with a grin, "You answer my questions, and I'll answer yours then."

"Well I liked all of it, but the Zambesi Croc-tail was very tasty, and both the desserts were superb." said Cher.

"Very good," said he, and turning to Helen, "What about you my dear? What was your favourite course?"

"The Bafana Bafana was great, but again I'd say the two desserts were delicious." she answered.

"Obviously two ladies with a sweet tooth." smiled the stranger, as they waited for him to declare himself.

"My name is Chester Gannet, and I'm here looking at this interesting and inventive menu. I am the owner of the Skinny Pig restaurant in Great Baddow, and yes, I have been on telly."

"Oh, I remember now, you're the chef who invents all that very odd cuisine. I saw a programme a couple of weeks ago and you were cooking three very peculiar courses. Let's see, Yes, it was a starter of slug kedgeree, followed by trout poached in custard, and finishing with a dessert called pustulating cake." spouted Helen.

"You have a very good memory my dear," Chester smarmed, "But I'm always looking for new twists, right at the moment I'm working on a new selection starting with stickleback whitebait, and finishing with vole and vanilla vol-au-vents." He stopped and waited for incredulous looks and wasn't disappointed.

"But the piece de resistance," he said," Is the main course. This is Jumbo sausage rolls made with the meat from a bull elephant's penis."

Both of the hockey players began to giggle like two silly schoolgirls, and then Chester grinned and added," It's a very precise technique we've developed. You have to make sure that the good old elephant's got a stiffy at the time, to maximise the amount of meat that you can get."

He then rolled his eyes and put his tongue in his cheek, and the two silly girls both wet themselves laughing. "Nice to have met you, ladies," he concluded, "Here's my card, if ever you're in the area of Great Baddow, pop into my restaurant for some complementaries."

Then he disappeared back to his table at the other end of the restaurant.

Helen dropped her new friend off at the bungalow in Leiston about an hour later, just as her brother and her father were returning from the greenhouse, and her mother was re-surfacing after her alcohol induced post lunch nap.

"Hello. Hello, I'm back," began Cher, looking very pleased with herself," Where is everybody, come quick, I've got great news."

She ran into the living room like an excited child who'd just woken up on

Christmas morning, only to be confronted by a bleary-eyed Blue Nun imbiber, and a slightly damp ex-butcher and computer games genius.

"Really? What is it?" said Stanley.

"Well, I had a wonderful lunch with Helen, up at the Swan at Gillingham. Oh, she is such good fun, I really like her, we are going to be the best of mates, and the food was just delicious, and oh I'm so happy."

Everybody waited in anticipation of good news, and Norman pleaded, "And yes, what's the news?"

"Oh, yes, I must tell you. It's brilliant. I'm so happy I could die." she gushed, barely able to catch her breath.

The Yorkshireman repeated the plea, "Aye lass, what's the news?"

"It's wonderful. Helen is lovely. I'm so pleased. It's the best news I've ever had." she gushed again, now in danger of going into hyperventilation.

Lisalotte yawned, groaned, and swore emphatically, "For vuck's sake girl, vot is ze vucking good news?"

Cher took a deep breath, composed herself, and then blurted out, "I've been offered a transfer to Leiston Lionesses. I'm going to play for a proper hockey team, that doesn't lose every match playing on a makeshift dung heap." Then she raised her arms and jumped in the air, giving the floorboards a lot to worry about. Everybody smiled. They all knew how important playing hockey was to her. Hugs and kisses followed.

"Eee that's champion lass, I'm reet made oop for yer." said Stanley.

"I'm glad. Zat means ve von't haff to go to zat vucking shit-hole of a pitch at Gillingham every veek. Vell done liebling." said Lisalotte.

"Well done, Sis, you've always been too good for the Enchants." said Norman.

Over coffee they all sat down in the living room, while the hockey player continued to gush with enthusiasm for her new opportunity, and then she remembered her other news.

"I nearly forgot to tell you, there's something else. As we finished our meal today, this fellow came up to talk to us. We thought we recognised him from the telly, but we couldn't remember his name. Anyway it turned out that he was Chester Gannet, you know the TV chef."

A silence suddenly hung over the room like somebody had just switched off the sound system at a Guns and Roses concert. "I'm sorry, "said a confused Cher," Did you hear me? We met Chester Gannet this afternoon!"

"Zat's all ve vucking need, bloody Gannet, der arschloch." Lisalotte spat.

"Oh dear! Oh dear!" Stanley despaired.

Cher's brother looked puzzled, but it occurred to him fairly quickly that no one had ever talked to his sister about why the family had moved south from Yorkshire. She had only been 12 at the time.

"Er! Have I done something wrong, or are you all winding me up here?" she asked coming down with a bump from her earlier happiness.

"No Sis," said Norman," I think I had better explain.", and he looked at his parents for nods of approval.

So, for the second time in 24 hours he told the froggy sausages story, and revealed to his sister the dilemma that the family had allegedly suffered as a result of Chester Gannet's actions. She listened carefully, and when her brother had finished she thanked him for his patience. Then she hugged a tearful Lisalotte, and a very quiet Stanley. Having finished the story again, this time while carefully gauging his parent's reactions, the young man recalled what Clarisa had said the previous day about being absolutely sure of the part that Chester had played in his family's demise. Both Norman's oldies appeared to be certain in their understanding, but an inkling of doubt about the facts of the matter was beginning to grow.

Soon after, the man in the Porsche made his way home to Chelmsford. It had been a strange very reflective and contemplative day. Some important things were very likely to change in the lives of every member of his family as a result. Clarisa was waiting for him back at the Hub, and had prepared an Italian salad for their evening meal. She was the foundation on which his life was now built, and he was so glad to be back with her, surrounded by the certainty that in a few short months they had put together.

Earlier that day in Chelmsford, it had stopped raining when City's number one fan surfaced and looked out of the window wondering if the game at the Silverlake Stadium would go ahead. It was City's penultimate game, and they were away to Eastleigh, and to have any chance at all of staying in the playoff places they had to win. If that didn't happen, then either Dover or Basingstoke could rob them of their rightful place.

But first of all, Hugh had other problems to deal with concerning all the baggage he was carrying. He had a happy, cheerful breakfast with Millicent and the boys talking about family matters like holidays and schoolwork, and then went for a potter in the garden to think things through. Everybody knew him as a man who said what he liked, and liked what he said, and to hell with the consequences. He was seen as outspoken, forthright in the extreme and unafraid to express his opinions fully and frankly. But all these secrets he was carrying were beginning to get him down. At this time in his life he had to consider carefully what to do for the best, and he didn't know if he should reveal any or all his concerns or button his lip. After a while walking around and thinking, he steeled himself, and strolled over to the Ball's house.

He rang the door bell and at his second attempt Tina came to the door dressed as she always was like some gorgeous celebrity, totally the opposite of the poor bedraggled rain-soaked refugee she had appeared as 2 days ago.

"Oh Hugo, Hola hombre," she grinned, and added "Que va?" with her usual huge smile.

"Don't smile at me, senorita." He replied, kissing her outstretched hand.

She never varied their greeting routine very much, so she turned her back towards Hugo and wiggled her arse, and then looked provocatively over her shoulder with a smile.

"Does my boom look big in this?"

"Sure thing, sister!" he answered, with the expected and enjoyed playful slap, and then as usual they both fell about laughing. They moved to the kitchen where Tiny was drinking coffee and reading a business manual.

"Hello, mate", he said, looking up from the manual," To what do we owe this pleasure?"

"Oh, I just thought I'd come over and see if you needed any help with the garden now it's stopped raining."

"That's very kind, "said Tina," But I think the boys have it all in hand later on today. Did my darling tell you about my clever plans to bring the fish indoors, and just use the pond for las vacaciones?"

"Yes, sounds like a good idea," Hugo replied unconvincingly, "But what does the garden look like now?"

What Hugh wanted to do was separate his friend from his wife, to have a quiet word with him about what had been on his mind.

"Come and have a look." said the boss, moving towards the door. His Chica stayed indoors.

They surveyed the scene in the garden as if they were viewing the devastation of a tsunami, and it was certain that the beautiful garden that had been created only a few weeks before, was now partly destroyed by the recent deluge. The patio and pergola and most of the structure of the landscaping were still intact, but the fishpond was obliterated, and the trench that had been dug to remove the water had made an ugly scar across the lawn from one end of the garden to the other. But, as Mr Balls had reassured his distressed little rain sodden waif on the day of the great flood, "It was all repairable."

The fatman shook his head sympathetically, and made all the right noises of commiseration, but he wanted to turn his friend's attention to other things.

"I found it a bit confusing last night in the Brewers," he explained, "There didn't seem to be any problems between the gayboys. They seemed to behave as they always do, and I don't think there's much wrong with our accountant friend. Not enough to keep him off work for two weeks anyway."

Tiny thought for a few seconds and then replied, "I think we just have to accept that his G. P. has signed him off until early May. Hopefully he will return to work then, and get on with the job in hand. Let's for the time being keep our fingers crossed, and give him some breathing space."

"Yes, but...."answered Hugh.

The boss interrupted, "Listen, he's a mate, let's not be too hard on him."

"Yes but I....." repeated the fatman.

"No, mate, that's my last word on it. Leave it there please." Tiny replied raising his voice slightly and walking slowly away. Hugh followed his friend back indoors knowing with all certainty that was the end of the matter for now.

Later, in the afternoon, at about the same time as Norman was starting his journey back from Leiston to Chelmsford, City's number one fan's miserable buttons were depressed with a vengeance, when the crunch time match finished with a score of Eastleigh 1 City 1. His sense of doom was overwhelming, when he then learned that after that day's matches both Dover and Basingstoke were breathing down City's neck in the league table. This meant, that if Basingstoke won their game in hand against Hampton and Richmond on the following Tuesday, it would be almost an impossibility for City to reach the playoffs. It was unlikely that Basingstoke would lose to Hampton and Richmond, who were already doomed to relegation, and equally unlikely was the prospect of City beating Woking, already promoted as champions, in their final match of the season. The agony was complete, with his recognition that the whole season had now come down to a mathematical miracle being required for City to triumph.

On Tuesday 24th April, Hampton and Richmond were beaten 2 - 0 at home by Basingstoke, who jumped over City in the table, and only needed a draw in their last match to ensure that they, and not City, would progress to the playoffs.

CHAPTER 9

Pork Scratchings and Gaviscon

(Wednesday 25th to Friday 27th April 2012)

Wednesday lunchtimes had recently fallen into a regular routine for Tina and Millicent. They had discovered that every Wednesday at 1pm, there was a free concert at the Cramphorn Theatre in Chelmsford. Sometimes it was jazz or classical, saxophone, or piano, or guitar, or some other musical genre. The girls usually met at about 12 noon in the Wine Cellar Bar and Bistro near the Cathedral in Duke Street, and enjoyed a quick lunch from the Lite Bites Menu, before walking up Duke Street to the theatre. That particular Wednesday they were both looking forward to Happy Jazz, with Jeffery Wilson, and Peter Marshall, with a theme of "Birds".

Although Millicent had the exclusive use of her own car, when she was going into Chelmsford, she preferred to walk. So, shortly after getting back from taking Bimbo her crackpot labradoodle for his daily exercise, she was off again, making her way through the drizzling rain, to the wine bar via Stump Lane and the Bunny Walk.

Her Spanish beauty friend had set off much earlier in the morning, taking a PAMTAX taxi down to the city centre, to stroll round her favourite shops; Debenhams, River Island, and Monsoon. She had booked to have her hair done at Toni and Guy's a few days before. Unfortunately there had been a mix up over the time of her appointment, and they had contacted her on her mobile while she was in Debenhams, and moved her forward an hour. When she left Toni and Guy's at about 11 am it was raining again and she had time to kill, so she decided to buy a brolly in Marks and Spencer's and walk quickly to the wine bar. By the time Millicent arrived she had been there over 40 minutes, and was just starting on a second bottle of a very tasty Rioja Tempranillo.

Millicent was greeted, with Rioja fumes, and a kiss on both cheeks.

"Hola, Meelysont, que tal?"

She was always amused at her friend's pronunciation of her name. It sounded like a lot of money in some European currency. The former model was obviously by now a mite unsteady on her feet," I have been here a while, they mixed up my hair time." she exclaimed.

"Bueno! Never mind. I am here now," responded a slightly damp, smiling Millie, "You've started without me then? Your hair looks lovely."

"Do you want to share this delicious Rioja with me, or do you want something different?"

"No. If you don't mind, I'll have a glass of Chardonnay; I can't drink red wine at lunchtime. It goes to my head."

"OK, Meelysont, whatever you say. And what shall we have to eat?"

"Shall we try an option from the buffet menu; that gives us lots of nibbles to share?"

"Estupendo! That will be very nice." she agreed, slurring the orders to a slightly amused barman.

The girls sat down together, and went through the girlie small-talk ritual, and by the time the food arrived Tina was halfway through the 2nd bottle of Rioja. They began foraging their way through the buffet, and Miss Iberia was getting louder and louder. She began to talk about recent events.

"It has been terrible, Meelysont, such an upheaval moving to Chelmsford, and then with all the work going on while Tim was away it has been very stressful. I love it in Chelmsford, but we only moved here because of the stalker."

"The stalker?" asked Millicent," You had a stalker? That was back in East Bergholt then?"

"Yes, he was an old boyfriend. Simon was very dark and handsome. I went out with him for about 6 months back in Madrid. He was English though, and he tracked me down when I moved here. It was impossible to get rid off him, even after Tim and I were married."

"Did you get the police involved? Surely they could have done something?"

"We reported him to the police, but as we planned to move to Chelmsford within a few months, they weren't interested."

"That's terrible!" sympathised Millicent, "So what happened after you moved? Did he bother you again?"

She hesitated, and then confided," Yes, somehow Simon tracked me down again within days. I don't know if I should tell you this, even Tim doesn't know, but the man who the police arrested in my garden stealing my goldfish when Tim was away, was the stalker."

Shocked, her friend replied "No I don't believe it!"

"It is true, Meelysont, I couldn't tell Tim though." she then laughed and tossed her newly coiffured hair in the air, and added, "Simon was a lovely man when he was my boyfriend, very generous, and very good in bed."

Millie was slightly embarrassed, and after a small pause and a sip of Chardonnay tried to change the subject, saying "How are you enjoying the food, the olives are nice today, aren't they?"

"They're lovely, Meely." Tina answered, took a swig of Rioja, and continued, "Spike was very good, when Tim was away. He protected me, made me feel safe. When you first look at him he looks awful, but when you get to know him. Well!"

Then she did it again. She laughed and tossed her head in the air again, and then ran her hand through her hair smiling. She continued with a definite twinkle in her eyes. "He is a very sexy man. I don't believe that he's really a homosexual. It seems such a waste."

Again, her lunch companion was just a little uncomfortable with the conversation, but soaked in the Rioja, she was oblivious to the discomfort she was creating. She took a final glug of wine, looked briefly at the empty bottle, and then said, "You know, Meely, I've met lots and lots of different men in my life, especially when I was modelling in Spain. I love Tim in a different way to the others, and we have been married 6 wonderful years now. Oh, Meely, don't you ever find married life boring and just long for something different. What about that Polish taxi driver, Pavel. He is lovely. Eastern European men, they are very laid back, and he is very fit and athletic."

Even if it wasn't a rhetorical question, there was no answer expected. Millicent wasn't about to directly answer the question anyway. She was shocked at her friend's avalanche of revelations about her men and the way she felt. For a moment she just stared into space, then she answered softly, and without prejudice," No Tina, I'm very happy with my Hugh, and besides, I have three growing teenage boys to look after."

"Of course," slurred Miss Rioja 2012," Gracious me, look at the time; we'd better be going to the theatre."

They walked arm in arm up Duke Street, tiny Millie carrying most of the combined load, and took their seats in the theatre, just before Jeffery and Peter began the first number. A delightful collection of bird influenced jazzy numbers followed, interspersed with some terrible jokes about our feathered friends from Jeffery, which the slightly sober lady enjoyed immensely, while her sozzled friend dozed quietly throughout the whole performance. When the concert was over, Millicent managed to escort her companion out to the foyer, where she ordered and administered several black coffees, while they waited for their taxi to arrive.

Sometime later Tina was gently shoe-horned back into the living room of her house, and Millie went home. She reflected on what had been revealed in the Rioja haze, remembering that the Balls had only married 6 years ago, and that it was obvious that both of them would have history. But she was worried. She really didn't want all the information she'd been presented with, and she didn't know what was best to do with it.

By the time it was late evening in Avalon House, and Tom, Dick, and Harry had finished their X-box sessions and been sent to bed, the lady of the house had finished all her chores, and decided to have a little chat with her husband. She made two coffees, opened the favourite bourbon biscuits, and went into the lounge, where he was about to fall asleep in front of the telly.

She nudged him awake and said, "Darling, I need to talk to you."

"What is it, Reepicheep?" asked a sleepy Hugh.

There were two things on her mind, and she chose to raise the easiest one first.

"First, I need to ask you again about something."

"What's that?"

"One word! Babestation! You haven't talked to Tom about it yet have you? Since I last mentioned it, I've found him tuned in to that station twice. Darling, it's embarrassing for him and for me. Please deal with it. Will you?"

He grinned, and just said," OK, sweetheart, leave it with me, I'll talk to him."

"Please do it, darling," Millie replied, adding an insistent, "Do it tomorrow please."

She paused, before raising her second concern. She wanted to think very carefully about how to bring that day's conversation in the wine bar to her man's attention. Hugh started on the packet of bourbons and began dunking them in his coffee one at a time.

"I had an interesting lunch today. You know, we went to the Wine Bar and Bistro for a snack, and then to the Cramphorn for a jazz concert afterwards." she began

"I bet the jazz was great, that Jeffery Wilson bloke is brilliant isn't he? And Peter Marshall's a superb piano man."

"Yes, it was very enjoyable, but that's not what I'm trying to say. You see, Tina; well she was a bit squiffy. No, that's an understatement; she was what you would have called pissed as a fart."

He laughed, and almost choked on his biscuit," Really, what happened?"

"It's not funny, darling, she started talking about the men in her life. It was a strange conversation. Did you know that the fellow they arrested trying to steal her goldfish, was an old boyfriend called Simon from her modelling days, who'd been stalking her, even when she lived in East Bergholt?"

"No, Blimey! Does Tiny know?"

"No, and I don't think she wants him to either."

Millicent paused and sipped her coffee, and looked earnestly at her man.

"There's more isn't there, sweetheart?" he said.

Millicent was uncomfortable about what she needed to convey to her man. She chose her words are careful thought.

"Yes," she continued, "Then she went on about Spike being a very sexy man, and how he couldn't possibly be a homosexual because it was such a waste."

Now if Hugh had heard that, without his prior knowledge of what had occurred while the chairman was away, he would probably have laughed until he was sick. But given what he had been carrying around for a week or two, what his wife had just said stopped him dead in his tracks, or to be more precise in the middle of his biscuit. The soggy bourbon fell back into his coffee with a splosh. He sat up with a jolt and a very worried look on his face. But he knew he couldn't say anything.

"And then," she added, "After that, she started saying how fit and athletic that Polish taxi driver, Pavel is. She didn't say he looked fit. She said he is fit!"

The jolly fatman was still dumbstruck. Fortunately Millicent thought he was just mulling over what she'd said, and considering a reply.

"Do you think that Tiny and Tina are having problems in their marriage?" she asked," She does seem to have developed a roving eye. The way she was talking, you'd think she was a single girl playing the field."

Just as the jolly fatman had been beginning to doubt what he saw on the landing, his doubts were now swinging back the other way. And although it looked like Scruffbag's late nights at Tyrell's Close were vindicated by the prowler in the garden, it now turned out that the goldfish thief was stalking the Spanish beauty. A myriad of questions ran through his brain, like, "Did Gordon and Spike's relationship really appear to be back to normal?" and "What was that Pavel business all about?"

He had so many questions and no easy answers. After he'd ruminated carefully, he decided it was best to obscure the issue, even though at the back of his mind there was a tangle of dilemmas which seemed to be snowballing.

"No, I don't think their marriage is in trouble, Minnie Mouse," he reasoned, "You know she is an awful flirt. Look at the way she behaves towards me. And if she was, as you say "pissed as a fart", she probably didn't know what she was saying. It was the booze talking, so don't worry about it."

With that, the petite Millicent cuddled up to her man's massive bulk reassured, "Yes, you're right, darling." she whispered," Thank you for being so clever and understanding. What would I do without you to look after me?"

At that particular moment Millicent had conveniently forgotten that only a man of her husband's gigantic alcoholic experience would know exactly how much of a truth serum the demon drink could be.

NerdiSoft had been a hive of activity since the chairman's return from his trip to China and the U. S. A. and everything except for the accounting was now moving apace to get 1stCitySoft launched. On Friday, despite the obvious absence of Gordon on sick leave, there was an impromptu board meeting, to consult the team informally about their individual progress, and to bring them up to date. Compared to the previous, very professional meeting, this was to be quite relaxed. Good news, social issues, and future plans were all on the agenda. The boss was aware of the pressure he had placed everybody under, and the unfortunate way the previous meeting had ended with a berating of their accountant, and so the meeting took place over coffee in his office.

"Come in and sit down, boys," he began, "First I want to thank you for your sterling efforts. I'm so pleased with the way things are progressing."

There was no need to respond.

He then added, "I know that we're on track here, and that 1stCitySoft is moving ahead nicely. So from today on were going to refer to ourselves as 1stCitySoft not NerdiSoft, and we'll give that name to what so far we've called the global project. The premises in the Hedgerows Business Park in Chelmsford are under contract, and the workforce had been brought up to date with plans for the future, including the relocation of the current operation. The selection of games we are marketing globally is all ready to go, so unless you've got any issues you're worried about, we'll cut to the chase."

They both shook their heads and remained quiet. Tiny continued.

"Our associates in the 1stCitySoft project are coming over to the U.K. in June to seal the deal, and they are very keen to do it over a game of golf. I know that the Yanks, Carlton and Bates are keen golfers, but I'm pretty certain that Mr Wang and Mr Wu haven't played before. It should be interesting. It's probably best if Gordon and I play with our Chinese friends, and you two give the Yanks a game."

Hugh was relieved that he wouldn't have to play golf with absolute beginners, but Norman wasn't too concerned.

"Now, we need to think about our plans for phase 2." said the chairman.

The marketing director knew exactly what his boss was talking about, but couldn't help pretending ignorance. "Phase 2?" he asked, "What's that all about then?"

"Well, we operate in a continually evolving market, and things move very fast in the world of technology. If we don't keep up to date, we won't survive in the ever-changing business environment. Therefore we must adapt to keep pace. Look at HMV, how they've had to change. Where have all the little record shops gone? I'll tell you, they've disappeared, because they couldn't adapt. HMV are struggling because the younger generation are no longer quite so keen to buy CDs and DVDs, and pretty soon they won't want to buy silicone chips either. And they don't have to because everybody's moving to online downloading. The pop music charts, what they used to call the Hit Parade, has been based on downloads for years."

"Well I like CDs and DVDs," said Hugh as his nephew nodded in agreement, "When I buy something, I want to hold it in my hand. It gives me a feeling of security that I can't get with a download. I like to buy something physical, not digital streams in the ether or fibre-optics."

"Yep, me too, "Tiny answered," But we are dinosaurs, and our target market is mostly youngsters and younger people, and they are going to want downloads."

"So what's phase 2?" enquired the joker, knowing the answer already.

"I'll explain." the boss went on "As the world market moves we'll need to set up our business differently. There'll be a gradual move away from media to download. We'll be selling online, and from something amounting to a call-centre. So we'll need to plan ahead for that. Our Chelmsford office will handle the UK, Europe and Africa, SSCM, that's Softly Softly Catchee Monkey, will handle the Americas, and WWHD, that's Wang Wu Hoo Doo Production, will handle Asia and Australasia. Norman, you are going to be our key man in Phase 2. I talked to the guys in Columbus about this, and we're going to send you over there to talk to their distribution experts. Then we'll send you on any courses you might need to be able to set up the software, websites, interfaces right here in the U.K. and whatever you implement here will be adapted for our sister operations in China and America."

The development director's face was a picture, he was speechless. The opportunity to develop the required software as well as the games was a challenge that he would relish.

The marketing director was equally pleased with the way his substantial investment in the company was now going to pay big dividends.

"I can see you're both pleased with what I have said, "Tiny added, "And I think we can anticipate that within a few years our small staff of 10 here in Colchester, will grow to over 50 in Chelmsford to handle our expansion, and to cover the administration for our partners at SSCM and WWHD."

Then he stopped, gave a whoop and shrieked with his hands in the air, "Full steam ahead for 1stCitySoft, we're going global boys!"

All 3 of them shared high fives, and then the most casual board meeting they'd ever attended was over. They returned to their work elated, all of them aware that this was a big step in a big year for the company. Somebody couldn't resist a joke about it all though.

"I wonder if Phileas Fogg did that." he mused,"

"Phileas Fogg did what?" Norman replied.

"You know, Fogg went round the world in 80 days. Our chairman went round the world in 8 days. I wonder if he changed everything after he returned from his round the world trip."

"Well he invented those fancy expensive crisps." was the tongue in cheek reply.

"Yeah, I love those Mexican ones with cheese and jalapeno, but I don't think that was his phase 2. I just hope that our chairman isn't now planning a journey to the centre of the Earth."

The young man returned to working on "Secrets of the First City", implementing a new idea in the program that had just sparked off from the conversation. He googled "Phileas Fogg" and "Round the World in 80 days", and ploughed through the search results finding some very useful and interesting twists for the program he was writing.

He was looking forward to the future immensely. Even though he wasn't the best golfer in Chelmsford, he was even looking forward to the sealing of the deal in June over a game of golf, especially as it would give him a chance to meet his new colleagues in the global setup. Being sent over to the U.S.A.

so that he could extend his expertise into writing the software for Phase2 was even more exciting.

Soon it was the end of another week at work, and there was another Friday night in the Brewers to savour. Norman and Clarisa were closer than ever. For them life was good, and looked as if it could only get better. The man in the Hub was ready to walk off to the pub, but he was awaiting the scheduled Friday evening phone call from Leiston. Usually you could set your watch by it, but for some reason not yet known it was late. Just before 7:40 pm the phone rang. At long last there was the familiar Friday voice.

"Ey Oop, son, 'ow yer diddlin'?"

"Alright, Dad, how are you?"

"Mustn't grumble, nobody listens anyway."

There was something not quite right. Stanley's tone was somehow different, but the conversation continued as normal. "Mum alright, is she?"

"Aye, son, same as ever."

"What can I do for you, Dad?"

There was more than one moment's hesitation before the ex-butcher went on.

"Well, I'm just phoning up t' tell thee 'bout t' game tomorrow, t' 'ockey match. They're not playin', postponed due t' a waterlogged pitch."

There was another pause as he seemed to be struggling to speak.

"But there's somethin' else, son, I need t' ask yer a favour."

He coughed, and from the sounds coming through the line, appeared to be crying. Then he blurted out painfully," Yer remember me sayin' 'bout me old friend Arthur Fartworthy bein' in poor shape. Well now 'e's died, and t' funeral's next Tuesday, and I was wonderin' if yer'd take me oop there?"

Norman knew his father very well, and could hear the obvious sadness and distress in his voice. He thought quickly and answered quickly.

"OK, Dad, it's a long way. How about we take our time, go up Monday, and come back on Wednesday, and you could visit some of your old haunts while we're up there, instead of trying to do it all in a tear arse rush?"

"Aye, son, that would be nice, and I could pay me proper respects to my old mate Arthur. Eee! Yer a good lad."

"Well, Dad, you're not getting any younger you know. I'm sure I can get the time off work, they owe me some leave. I'll make all the arrangements, and book us a nice hotel. You can leave it all to me."

"That'll be champion, son, and I'll be able t' get away from yer mum for a few days, she's doin' me head in."

"Right, Dad, I'll give you a ring tomorrow when I've sorted it all out. Love to Mum. Got to go!"

"Bye, son, and thank you."

"Don't mention it, Dad. Bye for now."

The young man was pleased that he didn't have to go and watch yet another hockey match, and also pleased that he could take his father away for a few days, even if it was going to be a sad occasion for him. He was determined that he would make it as enjoyable as possible, and started thinking about making arrangements that would suit his dad.

Just before the customary trek down to the Brewers, Hugh resolved to deal with the one issue that he had been saddled with, that was unlikely to end in tears. He went to extricate Tom from his X-box, and have a word with him about his interest in Babestation. In the Ramsbottom family all the necessary safe-guards were in place to ensure that online pornography was not accessible to the boys, and Babestation on TV was regarded as a safe enough option. Hugh had decided that he didn't want to take a schoolmaster type approach to the issue, and call his eldest son into his study, so he led him gently out to the bottom of the garden where they both sat down with orange juices, man to man, father to son.

"Tom, you're growing up, and soon you'll be a young man. We need to have a chat."

Ramsbottom junior was at least a partial, perhaps embryonic, chip off the old block, and had a genetic disposition to the same sense of humour as his father. He sighed, and looked at his him with some resignation.

"Oh, Dad," he said, "You're not going to give me a lecture about the birds and the bees, the ins and the outs, are you? Only we've done all that stuff already at school."

The fatman chuckled. "No, son," he replied with a fatherly wink, "I'm sure you already know more than me. I'm so old now; I've forgotten most of it."

"Yes, sure thing, Dad." Tom yawned.

There was a pause.

"Son, I'm glad that you're interested in looking at Babestation. Especially as it's girls you are interested in."

Tom blushed, but he didn't reply, and his dad noticed.

"No need to be embarrassed, Tom. It's just you growing up. But I'd like you to be more careful about it. Mum has come into the playroom a few times when you've been looking, and I don't want Dick and Harry to share your interest until they are ready. So all I'm asking you to do is to be discrete about it, and make sure your mum doesn't catch you looking again. Can you do that for me, son?"

"Yes, Dad, of course. Don't worry." Tom answered, feeling uncomfortable enough to want to end the discussion.

Hugh was happy to have done a good job, and concluded, "And Thomas, if you ever need to talk about the birds and the bees, the ins and the outs, then don't hesitate to come and have a word with me, will you? Remember, whatever you, and Dick, and Harry need, me and your mum, are on your side."

"Thanks, Dad," Tom said, finishing his orange juice, "Can I go back to the X-box now?"

"Yes, OK, son. See you later." was the reply.

The proud father sat there for a while, at the bottom of their garden, wishing that all the other problems he was carrying like an albatross around his neck, could be as easy to deal with.

An hour later he was strolling down Springfield Road with Tiny, popping into the Red Lion for a quick Guinness, and the Oddfellows for a pint of Doombar, before making it to the Two Brewers for the Friday night session, and several pints of Fuller's Pride. Norman was there, minus Clarisa as she was out with a girlfriend in Colchester, and despite his continued sick-note, Gordon was well enough to arrive with his harem in tow. The fatman bought a round for everybody, and started to chat about the earlier informal board meeting. He was a bit more gentle than usual with his arch enemy, and avoided all the gayboy banter.

"How are you now, Gordon, feeling any better?"

"I'm OK, thanks for asking, but not ready to come back to work yet."

"Exciting things happening at work. Everything's right on schedule. We were talking about phase 2 of 1stCitySoft this afternoon."

"Phase 2? What's that then?"

"Basically, it's all about preparing for the future, as the world moves from media to download we must keep up to date."

"Oh, I see, and has anybody done a cost assessment on that grandiose plan?"

"Well, you can put that on your to-do list when you get back. But it doesn't matter what the cost will be, because if we don't adapt to that change, we'll probably go under as a company, and we don't want that do we?"

Gordon didn't answer, and Spike then sidled up to Hugh, changing the subject to the slim chance of City making the playoffs.

"Your beloved Carrots seem to have buggered it all up. No chance, mate, Basingstoke are in the frame for the playoffs, and your lot can't do anything about that."

"I've told you before, Scruff, it's Clarets not Carrots, as in wine not vegetables." he answered with some irritation.

"They've played more like vegetables though, haven't they?"

"Yes, I suppose so. They blew it in the game against Salisbury, but that was not the team's guff. I blame chief vegetable Pennyfather for that."

"And even if they beat Woking tomorrow 6-0, it won't matter a jot, unless Basingstoke lose?"

"Yeah, don't rub it in, Scruffbag. I'll be there supporting them whatever. When was the last time you showed any interest in your local team?"

"My local team will always be Inverness Caledonian Thistle. I'm only down here in England on missionary work. My heart belongs by yon bonnie banks and yon bonnie braes."

"That's song is about Loch Lomond, you Scottish dimwit. And doesn't it say that you and your true love will never meet again? Aahhh!"

"Whatever!" concluded the decorator. Then he disappeared into the gents'.

The discussion with Gordon was resumed.

"We've found the new premises, on the Hedgerows Business Park. We get the keys on Monday. Why don't you come and have a look?" Hugh enquired.

"Maybe, if I'm up to it." the accountant replied with a distinct lack of enthusiasm.

"Do you know they measure up in square metres these days, not square feet anymore. Gave me some grief, I can tell you."

"Sure thing, fatso, mathematics not your forte is it."

"It's just that everything has to be effing metric these days, and I'm an Imperial man."

"You said it, mate, never a truer word. Would you care for a pterodactyl sandwich?"

"No, listen! They're doing it with all our measurements. I understood all the Imperial stuff, I could relate to it, visualise it. We've gone from pounds to kilos, yards, feet, and inches, to metres, and centimetres, and I know for a fact they're trying to sneak in kilometres instead of miles for our road measurements."

Spike returned, and was joined by Ike and Mike, while Tiny was sitting down separately with Norman discussing the plans for his trip to the U.S.A.

"I don't bloody like it." the fatman moaned on, "Do you know I'm not 6 foot tall anymore, I'm 1.828 metres tall, and I don't weigh 18 stone anymore, I weigh 115 kilos?"

The scruffy decorator choked on his drink. "You don't weigh 18 stone, Rambo, more like 24 stone, or should I say, what is it 400 kilos?"

"Shut up, queer boy, or I won't order you another pint. It'll be 0.563 of a litre. Doesn't sound that appetizing does it?"

"What are you moaning about, fatso, we're in the EC for keeps, and we don't have any choice about these things. Everything's decided in Brussels nowadays." interjected Gordon.

The answer came quickly and with irritation," Yes, and if those idiots have their way, soon we'll be driving on the wrong side of the road, and all speaking German. My granddad fought in the war to stop that happening, and now all our bloody crackpot politicians just give in to the slimy European bureaucrats. I tell you I'm voting for UKIP at the next election."

"Swapped your allegiance from the British National Party then have you?" Mike said winding him up still further.

"Very funny, Mikeypoo, at least I'm not a Communist like you. That's a totally discredited political system, if ever I saw one. Even the Russians couldn't make that work. Nearly 25 years after the collapse of their system, what have you got? I'll tell you. Now all the KGB and Politburo gangsters are the biggest capitalist moguls in the world."

"The Chinese are still Communists though, and there's nearly one and a half billion of them." offered Ike.

"Don't make me laugh," the joker answered," Since the Chinkies took over Hong Kong in 1997, they've learned how to be capitalists too. The sad thing is they're so much better at it than we are."

"Isn't that why we are doing so much business with them though?" asked Gordon.

"Sure thing!" said Hugh, and he then wound up the argument with a Ramsbottom statement, as he was inclined to do when he tired of every Brewers discussion.

His conclusion this time was," Since the yardstick we used to understand and measure with, became a metre-stick, that extra 4 inches, or should I say 10 centimetres, has just become an excuse to allow more scope for mediocrity."

"You know what Bob Dylan said, don't you?" replied Ike, wishing to continue the debate.

"Bob Dylan's got sod all to do with it you wally. What the effin hell does he know about metric, he's an American, and they still use their versions of Imperial measurements."

The fatman was annoyed at not yet having the last word.

"That's interesting," smiled Ike, "What do they call them Confederate or Yankie measurements?"

"I don't know, and I don't care, but Bob Dylan's still got naff all to do with it."

"But Bob Dylan did give people like you, fatboy, some good advice, when he said - don't criticize what you can't understand. For the times they are a-changin." insisted Ike.

"Yeah! Like I said, so what! 'Cause Carl Perkins and Elvis Presley gave people like you some better advice. Both of them said - don't you step on my blue suede shoes, and it's just about as relevant."

Hugh had his wish to have the last word.

Throughout the whole boozy evening it was obvious to all concerned that their resident comedian was not his expected jovial self. In fact the whole time seemed to be an extended Ramsbottom episode exclusively featuring one grumpy old man. But then none of the usual crew was in the least bit aware of the secret baggage that he was carrying about them and their complicated relationships. Tiny and Norman spent most of the evening together talking about all the exciting aspects of phase2, and particularly the planned visit to the U.S.A. It was unusual for a Friday at the Brewers to be substantially used up by any of the lads in directly discussing work related issues, but if truth was known the chairman was on a huge high with his plans for the future, and he didn't mind.

Gordon's thought processes seemed to be completely at odds with his work colleagues. He'd lost interest in 1stCitySoft, without making it too obvious, and nobody really knew whether he was swinging a leg going on sick leave, or if he was genuinely suffering from stress. At this time, perhaps only one man had suspicions about that.

Norman had unloaded his concerns about the accountant on his uncle a while ago, and besides he had bigger fish to fry.

Spike wasn't giving anything away, and he and the jolly fatman seldom saw eye to eye on whatever issues, least of all if it had the slightest thing to do with his relationship with his partner. Hugh couldn't see any rift in their relationship that would necessitate time off work with stress. Perhaps, in the overall scheme of things, only Ike and Mike were not creating dilemmas for the Brewer's comedian.

All too soon for some the end of the evening's boozing came round, and there he was, walking into the bar, and asking Caroline to shout out, "Taxi for Mr Ramsbottom!" Pavel was another potential fly in the ointment. Pints were quickly finished, casual goodbye waves made, and the taxi made its way up Springfield Road. There wasn't even a last minute jibe for gay Gordon's entourage, and for once in a blue moon, when they set off for Vicarage Road, the four men didn't have their middle fingers in the air.

"Have you had a good evening, Zirs?" Pavel asked.

"Yes, thank you," answered Tiny, "A quiet one for a change."

"Yes, we've been discussing how we have to tolerate changes to so many important and traditional things in Britain to suit those rule obsessed EC bureaucrats in Brussels." interrupted Hugh getting back on his soapbox.

"In my country we have had to change many things also, and in so short a period of time." Pavel said.

One passenger couldn't help it. He had to have his say on a subject close to his heart, and to educate at the same time.

"Do you know why we drive on the left in Britain?" the cabbie was asked.

"No Zir, Mr Ramsbottom, but I am sure you are going to tell me." he dared to answer.

Hugh paused, and then retorted with irritation, "So you can hold your sword or your lance in your right hand to tackle the oncoming enemy."

Pavel thought for a few seconds, and then came back with, "But I don't need a sword or a lance, and in this taxi I don't have any oncoming enemas."

The 2 friends laughed at the bad pronunciation, and the driver didn't know why.

When the taxi arrived at the mutually convenient corner, the passengers got out, and Hugh gave a fiver tip, and said sarcastically," Have a good night my friend, and do watch out for oncoming enemas."

They stood for a moment in the drizzling rain, and then Tiny asked with concern," You alright, mate? You've been in a funny mood all night. Is there anything wrong?"

He was worried. His closest friend looked so old and grey

"Yeah, I'm OK, just feeling a bit tired that's all. See you tomorrow. Good Night!"

As soon as the tired fatman slumped through the door of Avalon House he suddenly felt very weak, had a violent raging headache, a strange tight sensation in his chest, and felt breathless and sick. He was convinced he'd eaten something that had disagreed with him. He thought it was the second packet of pork scratchings he'd scoffed in the Brewers. He went to the kitchen, drank a pint of water, took a large slug of Gaviscon, and went straight to bed.

CHAPTER 10

The Stuff of Dreams

(Friday 27th to Saturday 28th April 2012)

Many times during his childhood, Hugh had enjoyed walking with his parents across their most favourite area of the South Downs, all the way from Eastbourne to Cuckmere Haven, taking all day to cover the 8 or so miles, and having a picnic somewhere along the top of the Seven Sisters. There were always ham and pickle sandwich rolls, cheese and onion crisps, lemonade, and lovely red apples. After the walk, with tired legs and sunburned faces, they caught the bus back to Eastbourne, where Ramsbottom senior would take his son on the pier and buy him ice-cream and candyfloss, and give him a big bag of loose change for the slot machines. The sun always shone, and the chalky meadow flowers were always in full bloom, spreading a sickly sweet scent of wild flowers and grasses wafting through the warm breezes on the cliff-tops. He loved this part of the world, the dizzying heights of Beachy Head 500 feet above the waves, and the red and white striped lighthouse, like a big stick of Eastbourne rock at the foot of the cliffs. He was fascinated by the way the South Downs seemed to roll their way across the top of the Seven Sisters, undulating in proud, sweeping, uneven, folds over the land. Hugh's dad had taught him all the names of the Seven Sisters, from Michel Dean near Birling Gap; to Haven Brow near the River Cuckmere, and the boy remembered how many of the names were brows or bottoms. He, being a Ramsbottom boy quickly developing his sense of humour, was much amused by names like Short Bottom and Rough Bottom.

His favourite spot was just west of the Beachy Head lighthouse. Here, where the land swept majestically and gently downwards, before climbing steeply up again towards the Belle Tout lighthouse, he would always want to sit and just stare for a while, and breathe in the sights, and sounds and smells. Further into the distance beyond Birling Gap, his gaze would follow the irregular lines tracing the tops of the Seven Sisters and their chalk faces daring to peep out just slightly into the sea. His eyes would trace their ending into the distance at Seaford Head, and he would look forward to the final easy part of the long walk in between the cliffs, where the land went plunging down to the beach at Cuckmere Haven.

Now, he was here again, no longer a boy, a grown man, with a family of his own, and it was very different. Everything seemed darker, bigger, more foreboding, and far more dramatic. He was walking along the cliff-top, wearing shorts and sandals, seeing through his own eyes, but at the same time he had a huge panoramic view of the whole scene like a widescreen shot from an airborne helicopter. Whenever he focussed on any small aspect of the scene, it was like someone was holding a giant magnifying glass in front of him. He could see everything so clearly, but it was all so confusing. The sun was shining brightly and burning his face, but it was raining and hailing through an immense rainbow, so solid and vivid he could feel the colours as they drifted over him. To his right hand the Downs were a perfectly manicured, green, undulating, swirl like Tellytubbieland. As his feet tiptoed along the very edge, he could see Gordon dressed as Tinkywinky, the purple tellytubby with a triangular antenna, running along in front of him. He was taking bunches of 50 Euro notes out of his red bag, and throwing them over the cliff, while his eyes were rolling like big green gobstoppers, and he was singing "Money, money, money. It's a rich man's world."

Just up ahead of him was Spike, and he was Laa-Laa, the yellow tellytubby, with a curly antenna which kept changing into a tiny paint roller. He was bending over and painting the grass a more luscious shade of green, and immediately behind him was a gorgeous Tina rolling nude in the paint, smiling and saying over and over again, "Spike is a very sexy man.

Does my boom look big in this?"

As Hugh was walking along he answered repeatedly "Sure thing sister, sure thing sister."

Ike and Mike were the other two tellytubbies Dipsy and Po, and they were laying a gravel path and planting daffodils and tulips along it. Every now and then they stopped and planted an apple tree. As soon as they watered each tree, it instantly blossomed and quickly grew huge red apples, which fell from the branches and toppled in wide torrents over the chalky cliff edge, just in front of the fatman so that he had to avoid slipping on them.

Hugh stopped walking as he reached the top of the cliff over the Beachy Head lighthouse, and sat down looking in the direction of the Belle Tout lighthouse 2 miles away. On the down-land opposite which was strangely covered in deep snow, coming towards him he could see his mother and father skiing down the slope, waving at him and smiling, and then falling over the edge. He felt pain in his heart, and started to cry like a baby, and looked away, but whenever he looked back the scene was repeated like it was on a short continuous video loop.

When he looked at the beach below, the sands and pebbles were replaced by computer chips, all the rocks were CDs, and DVDs, and vinyl albums, and cassettes. The larger boulders were CRT TVs, and Computer screens. Along the wet-line there was what looked like seaweed, but on closer inspection it was black unravelled video tape, blooming up in huge piles as the waves crashed on the shore. The sea was brown like beer, and the foam at the edge was like beer froth. Hugh breathed deep, and for a moment thought he could smell the salt of a sea breeze, but it struck in his throat, and turned to the smell of stale beer. Looking closer at the beach he saw Tina's goldfish, millions of them, washed up, and struggling for air, as Pavel strolled along at the bottom of the cliffs spearing them with a lance in his left hand, singing in a Polish accent "You shall have a fishy on a little dishy, you shall have carassius auratus when the boat comes in."

The fatman got up again, keen to move on and get away from the confusion, and now he found he was wearing an enormous, black, woolly great coat, with a very long, very wide, claret and white Chelmsford City scarf draped around his neck. The rainbow had disappeared, and it was now very windy, but oh so warm. He struggled against the wind to push himself forward over a rise, and looking as the down-land swept away, he saw Millicent ahead of him in a wedding dress. She was young and beautiful, running along the edge, with the 3 boys all hand in hand dressed as the Blues Brothers, complete with the characteristic black hats and dark sunglasses. As they ran in panic they sometimes glanced back over their shoulders. They were being chased by a giant black and red steam roller, which was so close to the edge it was breaking bits of the cliff away, which could be heard crashing down to the beach below. They were running very quickly, and the steam roller was just clanking along, but it always seemed to be nearly catching them up. Millicent and the boys reached the bottom of a dip and started to run uphill towards a rift in the cliffs, and at first Hugh couldn't see a way across. He became frantic, and shouted out "Reepicheep! Reepicheep!" Then he started to run after them, and the giant moving magnifying glass showed him a rickety rope bridge over the ravine crossing the cleft in the cliffs. He felt the steam on his face, and smell coal and hot oil burning as it was wafting up towards him making him cough and splutter. He was running alongside the steamroller, but didn't seem to be catching his family up.

On this side of the ravine the City striker Jamie Slabber was standing on the edge. He was crying out "Salisbury! Salisbury!", and kicking footballs over the cliff. On the other side Glen Pennyfather and Captain Claret the City Parrot were both playing keepy uppy with carrots. They were laughing and saying "Bad day at the office, Bad day at the office." over and over again. Hugh looked away from Millicent and the boys, towards Birling Gap, and there he saw Norman and Clarisa sitting in the Porsche next to the Statue of Liberty shouting "Run! Run! Don't look back!"

Elvis was standing on the top singing "Blue Suede Shoes." Under the statue Tiny was sitting at a huge desk surrounded by giggling Chinese men, and they were watching a massive TV screen displaying Babestation. Behind them was an army of terracotta warriors standing to attention, and waiting as each one had a Yorkshire pudding placed on his head by Chester Gannet.

The fatman looked behind him and saw Phileas Fogg flying above the cliffs in a huge balloon with the new IstCitySoft logo emblazoned on the side. A young Bob Dylan was in the balloon singing "Don't understand what you can't criticize.", and dropping rainbow coloured micro-pigs out of the balloon to block the way. Hugh watched himself knocking them over the cliff with a giant golf club. Suddenly the balloon burst and showered him with bits of exploded micro-pig. He fell to the ground, and had to scramble his way out of a pile of pork scratchings. As soon as he got up he started to run again, but it was hailing golf balls, striking him on the top of his head, so he put up his hood. Struggling to move, he tripped over the bottom of his greatcoat, and ended up crawling inside the coat. As he fought more and more to get back upright the coat developed into a narrowing coalblack tunnel, which smelt like Gaviscon, and he was getting nowhere. He felt like he was being strangled by his Chelmsford City scarf, and then he couldn't hear, or smell anything at all. This got worse and worse, gripping him tighter and tighter, and he panicked more and more feeling himself sweating profusely, as he could no longer see Millicent and the boys. He wrestled with himself until it felt like he was swimming through treacle. The treacle solidified to become fudge, and then he was truly immobilised, and he gave up exhausted.

Then he woke up bathed in sweat, breathless and very, very agitated.
"Hugh, darling, are you OK?" Millicent pleaded, "I've been so worried about you. You had such a restless night thrashing around; I had to sleep on the floor, and some of the things you were saying....? Where have you been?"
He stirred like a sloth on tranquillizers, his head was pounding like a steam hammer, his mouth was a dry as the Gobi desert, and he ached all over. He took an unsteady slurp of the coffee that his wife had passed to him, swallowed hard, gulped, and spluttered,
"I had, I had, an awful, v - very confusing, but, but very vivid dream." Then tears filled his bleary, bloodshot eyes, and his face contorted as he looked at the love of his life and whined, "I nearly lost you Reepicheep, I nearly lost you and the boys."
Millicent had never seen her man behaving like this before. She held his hands, and sensed they were shaking. Her extrovert, confident, happy-go-lucky man was a wreck, a hollow shell, and she was so worried about him. "I can see you're upset sweetheart, but let's not talk about your dream now. Stay in bed, have a little doze, and in a while I'll bring you breakfast."
He was totally whacked, and he wasn't going to argue. He did as he was ever so gently instructed.

A short while later she returned and gently woke him up. He felt much better, and sat up to eat a healthy breakfast of muesli, yogurt, and orange juice. Slowly, he began to relate what he could remember about the dream.

His most vivid memory was the image of Millicent and the boys running from the giant steam roller, and of him not being able to help them get away. She listened intently, and then ran him a bath, and while he was relaxing in the bubbles talked about calling the doctor. He insisted it wasn't necessary, but she made him promise to go for a check up as soon as possible. Shortly after 11am he had made it down to the lounge, and then Tiny arrived.

"Are you OK, mate?" he asked, "I don't think you were on your best form last night. I was worried about you when we came back. You looked very pale and drawn."

"Yeah! I'm OK now thanks. I was a bit tired last night. Had indigestion I think. Had a bloody awful night, bit of a nightmare. Hey, you didn't see any terracotta warriors with Yorkshire puddings for helmets when you were in China did you?"

"No! Why?" replied an amused Tiny.

"Oh nothing, take no notice of me, I've gone round the twist." Hugh answered quickly, while Millicent noticed with some relief that her man seemed to be returning to his normal jovial persona.

By the early afternoon he was almost his old self, and despite his wife's by then half-hearted protests, he insisted that he would go to the game at Melbourne. If wasn't just for the match, because he enjoyed the banter, the atmosphere, and the Old Speckled Hen in the bar before and after. It was the last match of the season. Predictably City lost 3 - 1 to champions Woking, while Basingstoke drew 1 - 1 away to Welling United, coming 5th in the league table, and qualifying for the playoffs and thus denying the City faithful something they regarded as their divine right. The gloom and doom was complete. The Clarets number one fan would be difficult to console, as he was totally pissed off with the failure to make the playoffs for promotion to the Blue Square Bet Conference National. This was first time since they were promoted in 2008 that they had failed to do so. The distressing defeat brought him back down to earth with a huge bump, and his mind played tricks on him, as he recalled more bits of the previous night's dream.

The Ramsbottoms had a quiet reflective evening talking about their good old days.

Despite his giant public persona, and his inimitable speed of thought and riposte, he knew that that the diminutive Millicent was his rock, and without her he couldn't be himself. She knew that behind every big man is a little woman, who keeps him on the tracks. But now she was even more worried about what a big man he had become, not just weight-wise but also in terms of responsibility. A combination of his intelligence, flippancy and sheer bravado would usually carry him through, but she saw there was more to the situation than that required. Millicent was adamant that he should see a doctor as soon as possible, and to avoid any attempts at avoidance from him, decided to make him an appointment to see Doctor Harriman the following Monday evening.

CHAPTER 11

The Great North Run

(Saturday 28th to Monday 30th April)

Over the same weekend that Hugh had been having his nightmare, Norman and Clarisa spent the whole of Saturday and Sunday together. They went to the flat in Sandon, where the young man was introduced to a massive moggy called Phyllis, the Queen of Sheba, and the Empress of all she surveyed, who looked at him like he was an inferior being, and then turned tail and disappeared under the bed. The couple had lunch in the Crown Inn on the village green, and then despite the continual threat of rain, went for a long walk through the Sandon quarry, and out across the fields up to Danbury Country Park. On the way back down the hill it rained buckets but they didn't care. They gave Sugar Hut a miss on Saturday evening, and instead had a long leisurely meal in Prezzo, and then stayed up late in the Hub listening to the sounds of Stereophonics, Coldplay, and Adele. On Sunday morning they had a romantic lie in, and then went ice skating at Riverside Ice and Leisure. As it came to Sunday afternoon, it would usually have been time for Norman to go to the Ramsbottom's for a roast dinner, and so he wanted to ask Clarisa a question.

"Hey, sweetheart, are you ready to forgive my uncle yet?"

"Why do you ask, my Elfie?"

"Well, my little pixie, I usually go to Avalon House about once a month for a Sunday roast, and I'd be dead chuffed if you'd come with me. I'll never get away from the fact that Hugh and his family are a big part of my life, and I want all the people I love to be happy together."

"Do you love me then?" she asked, looking at him smiling and already knowing the answer.

"Of course I do. I've never said that to anyone before, but then I've never felt like this about anyone before."

"Felt like what, Elf?" she said mischievously.

He thought for a second, wanting to choose his words carefully.

"This weekend has been very special, and I just feel that I want to be with you all the time."

They fell together, eyes to eyes, lips to lips, grinning, ecstatic, the only two people in the whole Universe, and if there had been room for an orchestra in the Hub flat, the violins would have played in sweeping breezes of flaming fire.

The Sunday roast was a delightful family occasion. The unfortunate incident in the Brewers was quickly forgotten. Clarisa and Millicent seemed to like each other from the start. The only woman in the Ramsbottom household was so pleased to be able to indulge in some girlie talk, while the 5 boys went about their laddish business playing computer games. Norman told his uncle about the need to take his dad to the funeral in Yorkshire, and it was agreed that time off would not be a problem.

In the late evening the young couple walked back to the Hub from the Springfield mansion in the continuing drizzling rain. It had been a lovely weekend for both of them, and neither wanted to separate. He drove her home late Sunday evening, and it seemed to take ages for them to say a damp-eyed goodbye to each other.

The next day the clock radio alarm burst into life, and the familiar voices of Martin and Sue on Heart FM introduced another play of Olly Murs singing "I just want you to dance with me tonight." It was an overcast May morning, a Monday 8 am, and the city centre of Chelmsford was beginning to stir. The alarm said 7.59 am, and it was time to get up and get ready for a journey northward to what Norman called "The land of my father". The morning routines and healthy breakfast were quickly over, and then he packed a small suitcase ready for the trip, not forgetting his laptop, fully charged mobile, and satnav. He hoped that his dad wasn't intending to travel with the kitchen sink, because his pride and joy motor wasn't designed for people with lots of luggage.

Just as many times before, at 8.45 am precisely the Porsche Carrera 911 engine roared and the car slid out onto Springfield Road, making for the A12, but this time past Colchester and onward to Leiston. Since he was going beyond his usual destination at this busy time of a working day, Porscheman didn't expect to make the drive all the way without a hold-up or two.

"75 minutes, to Leiston." he guessed.

He popped out an Adele CD, and pushed it into the player.

"We could have had it a-a-all, Rolling in the dee-ee-eep.", sang Adele, and Norman couldn't help but think of how lovely his Clarisa was, and how she was just unique and perfect.

There were a few minor blips in the journey, some road-works around Ipswich, and a road rage renegade in an old Escort Cabriolet whose one brain-cell thought he might compete with a Porsche on the Wickham Market bypass. But he arrived at the bungalow in Leiston at 10 am, give or take a minute or two.

Cher was still in bed, and didn't bother to get up, but Lisalotte was pleased to see her son, giving him a big motherly hug, and Stanley was almost ready for his journey. At about 10:30 am, after a quick cup of coffee, and some chitchat with his mum, his dad had smoked his 2 fags, and so he was installed into the car, and they were ready to go. Since the government had declared a drought on 16th April, it had hardly stopped raining, and true to form it was now raining pussies and pooches.

The Yorkshireman wasn't very talkative at first. There was a peace in his own silence that he seldom achieved in his wife's company, and Norman was content to just concentrate on his driving for a while. The 30 odd miles around the A12 and north of Ipswich to the A45 were eaten up in little time, and apart from a few grunts the passenger was contentedly quiet. But his son was aware that every hour or so Noble senior would need his nicotine fix, and smoking in the car was "streng verboten". So they made the first quick stop for a fag break after about an hour in a lay-by on the A14 near Bury St Edmunds, and after that Stanley started to come alive and began to talk.

"Thanks for this, lad. It'll be good t' be back in God's own county." he began.

The young man just glanced at his father, smiled, and put his eyes back on the road.

"It's goin' t' be a good break for me. Just lately yer mum's bin gettin' on me nerves. We've bin married now for 32 years, and like t' old song sez, it don't seem a day too much. We spend too much time together. She sits and watches whatever crap is on t' telly nearly all day, even those bloody shoppin' channels. There's nothin' that challenges yer brain. It's Jeremy Kyle, All new Trisha, Loose Women, Dickinson's Real Deal. I wish she'd watch some of those cookery programmes like Jamie Oliver's 30 minute meals, and then we might get summat decent t' eat. I've got nothin' t' do but listen to 'er goin' on, and because she's a bit deaf telly's always on so loud it gives me a reet 'eadache. When I want t' go out for a few beers she moans, but she won't come with me, or go out anywhere. This bloody weather's stopped me doin' much in t' garden, and ever since that prize berk t' Minister of Bugger All announced that we were 'avin' a drought it's done nothin' but bloody rain. They've got billions of pounds worth of satellites and computers t' predict t' weather, and they gets it wrong all t' time, They're not as reliable as t' old fella wi' a bit of seaweed, who looks at what t' sky's doin', and see's 'ow birds are behavin'."

Noble senior was on his soapbox, and Noble junior just listened and drove.

"I can't move in t' greenhouse, 'cause it's full of Sid's bloody 'erbal plants. D'yer know 'e 'arvests 'em every month, and 'e's got a kiln for dryin' 'em? 'E even stores t' dried leaves in me' shed, but I can't believe it's all for 'is personal consumption, I think 'e's sellin' it as an 'erbal remedy to all 'is cronies in t' Parrot and Punchbowl. I'm a man of simple pleasures, I like me garden, me roses, me green'ouse, a few beers, and a bit of clay pigeon shootin', but yer mother's difficult t' live with sometimes, and when I can't do me fav'rit things I get as grouchy as she does."

Again the young man driving just smiled and listened.

"And yer sister's got a new girlfriend, so she's not interested in anythin' but 'er, and bloody 'ockey. Mind you, Helen's a good sort, works at t' Adnam's Brewery in Southwold, and she can shift a few pints. She reminds me of yer mother in 'er 'eyday. When yer sister gets 'old of telly remote it's Deal or no Deal, Pointless, Eggheads, and Mastermind. That's a bit better, but all day quizzes? No! Eee! I wish sometimes I could go back t' me butcher's business, but we ent got t' money t' start t' business oop again."

The father paused for a moment, and the son chose to butt in, before it became like a continuous episode of "Grumpy Old Men".

"Well Dad, I'm going to do my best for you to make this an enjoyable experience, even if its raison être is the funeral. We'll stop for your fag breaks, have lunch somewhere on the way, and I've booked us into the Golden Lion Hotel in Northallerton Town Centre for a 2 night stay. How's that?"

Stanley's face lit up, "Eee! That's grand lad, did yer know me and yer mum stayed there after our wedding?"

"No Dad, that's just a coincidence. I picked that hotel on the Internet because it's right in the High Street, and we can go to some of your favourite old pubs."

"Like t' Tickle Toby Inn and t' Nag's Head?"

"Yes Dad if that's what you want."

Father was grinning fit to burst.

Soon they pulled into the Cambridge service area on the A14. The satnav displayed 92 miles; about a third of the way. Stanley's sudden cheerfulness meant he needed a pee, a pot of tea, and another fag or two, and Norman wanted a coffee. As they sat down in the cafeteria the young man asked, "Did I know Arthur Fartworthy then?"

"Probably lad, yer might 'ave, 'cause 'e lived in Ainderby Steeple all 'is life. We'd always bin big friends, but when we went south yer were only knee high t' a grass'opper. Arthur ran butcher's shops all over t' North Riding, but mainly in Catterick and Northallerton areas. 'E taught me everythin' I knew about butchery, must 'ave bin doin' it for over 60 years. 'E bought me old shop in Ainderby Steeple when we came south after t' Chester Gannet fiasco. Actually it weren't in Ainderby t' be exact, it were in Morton on Swale, but Ainderby and Morton are almost one continuous village along t' A684 only a few 'undred yards apart, and I've always thought of 'em as one village. Arthur was kingpin in our local association. That's Butchers and Meat Provisioners of Excellence. 'E were t' founder member of t' BuMPErs, together wi' 'Ector Blunt from Catterick. Funny bloke 'Ector is, you'll no doubt meet 'im tomorrow."

Tea and coffee were over and they got up to leave.

"Next stop for lunch, in about an hour?" said the driver.

"Aye lad, that'll do nicely." answered the passenger.

The Porsche was burning up the miles on the A1 and A1M, and released from the bondage of the daily drivel the Yorkshireman was in good form. He ran through a list of his butcher friends, but his driver was only half listening.

"I'm sure all t' old crew will be there tomorrow. "Lamb Chop Charlie", Charlie Sidebottom from Ripon, old "Dew Drop", Edward Pickleswick from Sowerby, "Porky Jed", Jeremiah Girdlestone from Bedale, and "Sadface Sid", Sidney Thornthwaite from Masham."

There was an interruption, "Is there anywhere else, you'd like to visit while we're up in God's own country?"

Noble senior thought for a while and then replied, "Well t' Durham Ox is one of me old 'aunts in Northallerton, and opposite t' Golden Lion Hotel, if I remember rightly, there's a reet lovely place called Betty's Cafe Tearooms, best cup of tea in England. I'd like to 'ave a butcher's in there."

"OK Dad, we'll find those."

"What about you lad, d'yer want to visit anywhere?"

"Only a few places like our old house and my school in Ainderby Steeple, and Northallerton Grammar School, where I did my GCSE's."

At lunchtime, just after 1.30 pm, they pulled into the A1 service area at Grantham North with the satnav reading 152 miles. Lunch for a health conscious young man was a tuna and cucumber sandwich and a fresh orange, but he didn't mind watching his passenger tuck into fish, chips, and mushy peas, and another pot of tea. He was enjoying the time alone with his father, even though he was already missing his work, and thinking a lot about Clarisa.

"'Ow's yer love life these days, lad?" enquired the Yorkshireman.

"Better than ever, Dad, I've met a lovely girl called Clarisa, and we get on so well. We both like doing the same things, jogging, working out in the gym, eating healthy, and listening to the same music. I've never met anyone like her before. She is very special."

"I'm made oop for yer, son, it's about time yer settled down, and made a granddad out of me."

Nothing was further from the young man's mind. He didn't reply.

Before they left Grantham, he had to fill up with petrol, and so by the time he was slipping back onto the A1, Stanley's lunch had settled, and he was snoring like a sawmill. The driver put his foot down. There was another 81 miles to his next planned stop at Wetherby, and with his passenger fast asleep, and not contemplating another fag break, all being well, he was confident he could make that in about an hour. It had stopped raining while they were at Grantham, and the traffic was fairly light, and Norman was keen to get the journey over now, so they could both relax for a while.

The Yorkshire miles passed swiftly under the Porsche's wheels.

Eventually, after sawing planks for well over an hour, the Yorkshireman began to wake. Things had gone even better than expected, and they had just turned off the A1 onto the A684,

"Alright, Dad?"

"Aye, lad. Where are we now?"

"Well into God's own country. You have had a good kip! Six miles to Northallerton, and in a few miles we'll be going through Ainderby Steeple."

Stanley was like a small child who'd just been given a birthday present. He sat up, wide-eyed, and alert. "Look, lad. There's t' River Swale, blimey it's oop a bit, must 'ave bin rainin' for days on end 'ere. There's me old shop. I wonder who's runnin' it now Arthur 'as gone? See, I told thee, not much green grass between Morton and Ainderby, just along 'ere there's t' church, St Helen's, and opposite'll be t' Effin Boot, or t' Wellie as locals call it. Blimey, it looks a bit sad and derelict. I wonder if it's closed Eee! That were right champion lad."

And so he went on and on all the way into Northallerton like a tour guide with verbal diarrhoea. "On t' right Nag's Head, and just a bit oop on t' left Durham Ox and there's t' hotel on t' right. I was right it is just opposite Betty's Cafe Tearooms."

It was just about 4:30 pm, the satnav read 264 miles, and they'd arrived.

After checking in to the hotel, and finding they had 2 very comfortable adjacent rooms facing the High Street, Norman phoned Clarisa, and then his mum, to report their safe arrival, and then took a quick nap to recover from the journey. The other traveller, who had been sleeping like a newborn baby for the previous hour and a half was wide awake, and made his way quickly to the hotel bar for a good old pint of Yorkshire ale. While he was there he began talking to the barman.

"We passed through me old village at Ainderby Steeple on t' way 'ere, and it looked like t' Wellie, t' Wellington Heifer, my old waterin' hole, was closed." exclaimed Stanley.

"Aye, that's right. A few years ago it was sold t' a large pub company, I forget their name, but they didn't last long, t' locals didn't go there anymore." the barman offered.

"Last pub in t' village gone up t' Swale then?"

"Aye, middle of August 2011 it were, and for a while, that were a bad area for ale drinkers, 'cause t' New Inn at Thrintoft, 'ad closed in 2009 as well. But if I remember it right, it reopened in t' Spring of 2010."

"Eee! T' Wellie were a grand 'ouse in its day, I were a regular there for 20 odd years yer know?"

"We 'ear that it's gone private again now, and they're refurbishin' it, goin' t' do bed and breakfast as well after they reopen."

"Shame they 'aven't reopened already. We're goin' to a funeral tomorrow at St Helens church in Ainderby, and I know Arthur would 'ave wanted 'is wake t' be 'eld in t' Wellie if it could. It were 'is fav'rit' boozer, and me and me son could've stayed there. Shame!"

"Aye, sir, but their loss is t' Golden Lion's gain. Another pint sir?"

Norman woke up after about an hour, showered and changed, and went looking for his father. He knew he'd find him in the hotel bar. He was enjoying himself, drinking good Yorkshire ale, and talking to real Yorkshire people. The young man ordered himself a Perrier water, and got a disdainful look from the barman as if to say "And what's wrong with our ale, or even our tap water, in Yorkshire?" He sat down next to his dad, who was talking to a local couple about his butcher's shop, and the village as it was in t' good old days, when it had 3 pubs.

When they had finished their dinner at the hotel in mid-evening, Norman suggested a small pub crawl to take in a couple of favourite Northallerton pubs. Stanley was relaxed and totally at home, but after a pint in the Tickle Toby Inn and another in the Nag's Head, the exertions and excitement of the day started to tire him. It was 10 pm when they went up to their rooms for a good night's rest. Noble senior fell asleep almost immediately, but Noble junior lay awake with a big smile on his face, listening to the contented sounds of a nearby sawmill in the adjacent room.

CHAPTER 12

Ainderby Steeple Revisited

(Monday 30th April to Wednesday 2nd May 2012)

The day of the funeral started with breakfast in the hotel. Stanley had the full English including several slices of fried bread, and Norman had the muesli, fruit and yogurt option, with fresh orange juice. After some relaxation time reading the local newspapers, they then went to their rooms to dress appropriately for Arthur's funeral. Both adorned in dark blue suits, white shirts, and black ties, and highly polished black shoes they returned to the hotel foyer with time to kill. The ceremony was at 1 pm, and it was only 11 am, but fortunately the well organised son had a plan that he knew his fellow traveller would highly approve of.

First they headed off to find a hand car wash. They may have looked very smart, or perhaps like two very bad Yorkshire imitators of the Blues Brothers, but Norman was determined that they wouldn't go to a funeral in a dirty car. When the Porsche's silver grey paintwork was gleaming again, they drove back to the High Street and parked.

"Where we goin' now, lad?" was a question.

"Just follow me, Dad." was the instruction.

Within a few minutes they were sat at a white clothed table in a Grade II listed building on the wide Georgian High Street, in the place that was widely acclaimed as Betty's Cafe Tearooms.

"Cor! It's reet nice in 'ere, 'int it? It's posher than I remember." said Stanley, looking at the fine bone china, and tastefully decorated very welcoming decor of the tea rooms.

"Yes, Dad, and did you see that display on the way in?"

"What was that, son?"

"You mean you didn't notice? Father, you drink too much. Look! There are a few plaques and newspaper displays on the wall. Can you see them?"

Rightly proud of their reputation, the tearoom proclaimed "Against competition from a high standard of entrants, Betty's Northallerton scooped The Tea Guild's prestigious award for Top Tea Place 2012 – the highest accolade in the tea world."

Elsewhere in the tearooms there were bills posted declaring "Northallerton, named the best place in the UK to enjoy Afternoon Tea. Posted on 30th March, 2012."

The waitress waddled over to take their order. Norman asked politely for a pot of Lapsang Souchong and couldn't resist a small piece of carrot and walnut cake, and Stanley winked at the waitress and ordered English Breakfast Tea, and a mega-slab of rich fruit cake. Then he grasped the waitress' hand and exclaimed "Tha' knows me lass! It's Doreen, Doreen Heckmondwyke 'int it? I'd recognise that pretty face anywhere."

The Essex boy was a little embarrassed. He wasn't used to hearing his dad's chat up lines, and the waitress, although she was a fine looking well-built Yorkshire lass, must have been 60ish. All was quickly revealed.

"Stanley! Stanley Noble! It is you, isn't it?"

"Aye, Doreen, it must be 10 years, and yer don't look a day older."

Doreen blushed, and then asked." You're looking very smart; you must be here for the funeral?"

"Aye, lass, Arthur's funeral, yer'll be there, won't yer?"

"Yes, love. A lovely man Arthur was. I've been his housekeeper for the last ten years. Look! I'm working now, but we'll have a chat this afternoon at the wake. You probably know it's in the New Inn at Thrintoft. OK?", and then she waddled off to get the teas and cakes.

The Yorkshireman leaned over to his son and quietly explained," Me and Doreen went t' school together. I've known 'er since we were nippers. She were my first love. We used to 'old 'ands in t' bus shelter. She's lived in t' village all 'er life, probably still does."

The young man felt good. His dad was like a new man, rejuvenated by all the lovely experiences he was having on this little excursion to his beloved birthplace.

A little while later, they left Betty's, and a revitalised Yorkshireman blew a kiss to Doreen, making her blush again. After a slow drive up the High Street, and along Grammar School Lane, they took a quick butcher's around the area of Northallerton Grammar School (which had been renamed Northallerton College), and then drove the few miles out along the A684 to Ainderby Steeple. At 12:50 they parked outside the parish church of St Helens, and then walked up the path towards the entrance. The Bedale Brass Band were playing "Abide with Me" in the church grounds, it was a bright and dry early May Springtime day, and as they walked Norman could see his father was choking up with the emotion of the occasion, both sad and joyful. Sadness came with the sense that it was the passing of one of his oldest and most revered friends that had brought him back to this place. Joyfulness was because here he was at home, in the village of his birth in t' best county in England, and he was soon to meet up again with many of his oldest friends.

As they entered the church and crept into one of the back rows of pews, there were turned heads and polite waves and smiles of recognition for the Yorkshireman from faces he hadn't seen in many a long year. They were faces that his son didn't recognise at all.

The Ainderby ex-patriot nudged his son with his arm and whispered, "See that lot over there on t' left, lad; they are t' BuMPErs, our local association. That little short arse on t' end is 'Ector Blunt, and 'e's a........"

Before he could finish, the church organ played and everybody stood up, and the poll bearers carried the coffin slowly up the aisle accompanied by the sobs and coughs of the congregation. The vicar was the Reverend Raymond Robinson, a broad fellow built like rugby scrumhalf, who all the locals knew as old triple R's. He knew the deceased very well, and the locals were confident that he would conduct the service with appropriate reverence for a man who had been well loved in this area of Yorkshire.

"Good afternoon, "he began, "Welcome all of you. There are a lot of faces here today that I recognise, and for any of those that I haven't met before, I'd be delighted to meet you later. We are here today to celebrate the life of Arthur Fartworthy, who I personally knew as a pillar of the community, a regular churchgoer, and a man who will be sadly missed by all of us."

From his own personal experience he then went on to illustrate Arthur's life, precisely and accurately. The vicar then paused, before he introduced one of Arthur's favourite hymns. Everyone stood quietly and listened as the choir sang a cappella.

"Morning has broken, like the first morning,
Blackbird has spoken, like the first bird............"

Because the song was unaccompanied it added to poignancy of the wonderful feeling of hope in the lyrics.

"Sweet the rain's new fall, sunlit from heaven............

Norman remembered he had heard the song before on a Cat Stevens CD.

"............Praise with elation, praise every morning,
God's recreation, of the new day."

At the end of this song the vicar then said, "I remind you that Arthur would have wanted us to celebrate his life, and to me the only sad thing about today would be that we can't do that in the Wellington Heifer. T'Wellie was Arthur's favourite pub for all his life, and it's a shame that we can't send him off to Heaven raising a few glasses in there. For those few of you here who might not know, our much loved late 18th century inn was the last remaining pub of three that used to be in the village. Unfortunately, it was closed on the 19th August last year. That was a very sad day for the village."

Many of the congregation shared concerned looks, and made nods of agreement at that point, and then the vicar continued with a warm and confident smile.

"But, the good news is that t' Wellie is expected to reopen this August."

The congregation shared the delight of something that they already knew and looked forward to, and but for the solemnity of the occasion they would probably have all cheered.

Soon the Brass band joined with the church choir to perform a well known hymn, and Norman watched his dad standing straight and staring forwards, tears streaming down his face and into his bushy moustache, as he sang embarrassingly out of tune.

"The Lord's my shepherd, I'll not want;
He makes me down to lie
In pastures green; he leadeth me
The quiet waters by.

My soul he doth restore again,
And me to walk doth make
Within the paths of righteousness,
E'en for his own name's sake.

Yea, though I walk in death's dark vale,
Yet will I fear no ill:
For thou art with me, and thy rod
And staff me comfort still.

My table thou hast furnished
In presence of my foes;
My head thou dost with oil anoint
And my cup overflows.

Goodness and mercy all my life
Shall surely follow me;
And in God's house for evermore
My dwelling-place shall be."

"Now!" smiled the vicar, "We couldn't see Arthur off on his journey, without a bit of Frank Sinatra. If you knew our friend, then you'd also know he was a lifelong fan, and I'm sure you'd agree about the aptness of this song."

After a few crackles from the old scratchy record that was playing, Frank's voice filled the church:-

"And now, the end is near, and so I face the final curtain,"

Arthur had been very precise in his dying wishes, and he had insisted that his favourite Sinatra song should not be cut short.

Old triple R's certainly wasn't going to tamper with a man's final wishes whatever time constraints there were.

Nearly everybody was visibly moved by the poignancy of the words of Arthur's favourite Sinatra song. Only Hector Blunt remained completely expressionless.

The Essex boy watched all these people that he didn't know at all, pay their respects in a most dignified and loving way to their dear departed friend, and couldn't help but be moved by the torrents of emotions wallowing around the walls of this old church. There was such warmth and depth of feeling here. Arthur's was a long and fulfilled life, serving the community he grew up in and loved with true passion. He would be widely regarded as a great loss.

When that part of the service was over, the congregation streamed out into the churchyard to the sounds of the choir singing "All things bright and beautiful".

There was still an aloofness, a detachment, an unspoken, but fully understood protocol, between all present as they prepared for the most emotional and finalising part of the funeral. Everyone remained quiet and respectful towards their dear friend Arthur. At the graveside the vicar performed the standard ceremonial rites.

"Man that is born of a woman hath but a short time to live, and is full of misery. He cometh up, and is cut down, like a flower; he fleeth as it were a shadow, and never continueth in one stay. In the midst of life we are in death: of whom may we seek for succour, but of thee, O Lord, who for our sins art justly displeased?"

Then finally the vicar concluded with:-

"Earth to earth, ashes to ashes, dust to dust; in sure and certain hope of the Resurrection into eternal life."

Each and every person present threw his handful of earth into the grave where Arthur had been lowered, and by this time the Bedale Brass Band had reassembled in the churchyard and began to play "Land of Hope and Glory". Now the solemnity was over, and there were two more tunes from Frank Sinatra that all present would have recognised as Arthur's favourites.

As the strains of "Strangers in the Night." and "Love's been good to me." floated across the churchyard, the bonds of ceremony and sadness began to break, as if in satisfaction for a job well done. A palpable release of tension descended upon the throng, and hugs and handshakes were exchanged. Some broke into smiles and laughter with a welcome sigh of relief. Stanley almost ran forward to greet someone, who looked the spitting image of Captain

Mainwaring from Dad's Army, and shaking him warmly by the hand introduced his son.

"This is Lamb Chop Charlie, Charlie Sidebottom from Ripon. Charlie, this 'ere's my lad, Norman." said Ainderby's lost son.

They shook hands, as Charlie replied with a huge grin missing two front teeth, "Last time I saw thee, lad, yer were a spotty teenager."

"'E's a director now, in a computer company. 'E writes computer games for a livin'." continued the father with pride.

"Couldn't get a proper job as a master butcher then?"

Charlie smiled the toothless grin again.

"Nay, Charlie," mocked Norman, in his best Yorkshire accent," I'm t' world's biggest layabout. Couldn't do a proper day's work if yer paid me."

Stanley was a little embarrassed, but Charlie got the joke.

"'Ee's a chip off t' old block after all. Kick me if 'e 'ent." Charlie said slapping him on the back.

Soon they all tumbled through the churchyard gate and out onto the highway, ready to get into the cars for the short ride to the venue for the wake. T' Wellie looked a sad travesty of its former glory, boarded up, and bedraggled, waiting for the much anticipated refurbishment.

Predictably all the oldies were moaning about not being able to go to the wake in there, as they'd have to travel from St Helens to the New Inn at Thrintoft. But it was less than 2 miles away, and only a 5 minute drive.

The stream of cars made their way to the wake, and there was another opportunity for pointing out places of interest, as they passed the former butcher's premises and the Old Royal George pub on the way through Moreton on Swale. When a few minutes later, the cars all spilled out at the New Inn, the Bedale Brass Band were playing "Lord of the Dance" in the car park and a weak spring sunshine was spreading its fleeting intermittent rays across the nearby fields.

"Eee! I don't know, 'e could've waited t' die, until t' Wellie was open again. I've never thought much of this place." spouted another of the butcher's clique, as he came to greet Stanley. Edward Pickleswick from Sowerby was known by all as "Dew Drop" owing to there always being one on the end of his large and very pointed nose. Not the best thing by far for a butcher.

Edward continued, "I suppose, we 'ave to count our blessings, that they've still got an inn open 'ere in Thrintoft. It's not t' liveliest place in t' world, and if I remember rightly this place was closed for a while just like t' Wellie."

"Aye! If Arthur had to pop 'is clogs now, what's wrong wi' t' Old Royal George? They've always served fine ale in there," offered Jeremiah Girdlestone, looking at his old friend.

"Old Dew Drop's reet tha' knows? T' New Inn closed in 2009, and only reopened in t' Spring of 2010."

"That's "Porky Jed", Jeremiah Girdlestone, from Bedale." father explained to his son, "Finest pork butcher in t' 'hole of North Yorkshire. 'E more than likely organised t' brass band. 'Is son Laurie plays trombone for them."

Norman would remember all the names, and the nicknames would definitely stick. It didn't really matter because, although they were politeness itself to him, it wasn't him they were all connected to. The wake was destined to be like a butcher's convention, like an informal AGM for BuMPErs, and the young man was quietly contented that his dad was having a roaring good time meeting all his old cronies again.

"See that prize prat over there?" indicated Stanley to his son, nodding in the direction of a little fat man with huge ears and no hair, "That's 'im, 'Ector Blunt, 'who I pointed out earlier. 'E and Arthur founded BuMPErs in t' 60's. 'Ector's dad and 'is granddad were butchers before 'im. They say 'e was born wi' a meat cleaver in 'is hand, 'E is supposed to 'ave shot and skinned 'is first rabbit when 'e was 6. At 9 'e was wringin' chickens necks, and 'e was workin' in an abattoir at 14. Slaughter, you could say, was in 'is blood. It's said that 'e loved t' killin' so much that 'e would 'ave chopped oop cats and dogs if it was legal. It's even rumoured that 'e spent time in France learnin' t' butcher 'orses. People used to joke that 'e would make donkey burgers and palomino sausages given 'alf a chance. I 'ope I don't 'ave to speak to t' little short-arsed prat."

The spread in the restaurant of the New Inn was superbly impressive, if you were a rampant carnivore that is. Arranged across a massive white tablecloth, there was everything you'd expect of a butcher's get together. Handcrafted steak and ale pies, beef and stilton pies, sausage rolls, pork pies, ham on the bone, and probably the finest selection of sausages of all varieties ever assembled in Yorkshire, all made by this illustrious tribe of master craftsmen. The hot food was laid at opposite ends of the table; huge cuts of top quality roast beef, and a classic suckling pig complete with the russet apple in its mouth. There was a cheeseboard the size of a barn door, with a huge range of English cheeses and chutneys, and thankfully, a few plates of crudites, celery, carrots, tomatoes, and lettuce. Norman found a little to satisfy his less animalistic dietary needs, as he nibbled politely at some of the leaner sausages and the crudites.

Noble senior's pals were all a little surprised that his son wasn't a chip off the old block beverage-wise, when he ordered mineral water at the bar, and declined all offers of the fine Yorkshire ales on offer. Even "Sadface Sid", Sidney Thornthwaite from Masham, piped up with "Ne'er trust a man that sups no ale." But the teetotaller was confident that this lot would not need any help from him to have a valiant try at drinking the place dry if that was at all possible. They began stuffing themselves with fine carnivorous fare, and indulged in copious quantities of ale, and the Essex boy drifted away to a quieter corner where he recognised Doreen Heckmondwike.

"Hello again, Doreen." he introduced himself politely, "I'm Norman, we met at Betty's Cafe Tea Rooms earlier."

"Yes, I remember," she answered, "It's nice to meet you, and to see Stanley again after all this time. He looks as if he's having a whale of a time over there."

She pointed at those assembled at the bar.

"How's your mum? Lisalotte, isn't it? I haven't seen her in years."

"Oh, she's fine thank you. Still as German as an oompah band at a Munich Bier Festival. She doesn't change much."

"That's where she met your father, isn't it? And she's got a sister, what's-her-name? Brunhilda!"

"Yes, they met at the Munich Bier fest, and my auntie Brunhilda lives in Scotland now."

"Me, and your dad, were childhood sweethearts, went to infants school together."

"And you still live in Ainderby Steeple. Don't you?"

"Yes, lived here all my life. It's a lovely place, my home, couldn't live anywhere else. Nor would I want to."

"The BuMPErs crew all seem very unhappy that the Wellington Heifer's closed. Do you know what's going to happen to it?"

"No need to worry, love. Word on the grapevine is that somebody called Rob Gilpin is planning to refurbish it, and reopen in August. They're even planning to do bed and breakfast later on next year. If you come up here again, just think, you might be able to stay there. Arthur was such a well loved man in the village, the lads over there were talking about having another little celebration later on, when t' Wellie reopens. I can't think of a better excuse for you two coming back to visit us again."

As the wake got into full swing, the brass band played on in the car park at the New Inn, running through "Lord of the Dance", "The Floral Dance", "The Liberty Bell" better known as the Monty Pythons theme, and "The Dambusters March", as well as repeating Arthur's favourite Frank Sinatra tunes.

After a long while Stanley arrived at Norman's shoulder, slurring and unsteady on his feet, and planted a big, wet, beery moustached, kiss on Doreen's cheek.

"I think I'd better sit down, now, and take a little breather." he said, "Not as young as I used to be."

"None of us are, "replied Doreen, eyes fixed softly on her childhood sweetheart, "But we do our best to keep lively."

"Eee! Doreen, you're still a fine figure of a woman. If I were 10 years younger..." slurred the wide eyed butcher.

"You would still be married to Lisalotte. It must be 30 odd years" replied Doreen, not annoyed, just amused,

"Aye, lass, that much is true." he sighed.

"Anyway, before you fall asleep, or fall over, I've got something for you." smiled Doreen, opening her large black handbag, and rustling her way through the contents. She then passed over a brown envelope with two words "As promised" written on it in Arthur Fartworthy's handwriting.

"What's this?" he asked; holding the envelope up.

"Put it away and open it later, Love. Quick, before Hector comes over." said Doreen. They were suddenly aware of a wet blanket sensation, a black cloud descending, almost as if Albert Pierpoint had arrived unexpectedly with a death warrant, as Hector approached, and interrupted with a curl of his upper lip. "Hello, Stan. Having a good time, are we?"

"Yes, nice t' see thee, 'Ector. It's so sad about Arthur. Still, 'e 'ad a long and illustrious innings, didn't 'e? And what a cracking celebration, lovely service, and a good wake."

Thus spoke the exiled butcher suddenly becoming more coherent.

"Good innings for a fine man. We'll all miss him. Best butcher that ever walked in these parts, that's no mistake. You'll have to excuse me." snorted the little prat sidling away towards the gents' much to everybody's relief.

Much later in the afternoon the proceedings were winding down and everybody was saying their goodbyes and best wishes in the car park. Norman ran through the handshakes, and remembered all the names and faces of the people he'd met. It had been a lovely day for his father, but by now the son's placid nature was being stretched to the limits. As they drove away it felt like he'd just stepped out of an episode of "Last of the Summer Wine" with a bit of "Dad's Army" thrown in for good measure. Before very long, they arrived back at The Golden Lion Hotel. The elder Noble went up to his room for a well earned rest, and the younger drove a little way back out of town and parked at the Sacred Heart Church, and went for walk all the way along to the end of Grammar School Lane and back, so that he could have a better look around the area of the Northallerton College. As he walked, he enjoyed the solitude, and tested his memory again, asking himself questions about his recent acquaintances. He remembered that the acronym BuMPErs stood for "Butchers and Meat Provisioners of Excellence." God knows he'd heard it often enough that afternoon. He also recalled all of the members, and chuckled to himself at the nicknames he'd collected for them. They couldn't fail to stick in his memory with labels like "Dew Drop", "Porky Jed", and "Sadface Sid". Most of all, Hector Blunt, the man who required no nickname, but who had been referred to as a short-arsed prat would stick in his memory. He stuck out like a fish out of water.

Then he remembered the affection between his father and Doreen Heckmondwyke, and how she had given him a sealed envelope from Arthur. Then she'd quickly made him hide it as soon as she saw the butcher Blunt approaching. Noble junior wanted to remind himself again and again how happy the get together had been for his father that afternoon.

At 7pm he went to the room to wake Stanley up. After the lavish feast they had enjoyed at the wake, he was sure that his dad would nevertheless be hungry again, but would more than likely be content with a sandwich for his evening meal. He was awake, and sat in an armchair reading that week's issue of the Northallerton Echo. They stayed at the hotel and shared a large plate of freshly made ham and mustard sandwiches, and talked at length about all the butcher friends, and how much they had enjoyed the day.

"Eee! That's really made my day today lad, meeting Charlie, and Edward, and Porky Jed".

"That's great Dad, It has been a good day, and I've enjoyed meeting some of your old friends, especially that one who's the spitting image of Captain Mainwaring in Dad's Army".

The father chuckled, "Oh, Lamb Chop Charlie, yes lad I know what yer mean."

"And they're all brilliant characters with cracking nicknames. I wondered what nickname they had for you."

"I used t' be called "t' Stanley Knife" or just "t' knife", but after that Chester Gannet nonsense they renamed me."

"Oh I get it. Did they call you "Froggy" or "Frogs Legs"?"

The butcher nearly choked on his sandwich, as he burst out laughing, "Nay, not quite, lad, you're on t' right track. Me new nickname was "t' Ainderby Frogman", and that came about courtesy of t' local newspaper. But me career in Yorkshire was over, and so luckily it didn't really stick. So this afternoon they all thankfully reverted to using "t' Knife" as me nickname."

The son had never heard that tale before, and it pleased him that his dad had relaxed so much in the 2 days they had been away. It was still at the back of his mind as to exactly what part Chester had played in the family demise, and they were both in such a relaxed frame of mind that there appeared to be no harm in discussing the matter.

"Do you know for a fact that Chester Gannet screwed things up for your old butcher's business?" he asked.

There was a moment's thought and then a response, "Well, we were on that TV programme wi' 'im, and t' shit 'it t' fan soon after that. Yer mum 'ad taken an instant dislike t' im even before she dropped 'er clanger and called me Seasonal Burgundian sausages those froggy bangers."

There was a moment's pensive silence while they both thought about the incident, but there didn't appear to be any need to continue the subject.

"Come on, let's take a little walk, stretch our legs, not too far, it's been a long day." said the young man.

So they took a five minute stroll along the High Street to another old drinking spot, which they had found out that afternoon was also a favourite of

Arthur Fartworthy. As they entered the bar of The Durham Ox and ordered their drinks, a J2O and a pint of best Yorkshire bitter, they both suddenly wished they hadn't bothered. There he was in the corner, that miserable malevolence, Hector Blunt, who came over as soon as he recognised them.

"Hello again, Stan," he sneered, "I didn't expect to see you in here. I'll get those."

Norman now noticed that unique among the butcher friends, Hector didn't have a Yorkshire accent, but he couldn't exactly place his accent either. He also wondered why the obnoxious Mr Blunt addressed his dad as "Stan".

"Oh, 'ello, 'Ector" was the reply with a barely disguised resignation. There was an obvious inability to hide not really wanting to be in the same place as the short-arsed little prat, let alone drinking a pint with him.

The drinks were poured, and they sat down, and made small-talk for a while about the Durham Ox and about Arthur, and then the bald prat said to Stanley "Tell me, did I see Doreen give you a brown envelope this afternoon from Arthur?"

"Er, did she, I can't remember," he replied, deliberately being evasive, "If you say so, I suppose she must 'ave done."

He hadn't forgotten about it, but as he had changed out of his black funeral suit into a more casual tweed jacket, and he'd also been a bit "in his cups" earlier on, he wasn't about to find the envelope on him, or remember where it was without a bit of mental backtracking.

"Oh, come on, you've got it haven't you?" Hector snarled, "Have you opened it? Do you know what's in it? Don't play dumb, and keep winding me up. Come on be honest."

The Yorkshireman had heard enough. He'd never got on with the little bald one, and this haranguing was too much. His face was puffed up red with anger, and Norman had never seen him so agitated before. Something was about to ruin a great day, and Noble junior was helpless to prevent it. Suddenly, Stanley stood up, put his pint down, and stared his antagonist straight in the eyes. It seemed as if all other business and conversation in the pub suddenly came to a halt, and there was silence, as he ranted.

"I've never liked you, Blunt. Yer an obnoxious, ignorant, fat, big-eared, short-arsed little prat, and if I never bump into yer again it'll be like Christmas every day. Now take this pint and shove it oop your flabby, lazy, spotty arse. Sideways! Come on, lad, we don't want t' drink in 'ere wi' this pillock."

Then he got up and barged through the door, followed by his extremely bemused son. A few paces along the High Street son caught up with father fully expecting him to be very upset. But he was laughing his chubby Yorkshire head off.

"Dad! Dad!" said Norman, "I'm sorry we went in there, I didn't know that horrible man would be there, I hope it hasn't ruined your day."

The butcher stopped in his tracks, turned and gave his son a huge bear hug, and still laughing spluttered, "Nay, lad, that's made my day. I've always wanted to tell that useless pile of shite exactly what I think of 'im. And this little event 'as bin t' jam on today's Yorkshire puddin'. Come on, let's 'ave a drink back in t' Golden Lion, and I'll tell yer what's 'appening."

Back in the Golden Lion a few minutes and an easy stroll later, with a pint in his hand, Noble senior began to explain.

"Well, lad, yer remember that business with the Seasonal Burgundian Sausage, that came to a sticky end with bloody Chester Gannet?"

There was a nod of recognition from the butcher's son.

"Well, Arthur 'elped me wi' t' recipe for that. We worked on it together, because 'e was t' finest master sausage maker that ever lived, and me being like 'is apprentice, 'e wanted me t' take over t' reigns after 'e'd gone t' sausage heaven. Arthur was gutted when it all fell over. That's why 'e 'elped us buying me old shop in Ainderby, and t' proceeds for that sale set us oop in anonymity in Leiston. But you were in t' middle of yer schooling, just passed them GCSE's, and we would 'ave loved t' keep yer at Northallerton Grammar, but we couldn't afford it. So we 'ad t' ship yer off t' yer Uncle Hugh in Chelmsford. Besides which yer mum was in an awful state. She 'ad a nervous breakdown, and so we 'ad to retire, and take it easy for a while. Leiston was ideal. It was quiet, out of t' way, and t' countryside was a slight reminder of Yorkshire. Anyway, I digress."

He took a large swig of his beer and then continued.

"'Ector Blunt never liked anybody being friendly wi' Arthur, and that goes back to t' days when they formed t' BuMPErs together. 'E always thought 'e 'ad some 'old on Arthur, and that 'e'd get all his famous sausage recipes when 'e died. So that's what's in t' brown envelope lad. It's all the Fartworthy secret sausage recipes. 'Ector knew that, and that's why 'e was so disgruntled and pushy with me at t' Durham Ox just now. 'E must 'ave seen Doreen give me t' envelope this afternoon at t' wake. But what 'e didn't know was that Arthur had promised me t' recipes when we moved south. Also 'e wasn't aware that by t' time we'd just bumped into 'im again, I'd already opened t' envelope. I knew what was in it."

Father stopped and beamed a mischievous smile, which his son returned. Then he went on.

"Eeee lad, I'm so glad we've seen all me old mates again, but 'Ector Blunt's a totally different kettle of fish. 'E always was an obnoxious little prat. You wouldn't know that 'e 'as a brother called Rex who's an undertaker. 'E's known all over t' North Riding as Vaginosauras Rex because 'e's t' biggest twat in North Yorkshire."

Norman's dad didn't often crack jokes, and especially those that mentioned body parts. It must have been something to do with a butcher's creed. They both laughed, and then the old man beamed the widest smile, and carried on talking.

"These few days away, 'ave done me wonders, lad. I've got a better balance in me mind now. I'm going t' go home a new man, sort things out w' yer mum, and see if I can find a way to start up me business again. Maybe keep it small, and just specialise in sausages, armed with all Arthur's expertise that could be successful. Eee! It's an ill wind that blows nobody good."

He finished his pint, stood up, and just said "Reet, lad, it's bin quite a day all in all, and I'm reet knackered. I'm off to' me bed; see you at breakfast in t' morning' about 8 then?"

The young man nodded, and said, "Goodnight, Dad, sleep well."

It wasn't long before Norman also went up to his room, and after calling Clarisa, he too was soon sleeping like a baby.

The next morning at about 8 am a very happy Yorkshireman, and a contented adopted Essex boy, had breakfast, checked out of the Golden Lion, and made their way back south. On the way they chatted about their recent experiences, all of the butcher friends, and the Chester Gannet business.

"That were such bad timing, lad. You'd just got yer GCSE's at t' Grammar School."

"I wasn't that brilliant at school. I only got D's and E's in most subjects. I was only any good at Technology and Computer Studies. I got A's in both of those."

"Yer did alright down at Boswells though, lad?"

"Yes, when I'd finished the 6th form there I had A's in Sociology and Technology. But I didn't want to go to Uni. I was only ever any good at computer related stuff, and I wanted to write my own computer games."

"We 'ave yer uncle to thank for lookin' after yer, lad. And 'e 'elped t' turn yer into a success in yer chosen business. 'Ow is 'e these days? Must go down to see 'im one day."

"Oh, you know, he's a one off, his own man, infuriating at times, but you can't help but like him. He's really a very kind man, got a great sense of humour, and loves to wind people up."

"He's no fool though, lad, 'e's a very clever man."

"Well he's very rich, and it's his money that keeps the company progressing, but I think he's got a bit of a weight problem."

"Bit of puppy fat lad, that won't do 'im any 'arm. Still forthright with 'is own point of view I bet?"

"That gets him into trouble occasionally, but everyone who knows him, knows what he's like. He trying to engineer his way into being a director at Chelmsford City F.C., but they remember that incident last year when he'd been on the mutton vindaloo."

"What 'appened then, lad?"

"Well, one of his farts cleared the Cro-ro end behind the goal. Dave Rainford was just about to take a penalty and the ref stopped the match because he thought there was a gas leak."

They both laughed like silly boys.

"I remember the Comedy Nights on the 1st Tuesday of the month in the Brewers."

"Aye, that's where they do the Fuller's London Pride, 'int it? Nice pint that!"

"Trouble was uncle didn't like one of the comedians they booked and started heckling, and then it turned out he was funnier than the comedian."

Another chuckling fit filled the Porsche as it zipped along the A1 to the south.

"'E can play a good tune on t' piano, Hugh can."

"Yes, I know that, but why does he have to be first up at the karaoke, when he can't sing a note in tune? Still most of the time he only sings Status Quo, so it doesn't matter 'cause everybody joins in and drowns him out."

"But 'e's getting a bit lardy is 'e, just like t' rest of us. We're not getting' any younger, and that just "appens, lad."

"No, Dad, I worry about him, we all laugh about it, but it's not funny really. A couple of weeks ago he was banned from the Imperial Chinese buffet. Now that's an eat-all-you-can place for a set price, but he was banned for eating too much, and that says it all. And I think auntie Millie is starting to get worried about him too. Honestly he doesn't just eat for England, he eats for Europe."

Fag breaks at Wetherby and Grantham service areas, and lunch at a stop near Cambridge, and the 264 mile journey was disappearing quickly. Around 4 pm they pulled up outside the bungalow in Leiston. Noble senior got out of the car saying, "Job's done, and it's a reet goodun."

Norman could now have a rest from driving, and "Yippee!" his mum had prepared his favourite again. Soon the bockwurst and sauerkraut were ready, and the Essex boy still hated them both, but scoffed enthusiastically to please his mum. It was a kind of noblesse oblige, maybe even Nobless oblige?

Later, father and son made for the garden, even more congested with Sid's therapeutic herbs than the previous visit, and Stanley sat down, and breathed a big sigh as he lit a fag. Then smiling he said, "I suppose yer'll be on yer way soon then, lad. Eee! It's bin bloody marvellous these last few days. I feel like I've been away a month. Can I ask yer 'ow yer feel about another trip oop North later in t' year, when t' Wellie reopens, and does bed and breakfast. I'd like to stay there, and see me BuMPErs mates all o'er again."

"And Doreen Heckmondwyke, no doubt,"

"Eee! Don't tell yer mother 'bout Doreen. She's a very jealous woman, yer mum."

"Yeah, OK Dad we'll go up there again. Why not? I enjoyed the break as well."

Sometime later, and the man in the Porsche was cruising homeward feeling good, and looking forward to being home and sleeping in his own bed. He'd been giving the car a bit of a hammering along the Wickham Market bypass, and was just easing off the accelerator as he was coming to the section of road where it went from dual carriageway to single highway, and then he saw a dark grey coloured Vauxhall Cavalier with a blue flashing light on top just before the lay-by. He was waved in by a police officer, and so he stopped and rolled down the window.

"Would you switch off the engine and get out of the car, please Sir?" asked the policewoman politely.

"What's the problem, officer?" said Porscheman switching off and getting out.

"Nice car, Sir, is it yours?" said the police officer not answering his question, "Have you got your documents with you, Sir?"

"Yes, it is my car, officer, and I'll get the documents." he replied, reaching for a file hidden under his seat. He handed the file containing his driving licence, registration document, MOT certificate, and insurance policy to the officer.

WPC 159 perused them slowly and deliberately, checking the registration, and then handed them back saying "That all seems to be in order, but I'm not too happy with your driving, sir."

"What's wrong with it, officer?" he enquired becoming a bit annoyed with the WPC's tone.

"Far too fast for a sleepy little county like Suffolk, Sir. You were doing over 90 miles per hour back there." she said pointing back down the road.

Norman was always wary of speed traps. Having a car like a Porsche, he knew it was a fuzz magnet, and he hadn't seen anyone or anything back down the road to suggest a speed trap. But it had been a long day, and it was now twilight, and he thought that maybe he'd just not noticed. "Was I really, officer? I'm sorry I didn't notice my speed. It's been a long day, and I've driven all the way from Northallerton in Yorkshire today." he said.

"That's as maybe, but it doesn't give you an excuse for tearing around our countryside like Michael Schumacher."

She paused and then said, "Where have you just come from? Yorkshire's not that way!"

"No I've just dropped my dad off in Leiston."

"And what's your destination now, Sir?"

"I'm on my way to Chelmsford, which my documents show is where I live and where the car is kept." he replied becoming exasperated.

"Calm down, Sir. No need to get agitated. I'm only doing my job." the WPC went on.

"Oh, just give me ticket WPC 159 what's-your-name. I'm tired. I've got miles to go, and I don't need this."

"WPC 159 Highwater, Sir. And if you keep calm I'll explain. You see, my Chief Constable's very keen on keeping our little county quiet, and we don't want a load of wide-boys from The Only Way is Essex thinking they can burn rubber on our country lanes. Do I make myself clear?" She explained precisely raising her voice slightly.

"Yes, officer, can I go now, or can you give me a ticket and get it over with please?"

"Providing you understand me clearly." the WPC uttered, "I'll let you off the ticket, this time. OK?"

"Yes, officer." he replied, trying to look humble, but seething inside.

"OK, Sir, Now fuck off out of my county, and don't let me catch you speeding again. Good evening, Sir." the WPC concluded.

He got back in the car, started her up, and drove slowly away. But the lesson was lost. He was just plain annoyed, and took it out on his pride and joy, and so less than 60 minutes later, much relieved to be home, he pulled into his parking space in the Hub back in the first City of Essex.

While Norman and his dad had been visiting Yorkshire, Millicent had made sure that Hugh paid a visit to somewhere a bit nearer to home. On the Monday she had made him an appointment to see their G. P. Doctor Harriman, someone who had been looking after him since he was a child. For Millicent it was an uncharacteristic mistake that she did not to go with him, but she had trusted her husband to be honest with the G. P.

He had no intention of being honest. He was Hugh Ramsbottom, the jolly fatman, and people had expectations of him. He laughed off everything bad, he took the piss out of the slightest weakness, and he always had the last word. His attitude was that if you were in trouble you could come to him, you could depend on him, and with a quick quip and a cheery wave he would solve all your problems, because he was strong, he was tough, he was reliable and he was a big man who didn't have any problems. He wouldn't dream of burdening anybody and especially a quack with anything as trivial as a bad bout of indigestion, and a vivid confusing nightmare.

"I haven't had the pleasure of your company for quite some time, my friend. So! What seems to be the trouble?" Doctor Harriman began.

"Oh, I've been having the odd funny turn, feeling a bit tired, and getting terrible indigestion. Most of the time I'm alright, but every now and again it seems to creep up on me. I get a bit crotchety, I'm breathless, and once I had a very disturbing dream."

"I see," said the G. P. "Hmm! You don't smoke do you? But you have put on a lot of weight over the years. Step on these scales please."

Hugh did as instructed. There was a sigh of resignation from the quack.

"Hmmm, you're over 20 stone. Still like a beer or six do you? And I bet you don't take much exercise. Let me take your blood pressure."

Doctor Harriman took a blood pressure reading, tested the patient's pulse, and sighed again.

"Hmmm, I see, 160 over 95, Blood pressures up a bit, but your pulse is regular. Is there anything else?

The fatman wanted to gloss over the whole episode; he didn't like doctors and didn't trust medication. "No. but there's been a lot of stress in my life recently what with the company going global."

"Well, it's good to hear that your business life is so successful, but I think it's time for you to take some tough advice, my friend. First I'm going to send you for some blood tests. When we get the results I want you to come and see me again."

The Doctor handed over a blood test form, and then said, "Right, in the meantime I want you to think very seriously about your lifestyle. You're going to have to cut down on the booze, eat less bad food and snacks, change your diet to a more healthy regime, and take a lot more exercise. You don't have to crash diet or start running 10 miles a day. In any case that would probably save the health service a great deal of money by killing you off. But it's clear that if you don't make changes your heading for a crisis, my friend. Diabetes, stroke, heart problems, just to mention a few big possibilities. Here! Read these leaflets, and I'll see you again in a week or two."

The patient took the literature offered, shook the doctor's hand and left the surgery glad that the trial was over. He threw the leaflets in the bin on the way out, and looked at his watch. It was 7 pm, the ideal time for a quick pint or two of Fuller's Pride to relieve all the stress before getting the taxi home.

A little while later Millicent was asking how he got on at the surgery. Hugh repeated the conversation with the doctor, and alcohol was clearly noticeable on his breath. She wasn't at all certain that he was going to take any notice of the advice the G. P. had given. Her husband was a stubborn man, and she was alarmed at how big a shock he would appear to need to make him realise that he was drinking in the last chance saloon. She was upset, and once he was otherwise occupied, she hid herself away in her bedroom for a while and had a little weep. He never knew that had happened. He was also unaware that from then on she had decided to keep a closer eye on him, and try to steer him gently away from his lemming lifestyle.

CHAPTER 13

Monsoon and Tellytubbies

(Tuesday 1st May to Friday 4th May 2012)

Hectic was not the word, it would have been better to say frenetic, to describe the frenzy of events beginning to evolve after the board meeting on 19th April which set the wheels in motion for the transformation of the company from NerdiSoft to 1stCitySoft and from small beer to global player. Norman's work had been well received, and he continued to finalise the latest batch of games software on schedule and entirely as promised. Tiny and Hugh had visited potential new premises in Chelmsford on the Dukes Park Estate, and the Hedgerows Business Park. They had made a choice to move to the latter of the two based upon the quality of the proposition, the budget they had allocated, and the image presented. Gordon had been off sick diagnosed with stress instead of being very busy pulling the accounts together, but only one man seemed to have reservations about that. Everybody looked forward to a rejuvenating weekend starting as usual with the Friday night get together in the Two Brewers.

The man with a Porsche was more keen than usual to get home, and even broke his normal pattern of driving back to Chelmsford via Stanway, Tiptree, Maldon, and Hatfield Peveril just to save a few minutes on the journey. He whizzed back along the A12, so that he could get half an hour in the Excel gym in between arriving home, and going for a meal in Prezzo.

So that he wouldn't miss his Friday evening call from Leiston he had his landline divert calls to his mobile, and just as he and Clarisa were finishing their meal his mobile phone played his downloaded tone, a clip from Bruno Mars "You're amazing, just the way you are."

Norman was surprised when he answered. Instead of his dad saying "Ey Oop, son, 'ow yer diddlin'?" it was his sister, whom he seldom spoke to on the phone, greeting him with "Hello, Bruv. Wha's Uuup?"

"Hello, Cher, this is unexpected. How are things with you? Is Dad alright?"

"I'm OK thank you. Yes, Dad's fine. He's at the AGM of his clay pigeon shooting club. So, I thought I'd give you a ring, and tell you my news."

"What's the latest with you then?"

"Well, I've now left the Norfolk Enchants. I was fed up with having to go up to Gillingham Dam to play, and then losing and getting covered in mud and cowpats every week. I've joined Leiston Lionesses. They play on a proper ground not a ploughed field churned up by cattle, and it's not far away. They're second in the league, and looking at promotion this season."

"Wow! That's brilliant, Cher. Well done."

Cher had obviously forgotten that her brother was in Leiston when she had first given the news of her impending transfer, but he just humoured her.

She continued. "And there's more. I've got a new girlfriend, Helen, and she's the captain of the Lionesses."

"Ah! I see! That's crafty."

"Oh don't be like that, bruv. I'm very happy."

"I'm glad for you, Sis'. How's Mum?"

"Still annoying me and Dad with her selective deafness, and her uncanny ability to misunderstand almost everything we say."

"Oh don't be like that, Cher. She's not that bad."

They both laughed, and then she changed the subject and said," There's no game this week, but Dad will be in touch soon, so you can come up to watch me play for the Lionesses."

"And win, for a change."

"Yeah, that'll be good. Right then, I'll let you go off to the pub then. See you, bruv."

"Bye, Cher. Love to Mum and Dad."

Norman and Clarisa left Prezzo, and skirted round the edge of the building keeping as much under cover as possible. It had been raining on and off all day, but as if to finish off the day with a grand evening crescendo the frequent showers had now turned into a full blown monsoon. People scattered around this part of town with umbrellas blown inside out, dodging puddles, and veering out of the target zone of cars splashing their way from the car park.

Back in the apartment, they both changed quickly into their chosen outfits, avoiding the temptation to enjoy a frenzied grope with each other. It was fancy dress at the Brewers, and they were going as Mickey and Minnie Mouse. Apart from the rain, that was another good reason for driving to the Brewers. Even with the windscreen wipers on maximum they were still unable to provide a completely clear view through the lashing rainstorm. Only the ducks and swans cruising up and down the Chelmer alongside the Hub revelled in the deluge.

At about the same time, a taxi arrived at Avalon House to pick up Hugh. He was dressed as Roy Chubby Brown, and if it hadn't been for the torrential rain he would have had no qualms about walking down to the Brewers dressed like that. He would no doubt have stopped off at all the habitual watering holes along the way as well. The Taxi driver, Pavel, expecting to see him in his normal attire, was becoming ever more convinced he would never understand the strange ways of the English. Not least of all because he was greeted with a tirade of over the top bad language. At this time the jolly fatman was going to play the part of Roy Chubby Brown as authentically as he possibly could.

One minute later Pavel drew up outside Tiny's, and things went from bad to worse when someone looking like Alan Sugar stepped into his cab, pointed at him, and said "You're fired!"

Soon the taxi arrived at the Brewers, at exactly the same time as the Porsche. Pavel sat in his cab agape as Mickey and Minnie Mouse, Roy Chubby Brown, and Alan Sugar greeted each other and wandered into the pub together. Gordon and Co. had not arrived yet, but already assembled was a perverse collection of characters, including tarts and tramps, Henry the Eighth, 2 Freddie Mercury's, Dame Edna Everidge, and a Fairy Queen. They moved to the bar, where Caroline was fittingly dressed as a French Maid, and ordered their drinks. It was 2 pints of Fuller's Pride, a J2O, and a white wine spritzer.

Then all present turned for the entrance of the Vicarage Road mob, which had just arrived in the car park. Speculation was rife that after the frequency of Hugh's jibes about it; they would turn up as the Village People just to annoy him. They were all wrong, but were not disappointed when instead they arrived dressed as the Tellytubbies to whoops of delight, and ripples of applause. For a few moments the Teletubby cluster caused the jolly fatman a panic pang as he had a flashback to his recent dream, but he didn't let himself worry about the strangely prophetic aspects of that for more than a few moments. It was his prerogative even dressed as Roy Chubby Brown to survey them all one at a time offering his usual acerbic wit.

"I'm confused," he said pointing to the purple tellytubby with a triangular antenna, "Which one of the Village people are you supposed to be?"

"None of them," a recognisable Gordon answered indignantly, "I'm Tinkywinky."

"More like Twankywanky." he smiled, and then added, "What have you got in the red bag? Is it the company accounts, or a stash of cash?"

The jibes were being ignored, and so the joker moved along to Ike.

"Good typecasting Tipsywipsy. You're a gardener, and you really are a stubborn sod, with a dipstick on your head."

"It's Dipsy, you moron." Ike replied, and turned away.

Next it was Spike's turn, and Hugh was totally delighted that he was Laa-Laa, yellow, with a curly antenna, which he felt was another probably accidental typecast. But he had to be careful not to imply anything untoward with regard to recent events at the Ball's house. So he just stared at the scruffy decorator and said, "How do you do La-di-da? Can you get police broadcasts on that curly aerial?"

They continued their healthy disrespect for each other, and Scruffbag just ignored him for the moment.

"And finally," reported the fatman, "We have a red Poo. No, I'm wrong; it's a poof with a ponytail blowing bubbles."

There was no response from Mike, as he moved off towards the dartboard, and soon the Tellytubbies were playing Killer with one of the Freddie Mercurys and Dame Edna Everidge.

Many pints of Fuller's Pride flowed, and the entertainment was provided by guest comedian Roy Chubby Brown, slightly more disgusting than usual, but only to remain in character. Norman told all who would listen about his recent trip to Yorkshire with Stanley, and the characters that he'd met there, and Roy Chubby Brown seemed pleased to hear about the confrontation between Noble senior and Hector Blunt at the Durham Ox. When the idea that they would be returning to Yorkshire later on during the year, when the Wellington Heifer reopened was introduced, he insisted that he wanted to accompany them.

Again the evening eventually developed into the Ramsbottom Olympics. The darts match started normally, if it was possible to picture 2 Freddie Mercurys battling it out with Twankywanky and Poo, but when the fatter of the two Freddie's mis-threw a dart that landed on and pierced Twankywanky's red bag he wasn't very happy. The Tellytubbies outfits were on hire and had to be returned intact and undamaged. But by the time the darts had been won by Twankywanky all was forgiven. Then followed another incredibly messy pints of lemonade drinking contest, during which one Tellytubby was drenched from head to foot, and resigned to losing his deposit. Roy Chubby Brown was the winner this time, and he managed to avoid showering everybody with a lemonade stream shooting out of his nose. He was very pleased to defeat his archrival gay Gordon. When the night concluded with the arm wrestling contest, Roy Chubby Brown beat La-di-da in a rasping, vicious, very loud, and disgusting fart finale. But that was after there had been a fight between one of the Freddie Mercury's and Henry the Eighth. Freddy accused Henry of cheating by holding on to the table with his free hand. Henry won the arm wrestling heat but his opponent then punched him and shouted, "You fuckin' cheat. I want a rematch."

Caroline came over to adjudicate, and declared that they should start again, but they just carried on arguing. It was very amusing to see Freddie Mercury and Henry the Eighth both chucked out of the Brewers by a French Maid.

Altogether another riotous Friday evening in the Two Brewers was drawing to its close, but not before a dead-ringer for Alan Sugar had pointed his finger at, and fired everybody, and the jolly fatman began to hatch another joke at the Village People's expense.

Pavel turned up with the usual taxi, and instead of calling out "Taxi for Mr Ramsbottom" he attempted some humour and blurted "Taxi for Roy Chubby Brown and Sir Alan Sugar. Yes! Brown and Sugar. Ho! Ho! Brown Sugar, I think that by the Rolling Stones."

His word association humour, which he thought was hilarious and very British, got a tumbleweed response from his passengers. He stood, confused and disappointed in the midst of the pub revellers, still wondering if he would ever understand the British sense of humour, and then with a look of disappointment on his face he reverted to "Taxi for Mr Rambottom!"

As they went to the taxi, Hugh turned to the Tellytubbies and shouted out, "Hey, you lot are you going back to the Tubbytronic Superdome now for a bit of tellytubby rumpy-pumpy?" Seconds later a car turned on to Springfield Road carrying the Tellytubbies all with their middle fingers in the air.

The taxi driven by a confused Pavel, made the short trip homeward in the pouring rain. Then it stopped on the corner of Springfield Road and Tyrell's Close. The joker had been hatching a last quip of the night at the cabman's expense, but before he could say anything Pavel spoke up, "I have him in my taxi, Mr Sugar, he very nice man, give me big tip."

Hugh looked at Tiny as if to say" Shall I? Yes, I will, it's too good to miss." Then he shook his head and said," Pavel, you are a little liar. I don't believe you about Alan Sugar. He's got his own chauffeur driven Rolls Royce. Don't you ever watch The Apprentice?"

Pavel looked as if he'd just had the rug pulled out from underneath him. Once again as the two friends got out of the taxi, they left the cabbie confused.

"By the way, mate, what happened to that bloke who the police arrested stealing Tina's precious goldfish?" asked the fatman.

"Oh, he got off with a caution for trespassing in the garden, not enough evidence to convict him of stealing." Tiny replied.

"I wonder what happened to the goldfish. I suppose he must have swallowed the little beggars then." Hugh laughed, "Goodnight, mate."

Then they both chuckled their way happily back to their homes.

CHAPTER 14

Traditions and Sweet Revenge

(Saturday 5th May 2012)

It was a long held tradition that all the boys would congregate at Avalon House for the F. A. Cup Final every year. This had started long ago when the rich kid on the block had the biggest house, with the biggest television, and the money to buy all the beer and fast food needed to indulge in, and possibly celebrate, such an event. Times had changed, and none of the lads were exactly walking on their uppers, but Hugh was still the richest man they knew, and so the tradition persisted. Now he had a top of the range high definition 100 inch screen television installed in his playroom, and all the technology for freeze frame, instant replay, zoom in and out, multiscreen viewing etc. ad nauseam. Millicent had been despatched over to Tyrell's Close, where she and Tina would enjoy a bottle of Moscatel de Valencia, some Thornton's chocolates, and a prolonged period of girlie chat.

Ramsbottom and sons, Tom, Dick and Harry, all perversely attired in Chelmsford City shirts, were installed ready for the action at 4 pm, as Gary Lineker and John Motson were plying their way through the BBC's version of the build-up. Football pundits from top teams watched clips from previous rounds, and offered their obviously biased views of who would play, who would win, who would score, who were the bad boys, good boys, sad boys. At least on the BBC there wasn't an irritating interruption every 10 minutes for the same adverts for the same companies, so annoying and repetitive that they might fuel a telly watching hooligan tendency. As the sponsor of the F. A. Cup for 2012 was Budweiser, the fatman wouldn't have approved at all. To him the oldest and best by a mile football competition in the world should be sponsored by a company making real ale, like Shepherd Neame, not Budweiser which he regarded as pseudo-European American brewed piss-water. He liked tradition as much as he appreciated history, and it also galled him that the kick-off was at 5:15 instead of the traditional 3:00 pm. This was claimed to be in order to fit in with residual Premier League games, but was more likely an indicator to future games kick-off times being influenced by, or perhaps determined by, television coverage requirements.

In quick succession the entourage arrived, and mine host took great delight as each of them rang the bell at the entrance to his substantial car park, and announced themselves into the intercom to be allowed entry through the automatic wrought iron gates. He watched on his CCTV as each arrived, and felt a delightful warm smugness as he delayed them all slightly. Soon they had all assembled. Tiny had walked from across the road, and was wearing a Chelsea shirt. The Village People came together. Scruffbag wore a Liverpool shirt, but the others were just casually dressed with no football allegiances illustrated. Norman was sadly missing, as life had recently changed for him in a big way. Since he had met Clarisa, he had turned up less and less at all the boy's get-togethers. Even the Friday night at the Two Brewers regular booze-up was now a less frequent affair for him. The Cup Final coincided with Clarisa's birthday and her Normie had planned a day out in London for the occasion. The jolly fatman was upset at his nephew's failure to attend this traditional event, but he had an ace up his sleeve, and once the usual crew had assembled he plied them with beers, and crisps, and nuts, and then explained.

"I know you fellas won't mind, but I thought it was about time that we got our revenge on that little prat Terry Smith for what he did down the Brewers a while ago."

"What are you on about, Rambo?" Spike sniped.

"You know, when I pulled that joke on Nobless about him going to the Sexual Health Clinic, and then had to cover it up when he brought Clarisa along to the Brewers. It was all going smoothly until big mouth Terry turned up and upset her."

"Hey, that was your practical joke going too far really," Gordon said, "But what is it that you've got in mind?"

"Well, I've invited Terry along to watch the match with us." he said, as everybody groaned.

"I can't stand the little shit for brains. Why did you do that?" Spike questioned, and Ike and Mike nodded in agreement.

"Patience, batty man, I will explain." Hugh replied. "I thought we would get him absolutely shit-faced, out of his tiny brain, and then put him on the train leaving Colchester at 9:30 tonight bound for Norwich. By the time he gets there and comes round he'll be stranded in Norfolk for the night. I've arranged for Ahmad and one of his brothers to pick him up and take him to Colchester in a cab, and then they'll drag him on to the train."

The gang all broke out in smiles to cries of "Yes! Yes! That'll teach the little prat a lesson."

"Oh, and I thought we'd first of all dress him up in this before he goes." he went on, holding up an Ipswich shirt and shorts, "That'll make him popular in Norwich."

There were more grins and much delight at a well thought out plan, and when Terry arrived a few minutes later he had no inkling what was in store for him. Everybody hated him, but they greeted him with polite small talk, and an apparently warm welcome to the event.

"What can I get you?" asked mine host. Terry wanted a bottle of Old Speckled Hen.

The joker had the thought, "Wasted on that useless little dickhead, Budweiser was made for idiots like him.", but provided the requested beer with a smile.

The match began, but the football was incidental. Really, this was just another excuse to have a few beers and let off some steam. Mine host worked his way through a crate of Old Speckled Hen, partly assisted by his best mate, but the rest of the crew were content with the stack of Budweiser that he had bought almost as a joke, and the 3 boys were strictly limited to fruity soft drinks.

Chelsea's early dominance showed with a goal in the 11th minute by the Brazilian Santos do Nascimento Ramires, quietly celebrated by Tiny. Liverpool failed to live up to the footballing talent they had on display.

At about the time that Chelsea scored Norman and Clarisa were walking hand in hand along the Mall towards Buckingham Palace. They had booked a table at a lovely Italian restaurant in Westminster, and later on in the evening as a surprise the young man had arranged a romantic twilight flight on the London Eye.

Soon it was halftime, and the right time for a top-up of the beers for the boys, including a 2nd Hen for Terry. The eager prank player's thoughts were," OK, he's pacing himself a bit, but he'll get a taste for it and show his true colours eventually, and then we'll really load him up, and get him pissed."

Typically for Hugh halftime was also time to educate.

"Did you know this was the 131st F. A. Cup Final?" the fatman said to no one in particular, and everyone present "And that means the first one was when?"

The company accountant was quick to fall into the trap.

"It's obvious, isn't it?" he replied," The first Cup Final was in 1881, that's 2012 minus 131!"

The quizmaster grinned inanely, delighted that the bean counter had fallen so easily, and retorted, "No, gay-boy, you're wrong, it was 1872, because they didn't play the finals around the 1st and 2nd World Wars."

He then cheekily added, "That was 1916 to 1919, and 1940 to 1945."

He knew that that statement would result in further confusion and disagreement.

"No, you're wrong, that can't be," was the insistent reply, "The 2 World Wars were 1914 to 18 and 1939 to 45."

"Yes, but you're forgetting the F. A. Cup competition begins each year in the summer of the year before the final is played. It's not just for the big boys you know; almost any team affiliated to the Football Association can enter."

"You smug bastard." was the reply with a snarl. That was round one to the joker.

"Did I tell you how well Chelmsford City did in the F. A. Cup?" City's number one fan continued, "This year they reached the 2nd round again, and took Macclesfield to a replay." "Groans all round." snorted Gordon, "We've heard that a dozen times already."

Hugh changed the subject, and continued," You know why Liverpool are losing don't you?"

"Because Chelsea are the better team?" enquired Mike.

"No, it's because half their fans are stuck in transit. Bleedin' Richard Branson's Virgin Trains mob have cancelled nearly all the direct services between Liverpool and London for maintenance work. I think Branson's probably a Chelsea supporter."

"I still think Chelsea are the better team, and they'll win it." Mike concluded, and sure enough early in the 2nd half Chelsea emphasised their superiority when Didier Drogba doubled their lead in the 52nd minute. It was 2 - 0 to Chelsea and for once Spike was completely silent brooding in the corner, but not the least bit embarrassed to be wearing a Liverpool shirt.

Every dog shall have his day, and Scruffbag had a brief moment of his in the 64th minute, when Andy Carroll scored for Liverpool. The decorator jumped up and punched the air with a burst of enthusiasm, and even Mike briefly showed some excitement. A very amused host had to respond in his usual vein with "Steady on there, boy. He may have a better ponytail than you, but that doesn't mean he's a candidate for Gay Pride."

Mike looked him straight in the eye, with a snarl, and held up a middle finger in salute. Mine host laughed and went off to refill the crisps and nuts.

Controversy raged over a header from Andy Carroll in the 81st minute that appeared to be palmed onto the underside of the bar and then away by goalkeeper Petr Cech. The referee consulted with a linesman, and decided the ball had not crossed the line. Despite late pressure from Liverpool, Chelsea won in the end, and nobody in Avalon House really cared.

For City's number one fan it wasn't real football, like his beloved Clarets. It was just a team owned by and assembled with the money of a Russian billionaire, playing a team owned by a rich American.

Terry Smith had been quiet throughout the game, almost inconspicuous, and the plan to get revenge appeared to have backfired, when at the end of the game, he refused a 3rd beer explaining, "No, mate, I'm on soft drinks from now on. I'm on a promise tonight. Got something exciting lined up."

All the rest of the gang were listening in, and there was a definite sense of deflation.

"Exciting? How's that? Still trying for a baby, you and Sharon, are you?" the prankster enquired with a nudge.

"Yes, mate, that's the problem." Terry explained, "The missus is pregnant, and the shop's been shut ever since she found out. But I've got alternative plans. I bumped into an old flame, Teresa at a wedding a few weeks ago, and she still fancies me. So, seeing as Sharon's staying at her mum's tonight, well

I've booked a Travelodge in Needham Market, and I'm away for a dirty night. I've got to go about 8:30 and pick the lady up."

Immediate thoughts were, "That's no lady if she wants a dirty night away with Terry." and secondly, "Shit! That's the plan to dump him pissed in Norwich scuttled. We need a plan B." But Hugh didn't voice his thoughts, he just played along with Terry's bravado in announcing his dirty little plans to everyone and said," You randy little sod, Terry. Shall I get you a fruit juice or something?"

With the match over, mine host invited all present to move to the boys playroom, and make use of the X-Boxes to play computer games. Tom's X-Box was set up to play the new version of Viking Ninja Holocaust 9, Dick's played R. McGeddon's Nerd World Apocalypse, and Harry's was set up for Beer Festival Bastards Final Frontier. Due to the fact the Ramsbottom juniors were super techno-brats, and everybody except Terry had now had several beers, it was a foregone conclusion the youngsters in the Ramsbottom household would have enough expertise, not to mention sobriety, to win.

Once installed in the playroom, the jolly fatman took orders for takeaways, Pepperoni Pizzas for the 3 boys, and curries for the grown ups, Chicken Jalfrezi, Lamb Bhuna, and Beef Madras, with a huge side order of onion bhajis, samosas, pakoras, poppadoms, and chutneys, and as he phoned the orders in to the Papa John's and the Sitar Tandoori, he had a brainwave.

"I'll get that snotty arse-wipe. He'll be sorry," he chuckled to himself, as a plan B formed in his pickled, but still highly inventive brain cells.

After the takeaway meal arrived they all sat down in the kitchen, at the massive antique oak table, cracked open a few more beers, and indulged in the Indian feast to their heart's absolute and satiated contents. Despite his arrangement to spend a dirty evening at the Travelodge with a lady of dubious taste, Terry also joined in with the curry fest, a fact that prompted a big smile from mine host, and helped enormously with the deception involved in plan B. But Terry's request not to ply him with any more alcohol was honoured, so the joker mixed him up a pint or two of fruity cocktails to go along with the food.

It wasn't long before 8:30 rolled round and Terry had to go. The householder went out to the car park with him, opened the gate for him, and waved him on his way with a, "Bye, Terry, hope you enjoyed it. Have a good time tonight in Needham Market, you dirty little rat."

By the time Smithy had disappeared up Springfield Road, the prankster had all but exploded trying to hold his laughter in, and he couldn't wait to go back in and tell the crew what he had done. After nearly being sick with laughing, he composed himself, put on the straightest face he could muster, and returned to the kitchen.

"Shame about the plan backfiring, "said Gordon, "Makes you wish you hadn't invited the slimy little bastard here, doesn't it?"

"Er, Yeees," replied the joker," Cracking his face into the biggest grin, and causing a breakout of confused looks all around the table. The head of the gay clan was most confused, and Ike and Mike just looked at each other, both probably thinking that their mate had finally slipped into insanity. Only Tiny remained unperturbed, smiling quietly to himself, because he knew his long term friend only too well. Hugh was by this time rolling about on the floor, holding his stomach, aching with mirth, and almost foaming at the mouth.

"What's going on, fatboy? Have you lost your marbles or something?" Gordon pleaded in exasperation, as the belly laugh became ever more intense. Hugh's face was split literally from ear to ear, and he was laughing so much, he was truly in pain.

"Well, I...I...I..." the fatman corpsed, trying to get his words out, and then broke into violent hiccups, which made things even worse, "Oh God! Hic! I..., Well..., Hic! You... Hic!" and then he rushed out of the room heading for the big white telephone.

The bean counter was becoming annoyed and said," What's a matter with laughing boy? I've never seen him like this before."

The 1stCitySoft chairman put a finger across his mouth pointing upwards, and replied, "Patience, wait and see! When he's composed himself, he'll be able to tell us. He's obviously very pleased with himself over something, probably something to do with Terry."

After a few minutes mine host came back through the door still grinning, and saying, "Sorry about that, Hic! I don't know what came over me." and then just sat down and stared at the wall taking deep breaths There was a brief silence, and then all present simultaneously turned in his direction and pleaded loudly, "Well, come on. Tell us what's going on."

He could hardly speak it out amongst the insane tittering, but he started as best he could. "Well...... You know Terry was planning a spot of... Hic! Of playing away from home tonight?

Hic! And so I couldn't get him to... Hic! to drink more than 2 beers.

There was a collective, "Yeees."

"And.... and.... and Hic!"

"Here he goes again, get the bucket," advised Gordon.

"And.... and.... and Hic!" repeated Hugh and then took another deep breath, "And he wanted fruit juice, Hic! Instead of beer."

They all hung on every word by now, waiting for the blood of realisation to pour from the stone of an inability to get the words out.

"Well.... that's what he got, Hic! And remember how he commented about how delicious it was? Hic! He said it was the best fruit cocktail he'd ever tasted."

There was another collective, "Yeees.", followed by Mike adding, "God, this is like pulling effing teeth!"

"Well...Hic! Shall I tell you what was in his fruit cocktail?"

He began to dissolve into uncontrollable laughter again.

There was another louder collective, "Yeees.", followed by Ike adding, "If you don't get on with it, I'm going to take you outside and kill you. Slowly!"

He went over to the kitchen cupboard, opened the door and brought 2 bottles out, and was laughing fit to burst, as he only just managed to put them on the table without dropping them. He held the first one up, and said," This is called Chasteberry, real name Agnus Castus, also known as Monk's Pepper, which you can buy in Holland and Barretts. Millicent uses it to help with her PMS, and I crushed some of these capsules into Terry's fruit cocktail."

"Really, what does it do if you're a bloke then?" Tiny asked inquisitively.

The joker was still grinning like a deranged feline monster, but managed to blurt out," It suppresses the libido in men, Hic! It's what's known as, Hic! An anaphrodisiac, it reduces, Hic! testosterone levels."

He was about to explode again, but the penny was at last beginning to drop, and all the crew broke out in wide grins.

"And how much did you give him?" the accountant asked.

"Oh, not many......Only 7or 8 capsules."

They all looked at each in utter disbelief, mouths agape.

"That'll stop the dirty little git having his evil way then," asserted Ike beginning to giggle.

"Well, maybe. Hic! So I thought I'd add some insurance. Hic! Because I don't know how quickly the Monk's Pepper works. Hic!"

They all waited grinning for the next instalment, wondering what was in the other bottle, and then he continued," Here we have something you may be familiar with, it's Senokot syrup. Hic!" He began to giggle uncontrollably again.

"We had it leftover from a recent prescription for Tom. Hic! You're supposed..... You're supposed to take..... take 2 teaspoons. Hic! But I gave him ...... half a bottle in his fruit cocktail. Hic! All in all....... I think that Terry's very unlikely.... Hic! to be coming tonight...... But he surely will be going."

At his point, the jolly fatman couldn't control his laughter any longer, and began rolling about on the floor again, but this time he wasn't alone. Everybody erupted into a relentless spate of unrestrained giggling. Tom, Dick and Harry came back from the playroom wondering what all the noise was about, and just at the moment when all control was lost in an orgy of laughter, Millicent and Tina arrived, to find 3 young boys staring goggle-eyed at 5 grown men with tears rolling down their cheeks thrashing about in an amorphous giggling heap on the kitchen floor.

"Just another Cup Final night, at the Ramsbottoms!" she smiled making for the kettle.

So, the kettle boiled, the coffee was made, and eventually the 5 grown men stopped being silly, and came back to some semblance of normality. The sensible wife set about getting the 3 boys off to bed, Tina took Tiny off home, and only the the gay entourage remained in Avalon House. Quickly realising the situation the joker couldn't resist reverting to his usual standard of jibe.

"Hey!" he piped up jovially," Just because it's me and you bunch of poofs left, don't jump to the conclusion that we can turn this into an unofficial Gay Pride convention."

"Why do you do that?" was the annoyed retort from Spike.

"Do what?" answered Hugh, being unperturbed at ruffling the Scruffbag's feathers after what he had witnessed over at Tyrell's Close a few weeks ago.

Feathers were truly ruffled, mostly due to the booze, and he went on, "You always revert to your homophobic prejudices whenever it suits you to crack a joke at those present. We are all just people, with feelings and sensitivities you know, and I'm getting well fed up with all this anti-gay stuff."

"I'm not anti-gay. You're too sensitive. You're all my mates aren't you, or why would you be here?"

"But why do you have to persistently take the piss out of us being gay? Are you homophobic?" the scruffy decorator continued.

The joker wasn't ruffled, but he was about to enjoy what was occurring, and replied," You fellas know me, and you also know I take the piss out of everyone, not just gays. Look at Nobless, he's a continual target of my jokes and my pranks, and most of the time he just turns the other cheek. Why can't you all do that as well? Like I said you're all too sensitive about it, and homophobic isn't a proper word anyway."

"What do you mean?" asked Spike.

"Well," he said, "A phobia is an irrational fear or hatred of something, and I don't fear or hate any of you, you are all my mates. You've been invited here today by me, to eat my food, drink my beer, and enjoy my hospitality in my house. Every one of you has been helped by me in some way. Isn't that true?"

There was silence and downward looks from them all, but the subject wasn't stopping there. "Scruff, I loaned you money to start your business. Ike, I paid your garage bill when your van broke down in January, and Mike, I got the credit card company off your back when you screwed up your finances last year. When it comes to Gordon…..,"

He had to be careful here because he hadn't let the cat out of the bag yet as to his suspicions about the reluctance to produce the company accounts.

He repeated, "And when it comes to Gordon, well he owes his job at 1stCitySoft to me and the boss. That's a fact!"

The accountant looked at the other three and then at the Hugh, and asked, "What have you got against gays though, fatso?"

"Absolutely nothing, but us straight people have this gay liberation bollocks shoved in our faces every fucking day of the week, and every hour of the day. On top of that political correctness says we're no longer allowed to take the piss out of each other. Well, I say arseholes to political correctness. I will take the piss out of what I want."

"So that means that you can take the piss out of our sexuality does it?" asked Mike.

"Yes," said the fatman, "And likewise you can take the piss out of mine."

That made the collective gay entourage think a bit. There was a pregnant pause.

The chairman of the debate felt the need to lighten the conversation, and replied smiling convincingly, " I have nothing against gays, my friends, except that you've high-jacked the word gay for a different meaning. Not many years ago, gay meant cheerful and brightly coloured. So you, my pink friends, need to bloody cheer up to live up to the label you've misappropriated. Anybody want another Budweiser?"

The tension was broken; they all smiled and raised their middle fingers in the usual salute, and to a man all gratefully accepted another beer.

"Look!" said the joker, wanting to draw the discussion to a conclusion, and to have the last word for a second time, "As I said, you're all my mates, and I wouldn't hesitate for one minute to offer you help when you need it. I take the piss out of everyone and everything, and I don't give a hoot about political correctness. I'm unconcerned if you want to be heterosexual, homosexual, bisexual, transsexual, or bloody dodecahedral sexual. Whatever floats your boat, that's OK with me. I don't care if anyone wants to stick light bulbs up their arse, or bloody lighted roman candles, or doner kebabs with jalapeno peppers, but please don't call it alternative sexuality. Live and let live, each to his own, and have an effin' sense of humour about it will you? And for fuck's sake stop shoving your sexuality in my face every second of the day."

This time there was a silence with a warmer glow. It might have been the beer, but more than likely this gay lobby had seen a light. Hugh was Hugh, and he had his own view on the world, and it seemed that nothing or no-one was ever likely to change that.

Then the jolly fatman mischievously added," Now, if anyone wants to accuse me of being xenophobic, then I'll hold up my hands. I hate bloody Germans, especially when we meet them in a penalty shootout."

He grinned again. They all knew he was joking; after all, via his nephew Norman, their host had a German side to his family.

CHAPTER 15

Luftwaffe Reprise

(Tuesday 8th May 2012)

Brunhilda Doenitz had arrived in Scotland in December 1980 by accident, an irony that wasn't lost on her. She had been on her way to the wedding of her sister Lisalotte, to Stanley Noble in Yorkshire, when her plane was diverted from Leeds/Bradford by dense fog, and she landed late and annoyed in Glasgow. Certain that she would miss the wedding, she sent a terse wedding telegram to Lisalotte and Stanley which just read "Have a nice wedding. Staying in Scotland. See you later."

She decided to make good use of her bad fortune, and to visit Eaglesham where one of her many heroes had parachuted from his plane in 1941. She knew the story well of how Rudolph Hess had been stupid enough to fly solo to England, so that he could negotiate with Churchill for peace before Hitler launched Operation Barbarossa against Russia in July 1941. How he was only 400 hundred odd miles off course for Chartwell, and his plane had eventually crash landed near Eaglesham, south of Glasgow. Then he was arrested and became a prisoner of war. At the Nuremburg trials he was sentenced to life imprisonment, and spent the rest of his days languishing in Spandau Prison, Berlin, until his death in 1987. When Fraulein Doenitz landed in Glasgow, she saw a parallel with her hero, and it was too good an opportunity to miss, to be able to visit the town where one of her heroes had met his early and humiliating demise. As a lady of genuine Teutonic stock she was proud of her German roots, paradoxically her strength and her weakness at the same time. Her personal heroes were nearly all Germanic icons, and it would be true to say that all of them had flaws, a fact which she found somehow endearing.

She was immediately enraptured with the rugged beauty of the Scottish terrain, and was amazed at how the lack of light pollution in the countryside, and clear, crisp air, displayed the glory of every star in the Milky Way filling the skies. After 2 weeks touring around, and visiting Glasgow, Loch Lomond, Edinburgh, and Perth she eventually settled in Blairgowrie, and found herself a job as a German/English translator. She quickly grew to love her adopted country, and after spending 32 years in Blairgowrie, she considered herself at least a bit Scottish. Sister Lisalotte had maintained some German traits, including bleached blonde hair, and learning pigeon English at best, but Brunhilda had made concessions to her new Vaterland. She liked to wear tartan, and had adopted a gingerish tint to her natural blonde locks.

If little sister was all mouth and trousers, all front and no substance, lots of red lipstick and little grey matter, then big sister was as different as could be. When they were younger they were recognisably sisters, definitely honed from the same fine blade, and both were amply proportioned big-bosomed, blonde women, but over the years more than subtle differences had been accentuated between the two of them.

While they had been working in the Bierkellers at the Munich Beer Festivals, they could both be described as great bustling clod-hoppers of girls. But it was clear which sister was the fairy elephant. Whereas one of the sisters could carry 8 huge steins of beer without spilling a drop, the other had, despite her size, a gazelle-like lightness, a daintiness about her, and only managed 6 at best. She was ambidextrous, and could write equally well with both hands. Her sister was single-minded, but could get muddled equally well with both halves of her brain.

The older sister by just under 2 years WAS fur coat and no knickers, red hat no drawers, strong of arm but certainly not thick of head. She was a positive, extrovert and intelligent woman. To her, political correctness was utter nonsense, and she called it as it really was. She took no prisoners, and would have been a perfect foil for Hugh Ramsbottom.

The little town of Blairgowrie, nestling at the foot of the Grampian Mountains had grown in the intervening years, so much so that by 2012 it was the "twin burgh" of Blairgowrie and Rattray. It was the raspberry growing centre of the Universe, and himbeere as they were known in Germany were the exiled German lady's favourite fruit. Blairgowrie was also only a short distance from the village of Bankfoot, the location of the Macbeth Experience, where she worked part time every summer season. She adored the intrigue and mystery surrounding Macbeth. The question as to whether he was the murderer portrayed in the "Scottish Play" by William Shakespeare, or an 11th century Scottish warrior king fascinated her. She was a romantic soul, and also loved the connections with and proximity to Glamis Castle, which was not only the setting for Shakespeare's Macbeth, but also the childhood home of Elisabeth Bowes-Lyon, the Queen Mother. Despite the overtly republican credentials of her many heroes, she was resolute in her admiration for the British Royal Family.

She thought, "Weren't they really all German anyway?"

On the evening of her birthday on May 8th she had been at a local protest meeting, to campaign against plans to erect a wind turbine on the top of Balduff Hill, so close to the local beauty spot of Reekie Linn, a beautiful and impressive waterfall in Genisla. She had two very strong personal reasons for resisting this planned project.

First of all, Balduff Hill was a favourite launch site for her hang gliding exploits, one of her various aeronautical pursuits. Secondly, the Reekie Linn waterfall held great sentimental significance for her. A long time ago, shortly after her accidental adoption of Scotland as her new home, she had fallen in love with a young man called Henry McVitie, and they had often made their way up to the waterfall in the twilight of the long Scottish July evenings, They were "roaming in the gloaming" as the well known song would have said. And it was there that she was certain she had conceived her only son Duncan, lying on a dark green and blue Mack tartan blanket listening to the incessant, powerful, overwhelming rush of the waterfall in heavy spate, as a balmy evening lingered on into seductive, quieter semi-darkness. She didn't have any "green" disagreements with wind turbine construction. She thought they were an excellent idea. It was just a case of NIMBY- "not in my back yard" and she was determined to stop the erection of a wind turbine on HER hill next to HER waterfall.

During her time in Germany she had been an ardent fan of an electronic music band called Tangerine Dream, and particularly their famed work Phaedra released in 1974. When she became an accidental Brit, with an uncharacteristic capriciousness she switched her allegiance to Hawkwind, a space rock group, and as they had gone "In Search of Space" in 1971, so she went in search of Hawkwind in 1980. She found them in concert at the Perth Theatre, and it was there that she met the brawny, handsome 20 year old Henry McVitie, who at that time had the nickname "Biscuits" for rather obvious reasons. It was this Scottish patriot who would become her son Duncan's father.

A few years before he had become disillusioned with his job as a builder's labourer, and having learned to play blues guitar, and equipped with an abundance of youthful audacity, he had engineered bumping into Dave Brock the leader of Hawkwind, with the idea of persuading him to let him join the band. The space cowboys were nothing like a blues band, but Dave was amused by the boy's bravado, and offered him a job as a roadie. When Brunhilda cheekily sneaked backstage and into the green room at the Perth Theatre, Henry was three sheets to the wind, and so wearing his beer goggles he mistook her for the legendary Stacia. She was a big Irish girl who had been a regular attraction at early 70's Hawkwind concerts, dancing nude and often adorned by iridescent paint. He was ribbed by the band members for uttering the classic, "Hello Babe, I didn't recognise you with your clothes on!"

She didn't mind his drunkenness, she'd seen plenty of drunken men in the Bierkellers, and he was her kind of man. He wore a kilt, rode a motorcycle, and was a ginger-haired, long-bearded Scottish patriot. Soon they were inseparable, and she followed him all over Scotland and the North of England as the band continued their tour. But she knew he was tied to his touring life with the band, a nomad who wouldn't be shackled, and so when she found she was carrying his child, there was no way she was going to tie him down.

Her only beloved son wasn't the sordid product of a one night stand however, because through the years groupie and roadie had frequently met up again, and rekindled their fire, whenever Hawkwind, and later also Motorhead were on tour. He became the love of her life, and she was willing to make this sacrifice for him.

Although when they met, he bore the nickname of "Biscuits", throughout most their long intermittent relationship she knew him by the name of "Tusker".

This came about when Henry worked as a roadie for Lemmy and Motorhead. He lost the epithet "Biscuits" one night when the intimacy, craziness, and camaraderie of travelling on the road together with the band led to a drunken willy measuring contest. Bernard, one of the other roadies, who claimed to have the biggest plonker in Scotland, was devastated to find that "Biscuits" was such a big boy, a well endowed, indeed, donkey-blessed individual. He immediately renamed the boy because of his elephantine proportions, and he adopted his new name with pride, and so became known by all as "Tusker".

The day after Brunhilda's 60th birthday, a Tuesday, was a fresh and breezy May morning, and she awoke happy and content. After a breakfast of pumpernickel black rye bread with marmalade, and strong coffee, she said "Aufwiedersehen" to her son Duncan as he made his way off to work in Perth. She was proud of her son, who had qualified as an accountant 7years ago, and was now working at a company called Perth Open Office Services.

P.O.O.S. were a major company, with contracts all over Scotland for the generation and installation of office premises, covering everything from office furniture and computers, to paperclips, and coffee machines. As he left his mother with a routine nonchalance, to enjoy her daily interests, neither of them knew how significant this day would be in their lives, and how their lives would change forever.

After Duncan had left for work, she went down to her den in the cellar, in her small, tidy bungalow on the outskirts of town. It was a place that was habitually out of bounds to her son, her secret place, where she was able to indulge in another one of her passions. She emerged from the cellar an hour later, and loaded up the trailer of her Freelander with her hang-glider. The springtime sun had warmed the heather-clad hills of Angus, sucked up the early morning dew, and it looked like the perfect day for flying had arrived.

Soon she was on her way, fully equipped for another beautiful solo flight. She had many passions, but flying was her most satisfying, and most rewarding. It was flying with a difference, because she combined it with her passion for naturism. She was a founder member of the Blairgowrie and

District Naturist Aeronautics Club. The BADNACers - as they were known, supported many flying disciplines, and these included hang-gliding, micro-lighting, free-fall parachuting, and gliding, all of them nude, and with their own unique risk elements. It was clear that with all of these pursuits, the flyer had to be very, very careful especially when landing. Landing in the wrong place was risky anyway, but even more so when naked.

Brunhilda had always been fascinated by the prospect of being able to soar through the skies, but just ordinary flying on a scheduled airline flight was far too tame, and removed all that was best from the experience. To her it wasn't real flying, it was a boring undertaking. She just considered it as being cocooned in a sterile cylinder together with a hypnotised collection of ignorant morons, whose only purpose in being there was the destination, and to whom the flying experience was mostly a claustrophobic time-consuming nuisance. She just thought "Where was the freedom, the excitement, the wind rushing through your nostrils, and across your bare skin, and the over all feeling of being in control of the elements, and ultimately your own fate?"

Her first introduction to the thrills of real flying came when she had met her kindred spirit, the love of her life. She and "Tusker" had discovered that they had a common interest in flying, and it happened that he regularly went gliding from Portmoak Airfield at Scotlandwell, and was a founder member of Flying Unhindered Club Kinross. She remembered the absolute thrill of that first flight over the Ochil Hill ridges and high over Loch Leven, and the Lomond Hills. On an outstanding clear day with superb visibility, she was ecstatic to see across both the rivers Forth and Tay and as far afield as the Grampian Mountains, all the time mesmerised by the almost silent swooping and soaring of the glider. She was nothing short of knocked-out, hooked, and from that point on flying in all its free forms became a lifelong obsession. Not much later when she had learned to fly solo, she added the naturist element, and that came about because she believed that another one of her heroes had been very fond of flying nude.

Hermann Goering might have been best known as a swaggering, fat, arrogant, Nazi bullyboy, the Luftwaffe chief, who stole art treasures from all over Europe in World War 2 for his personal art collection, and when indicted for war crimes at Nuremburg escaped justice when he managed to commit suicide the day before he was scheduled to be executed. But Fraulein Doenitz preferred to remember him as a veteran of World War I, as an ace fighter pilot with 22 victories, and a recipient of the coveted Blue Max. He was also the last commander of the "Flying Circus", Jagdgeschwader 1; the fighter wing once led by Manfred von Richthofen, "The Red Baron", another of her heroes. In line with her adulation for failed heroes, she also liked Hermann's sense of humour. She was amused that apparently he once wired Hitler after his visit to the Vatican "Mission accomplished. Pope unfrocked. Tiara and pontifical vestments are a perfect fit."

She was unamused that when he had degenerated from the once-dashing and muscular fighter pilot, into a corpulent, even obese, figure of fun, Germans joked about his ego, saying that "He would wear an Admiral's uniform to take a bath.", and joking that "He sits down on his stomach."

Soon after getting her solo gliding credentials, Brunhilda enjoyed the thrill of parachuting from the Perth (Scone) Airfield, and shortly after that from a Dundee airfield near the Tay Bridge. She then became a pioneer of the practice of nude free fall parachuting. Personally she found no difficulty in this, but in training others to enjoy this experience, she quickly discovered there was a requirement for some sort of qualification, and certification. This came about after a series of nude parachuting "accidents" which occurred when participants who had become very excited during the freefall, suddenly relaxed as soon as the parachute opened. The result was a high incidence of what was known as high altitude muck-spreading at 3,000 feet.

She drove confidently, as she had so many times before, from her bungalow in Dunkeld Road through the Blairgowrie town centre, and out along the A926 towards Aylth, then left along the B954 up to Bridge of Craigisla next to Reekie Linn. She then opened a gate onto the farmland that took her off-road up towards the summit of Balduff Hill at 1394 feet above sea level. In brilliant sunshine she carefully assembled her hang-glider, which she had painted red in homage to another of her heroes, and sported a brilliant red sail, and then donned her specially adapted crash helmet. This had been modified to include an MP3 player, which played her favourite gliding tune on a continuous short loop. She never took to the skies without this little extra. Her music of choice was a song she had first heard as a young girl of 14, back in 1966. It was the Royal Guardsmen singing Snoopy versus the Red Baron. Whilst hanging in the warm air, searching out a friendly rising thermal she would sing at the top of her voice.

"After the turn of the century,
In the clear blue skies over Germany………"

She loved the song, almost as much as she loved her ultimate flawed hero. Manfred Albrecht Freiherr von Richthofen was widely known as the Red Baron, owing to the fact that he had his aircraft painted red. He was another World War I ace fighter pilot, another recipient of the Blue Max, and considered the top ace of that war, being officially credited with 80 victories. She delighted in Richthofen's many other nicknames including "Le Diable Rouge" ("Red Devil") or "Le petit Rouge" ("Little Red") in French, and the "Red Knight" in English.

Fully kitted up, she stripped off stark naked, and placed her clothes in a rucksack, which she strapped tightly on her back. She picked up the hang-glider, and with all the bravado born of many years experience, and despite her 60 years, she dashed headlong towards the edge, taking off into the wildest, bluest yonder singing away at the top of her voice. It was an excellent flying day, and the thermals were kind. She had wonderful views over Cairn Gibbs and Loch of Lintrathen, and then she circled back towards Alyth, and on in a wide arc back towards Balduff Hill still singing away. Many times she chuckled her contented flying ace way through the song's chorus.

Replete with her success, she decided not to land, but to fly on, and complete the circuit again. The views at first were better than ever. She flew on, and sang on.

As she tried to make the turn back towards Balduff Hill for the second time, there was an abrupt change in the weather. The sunshine had suddenly gone, and she found herself shivering in the first spray of a light rain. Struggling to control the hang-glider she resolved to land as quickly as possible. The continuous loop of her favourite flying song still played, but she had stopped singing as she struggled for control.

The MP3 player never got to the chorus, before she found herself swirling continuously round in a freak tornado. In a very short while, totally out of control, she came down in a huge thistle patch close to the Devil's Elbow, on the 17th fairway of the Blairgowrie Lansdowne Golf Course. And here she died the death of a thousand needles as she was prickled to death being dragged round and round, in and out of the thistles for more than 10 minutes. Up in heaven she would probably have seen the irony of dying on the wing au naturel, whilst listening to a song about her beloved ace fighter pilot.

Brunhilda's G. P., Doctor McPherson just happened to be playing the golf course at the time, and he was sheltering in the trees at the edge of the fairway when the tornado swirled its way towards the thistles. He and his golfing colleagues had seen the hang-glider crash, and had witnessed the prickly demise. She was pronounced dead at the scene, and her remains were removed to a local undertaker immediately. Details for contacting her son, Duncan, were found in her rucksack, and he was informed of the accident at about 1 pm.

Duncan made his way back to Blairgowrie as quickly as he could. He visited his mother at the undertakers, cried quietly, and then went home shocked and devastated. He might have been 30 years old, but he was a "mummy's boy" in the sense that there had only been one significant woman in his life. He had never had a girlfriend, but he wasn't stifled by his mother, and otherwise he was no habitual social misfit. A complex character, a Scot with German undertones, unperturbed by being the illegitimate son of Henry, a father he never knew, he accepted these building blocks, and they never really bothered him too much.

His first thoughts back at the bungalow were how casually he had left home that morning, going through the daily routines, and unaware of how his life would change that day. The undertakers had returned the rucksack, and when he went through the contents he found instructions on how to carry on with his life. His mother, organised and methodical to the last, was always aware of the risks she encountered with her flying pursuits, and she had prepared everything for the possibility of her demise while flying. Amongst her effects was an envelope for her son. It was addressed:

"To Duncan, my lovely boy. To be opened after I have flown to Heaven. xxx"

He sat down, his hands were shaking, and tears rolled down his cheeks as he fumbled with the envelope. Inside was a single sheet of paper, and a large brass key. The letter, in Brunhilda's handwriting read:-

"My dearest wee boy Duncan,
I am so sorry that I can't be with you any longer.
You are a fine, handsome boy, and I have always done my best for you. I have guarded many secrets from you for a long time. But I promised myself that one day, after my death the truth would be revealed. I want you to find someone for me, and make sure he is at my funeral. His name was Henry "Tusker" McVitie, and he was the only man I ever loved. He'll be in his 50's now. I have no address for him, but if you get in touch with Lemmy from Motorhead saying you are Brunhilda from Blairgowrie, then I am sure Tusker can be found. In this envelope is the key to my cellar, a secret place for me. What you will find in there will make you a very rich man.
Goodbye my precious lovely boy.

Love Mum xxx"

CHAPTER 16

A Madman on the Edge of Genius?

(Friday 11th to Monday 14th May 2012)

It was Friday 11th May, and the Fuller's Pride was flowing down at the Brewers, most of it into an ever expanding Ramsbottom stomach, and all the crew were there including Gordon, who had obviously benefited from his holiday from work. He didn't appear to be at all stressed now, in fact he was the most relaxed that anybody had seen him for quite some time. The jolly fatman didn't like that, he felt that the accountant was swinging a leg, and in the next few minutes that relaxed mood was about to change.

"You're alright now then, gay-boy?" he enquired, "Only we're expecting you back at work on Monday, and there's a pile of stuff on your desk about to fall over in a giant heap. Do try and get there before it makes a mess on the floor, won't you?"

"I'm feeling better, thank you," Gordon replied, "Not least of all because I haven't had to spend every working day with you breathing down my neck, fatso. I'm looking forward to coming back and getting on with things."

"That's good, because if you don't shift your arse and get on with all the important stuff for the 1stCitySoft, we'll be looking for another bean counter soon." The tormentor uttered taking no prisoners.

Tiny noted a surprising frankness in his friend's manner. This wasn't the lovable roguish comedian that everybody knew. Since he had gone home under the weather a couple of weeks back there had been a noticeable change in his demeanour. The chairman interjected slightly annoyed with the harshness.

"Come on, mate, that's not necessary. He's got the best interests of the company at heart, I'm sure." He turned to the bean counter with a look that said, "Is that true?"

"Of course I have, I'll be back raring to go."

But he knew that before he could tackle the work for 1stCitySoft he would need to clear the backlog that had accumulated on his desk in the 3 weeks he'd been away.

"Anyway Gord, my old buddy," the antagonist continued like a dog with a bone that he wouldn't let go of, "We've all been working our little arses off while you've been away, just so that you could sit on yours and twiddle your mathematic thumbs."

The gay accountant smiled, preparing to issue an equally acidic retort.

"Little arses don't include yours though does it? You could change the course of the Nile with the size of yours."

Again, there was a sense that this wasn't the usual banter between two close friends and work colleagues, there was a bitterness, an edge, to what was happening, and what the two of them were saying. With temperatures rapidly rising, the boss realised that he'd better try to get them off the subject, before it came to blows, but it may have been a little too late. Hugh was a whisker away from bursting into flames. His face reddened, and then he responded in anger and not at all in jest, "And you, you ancient faggot, with all your experience you'd be an expert on arses wouldn't you?"

The raised voices drew attention, and the room suddenly fell silent. Spike was quickly at his partner's side looking extremely agitated, grabbed him by the shoulder and tried to escort him away to the dartboard, and for once the fatman didn't have the last word.

Scruffbag pointed his finger and shouted, "Shut up! You lard arse, before I take you outside, and kick your podgy butt from here to kingdom come. Leave him alone. Do you hear? He's not been well, and you aren't making things any better."

In a few minutes the conversation had deteriorated from very relaxed to spontaneous combustion and Tiny was in the middle of it desperately trying to keep the peace. He darted in between his 2 friends, and said, "Right, that's it now. Everybody calm down. I thought we were all supposed to be best mates."

Gordon went off to the dartboard with his partner, and the chairman instructed his mate in no uncertain terms to sit down and be quiet, and then ordered another round of drinks. Hugh obeyed like a scalded child, and his closest friend sat down and watched his hangdog expression with a concern born out of more than 30 years of friendship. They both took long swallows of Fuller's Pride before one of them spoke quietly.

"There's something a matter, isn't there? I've never seen you like this before. You're expected to be the life and soul of any get-together, and here you are tearing strips off a work colleague and drinking buddy. What the hell is wrong with you these days? It can't be the demise of the Clarets. Even you know that in the great realm of things that's not so important. I know we've been burning the candle at both ends a bit work-wise, but we're making good progress. I'm concerned about you, mate, we are old muckers, and since that nightmare you had a couple of weeks ago you've been behaving different. Just tell me what is wrong?"

The unjolly fatman had so many things buzzing round his head, and he'd been keeping them secret for a while. Tiny was being a real mate, a true friend, but most of the concerns were sure to impact on 1stCitySoft, and on their long term relationship.

The troubled man tried desperately to unscramble all his problems in his head, in an acceptable way, but every time he wanted to say what was on his mind, it made him cry inside. It caused him physical pain, his heart ached, his stomach burned, his head went into a spin, his eyes filled with tears, and he didn't recognise himself. It was as if he tragically morphed into a different man, a less affable, more serious person, and he didn't like it one bit.

Tiny brought him quickly back from the maelstrom inside his head, by quietly yet firmly instructing him to take the tray of drinks over to the dartboard, and to apologise to both Gordon and Spike. Like a little child that had been scolded for a misdemeanour and told to go up to his room, he obeyed the instruction. The chairman watched, apprehensive that aggro would spark off again, and from the other side of the bar was relieved to observe awkwardness and tension turn to handshakes and smiles. When the miscreant returned, the boss put an arm over his shoulder and said, "There! That didn't hurt, did it?"

Then after a short while, he quietly asserted, "Right! Let's call a moratorium on discussing work matters. We are here to relax and have a few drinks. We'll have a chat at work on Monday morning. But for now, give me back the Friday night in the Brewers happy-go-lucky man please."

Just as he finished speaking Norman arrived. It was quite a bit later than usual because he had been over at Clarisa's in Sandon having one of her special aubergine and cheese pasta bakes, and he was going back there to spend the night afterwards. She didn't mind him popping out for a couple of hours, because she had things to do.

"Hello, Nobless, want a drink, where you been?" Hugh asked.

He was going to try to live up to the expectations of him from now on.

"Yes, J2O please, over at Sandon, having a very tasty vegetarian meal." replied the young man.

"Seeing a lot of your little lady these days aren't you? It must be love. When's the wedding?"

He laughed. "Yes, she is very special. She has changed my life, and I love being with her. But don't go off and buy any confetti just yet."

"Millicent thinks she's a lovely girl, and they get on really well. How's about you both come to lunch on Sunday? Tiny, why don't you and Miss Iberia come too?"

Both the boys nodded accepting the invitations, and the fatman continued. "What was it like on the London Eye? I know it's a fantastic view in the evening if it's not raining."

"Oh, we had a cracking day, just perfect, strolling around the sights, the weather was kind, we had a superb Italian meal, and the London Eye was the icing on the cake. What an amazing way to see London in all it's glory. I tell you, we would have stayed on it and gone round and round, again and again, all night if possible."

"The Cup Final was pretty ordinary and predictable, but we had a special guest and a great laugh at his expense. We invited Terry Smith along."

"What! Why did you want to associate in any way with that tiresome twat?"

"Hang on a minute, don't lose your rag. We wanted to get revenge on him over that night at the Brewers. The idea was to get him completely wasted, dress him up in Ipswich Town kit, and put him on the last train to Norwich. We even had Ahmad and his brother lined up to take him to Colchester. But it was going to backfire when he said he was playing away from home in Needham Market, and wanted to stay sober."

Norman smiled at the idea of dumping Terry in Norwich dressed in Ipswich kit, thought for a moment, then asked, "He was playing away from home? Who with?"

"Oh we don't know the lady in question; it was just an old flame called Teresa he'd bumped into at a wedding."

"So what happened?"

The jolly fatman's face cracked as he relived the delight of pulling his practical joke on Smithy, and then he explained. "Terry asked for fruit juice, so I invented him a cocktail, which I'd call Double Trouble, because you might say it had two stings in the tail. First of all I put 8 chasteberry capsules in it, that's an anaphrodisiac, and that would make him incapable of rising to the occasion. Then I worried about how long it would take to affect him, so I added some insurance in the form of half a bottle of Senokot syrup."

At this point he was beginning to giggle uncontrollably again, and Norman and Tiny weren't far behind him in the mirth stakes.

"He went off to Needham Market with a smile on his face, and we don't know what happened, but I think we can safely assume that his dirty night was a disaster."

Hugh couldn't resist repeating his previous statement that, "Terry was very unlikely to be coming, but he surely would be going.", and then the giggles definitely got the best of him as he nearly toppled off his bar stool.

On this occasion Norman was pleased that he wasn't the target of another practical joke, and laughed long and loud at Terry's misfortune. When the mirth had receded, he waited till his uncle had composed himself, and then added seriously, "That's brilliant, well done, but I don't want Clarisa to know anything about that. Neither of us really wants to be reminded of that night. Promise me you won't repeat that to her."

The uncle looked his nephew straight in the eyes still grinning, and replied, "No problem, I won't say anything to her.", and for once the young man felt he could be reassured that someone was telling the truth. Tiny was relieved that the jolly fatman had made a swift return. Relating that tale had changed the atmosphere completely and now the joker had returned to his comedy venue, and the Village People had finished playing darts and returned to the bar. The resident comedian had his full audience and he was on a roll, and the next item on his agenda was something he picked out of the Essex Chronicle.

"Have you seen this?" he asked of his assembly, reading directly from the paper," On Tuesday 8th May the Prime Minister, David Cameron, and the Deputy Prime Minister, Nick Clegg, visited e2v, the leading provider of technology solutions for high performance systems, to see the positive contribution that investments from UK Regional Growth Fund (RGF) are making to the UK's manufacturing and technology sectors."

"Oh No! He's going to get on his politics soapbox again." said Spike.

"So, Batman and Robin pay us a visit, and spout a load of bullshit about what their government is doing for us in the recession. They should have visited 1stCitySoft and found out what a company like ours is doing for them. And then they should have popped in to see Mike and his gardening business, Ahmad and his taxi firms, and finished up looking at Scruffbag's little company."

He looked at the decorator and smiled as he said that, and the last bit of the statement was hard for the speaker, but he was trapped between his philosophy of enterprise through small business honest toil, and his growing dislike for Spike. He continued.

"They're all either hopeless or pathetic or bent nowadays, politicians are. We need another Margaret Thatcher to lead us out of this mess. Now she was a real politician, a statesman, or is it stateswoman. Britain was great again under her reign, she was the best Prime Minister ever, better even than Churchill."

Yes," retorted the scruffy decorator sarcastically, "She was brilliant; she destroyed all our heavy industry and shut down all the mines, making the North an employment desert full of ghost towns and broken families."

Hugh ignored the comment. He had a point to his argument and he wasn't going to be diverted from it, especially by someone with Spike's incisive intellect. He went on.

"I've been a Tory all my life. I was 15 when Margaret Thatcher came to the throne and 28 when she abdicated. But since then we've had grey men, Tories like John Major, a clone of Oliver Cromwell if ever I saw one, and a string of champagne socialist Labourites like Tony Bla Bla Bla, and bloody Gordon Brown driving the country into a financial abyss. Now the Tories have blown it. I'm voting UKIP at the next election, before we find that by some sort of European Federal stealth, Angela Merkel becomes our president."

Everybody knew that this was one of their mate's pet subjects, and so the best course of action whenever he got on his soapbox about politics was to say very little and to let him get it over with as quickly as possible.

They all laughed at the rant, the Village People returned to the dartboard, and at the first opportunity Tiny changed the subject by saying "I wonder what happened to Terry Smith?", and that brought smiles and boyish giggles back to the scene.

At the end of the evening's boozing, Pavel turned up and simply waved to indicate that the taxi was waiting. There was a return wave of recognition, and then pints were quickly finished. The Village People left at the same time, and before there was a customary final jibe, jumped into the car and left with middle fingers raised.

"Have you had a good evening, Zirs?" asked Pavel as he drove up Springfield Road.

"Yes, thank you, have you?" answered the boss.

"I have only just started my shift, and will be working till 6 in the morning." was his answer.

The joker interrupted, "Hey, Pav, are you a communist or a capitalist?"

"I don't know Mr Ramsbottom. My country is changing quickly, and it's not all good or all bad. Poland has a long and mostly tragic history, being overrun and oppressed from all directions. All I hope for is a better future for our people."

"Not much different to us then are you? But, Pavel, what the fuck are you doing here in England?"

The cabbie had an answer ready, but the ride was over and Hugh got out without bothering to listen to any reply. This was a subdued fatman again. There was no witty riposte to end the evening. The passengers got out of the taxi at the usual corner, smiled at each other, and went their separate ways.

Meanwhile, Norman returned to Clarisa's flat in Sandon expecting to find her looking beautiful with newly tinted hair, freshly painted finger and toenails, and softened skin from a long lazy soak in the bath. He was not disappointed, but she was also curled up on the couch, knees up to her chin, with tears in her eyes.

"Whatever is the matter, Pixie, why are you crying?" he asked, greeting her with a kiss.

"Oh, Normie, it's Phyllis, she's been missing for 3 days, and we are so close to the Chelmsford bypass on the A12, I worry that she might get run over."

She looked at him with big mournful eyes. "I know cats are like that, and he has gone AWOL before, but not usually for more than a day or two."

"I'm sorry, Sweetie, do you want me to wander round the village and see if I can find her?"

He knew that even if he did discover Phyllis somewhere in the vicinity, she would more than likely run away from him, and so did Clarisa.

"No, we'll just have to wait and see if she returns overnight. I suppose sooner or later she'll get hungry, and she didn't get to her enormous size without enjoying her food."

Clarisa got up and threw her arms around her man's neck, and he carried her to the bedroom.

"OK, lovely little one, we'll sleep on it, and hope she comes home to her mum."

She fell quickly asleep with tears still filling her eyes, and he lay there looking at her face, so baby-like, and listened to her soft breathing, and thinking how lucky he was to be with such a wonderful sensitive girl.

At 3 o'clock in the morning, she awoke with a start, which quickly changed to a contented smile as she heard her beloved moggy climb in through the window. Then for a while, she lay awake, looking at her Normie, and coinciding her breathing with his, and thinking how lucky she was to be with such a wonderful gentle man.

Gordon felt a little strange going back into work on Monday 14th May. It was almost as if he didn't belong there. So many changes had occurred in preparation for the move to Chelmsford and the launch of 1stCitySoft. After his G. P. had signed him off suffering from stress until Monday 7th May, and then his sick leave had been extended for a further week, he had been away for nearly a month since the frightful end of that board meeting on 19th April. Now he was back, and the first sight of his office left him horrified. There was paperwork 3 feet high across his desk and spreading across the carpet, some of it tumbling in untidy heaps against the far wall, and that was before he'd even had the chance to assess what a month's worth of email would bring him. To his work colleagues he had good reason to bite the bullet and get stuck into the backlog. What better reason could there be now for delaying the long awaited company accounts required not only to progress the global project, but also to satisfy the end of year returns to Companies House.

"Let me know if you need any help with that lot. We'll hire you an assistant for a week or two if you need it." the chairman offered, knowing full well that the answer would be an emphatic "No!"

Then he reassured Gordon that he'd do all he could to keep the marketing director's attention focussed elsewhere, and went directly along to Hugh's office for an informal mid-morning chat.

"I think it's time we had a bit of a chat about whatever is troubling you at the moment." he began, "I've been worried about you. It's fair to say that you're not your usual happy-go-lucky self recently. So, come on, what's up, mate?"

The fatman slumped back in his leather upholstered office chair. He knew he could always relax in his oldest friend's presence. "Oh, I'm just a bit stressed out and tired at the moment, and I had that funny turn after the Brewers a few weeks ago, and that bloody awful nightmare I told you about. But I've been to see the quack, got all the standard bullshit about losing weight, cutting out the booze, and getting on me bike. I've got to go and see him again whenever, but he'll just repeat the lecture, and give me a load of pills, and you know how I feel about that?"

"But, mate, you know really what he's saying makes sense. None of us are getting any younger, and we're all just making it up as we go along. You don't get a guide book for your life, but there are some things that are so obviously staring us in the face. We can put all this 1stCitySoft business on hold if necessary, if that's the cause of your problems. In the great realm of things a few weeks delay won't be the end of the world. I want my old mate, the Brentwood School wind up merchant, the joker from the Two Brewers back, and everything else can wait."

Hugh was touched by what Tiny was offering, but he knew that he couldn't put the biggest challenge in both their lives on the backburner now. It wasn't quite a runaway train yet, but it wasn't far off becoming one in matter of a few weeks. He wanted to explain his thinking.

"I want this project 1stCitySoft to be an overwhelming success just as much as you do, so putting it on hold now isn't on the agenda as far as I'm concerned. But, what I'm worried about is gay Gordon's part in it. He's up to something! Did you know he was in here on Easter Saturday pretending to work on the accounts? Norman caught him, said he was very secretive, and looked shell-shocked when he was interrupted. He's a devious little bastard I'll tell you."

Despite this new snippet of information at last being revealed, the chairman seemed to want to let the bean counter off the hook for no good reason, and continued to stall.

"Let's give him a chance to catch up and do what we expect of him. We've got a few weeks to go before his work becomes critical. He hasn't significantly delayed the process yet. Like I say, let's cut him a bit of slack. And, mate, please stay out of his face for a while, don't go storming in and upset him again."

They looked straight at each other. It was one of those "We understand each other, don't' we?" looks, and they both knew that the line of conversation had expired. But the marketing director was becoming suspicious that there was more to the situation between his 2 work colleagues than he was aware of, piling up another worry for him. Obviously, if the boss wasn't about to act on reservations about Gordon and the accounts, there was little point in Hugh spilling the beans about what happened between Spike and Tina while he was away in China. Equally, there was no point in raising the matter of Tina's drunken chat with Millicent, and her apparent promiscuous attitude. So instead he changed the subject, and told his mate about the latest episode of Tom and the Babestation business, his recent talk with his son, and his relief that Dick and Harry weren't showing any interest (yet). They both had a good laugh over that. This was a good piece of flippancy for Tiny to end the conversation and return to his office. Back at his own desk at the end of the discussion he thought about his long term relationship with his friend, and reflected whether he was a genius on the edge of madness, or a madman on the edge of genius.

CHAPTER 17

Those Magnificent Men

(Friday 11th to Monday 21st May 2012)

The previous few days had been very difficult for Duncan. His mother was gone, and he had to organise her funeral, and on top of that find someone he'd not heard of before. For a time he avoided the idea of opening the door to the cellar, being somehow deliriously inquisitive, and also filled with a sense of dread at the same time. After 3 days of just sitting and thinking, not eating, not wanting to feel anything but grief, he burst his own self-imposed bubble, and resolved to start the rest of his life. On Saturday morning he contacted the Motorhead fan club, spoke to a very sympathetic secretary, and within hours had a phone called from Lemmy himself. He remembered Brunhilda from Blairgowrie with much affection, and surprised Duncan with his fondness for her and Tusker. He promised to make every effort to contact the roadie as soon as he could.

Pleased with his progress, the bereaved son took a deep breath, braced himself, and put the key to his mother's den in the lock. He turned it slowly and apprehensively, pushed the door open, found a cord-pull to switch the light on, and hesitated before entering. He closed his eyes, and took another breath. Even before he crossed the threshold to this place that had been a secret to him all his life, he could sense his mother's presence, smell her perfume, and know that he was close to something that had been precious to her.

Just inside the door was a cork pin-board, and this was completely covered by pictures of him from when he was a little boy, right up until a recent visit to Edinburgh Castle earlier that year. Next to that picture was an envelope upon which was written, "To be opened in the event of my death".

He didn't want to touch it, he feared to go through all the rituals of closure too quickly. He looked away, and scanned the walls of the room. They were adorned with pictures and posters of his mother's heroes, and photos of her many flying adventures. Rudolph Hess, Hermann Goering, The Red Baron, and Snoopy, were all represented, and there was a life-size poster of his mother and a red-haired Scotsman in a kilt, standing in front of a Cessna light aircraft. He paused to look at this closely for while, and wondered who the man in the picture might be. He looked somehow familiar. He sat down at the large desk, the room swirled like a vicious whirlpool, and he found himself swimming pointlessly round and round in the circles of his imagination.

When he returned to conscious thought, he began looking in drawers and cupboards, and opened 2 very large heavy trunks squeezed into an alcove on the far wall. Every space, every nook and cranny, was filled with flying artefacts from the 1st and 2nd World Wars, and an enormous collection of Luftwaffe memorabilia. Among the artefacts were Iron Crosses and other medals, ceremonial swords, swastikas, flags, emblems, badges, headgear, binoculars, and a huge collection of photo albums from both wars, containing pictures of aircraft, pilots, airships, and famous people from those eras.

Duncan had little knowledge of the artefacts significance, but he realised now that his mother had secretly provided him with a treasure chest of substantial value. She had appeared to be a frugal woman, living simply in a small bungalow, but the secret in the cellar would turn out to be one of the finest, most valuable private collections of flying memorabilia, and particularly Luftwaffe and Hermann Goering artefacts, ever discovered. After several hours in the cellar, he unpinned the envelope from the corkboard by the door, switched off the light, and locked the door. For just a few extra hours he had felt close to mother.

It had been a week since the flying accident had changed Duncan's life. He knew the secrets of the cellar, the funeral arrangements still needed to be finalised, and he was sitting down steeling himself to open the envelope from the cellar pin-board. A sense of relief came over him as he at last managed to do it. Inside there were two sheets of paper.

The first sheet itemised his mother's funeral wishes. He began to read. First she specified the music that she wished to be played at her funeral. Then she requested that at the funeral, Tusker was to read some words that she had written herself, and that she had provided on the second sheet of paper. Then she expressed the wish that she be cremated, and that her ashes were to be scattered at twilight at the Reekie Linn waterfall in Glenisla by the 2 men in her life. Finally as her sole executor her son was to read her will after the wake to be held in her bungalow. Just as he finished reading his mother's words the telephone rang, and when he picked it up, there was a Scottish voice that he didn't recognise.

"Hello, Is that Duncan?"

"Er, Yes! Who am I speaking to?"

"You don't know me, Sonny, but I knew you're mother. I'm so sorry to hear about her accident. I'm Tusker, Tusker McVitie."

"Sonny" was knocked sideways with the sudden speed at which things were happening.

"Er! They found you then?"

"Yes! Lemmy's been in touch, and told me the sad news. Listen, Sonny, when will the funeral be held? I have to be there."

"On Monday, Monday 21st May, at the Blairgowrie Parish Church, in Upper David Street at 11.00 am."

"OK, Sonny! I'll be there for sure. Good to talk to you."

"Er OK! Bye then."

"Bye!"

And that was it. The caller put the phone down. Final arrangements could now be made. It was coming together.

The day of the funeral arrived, and it was a small and unfussy affair. Fraulein Doenitz wouldn't have wanted a lot of fuss, but there were friends and neighbours at the church for the service. There were some members of BaDNACers, and F.U.C.K., some friends from the wind turbine protest group, but the only family present was Duncan himself. As the hearse glided up to the church, and he stepped out, he heard the roar of a large powerful motorcycle, and there amongst the dark suits and black ties, and formerly dressed ladies suddenly appeared a ginger-haired, long-bearded, kilted and impressively sporraned, Scottish patriot, looking like an extra from Braveheart. He wore the distinctive dark green and blue Mack tartan, with a black sash strung across his left shoulder, and after removing his crash helmet, he donned a Tam o' Shanter. Only one person there knew who he was, and as everybody else recoiled in hesitation or fright, Duncan stepped forward and spontaneously embraced him.

"Hello, Tusker, I'm glad you made it."

"Me too, it was touch and go. How are you, Sonny?"

"I'm OK. Look! Before we go in, I have to give you this," he said, handing over his mum's written words, "My mother requested that you're the only one she wants to read it at the service."

The tartan biker looked at the sheet of paper and the neat handwriting, and just said "That's fine, Sonny, I'll do it."

The poll bearers were ready, and the procession walked slowly into the church to the rather incongruous strains of Hawkwind's "Silver Machine".

"I just took a ride, in a silver machine, and I'm still feeling mean, I got a silver machine........"

The Braveheart extra smiled and whispered, "Your mother will be pissing herself laughing at that."

The service began, and the Reverend Ferguson did his bit with the 23rd Psalm:-

"The Lord is my Shepherd; I shall not want.
He maketh me to lie down in green pastures:
He leadeth me beside the still waters.
He restoreth my soul:

*He leadeth me in the paths of righteousness for His name's sake.
Yea, though I walk through the valley of the shadow of death,
I will fear no evil: For thou art with me;
Thy rod and thy staff, they comfort me.
Thou preparest a table before me in the presence of mine enemies;
Thou annointest my head with oil. My cup runneth over.
Surely goodness and mercy shall follow me all the days of my life,
and I will dwell in the House of the Lord forever."*

And the other bit:-

"Man that is born of a woman hath but a short time to live, and is full of misery. He cometh up, and is cut down, like a flower; he fleeth as it were a shadow, and never continueth in one stay. In the midst of life we are in death: of whom may we seek for succour, but of thee, O Lord, Who for our sins art justly displeased."

Then the minister did the job of knitting together a brief life history from the information that Duncan had conveyed to him. He finished with a statement that, "Brunhilda's life was one of excitement and obsession, brutally cut short by a tragedy which happened while she was indulging in one her passions."

After that he called for Henry McVitie to go up to the pulpit.

Tusker read slowly and deliberately from the paper he'd been given, at first advising all present, "This is something a great lady asked for me to read."

Then he proceeded to read the words that had been written for him.

*"My friends, I wish to leave you with a few thoughts;
First, to everyone here, thank you, for your support and love.
I am sorry to leave you all behind.
But one day we must all take off for our last flight,
And then find we've crash-landed on God's own airfield.
You know that my first great love was to enjoy the freedom of the skies,
And now I'm as free as the birds I envied so much,
I have my own precious wings, and a flight-plan that lasts forever.
And I can fly as high as I want,
So high I can touch the stars,
And yes now I can be as daring and spectacular as my great flying heroes.
The Red Baron sends his regards."*

The assembled congregation sighed in unison with a warm internal contented smile.

He continued.

"Secondly, to Duncan;

My lovely wee boy, you are the raspberry of my eye,
The best thing that ever happened for me.
You have grown into a fine, handsome man.
Go out now, into the big wide world, and make me burst with pride.
I will always love you, no matter what you do,
And whatever you do, do it with love, for I will be watching you."

Again, all present breathed in the compassion of the moment, and Duncan's grin was so wide it hurt his face. The reader was moved, cleared his throat, and resumed.

"Finally, to Tusker, I know that you are reading this:-
We fell, we flew, we always knew,
We'd soar the skies in perfect blue,
Set stars as precious stones to light the way,
If each day could have a thousand hours,
And each hour could have a thousand days,
I'd forsake them all to be with you today."

He stumbled from the pulpit unable to see clearly through a flood of tears. It was somehow very odd, but also comforting for the congregation, to see such a big, confident, traditionally attired, but conspicuously out of place man, reduced to tears by the words Brunhilda had written for him. The second chosen song began;

"She flies like a bird in the sky-y-y,"

By this time the Motorhead roadie's tears had turned to laughter, and he broke into another wide grin saying quietly "There she goes, I bet she's pissing herself again. That's a bloody Nimble bread advert."

Duncan just nodded, and smiled back, and while the song played took some time to compose himself before he went up to the pulpit. He was a man of few words, and he was nervous in having to deliver a speech. Visibly shaking, he was brief.

"We are here today to celebrate my Mother's life. So I am reminded of the words of the American sportswriter Grantland Rice, when he said,

'*For when the One Great Scorer comes,*
To mark against your name,

> *He writes - not that you won or lost -*
> *But how you played the Game.'*

My mother played the game with honesty, and enthusiasm, and most of all she played it with an infectious passion. She worked hard, played hard, and loved hard, and I'm going to miss her for being the best mum in the Universe to me."

He sat down, and the coffin slid through the curtain on its final journey, accompanied by the usual it's over, terminal music. But then the speakers crackled for a few seconds and the funereal sounds were replaced by a song perhaps only familiar to Brunhilda and a few others.

> *"After the turn of the century,*
> *In the clear blue skies over Germany……"*

Tusker was deep in thought about his great lady, "She would know now that she had glided off this mortal coil twice to the same tune." he smiled.

Somewhere up in Heaven, flying across God's own airfield, Brunhilda was probably laughing her socks off. If she was wearing any socks that is!

The ushers opened the doors and indicated for the congregation to make their way out. In this part of the world the expectation might then have been to hear a lone piper standing in the churchyard playing "Amazing Grace" or "Scotland the Brave", but somebody had other ideas. There was another slight pause, in that most reflective and significant mourning moment, and then the final song played as the congregation left the church to the triumphant sounds of:-

> *"Those magnificent men in their flying machines……"*

Brunhilda was sending a clear message to the congregation, that they shouldn't mourn her death, but rather celebrate her life.

Nobody but nobody in the small congregation would hesitate to be moved to joy at the triumphant atmosphere created by the song choice of their deceased friend.

By the time they were all outside, they were all either crying tears of joy, or pissing themselves with laughter. Duncan and Tusker, and a few of the closest friends attended the wake, back at the bungalow in Dunkeld Road. Due to the celebratory tone of the service, it was a bright and jovial affair, but soon there was only two mourners remaining. Duncan had drunk a few wee drams, and his tongue had loosened a little. He felt a peculiar affinity towards the stranger in his mother's bungalow and began to talk.

"My mother loved flying."

"I know, Sonny, so do I."

"You took her up in a glider for her first real flight, didn't you?"

"Aye! That's true. Over at Scotlandwell."

"And then you did free-falling together."

"Aye, Sonny, and then we started hang-gliding."

"She liked that best of all, hang-gliding, but I wish...." he stopped in mid-sentence, tears quickly filling his eyes.

"I know, Sonny, "said Tusker sympathetically, putting an arm over the younger man's shoulder, "I know."

Then he continued philosophically, "That which you love, will kill you."

There was silence for a brief moment, and then the question.

"Did you love my mother? I think she described you as the only man she'd ever loved."

"Sonny, she was a very passionate woman, and we shared some special times together."

He paused, and looked his son in the eyes, and said, "Yes! I loved her."

There was another pause as courage was gathered, and another dram sipped. Someone wasn't used to drinking much, and it was beginning to embolden him.

"You're my dad, aren't you?"

"Aye, Sonny. I am your father."

They emptied the bottle together. The son sunk a few drams and his new dad more than a few, and then some. They stayed together at the bungalow for a few days, during which time they both read and re-read the will. They ate together, they enjoyed a few drams together, they cried together, and laughed together, and for a new found father and son relationship it was a very special time, remembering the great lady who had been most prominent in both their lives.

Then, on a fine May twilight evening they travelled up to the Reekie Linn waterfall on the Kawasaki, and reverently and quietly scattered Brunhilda's ashes at that special spot. The next day Tusker travelled back to England, and Duncan prepared to tidy up the remainder of his mother's affairs, and to begin the adventure of the rest of his life. He couldn't stay at P.O.O.S., and now that his mother was free-falling in heaven he had no ties. Soon he would be a comparatively rich man, and he had an urge to go south.

CHAPTER 18

Brief Encounter and Man versus Food

(Friday 18th to Friday 25th May 2012)

As another Friday evening came around Norman had finished his evening meal, and was enjoying playing an early version of Interstellar Paranoid Overdrive when the phone rang. Even though Cher's hockey season was now over, the man in the Hub knew his dad would still phone him every Friday evening to check if he was coming up to Leiston the following day.
"Ey Oop, son, 'ow yer diddlin'?"
"Alright, Dad, how are you?"
"Mum alright, is she?"
"Nay, son, she's not reet! She wants to speak to you, 'old on a sec and I'll put her on."
There was something very wrong. Lisalotte never spoke on the phone; she had a very acute case of telephonophobia. To her, using a phone was so scary it compared to other people's fear of spiders, even to the extent that she couldn't touch a telephone, and she would panic if a phone rang. There was a succession of fumbles at the other end of the line as attempts were made to switch to speakerphone, and then Stanley said "Just pretend Norman's in t' room with yer. 'Ere 'old this photograph of 'im if it'll 'elp. No! Don't be silly lass, it won't bite yer, just do what I say and it'll be fine."
After what seemed like ages the Yorkshireman spoke again, "OK, son, we're all ready at this end. Yer knows I'm not very good wi' t' new-fangled gadgets, but we've got this gizmo on't speakerphone, and Helen showed me 'ow to use it, so we can both speak to yer and 'ear what yer sayin'"
"OK, Dad, what's the problem?" asked the young man.
"I'll let yer mum explain." said the Yorkshireman, and then he could be heard encouraging his wife to talk. As she began to speak there was a whine in her voice that her son had not heard much before. She took a deep breath before she said, "My dearest boy, I haff some very sad news about your tante Brunhilda. Can you hear me?"
"Yes, Mum I can hear you, what is wrong with auntie Brunhilda?"
"Ve had a letter zis morning from her son, Duncan. Oh it is so sad. I just vish ve had seen her more often, but she liffed in Blairgowrie, and Scotland iz so far avay. Ve vere very close vhen ve lived in Germany. Ve vorked ze bierkellers in Munchen togezzer for many years, and she came to liffe in

Scotland after me and your farzher vere married."

She was rambling away, and not getting any nearer the point, but her son was used to it. Smalltalk was her forte, and she wasn't an expert at making conversation with a purpose.

An interruption was attempted," What does the letter...?"

"Your auntie vas such a clever girl. She vas ze one blessed wiz ze good looks and wiz brains. Ze boys alvays chased after her vhen ve vere younger, and she vas such a naughty girl. I sink she vas tri-sexual."

Noble junior stifled a giggle as he heard a voice say gently," Get to t' point, lass, get to t' point."

Meanwhile, he was chuckling to himself, at another peculiar and unfortunate misunderstanding. With some difficulty he tried to imagine what it meant to be a tri-sexual. And then he heard a harsh bark, "Shut up, Stanley, I am very upset, and you don't seem to understand."

There was another pause, as she composed herself, and then she went on," Are you still zere, my boy?"

"Yes, Mum I'm still here and I can hear you. You were telling me all about auntie Brunhilda. But please, what's wrong?"

"She vas angry dexters you know, she could write wiz bosth hends. She loved alvays, flying and everysing to do wiz it. But being in an ordinary flugzeug vasn't good enough for her. She said zat vas boring. She vanted to fly herself, small planes, gliders, anysing, even falling free and jumping wiz a parachute."

He attempted to interrupt again," Yes, Mum, but what does the letter say?"

There was another pause, and some whimpering, and then she rambled again, "Her sohn, Duncan vas illegible you know, she never married ze farzer, but I sink she knew who he vas. He vas called Henry, Henry McVitie. If I remember right he played in a famous rock band back in ze 70's. I sink it vas named after a bank. Yes! Barclays! Barclays Jones Harvest it vas."

It was clear that some of the things that Lisalotte was saying were either misinterpreted or misremembered, so the son just listened patiently as she carried on. He waited for a pause, and then asked again, "OK, Mum, please tell me what does the letter say?"

After another long pause and more whimpering, at last his mum suddenly and abruptly came to the point, and whined, "Your tante Brunhilda iz dead."

Norman didn't really know what to say, and just remained silent as he heard crying and blowing of noses at the other end of the line, and then a door slammed, and there was fumbling again as the phone was switched back to normal mode. After a pregnant pause lasting a few minutes, a different voice spoke, " 'Ello again, son, are yer there, I've put t' gizmo back t' normal. Yer mum's very upset; asked me t' take over."

"What's happened, Dad? How did auntie die?"

"Eee, lad, it were an accident, 'appened on t' day after 'er 60th birthday as well. Poor soul! Tuesday 8th it were. She crashed 'er 'ang glider on t' Blairgowrie Golf Course in a freak storm. Came down in a thistle patch, and were prickled t' death."

The young man thought for a moment that this was just the sort of scenario for one of Hugh's perhaps slightly too cruel wind ups, but he knew it could in these circumstances only be deadly serious. He was bemused, on the verge of giggling at the image of such an unusual accident, but at the same time concerned for his mother, and the obvious tragedy of the situation.

"Oh, that's terrible," he sympathised, "Will you be going to the funeral?"

"Nay, lad. It's already taken place. They 'eld t' service earlier this week, and she were cremated. But her lad's comin' down south t' see us Thursday week, once 'es sorted everythin' out. Sez 'es got summat for yer Mom. 'E'll be flyin' into 'Eathrow. I've got t' flight number for yer, 'cause we were wonderin' if yer could collect 'im and put 'im oop at yours for a few days. For some reason 'e sez 'is name is Doenitz, not McVitie, it's Duncan Doenitz."

This man was an unknown quantity, but he was family, and there was no hesitation to answer," Of course, that's no problem. I suppose you'll want me to bring him up to see you on the Saturday then?"

"Aye, son. That would be reet good of yer, and yer'd best give it a miss if yer were thinkin' of comin' oop tomorrow. Yer mum's in no fit state, best left t' mourn 'er own way. Me and Cher are goin' t' get out from under 'er feet. I'll be makin' meself scarce with t' clay pigeon shoot, and Cher and Helen are off on a day trip by coach to Sandringham."

"Yeah, that's OK, Dad, I think you're right."

"It's for t' best son."

"Right, Dad, I'll wait for your call next week. Love to Mum."

"OK, bye, son, 'ave a nice weekend," Stanley finished and put the phone down.

In the 5 days up to 25th May that Gordon had been back at 1stCitySoft, the pile of backlogged work had receded considerably. But much to Hugh's annoyance on Friday afternoon the bean counter had gone home at lunchtime with the flu. So when the fatman arrived at the Brewers on Friday evening it came as some surprise to find the complete gay entourage already there clustered around the dartboard as usual.

He ordered a round of drinks, partly to slake his insatiable thirst for Fuller's Pride, and partly to entice the company accountant over, so that he could go all K.G.B. on him.

"Glad you were back from twiddling your algebraic thumbs and putting in a shift at work these last few days. How's it going clearing the backlog?" he enquired as Gordon picked up his lager.

"Yes, it was good to be back in the saddle, but isn't it just Sod's law that I should come down with the flu now. My G. P. is getting right fed up with seeing my face, and he's signed me off until Monday week. Can't be helped. Sorry!"

The distinctly unjolly fatman wasn't amused; in fact he was incensed, and immediately exploded. "And if you've got the flu, what the fuck are you doing here tonight. You should be tucked up in bed with a hot lemon and Paracetamol drink and a hot water bottle, or maybe Spike could keep you warm. You, gayboy, are faking it; you're swinging your leg. You've just had a month off with stress and now you've conveniently got the snots and you'll be clicking your heels again until Monday week. Grow some bollocks, man, tear up your sick-note, and get your fucking idle little snout back to the grindstone."

Everybody present was surprised at this sharp tongued response, and for a few moments the victim was speechless. Tiny went to step in to calm things down, but before he could say anything, there was a reply.

"It's 25th May, and it's Julian Clary's birthday and I'm in the Brewers celebrating my idol. It's not my fault that I've got the flu. It's just bad luck, so stick that in your pipe and smoke it. Oh, and by the way Monday 4th is a Bank Holiday, so I won't actually be in again until Tuesday 5th."

Hugh was on the verge of punching the Gay Pride devotee, and then Norman uncharacteristically intervened.

"Cut it out you two, I'm fed up with all this squabbling. It's becoming a bit tiresome. You, go back to the dartboard, and you, Uncle, come outside. Now!"

The chairman just stood there and smiled, he was so pleased that the young man had defused the situation with his surprising interruption. The Village People reassembled at the dartboard as instructed. Uncle and nephew picked up their drinks and left the bar. Outside it was drizzling and a bit on the cold side, so the peacemaker made it as quick as he could.

"Listen! This has to stop. Whatever gripes you've got with our accountant friend you've got to leave them on the shelf. The Brewers used to be a laugh a minute, but you've changed just lately, and it's just not the same any more. If there's something wrong with you please get it sorted soon."

The unjolly fatman bit his lip, and looked tearfully at his nephew. Then quietly he answered.

"Yeah, you're right. OK, Nobless; I'll be a good boy from now on. I'm sorry, but it was the Julian Clary business that got my goat. I suppose the wooftah thinks he's Fanny the effin' Wonder Dog.", and then he smiled.

Norman smiled back, "That's more like it, uncle, come on let's go back indoors, were getting wet out here."

When they re-entered the bar Tiny had bought another round of drinks, and for the second time in a few weeks told his oldest friend to go over to the dartboard and apologise. Once again he was like child that had been scolded for a misdemeanour and told to go up to his room, but he obeyed the instruction. And just as before the chairman watched, apprehensive that aggro would spark off again, and was relieved when from the other side of the bar he observed awkwardness and tension turn to handshakes and smiles.

When the scolded child returned, the Boss put an arm over his mate's shoulder and repeated, "There! That didn't hurt did it?"

After the early altercation the next part of the evening continued a little subdued, but as the beer flowed tensions eased enough for the joker to have the usual pokes at his gay mates. So when a discussion about the Olympics began it wasn't long before he turned it around onto his favourite themes.

"I read that last week the Olympic torch arrived at Land's End, and the following day the torch relay began. It was on the 19th I think, and they'll be running it through Essex, and it's coming to Chelmsford in the first week of July." said the fatman.

"That'll probably be the best bit of the whole shebang; the torch relay. Have they got everything ready for the actual games? It's destined for a disaster, just like in Athens, and anyway in most of the events we don't have any quality athletes to compete with the Yanks and the Chinese, or dare I say the major nations like Uzbekistan." offered Spike acidically.

"Don't kid yourself, Scruffbag, we do the pomp and circumstance bit better than anyone, and when it comes to organising things like this we've got hundreds of years of pedigree behind us. What's more Seb Coe says it'll all be ready in time, and he should know. As for our athletes, well, we have got some world beaters. Wait and see."

"No, we'll be a flop just like in the World Cup. We just don't have the facilities, and we don't take the drugs."

"Why don't you get behind the Union Jack, and show us a bit of patriotism for a change. It's Britain competing in the Olympics not England. One nation united under the Union Jack."

"Not my banner mate. My flag is the Saltire, the St Andrews cross."

The decorator was being very picky, and very Scottish, and he knew it, and revelled in winding the fatman up about it.

"St Andrew wasn't even Scottish you dimwit; I think he might have been Greek."

"And your patron saint, St George was Turkish."

"Ah but there's large lobby that says we should re-instate St Edmund of Bury-St-Edmunds fame as the patron saint of England."

"That's all by the by, but as I said the Saltire is my flag not the Onion Jack."

"Ho! Ho! Anyway your flag's probably more likely to be the Jolly Roger, along with all the other gay boys in your harem."

This was more like the usual banter, and some small sense of relief fell over the assembly.

Then a more restrained voice piped up, "While we're floating around the subject of Scotland, I've got to tell you that my cousin, Duncan, will be visiting us next week. I've got an auntie Brunhilda who lived up in Blairgowrie in Perthshire, it's her son."

Hugh knew the family members but interrupted," Brunhilda's a good old Scottish name?"

"She was my mum's sister, and came originally from Germany. Anyway, she died a few weeks ago, and her son's coming down to see us. I'm picking him up at Heathrow on Thursday, and I'll bring him down here next week."

"I'm sorry to hear your auntie's died," Tiny sympathised, "What happened?"

Porscheman couldn't help but let out a careful chuckle, and then explained, "Well, she was keen on nude hang-gliding, and unfortunately got caught out by a freak tornado, and was prickled to death in a thistle patch on the Blairgowrie Golf Course."

For a moment there was silence. Then they all burst out laughing, while the storyteller was saying, "It sounds ridiculous, but I swear to you it's as true as me standing here."

The resident comedian found the story of the prickly demise absolutely hilarious, and he had more opinions on Scotland than he'd declared in the earlier conversation.

He interjected," The Romans had it right when they built Hadrian's Wall to keep the porridge gobblers out. Now the ungrateful freeloaders want independence. Give it to 'em I say."

Spike had to rejoin the argument," Thanks very much, my English oppressor. I think you've exploited us Scots for long enough."

"Well, not all the Scots are like Mel Gibson playing William Wallace in Braveheart, and by the way he's really an Australian. Some of them are barely civilised, they're savages, barbarians who eat haggis, herrings and deep fried Mars bars. Still, I suppose you bunch of poofs will be interested to see what Nobless's cousin will be wearing under his kilt."

Not too soon for some, the end of the evening's boozing was once more fast approaching, with the expectation that Pavel would arrive to take his fare up Springfield Road. But at the usual time it was Ahmad who entered the bar and introduced his arrival.

"Hello, Ahmad, we weren't expecting you. Where's Pavel." Hugh asked swilling down the remains of his pint.

"Oh, you won't see him again, my friend, he's been deported back to Poland. He was an illegal immigrant, and he didn't have the right paperwork to stay here." Ahmad replied.

"That's a shame. I always enjoyed winding him up."

"What's more he was working as a cabbie on a forged driving license whilst serving a 5 year ban in Poland for dangerous driving."

"Always drove us home very carefully. He was harmless lad and we were merciless with him."

"Yes, it's a pity, He was a hard worker. He worked as a plumber by day, and every evening as a cabbie. I met him when he turned up to service my boiler, and we got talking, and he asked me if we had any taxi jobs going."

"Your recruitment process needs a bit of closer inspection, Ahmad. How did that fau pas slip through the net?" asked Tiny.

"I don't know, but yes, you are right, we'll have to tighten up our interview procedures."

The Brewers devotees spilled through the door as they had done so many times before, and Hugh had his last word.

"Goodnight, girls. I know you're going to do something I wouldn't do."

Middle fingers were raised in the air as the Vicarage Road contingent drove off.

During the taxi ride the fatman had one more go at engaging his colleague on the subject of Gordon, and what he felt was his absolute brass neck in turning up at the pub when he was off work again. He thought it was getting beyond a joke, and seriously pleaded to have the accountant sacked and replaced by someone who they could depend on. But Tiny didn't want to discuss it. It was still drizzling miserably when they left the taxi, shook hands, smiled, and went their separate ways.

Up in Blairgowrie, the biggest adventure of Duncan's life was about to begin. Following the tragic death of Brunhilda, by 31st May he had tied up all his loose ends. The previously secret contents of the bungalow's cellar, a substantial collection of flying memorabilia from the 1st and 2nd World Wars, had been sold at auction and raised very nearly £300,000. The property in Dunkeld Road, Blairgowrie which he now owned was valued at over £150.000, and he was now suddenly a very rich man. He had finalised all his mother's affairs, and having relieved himself of the responsibility of working at Perth Open Office Systems, he was now ready to widen his horizons, and free to spread his wings.

At 30 years young, he had never travelled outside his native Scotland before. For the first time in his life he was boarding a scheduled flight on a real aeroplane. Previously he had only flown in small planes piloted by his mother, but he did not share her passion for flying. He was nervous and apprehensive, but also energised and excited. In a little over 90 minutes the Edinburgh to Heathrow shuttle would land in England, a country he had learned a great deal about, but never visited. There, he would be met by a cousin he had only met once 20 years ago, and he would start his visit to Essex, and then onwards to Suffolk to meet his aunt Lisalotte. He travelled light, armed only with a small flight-bag, in which was an important letter.

Standing in the Arrivals Hall at Heathrow holding up a sign for "Duncan Doenitz" stood the man in the Hub, looking forward to meeting the cousin he didn't really know.

On any flight from Edinburgh there might be a few Scotsmen wearing a kilt, a Tam o' Shanter, big socks, a sporran, all in their traditional tartan, and Norman had no clues to go on, so he was looking for somebody of about 30 dressed just like that. The stream of arrivals from the flight had started to dwindle, and he was getting worried that he'd somehow missed his cousin. When a traditionally attired Scotsman wandered through, the young man's gaze was briefly fixed on him as he breezed past and met some people holding up a sign saying, "William McPhee".

Then behind him he heard an unfamiliar voice saying, "Hallo, Norman, good to see you." in an obviously Scottish accent. As he turned back towards the gate, there was his cousin, dressed not as expected, but clearly a Primark man from head to toe; t-shirt, skinny jeans, cheap shoes, denim jacket, carrying a small flight-bag and wearing a broad welcoming grin. Only the bag and the grin didn't have the legend "Cedar Wood State" written on them.

"Hi, Duncan. How was the flight?" asked the Essex boy with a smile.

"Not a bad flight I suppose, pretty uneventful, actually a bit boring. Unlike my mother, I hate flying, it scares me shitless. But I must say it's not as frightening on a proper aeroplane."

They shook hands, and started to make their way out of the terminal.

"Good! Let's go. I've got the Porsche parked up in the multi-storey. It's a bit of a walk, so you can stretch your legs a bit."

There was a pause. This was always destined to be a little awkward especially at first. They hadn't seen each other since they were both little boys 20 years ago, and far from catching up on lost time, it was more like struggling to make conversation by finding some common ground. The new arrival appeared to be the strong silent type. He didn't have too much to say. Then Primark man spoke again. "By the way, you might be wondering why my surname is Doenitz and not McVitie, " he said as they walked on.

"No not really, my mum told me that auntie Brunhilda knew who your father was, but she never married him."

"Well, my father was Henry Tusker McVitie. He was a roadie for Hawkwind and Motorhead. You've heard of them have you?"

"Oh Yes! Not my taste though, I like Coldplay and Stereophonics. But do continue."

"Tusker was a wanderer, a nomad, a traveller I suppose you'd say in today's language, and in a way he and my mum were both free spirits. He was mad keen on all types of flying as well. She didn't want to tie him down when she fell pregnant with me, and so she decided that I would keep the family name, Doenitz."

They reached the car-park, found the Porsche, and soon were cruising along the M25 on the way back to Chelmsford. There were only snatches of conversation between the two men, during the go, crawl, stop, start, stutter, go, fly, stop again, process that typified driving on the orbital car-park. In a way the movement of the car, echoed the on/off nature of the interaction between them. Norman related his solitary memory of meeting his auntie

Brunhilda when he was 7, and being suffocated in her huge bosom. He didn't remember much at all about the short family holiday in Blairgowrie, least of all about his cousin.

Duncan revealed that he and his mother lived in a very small bungalow, and that she had accumulated the finest most valuable collection of Luftwaffe memorabilia hidden away in her cellar which he had been forbidden to enter. He explained that the collection had recently been sold at auction for about £300,000. He talked briefly about being qualified as an accountant, and how he'd now given up his job working for P.O.O.S. in Perth, after his substantial inheritance came through.

After a ninety minute drive they arrived at the Hub, and Norman introduced his cousin to Clarisa who had been waiting there. The visitor's few possessions were installed in the smaller bedroom, and then the 3 of them went down to Prezzo for a meal. The strange staccato basis of the conversation persisted until the lodger was on his second large Peroni beer, and then the awkwardness and shyness left him, and he showed charm, intelligence, and a very dry sense of humour.

"Phew! What a relief," thought the man in the Hub, "Primark man is human after all. Give him a drink and he comes alive."

"This isn't so bad after all," thought the nouveau riche Scot, "I think I'm going to enjoy myself in England. He's OK, my cousin Norm, and Clarisa, she's lovely, wonder if she's got a sister?"

During the next day, Duncan was taken to the 1stCitySoft offices in Colchester, and introduced to Hugh and Tiny. First impressions of the long lost cousin were not at all good. He appeared to be very introverted, shy, self-conscious and uncommunicative. Soon he was semi-abandoned in front of a game of Viking Ninja Holocaust 9. He'd not played computer games much before, but with occasional guidance he soon got the hang of it. Indeed, when lunchtime came, it proved difficult to prise him away from it. A few hours after lunch, the man in the Porsche took his favourite route back through Stanway, Tiptree, Maldon, and Hatfield Peveril to show off the new premises in the Hedgerows Business Park. Apart from a few questions about the accounting side of the business, Primark man had seemed not very interested. Norman looked forward to taking him to the Two Brewers on Friday evening to see whether he would switch to his other personality again.

Waiting for the family phone call on a Friday evening before the stroll down to the Brewers was a ritual. That Friday the cousins were enjoying playing a session of Beer Festival Bastards Final Frontier when the phone rang. It was the familiar voice of Stanley.

"Ey Oop, son, 'ow yer diddlin'?"

"Alright, Dad, how are you?"

"Mustn't grumble, nobody listens anyway."

"Mum alright, is she?"

"Aye, son, she's on t' mend now."

"What can I do for you, Dad?"

"Well, I'm just phoning up to ask thee 'bout tomorrow lad. Yer know bringin' oop yer cousin t' see yer mum. I take it 'e's arrived OK, as 'e?"

"Yes, Dad, no problem, he's here, and we'll see you tomorrow as planned."

"Champion! And yer mum says she'll do yer fav'rit for lunch."

"OK, Dad, We'll be there about 10, see you then, love to Mum."

"Bye, son, drive carefully."

Norman put the phone down, and turned to his cousin, "Right, now we're off to my local watering hole, for the Friday night session. The rest of the gang will be there. I hope you're ready to have your leg pulled mercilessly. Uncle Hugh is probably going to tear you to shreds for being Scottish. He is harmless, and it's all in good fun, so don't take it too seriously."

Duncan felt a little uneasy, and just replied, "OK."

"And then be prepared for the Village People. I don't know if you've had much contact with the gay community, but we have a bunch of gay friends, and they're very sociable. Our fat friend spends a lot of time taking the piss out of them, and they never hesitate to rise to the bait. There's Gordon, nickname Golden Bollocks, who is our company accountant, off sick at the moment, and his partner, Spike who runs a decorating company. We call him Scruffbag for reasons that will become obvious to you. Then there's the other two, Ike and Mike, nice couple, in a civil partnership, both work in the gardening business. All four of them share a house on the other side of town."

Primark man looked a bit shell-shocked. He didn't know if he was ready for what loomed ahead. Norman reassured.

"Don't worry, none of them bite, they're all house trained, and Tiny will keep them in order. He's our boss, you met him earlier, and he's a steady, reliable guy."

The resident comedian was just finishing his first rant of the evening, with nobody taking much notice, as they'd heard it all before. Besides which, Gordon, the target of his moaning was not in attendance.

"So, apart from a brief respite when he graced us with his regal presence for a whole four days, the bean counter had a total of six weeks off with stress and then the flu, while we've all been working our tits off to get 1stCitySoft off the ground running."

There were groans all round as the argument was concluded," I suppose we should be grateful that he's expected to put in an appearance next Tuesday. I wonder how long he'll last this time before he goes down with... with ... oh an in-growing toenail, or an ear infection."

There was a pause, as nobody felt inclined to mount a challenge, or indeed fight the accused's corner. It had all been said and done before. Boring! Even the chairman was tired of the subject. The arrival of Norman and Duncan broke the chain.

"Evening, Nobless, usual is it? And what will you have, my friend? The Fuller's Pride is excellent."

"Yes, I'll try that thanks." was the shy reply.

In truth Primark man was a bit uncomfortable, especially about meeting the Village People. Strange introductions over, the resident comic held the floor, while everybody waited for some invective about anything Scottish. He was usually very precise, but somehow he'd got the wrong end of the stick about his new target's name.

"Good name that Duncan McVitie. It certainly declares your pedigree as a porridge gobbler," the joker began, "Or maybe we could just call you, Biscuits?"

He quietly and nervously responded, "Aye! That was my father's nickname for a while, but it's never been mine."

"Really, opportunity missed. Shame!"

"And I'm not actually a McVitie anyway. My registered name is Doenitz. That was my mother's maiden name."

"You're a little German bastard then are you?"

"Yes, I suppose I am."

This wasn't at all a good start for the new arrival. At this point he was taking a distinct dislike to Mr Obesity. His cousin dragged him away to the dartboard before he burst into tears.

They played Killer with Ike and Mike, and the new Brewers recruit proved to be totally inept at darts, hitting the light above the board more often than anything else. Another round of drinks arrived, and while he was nearing the end of his 2nd pint miraculously his aim improved and he started to hit the target. Spike took a bit of a temporary shine to him as a fellow Scot, but Duncan was wary of the scruffy decorator and his sexual preferences, and so he remained aloof. Having enjoyed his 2nd pint, he returned to the bar where the resident comedian was still holding court. Suddenly the shy Scot became a different man.

"My round, fellas. Hey, fatboy, another pint for you is it?" he slurred. Everybody was astonished at the transformation, but smiled and Hugh was definitely set to cash in on it.

"Yes, Jock, that'll do nicely. Where's your bagpipes? Nothing scares the civilised as much as a good swirl of Celtic rock-n-roll."

"Can only be beaten by the incessant wail of a Sassenach's continual moaning." was the unexpected reply.

"What do you keep in your sporran, Jocky boy? Is it a deep fried Mars bar, or are you just pleased to see me?"

"Not as pleased as I'd be to see the back of you, porky."

"Oh no, you haven't been converted to a bumboy already by the poof brigade. You must have shown them what you've got under your kilt."

"No chance, my friend, I'm more interested in the barmaid. What's her name?"

With that they smiled at each other, and exchanged high fives. The jolly fatman seemed to be delighted with the banter rally, and Primark man once loaded with a few pints proved to be more than a match for him. Clearly, Hugh had learned that not all Scotsmen were cast in the image of ignorant, kilt wearing morons. The conversation continued.

"So, your real name is Duncan Doenitz then, is it?"

"That's right, porky" was the smiling reply waiting for the next instalment.

"Sounds like someone with a speech impediment saying Dunkin' Doughnuts."

Giggling broke out, and a moment later the now slightly drunk Scotsman found himself in full public view labelled with the epithet "Doughnuts!" He was unperturbed and made off to the gents' to unload a couple of pints.

"I like him once he's had a drink, even if he is a ginger-haired savage who's just jumped over Hadrian's Wall." declared his new best friend.

It was time for another rant from Hugh who seemed to be back to his old form, much to the assembly's relief. Perhaps it was because Gordon had not put in an appearance, or maybe he was just having a better day. Nobody knew either way but they were just so pleased to have their old joker back again. Tiny was especially pleased. He decided to turn the subject to something topical.

"I read in the Chronicle that now Chelmsford is becoming a City the Council has decided to spend £7 million on a revamp for the City Centre. They're going to dig up the High Street, Market Street and Duke Street, and the bit of New London Road this side of Parkway to redesign the streets and squares and the pedestrianised areas, and change the traffic control. Seems like an enormous heap of money to spend on that."

"Waste of our money, it's all OK as it is," interrupted Hugh, "There's no point in it. In the words of the wise, if it ain't broke don't fix it! Who is going to benefit? Is it all the pissed up vodka swilling morons who terrorise that area at night time?"

He fully realised the irony of his statement and then continued," The money would be much better spent on building the Clarets a prestige football ground suitable for league football, like Dartford Council have done for their local team." He was totally sincere is his assertion, but nobody wanted to discuss it, so the rant was cut off in it's prime.

The young Scotsman returned, and the fatman asked him, "OK, Doughnuts, apart from keeping your wallet padlocked, what are your hobbies?"

"Well, we have long, dark, cold winters in Scotland, and have to stay indoors a lot, but we're used to it, not like you southern softies. You have 2 inches of snow, and everything closes down or grinds to a halt. When the weather's bad I like to watch old films. I'm an ardent fan of classics like Casablanca, African Queen, and Brief Encounter, and I love all those Laurel and Hardy and Keystone Cops comedies."

"Anyway," he suddenly changed the subject, "The barmaid, Caroline, isn't it? Do you suppose she might be a bit of an old film buff?"

"You have got to be kidding, my ginger friend, "giggled the fatman, "Caroline's the type of woman who thinks that Brief Encounter is an underwear catalogue."

Time was soon approaching for the Ramsbottom Olympics, but before that something special had been organised. The night was uniquely set up for the Ramsbottom version of Man versus Food. Stacked in the corner were 12 tins of Ye Olde Oak Bockwurst Style Hot Dogs in Brine, the 1.2 kilo size, and 12 tubes of Colman's English Mustard.

The contestants had to open the tin, spread each hot dog with the mustard, and attempt to eat all of the 8 in the tin whilst being timed by the organiser. He had graciously, he considered, decided not to take part.

The contest began, and continued throughout, with whooping and cheering and raucous encouragement at each attempt to tackle the problem of defeating the Colman's.

Mike was first to go. He only managed 2 bangers in 3 minutes, before his eyes and nose became a continuous stream from the mustard, and he was forced to submit, to booing and shouts of shame.

Ike made an attempt to cheat by spreading mustard too thinly, but the judge intervened adding a very thick layer, and as a result he managed 3 in just over 3 minutes before streaming eyes got the better of him. He was annoyed at the amount of mustard Hugh had spread on his bangers as a response to his cheating, and wanted the contest abandoned.

Everybody thought that Caroline, with her extensive sausage experience, would have had no trouble if it hadn't been for the mustard, and even when her cheating was overlooked she only succeeded in eating 3 in 2 minutes 20 seconds.

Spike was next, and seemed to have a good technique to almost swallow the sausage in large chunks without too much chewing delay, but once again the mustard reigned supreme, and he was forced to give up after a brave 5 in 6 minutes.

The chairman wasn't even going to be persuaded to attempt the potentially disgusting feat, but several others did, with predictably disappointing results. Norman was even less keen to have a go, especially as recently Clarisa was doing a very good job of turning him into a part-time vegetarian.

Then it was Duncan's turn, and although he had to be coaxed into taking part, he impressively demolished all 8 of the hot dogs liberally spread with mustard in just under 8 minutes, with very enthusiastic encouragement and chanting of "Dough - nuts, Dough - nuts, go, go, go, Dough - nuts!" from all his new friends . Hugh was extremely pleased to present him with his prize, which just happened to be the 3 remaining tins of the bangers. He accepted them graciously, and 10 seconds later rushed full pelt into the gents' to expel the contents of his stomach with a series of violent wretches.

When eventually the standard Ramsbottom Olympics started, the strange partnership of Scruffbag and Hugh were the winners of the darts. The incredibly messy pints of lemonade drinking contest, was also won by the fatman, but then he'd saved himself by not taking part in the Man versus Food competition. Then it was a clean sweep, when unsurprisingly the expected contestant won the final of the arm wrestling contest. He competed against the new recruit but won easily with his standard gaseous finale. There was a large element of psychology involved in this final when Doughnuts was repeatedly ribbed about what a crap darts player he was, with jibes like, "Not very good with spears, the Scots, even miniature ones, much better at stabbing you in the back with their dirks."

All too soon, another Brewers session drew to a close, with the expectation that Ahmad would turn up to take his usual fare home. In his drunken haze the joker thought he saw Pavel enter the bar, and before he could say anything he went up to him, noticing something quite different about him. "Pav, I thought you'd been deported. What are you doing here, and what have you done to yourself, you look terrible?"

The man he was talking to was tall and bald, and dressed all in black like a Lithuanian gangster. On closer inspection he only bore a vague resemblance to Pavel, and Hugh wasn't at all sure, so he just stood there mouth agape in expectation of a reply.

He didn't have to wait long.

"You must be Mr Ramsbottom, and you and Mr Balls are going to Tyrell's Close. Correct?" enquired the man in perfect English.

They just nodded, and slurped the last few dregs of their pints. There was something rather sinister about this guy, and now he didn't look or sound like Pavel in the least. An explanation was forthcoming.

"My name is Stanislav. I am Pavel's older brother. Are you ready to go?" There was an insistence in the voice.

Out in the car park the last jibe was aimed in Spike's direction, "Hey Scruffbag, I had you down to win the hotdog eating contest. After all you must be well used to sucking saveloys." Middle finger in the air was the silent response.

The passengers were soon in the taxi, and the driver asked," I hear Chelmsford will become a City soon?"

There was no reply but the driver continued.

"I come from Krakow, one the oldest cities in Poland, dating back to the 7th century. It's not a bit like Chelmsford."

Hugh couldn't resist it, however sinister this bloke looked; he wasn't letting a history lesson go by without his input.

"Do you know anything about history Stanislav?"

"I am a professor of European history. But I left Poland because I could not get a job in Krakow. So here I am taxi driving."

The joker was desperately squeezing his buttocks, trying to avoid a huge fart, but it was too late.

"Funny name Stanislav; it sounds like an industrial strength toilet cleaner."

The smelly fart pervaded the car like a fog rolling over a flat morning meadow, just as it stopped at Tyrell's Close, and the occupants quickly spilled out holding their hands over their noses.

"And I my friend, most definitely need something of industrial strength to clear that fart from my cab." chuckled Stanislav as he rolled down all of the windows.

"Sorry! Good night, Sanilav." concluded the farting fatman.

In the meantime Norman had prised Duncan away from talking to Caroline, just as he was about to drop a clanger and invite her back to the Hub for a coffee.

CHAPTER 19

Lisalotte's Windfall

(Saturday 26th May to Friday 8th June 2012)

Saturday morning started badly and it really wasn't any surprise. Duncan had now been staying at the Hub apartment for only 2 days, but finding out that he came alive after a few drinks was accompanied by another less bearable discovery. Despite the second bedroom being at the opposite end of the hallway, it still sounded like somebody was sawing down a giant redwood whenever the ginger Scotsman started snoring. So on that Saturday morning Norman had hardly slept, and his guest had a hangover. Breakfast was simple enough. The muesli was easily turned into porridge, even if one of them fished out all the nuts and other non-oaty bits and left them on the side of the plate. In slow motion due to their distinctly different handicaps they were eventually ready to go on their way up to Leiston.

At 9.15 am most imprecisely the Porsche Carrera 911 engine roared, and slid out onto Springfield Road, making for the A12 and onward to Suffolk. Porscheman was definitely on autopilot as he gunned it on the slip-road at the Cramphorn flyover, looked at his watch, and gave it the turbo large.

"Shouldn't be too much traffic, e.t.a. 10:30ish" he thought, and then he slotted in the Hawkwind, Masters of the Universe CD that his cousin had brought with him. He didn't like it much, but then he was only playing it to irritate his passenger's hung over state, and at least most of it gave off a complimentary therapeutic chug in unison with the car's powerful engine There wasn't much conversation during the trip, the Scotsman reverted to his standard largely uncommunicative behaviour, and the adopted Essex boy was content to just drive.

Their arrival at the bungalow in Leiston was by no means greeted with bunting, flags and celebration. It was a low key affair, a bit awkward and slightly tense. After all, Duncan had not seen his relatives for over 20 years, and in all senses except a diluted bloodline they were strangers. Norman greeted his dad with a handshake, his mum with a kiss on the cheek, and his sister with a "Wha's Uup?", and then he just introduced their visitor.

"Mum, Dad, Sis, this is, Duncan."

The Scot repeated the form of his cousin's greetings, except with Cher to whom he just nodded.

"I vill make coffee for ous. How do you like it, Duncan?" asked Lisalotte.

"Oh black, strong, 2 sugars, please." was the reply.

They sat down while the coffee was made, and the hangover was still clinging on like a limpet, so even polite chitchat was difficult.

Stanley asked," Good drive oop, son, was it?"

Norman replied, "Oh, yes, no trouble, I think the car could find its way without me at the steering wheel."

There was a big pause.

The Yorkshireman went again, turning to the visitor, "Eee, lad, 'ow d'yer like it down 'ere in t' south?"

"It's OK, I suppose, haven't seen much of it yet. Essex it a bit flat compared to where we lived in Blairgowrie, and Suffolk seems very green and rural."

"That'll be t' rain lad, t' ent bloody stopped raining fer weeks on end. We'll all get washed away soon if it carries on."

Just then, Lisalotte reappeared from the kitchen with the coffee, and interrupted, " Yes, wiz all zis rain, I do hope ve don't have a satsuma like zey had in Japan last March, zat vas terrible, all zose people dying, zeir homes smashed."

Everybody in the room except Duncan knew that she meant to say "tsunami", but they wouldn't have corrected her, and the hangover was still biting hard enough for their visitor not to want to make a response. She set about pouring the coffee, and it hadn't passed her by, what condition her nephew was in, so she had made it extra strong. She continued," It is so vorrying, because ve only liff up ze road from Sizewell, and look vhat heppened to zat Fuckajimmy nuclear power station." This was her attempt at making intelligent conversation, but she clearly had absolutely no knowledge of the cause of a tsunami, or a satsuma for that matter.

There was an attractive gilded metal box lying on the coffee table from which she retrieved a number of old photographs, depicting herself and her sister in their childhood back in Germany, which she passed over one at a time, each with a lengthy description. She was trying very hard to build bridges with her only remaining connection with her past, and showed a hint of irritation with her visitor's booze inflicted headache, and apparent disinterest, while everybody else watched feeling slightly uncomfortable. However, after a while the coffee had its desired effect, Duncan perked up, and to great surprise suddenly started speaking with Lisalotte in what sounded like perfect German. Norman understood a little everyday German, but the ex-butcher only had a few important words in his foreign vocabulary. So there was a sense of relief, sufficient for everybody but aunt and nephew to leave the room, and let them continue in their foreign tongues.

Out in the greenhouse, Stanley lit a welcome cigarette, pushed aside Sid's lush vegetation, and after finding two boxes for him and his son to sit on, began," Well, lad, I'm glad t' ice 'as bin broken there. It was always goin' to be a bit awkward. Yer mum's bin even more difficult t' live with, after t' news 'bout Brunhilda. Eee, it's bin a great shock to 'er poor cow. As usual, me and Cher 'ave bin makin' ourselves scarce, and keepin' out of 'er way. Helen's bin good though, kept us all sane, and bin lookin' after yer mum as well. Nice lass, yer'll 'ave to meet 'er soon."

The Essex boy was relieved to be in the sanctuary of the greenhouse, and replied," Yeah, it must have been a rough time for you all. Thank heaven's the gout pills seemed to have worked, and Mum's Tourette's has receded, otherwise she'd be effing and blinding on top of everything else."

They both chuckled

"What's 'e like, yer cousin, all right is 'e?"

"Strange bloke, very quiet, until he's had a drink or two, and then he comes alive. Last night he was holding his own against Hugh, once he'd had a Fuller's Pride or two, and as you'd know, that takes some doing. Then he entered in some silly contest to eat hotdogs smothered in English mustard. He won it, but you could say he was unfortunate to enjoy the bangers twice."

They both chuckled again.

"Hugh, all right is 'e? Must make t' effort to see 'im sometime, and 'ave a few beers."

"Well, there's a lot of pressure at work at the moment, and I think he's feeling it a bit. It looks as if he's aged 10 years in the last six months. But you know him; he'll bounce back like he always does. Nothing gets him down for long."

"Eee, give 'im my best when yer see 'im, lad."

Father and son continued to hide in the greenhouse, talking over things including their recent visit oop north, and their planned return to the Wellington Heifer later on in the year. The friends of Leiston German club carried on in the lounge and then the kitchen until lunchtime rolled round. The family reassembled around the dining room table for Norman's favourite, which he had to pretend he liked again just to please his mum. By this time Duncan was on a roll, he loved bockwurst and sauerkraut, especially when it was accompanied by the very welcome hair of the dog in the form of a couple of pints of Adnam's. He even asked for seconds, much to his auntie's delight.

It was standard practice after their lunches for Cher and her mum to fall asleep on the sofa, after emptying 3 bottles of Liebfraumilch between them, and for father and son to retire to the greenhouse. But this was a different scenario.

Tears were shed when it came round to the subject of Brunhilda's unfortunate flying accident, and then Duncan brought out an envelope from his back pocket, and gave it to his aunt saying, "This is for you, tante Lotte. It is from meine Mutti."

With some embarrassment and awkwardness it was carefully opened. Inside were a letter and a cheque. The recipient perched her specs on the end of her nose, and read out loud.

"My dearest sister Lisalotte,

We haven't been together in a long, long time. Life goes so quickly, and none of us know when we will fly into the sunset, and land in a different dimension.

I wish we had seen a lot more of each other in these last 20 years, but we do have some wonderful memories of our good times back in Deutschland, especially in the bierkellers in Munchen. We will meet again on the other side, and we'll sit with the angels, and reminisce.

In the meantime, my lovely sister, I have left you a little something.

Aufwiedersehn liebling
Viele Grusse

Brunhilda xxx"

With that she burst into tears, and almost forgot to have a peep at the cheque she was holding. Cher put her arms around her mum, offered the box of tissues, and hugged her. When she had recovered her composure enough, she focussed on the cheque, and a big beaming smile appeared through the wall of tears. Brunhilda had left her £25,000. She focussed on her nephew, and just kept smiling and saying "Danke schon, danke schon."

He didn't know what to say, and the Yorkshireman sensed it was time to leave his wife of many years on her own. So he offered an invitation," Come and 'ave a butcher's at me greenhouse and garden, lad. Leave yer aunt to 'erself for a while."

The lads retired to the greenhouse, and the ladies talked for a few minutes and then customarily fell asleep on the sofa for a while. The visitor was amazed and slightly taken aback at the greenhouse, or more precisely its contents. He looked at his cousin, as the Yorkshireman was distracted looking for another box to sit on underneath all the profuse foliage, and whispered," Does your dad know what this is? I've never seen such a lot of it growing in one place."

Norman just shook his head and mouthed a quiet "No!"

He was surprised that his cousin knew what the greenhouse foliage was.

Stanley sat on the box he'd found, lit a cigarette, and said, "Sorry, lad, this plant's a bit of a bloody nuisance, grows so bloody quick. It's not mine, it's Sid's oop t' road. 'E sez it's therapeutic, 'elps 'im with 'is arthritis. He cut's it and dries it in a kiln I've got in me shed at the bottom of t' garden, then 'e stores it all in that drum." He pointed to a very large cylindrical container at the door of the greenhouse." But I think 'es selling it to 'is mates down t' Crown in King Georges Avenue. Eee, I wonder sometimes, they can't all 'ave arthritis."

The two cousins just looked at each other and grinned.

Soon the subject came round to football, and the forthcoming European Championships. The Essex boy wasn't that interested, but listened as his father and the novelty Scotsman debated the merits of several England players including Joe Hart and Wayne Rooney. Then Noble senior waxed as eloquently as he could after several pints of Adnam's about the Leeds United team that played under Don Revie in the 1970's, and included a number of Scottish internationals like Billy Bremner, Eddie Gray, and Gordon McQueen.

Duncan was equally enthusiastic about St Johnstone FC, the local football team in Perth, formed in 1884. He had followed them since he was a teenager, but confessed that he had never been to a match at McDiarmid Park. He compared his club to West Ham United, in that they were both yo-yo clubs historically floating between the top two divisions, with episodes of true glory being few and far between, although he conceded that the Hammers had enjoyed more glory than the Saints. He explained how his heroes had been promoted to the Scottish Premier League in 2009, and seemed to have successfully consolidated their position in the top league. Then he remembered a tenuous southern connection, in that the recent Southend United manager Paul Sturrock, had been St Johnstone's manager back in the early 90's, and had succeeded in getting them promotion to the top level in 1997. He referred to Sturrock as "Luggy", alluding to his large ears. The football discussion took over an hour, and since it became quite warm under the glass, the visitor felt the need to remove his jacket.

Eventually they moved around the garden, where the roses and the rhubarb had started to grow profusely under the short spells of sparse sunshine in between the long periods of torrential rainfall. The youngsters showed a polite if slightly detached interest. Then it was suggested it might be time to return indoors.

"Eee, lads let's go in and see if t' girls have woken up yet, shall we."

Unbeknown to all, when Duncan made a diversion back to the greenhouse, to collect the jacket that he'd left in there, he took the opportunity to quickly help himself to a generous stash of Sid's therapeutic dried plant.

When they returned indoors, they discovered that Helen had arrived while they were touring the garden. "This is my friend, Helen." Cher made introductions. But the focus of the gathering was always going to be elsewhere.

"Vhat haff you boys been talking about for so long?" slurred a bleary eyed Lisalotte.

"Eee, only football me dear, nothin' important," Stanley replied.

"Bloody football, stupid game, I don't know vhy you bozzer," she went on," I've only ever been to vatch football once, and I didn't understand it. Zhey keep shouting zat ze referee's an anchor, or somesing about him being from Kent."

All the boys and the 2 girls all looked at each other, and grinned at another typical misunderstanding.

Helen made and poured coffee, and they all sat down to chat again, and then Lisalotte announced that she was going to buy 2 dachshunds with her legacy, and then she was giving the rest of the £25,000 to her husband, so he could start up his butcher's business again. The Yorkshireman stood up with a start, and planted a big kiss on her cheek saying," Eee, lass that's reet champion. Now I've not only got all t' know 'ow wi' Arthur's recipes, but t' money t' set things oop again."

There was a catch, but it had great potential to be ignored when she added, "But zere must be no funny sausages and nussing for der arschloch Chester Gannet to complain about. I cannot go zroo zat again, last time vas a catch 23 situation."

Whilst this was going on, Norman was racking his brain, because he was absolutely sure he recognised Helen from somewhere, but try as he might his memory failed to provide him with a resolution.

Later on in the evening after they had all enjoyed a large selection of German style open sandwiches, the two cousins said a temporary Aufwiersehen, and took the short drive into Aldeburgh, where they were booked to stay overnight at the Mill Inn. This overnight stop had been recommended by Noble senior, because it one of his favourite haunts. The 16th century watering hole, with a history of smugglers, was situated in Market Cross Place, behind the ancient moot hall, and right on the seafront. Like great sections of the Suffolk coast the area around Aldeburgh was the victim of coastal erosion, and the Inn had once been in the centre of the small town.

It was a fairly warm, dry evening, and they made a constitutional stroll along the seafront before going upstairs to their separate rooms conveniently situated at opposite ends of the hotel. Nearly all the discussion was about Lisalotte and her amazing knack of getting things slightly and amusingly wrong. Norman explained how they were all so used to it, that they had given up attempting to correct her, preferring instead to enjoy the comical aspects of her misunderstandings.

"Yes, she's terrific my mum, it's all harmless, and she makes us laugh, but most of the time she truly doesn't know why."

"My mother was totally the opposite, always very correct and very precise, wouldn't let me get away with anything, and she taught me to speak German, like my life depended on it."

"Sometimes it just a little slip up, like instead of saying pull out all the stops, she says pull out all the crops. I'm sure her deafness has something to do with it. All those years standing too close to the oompah bands in the bierkellers."

"No, my mother never suffered from that, had perfect hearing as far as I know."

"She came out with a brilliant one, a while ago when we were talking about Chelmsford's Roman origins. She misheard Caesaromagus as Caesaradorus, and she thought for moment and said that it should have been a much bigger place if Caesar expected to be adored there!"

The ginger Scotsman laughed, and then his cousin carried on with," Not only is she a bit deaf, but that's not all, when she's got the gout she develops Tourette's syndrome, and then the air is blue. We could fill a swear box in one afternoon. Me and my dad are in stitches sometimes."

Duncan replied changing the subject," Yes, your father obviously has no idea what he's growing in his greenhouse, does he? This bloke Sid must be laughing. Not only will he be out of his tree, but he must be making a pot of money flogging off his dried arthritic potion."

"No, he has no idea that he's growing cannabis, and I don't want him to know. He's an exile from his beloved Yorkshire, and Sid's one of his best mates. So please don't say anything."

They walked a little further along the shoreline, and then turned back towards the Mill Inn, enjoying the fresh, salty, night-time sea air, and then came the question, "What do you think of Caroline? She seems to have taken a shine to me, and I quite like her too."

The Essex boy felt momentarily uncomfortable as he remembered the night he shared a bed with the lady in question.

"She's probably after your money mate. She knows you're a good catch with all that dosh. Not the brightest button in the box, our Caroline. She's the sort of girl who thinks that Sherlock Holmes is a block of flats, and that an itchy fanny is a Japanese motorcycle." They both giggled.

"Oh, I thought she was a bit like your Clarisa."

"Really!" offered the Essex boy disbelieving that such an inappropriate comparison could be made by any averagely intelligent person.

The sleeping arrangements were ideal in the Mill Inn that Saturday night. At the opposite end of the building, the persistent sawing of giant redwoods was not discernable, to a man with excellent taste in both cars and young ladies.

After breakfast on Sunday morning, and the return of the boys to the bungalow in Leiston, the day followed a similar pattern to the previous one. Again, Duncan reverted to his shy and introverted persona, and Lisalotte oscillated between ecstatic and tearful whilst continuing to amuse with her characteristic verbal gymnastics. Stanley as head of the household, attempted to hold everything together by keeping everyone happy. Norman blended into the background, and although he was confidently number one son, it was clear that at that moment in time his cousin was going to be the centre of attention. Cher and Helen seemed to drift off into their own little world oblivious to anyone else's presence, talking quietly amongst themselves, holding hands, and enjoying long lingering looks at each other. There was plentiful coffee, as Lisalotte and her nephew again indulged in long conversations in German about Brunhilda, and another opportunity for father and his son to escape to the greenhouse and garden.

When lunchtime came around, the lady of the house had prepared Wienersnitzel, with bratkartoffel, and a dessert of Rotegrutze, washed down with the habitual beverages. The Scottish visitor loved the German food, and again asked for seconds. Then the whole family settled down to watch the River Thames Diamond Jubilee Pageant, a maritime parade of 1000 boats, and the largest flotilla seen on the river in 350 years. Unfortunately this event, which already promised to be not the most exciting outside broadcast in Royal television history, was spoiled by heavy rain and the cancellation of the Air Force flyover due to a very low cloud-base and bad visibility at ground level. Both the Queen and Prince Philip exhibited a strong sense of good old British stiff upper lip, and a stoic resilience in the face of the torrential adversity. Nearly everybody watching fell asleep, or at least dozed off for a short while. Norman was still trying to tweak his brain into remembering where he had seen Helen before, but again it wouldn't come to him.

When late afternoon arrived, handshakes and kisses preceded the departure of the two cousins, with promises of further visits, and grateful thanks for the inheritance that had been conveyed from Scotland. The drive back was uneventful, and devoid of much interaction. To number one son's relief he was able to concentrate on his driving, and enjoy the experience of putting his pride and joy through its paces, as his passenger fell back into his non-communicative stupor.

The Essex boy had enjoyed his visit to Leiston, especially as there had been no hockey to endure, but he hadn't seen his beautiful Clarisa for too long, and looked forward to ridding himself of his lodger, and renewing his closeness with the love of his life. He hoped that now the trip to Suffolk was done, and the £25,000 legacy handed over to his mum, that his cousin would soon pack his bags and return north of the border. Duncan was family, but there was only so much hospitality that any blood relative would want to offer gladly.

Soon after they arrived back at the Hub, Clarisa came over; letting herself in with the key she had been given a few days before, and greeted her Normie with such enthusiasm and passion you'd have thought he'd been on duty in Afghanistan for 6 months. She gave a cursory recognition of the lodger's presence, and he took the hint, and decided to go off for a walk. While the lovers went straight to the bedroom, and renewed their acquaintance in the best possible way, the newly named Doughnuts went round to Caroline's little terraced house in Navigation Road, and shared some of Sid's famous foliage.

And that's the way it stayed for the whole night; two very diverse couples, in two separate locations, one couple lost in their love for each other, and the other couple stumbling mindlessly around the narcotically induced landscape of a different planet.

Clarisa was now a fixture whenever the Ramsbottom's had one of their Sunday or Bank Holiday roasts. Hugh had asked Norman and his lady along for lunch on the Monday, politely including the ginger barbarian in the invitation. Tiny and Tina were also invited.

It came as some surprise when a dishevelled and unshaven Doughnuts turned up at Avalon House, with the Brewer's barmaid in tow. Mr Ramsbottom wasn't pleased, but he had an abundance of sociability, and primed Millicent to lay an extra place at the table. Lunch was followed by a long session of computer games on the 3 plasma screens in the boy's playroom. The chairman's prowess as a game player had fallen away dramatically while he had been concentrating on 1stCitySoft, so he was an early dropout from the competition. Duncan was showing signs of the superb quality of the Jamaican woodbines he'd been smoking the previous evening, and didn't last long either.

They found themselves together, the smart, always correct, company chairman, and the nouveau riche, surprisingly intelligent, but nevertheless largely unknown quantity accountant. They didn't have much in common, but had a staccato discussion about accountancy matters, in between whoops and cheers and boos from the more proficient game players. In his heart of hearts the chairman would have dearly loved to have asked him, or any other accountant for that matter, to take over from Gordon and then complete the necessary work for the company accounts. But only he and Gordon knew the reasons why that was not possible at the moment.

While the boys were enjoying their laddish pursuits the girls enjoyed some wine and Thornton's chocolates, and discussed their respective jobs, relationships, and different roles in their lives. It wasn't that Caroline was unsociable; as a barmaid that was very unlikely, and she did have interesting and amusing things to say and tales to relate about her life and work. Perhaps she was just not what might be called "People like us". Nevertheless, Millicent made her very welcome, and despite having a cuckoo in the nest, she and Clarisa continued to develop their close friendship.

As afternoon quickly merged into evening, the supreme master of ceremonies invited everyone to watch the Queen's Diamond Jubilee Concert on the TV. All agreed what a strange mixed bag of good and bad performances the range of ageing artists presented. A large consensus were embarrassed by Rolf Harris, but grateful when he was interrupted mid-flight, disappointed with Cliff Richard, and considered Will I Am to be a waste of stage time. Everybody concurred that Tom Jones stole the show, and that the Madness set accompanied by fantastic visuals, especially for the song "Our House" was quality entertainment. The Queen smiled and jiggled her way through the various performances, but poor old 91year old Prince Philip had a bladder infection, and did not attend.

At the end of the evening the two young couples walked back towards the Hub together via Stump Lane and the Bunny Walk. But one couple glided through the moonlight only having eyes for each other, not noticing that the other couple had stopped and sat down on a bench to indulge in another hit of Sid's wacky baccy.

Once again the Hub apartment was lodger free, and Norman was so glad to be alone with his lovely little one. So, maybe the lodger wasn't high-tailing it back across Hadrian's Wall just yet, but at least he was making himself scarce. Without making any contact, he stayed away for another 3 days. He was a grown man, and his cousin had no need to be worried, because the Scot was now inescapably trapped in the clutches of Miss Bangs, and enjoying every minute of it.

On the following Friday, just before his dad's customary trek down to the Brewers, Tom resolved to deal with an issue that had been bothering him for a few days. Ever since the fatherly chat about Babestation, Tom had been more careful when furthering his interest, but something had been on his mind that needed discussing with his father. He went to extricate Hugh from the paperwork in his study. He had decided that he didn't want to take a superior approach to the issue, and call his dad into the playroom, so he led him gently out to the bottom of the garden where they both sat down with orange juices, man to man, son to father.

Tom began," Dad, I'm growing up, and soon I'll be a young man. We need to have a chat."

Hugh was more than delighted that his son was a chip off the old block, and had a genetic disposition to the same sense of humour as him. He sighed, and looked at him with some recognition of a situation repeated.

"Oh, Thomas," he said, "You're not going to give me a lecture about the birds and the bees, the ins and the outs, are you? Only we've done all that stuff already down the pub."

The son chuckled, "No, Dad," he replied with a cheeky wink, "I'm sure you already know more than me, even though you're so old now, you may have forgotten most of it."

"Yes, sure thing, son." Hugh yawned. There was a pause.

"You told me you're glad, " the youngster continued, "That I'm interested in looking at Babestation. It is girls that I'm interested in."

The father pretended to blush, but he didn't reply, and his son noticed.

"No need to be embarrassed, Dad. It's just me growing up. But there is something that you should know. You said that you don't want Dick and Harry to share my interest until they are ready. Well, I can tell you that Harry is far too absorbed in Playstation games at the moment, but Dick has a problem. He's not interested in Babestation like I am, but I have seen him tuning into Gaystation. So all I'm asking you to do Dad is to be discrete about it, and make sure Mum doesn't catch him looking at it. Can you do that for me, Dad?"

"Yes, son, of course, don't worry." Hugh answered, feeling uncomfortable enough to want to end the discussion.

Tom was happy to have done a good job, and concluded, "And, Dad, if you ever need to talk about the birds and the bees, the ins and the outs, then don't hesitate to come and have a word with me, will you? Remember, whatever you, and Mum need, me and Dick and Harry, are on your side."

"Thanks, son," Hugh said, finishing his orange juice, "Can I go back to my study now?"

"Yes, OK, Dad. See you later." was the reply.

The proud son sat there, at the bottom of their garden, while the father returned to his study filled with pride for the humorous way in which his eldest had passed on a problem. At the same time, he wondered how he was going to deal with the prospect of his second son perhaps being gay.

It had been an eventful week for Britain with the Queen's Jubilee celebrations taking place, while the Olympic torch was travelling on a tortuous route across the length and breadth of these fair lands. Lands that grew increasingly soggy day by day, as the heavens continued to open with by now, monotonous regularity. On Wednesday 6th June the granting of City status to Chelmsford by the Queen became official with the receipt of the Letters Patent. Not that anybody needed it, but what a great excuse for a celebration, and so the jolly fatman bought dozens of whoopee cushions and put one on every seat in the Two Brewers which was decorated with Union Jacks and pictures of Her Majesty the Queen. Obviously Hugh was very keen to show his blatant patriotism and in particular to have another lengthy boast about his home town of Chelmsford succeeding in its quest for City status ahead of not only Colchester, but also Southend, and not to mention Middlesborough and Reading.

Just as the previous week, it took time and a few pints of Fuller's before Doughnuts got going. He'd only spent a week down south, during which time he'd declared Essex a boring, flat and largely featureless wilderness, been unimpressed with Chelmsford itself, and had identified only a few saving graces in its location. These were; its closeness to London, which he seemed to have taken a liking to, after a one day whirlwind tour there with Caroline, and what he described as the cute tranquillity of the neighbouring county of Suffolk. There was a paradox in there somewhere which nobody seemed at all bothered to fathom.

The fattest old Chelmsfordian was inflated with pride for what was now his home City, "Been here on and off since Roman times, Chelmsford has. Bet you didn't know that, Doughnuts my friend. We were civilised when you lot were still living in caves and eating brontosaurus sandwiches."

"Perhaps, fatboy. Your pride is understandable, even though your claim is obviously scurrilous." the Scot retorted.

The jolly fatman was beginning to like this new recruit to the Brewers debating club, and within a few minutes he was going to discover that he was talking to someone who may have surprisingly been his intellectual equal, at least where some historical matters were concerned. He just smiled and said, "Oh please do explain that assertion, my ginger topped savage."

A deep breath was all that was necessary before the words of wisdom came forth. "Well, I'll congratulate your nondescript little town on conning the Queen into giving you City status, and you're probably not interested in hearing about far more legitimate claims, but I'm going to educate you anyway." He looked straight at the joker, who was grinning with delight, and then continued.

"You see, Chelmsford didn't beat Perth, which was also granted city status as part of the Jubilee celebrations, and has a more legitimate claim than Chelmsford. The City and Royal Burgh of Perth was the capital of Scotland from the 9th Century until 1437, and then officially the second City of Scotland until 1975. But probably due to a conniving Sassenach conspiracy our city status was summarily removed in 1975 in a local government shake-up. We celebrated our 800th anniversary last year, and it was still an "ecclesiastical city" because it had a Cathedral, but was legally considered a town. But we in Perth have continued to call it our 'Fair City'. It is now Scotland's 7th city and I know that the full restoration of its ancient dignity was long overdue."

Hugh continued to smile. It seemed that Duncan's knowledge of history, at least relevant to Scotland, could rival his own, and for that he would be afforded a non-grudging respect. This little statement had conferred a true sense of belonging from the regular assembly on their ginger friend. The Village People were pleased that the their tormentor had another foil for his leg pulling, diverting attention away from the relentless nature of his anti-gay posturing, but they were equally delighted that their new friend could hold his own intellectually against their giant fellow boozer, albeit after the 2 pint threshold had been reached.

The new Brewers recruit was intent on finishing the statement with a rounded conclusion in true Ramsbottom style, "And the best thing over all to come out of the restoration of Perth's city status is that now my home town, which is the twin burgh of Blairgowrie and Rattray, has become the largest town in Perthshire. My mother, God bless her little flying socks, would have been dead chuffed at that."

By all measurements this was a relatively quiet session, and although

Gordon had returned both to work earlier that week, and to the pub that evening, Hugh didn't have a go at him. In fact he seemed to be in a very generous and mellow frame of mind, certainly in comparison to some of the unfortunate outbursts the others had all recently witnessed. The gay entourage, clustered mostly by the dartboard, got away light for a change, as the joker held court by the bar, spending most of his time talking to Norman. Duncan was spending more and more time distracting Caroline from her barmaid duties. Nobody knew that that another little problem was niggling at the fatman's heart as he looked at the Village People and worried that his son Dick might be "one of them".

All too soon for some the end of the evening's boozing came round, and Stanislav entered the bar and called out "Taxi for Mr Ramsbottom!" The final dregs of Fuller's Pride were finished, and then the joker waved a limp wrist at his pooftah mates, but there was no last minute jibe for gay Gordon's entourage. There was no necessity for the middle fingers in the air gesture.

The taxi set off up Springfield Road, and the taxi driver asked," I suppose, gentlemen, you are very pleased that the letters patent have been issued to confer city status on Chelmsford?"

Tiny said nothing, and looked at his mate who rose to the bait, "Yes, I'm delighted, couldn't come too soon, and beating the Colchester mob to become the first City of Essex was the icing on the cake."

"I have studied European history for nearly 20 years, including that of Great Britain, and I believe Colchester's claim was legitimate for obvious historical reasons, and Reading's was also based on sound reasoning. But it appears the Queen was intent on granting prestige to smaller places, and that's partly why she chose Chelmsford and St Asaph." Stanislav asserted.

"Both St Asaph and Perth were effectively reinstated as cities. Both had ancient cathedrals and both for different reasons had lost their previous city status. Interestingly St Asaph only had a population of about 3,500 at the 2001 census." Hugh informed, not wishing to be outdone.

"We don't have a Queen in Poland to do this job of choosing cities, but our cities are much bigger. My home city of Krakow has a population of 750,000." concluded Stanislav.

This was the most intelligent conversation to take place in the homeward bound taxi for many a year. Again the jolly fatman was developing a grudging mutual respect with someone else for their command of historical knowledge. But, as the taxi stopped on the usual corner, he still couldn't resist a dig with "Have a good night Sanilav."

There was a response with an assertive grin. "Thank you, my friend, for not farting again in the cab." he said.

After a moment standing in the drizzling rain, Tiny smiled and said "Quiet sort of a night for a change, wasn't it?"

"Yeah, see you, mate. Good Night!" replied a fatigued fatman, and then they went they're separate ways.

The Brewers biggest boozer felt very tired and a bit dizzy, and this time he hadn't eaten any pork scratchings. He went to the kitchen, drank a glass of water, and went to bed, thinking he ought to go back and see his G. P. again.

CHAPTER 20

Dilemmas and Delegations

(Saturday 9th to Tuesday 12th June 2012)

By Saturday 9th June a week of ups and downs had just passed at 1stCitySoft. The ups were many. The company project was progressing in most areas roughly according to plan. Chairman and Marketing Director had established a plan for moving the existing operation and staff in Colchester, to the new premises in the Hedgerows Business Park in Chelmsford. The weekend beginning Friday 13th July was set for the move so that Monday 16th July would be the first day of the new era of 1stCitySoft in the 1st City of Essex.

The Development Director had continued to work on his two new games. Interstellar Paranoid Overdrive was almost complete, and currently in benchmark testing. The renamed Secrets of the First City was based around 2012 and Chelmsford's new city status, and was progressing well, and had now become First City Secret Phantom Invasion.

The Chairman had meticulously planned the forthcoming visit of Mr Wang and Mr Wu from Wang Wu Hoo Du Production in Wuxi China, and Carlton Schuman and Bates Masters from Softly Softly Catchee Monkey in Columbus, Ohio U.S.A.

All the downs related to the continuing unresolved situation regarding the full accounting review, auditor's reports, and Companies House returns, and making sure all the paperwork was fully up to date for the 1stCitySoft launch. And those downs solidified like a lump of hardening concrete across the broad shoulders of a very unhappy fatman.

He had been idling in his office, staring out of the window, and mulling over the situation with regard to this major thorn in his side. He thought first of all with pleasure, how fortunate it was that Golden Bollocks was just salaried senior staff as the company accountant, and not the Finance Director. That way it would be easier to dispense with his services. But that wasn't exactly the strict terms of what he was plotting to do. It would have been true to say that if he had his way he would "Sack the cheating bastard!" But he didn't know why his long-term friend and company chairman was being so lenient with the bean counter, and he was gradually becoming convinced that there was something going on which was completely unknown to him. As far as he was aware, the two of them had no secrets, not in their business lives, and not in their personal lives. It was only recently that circumstances had created a situation where Hugh had secrets to guard. Normally he held no secrets from Tiny or anyone else for that matter. He was uncomfortable about that, it wasn't in his nature, he told it like it was, and everybody who knew him, knew and expected that.

Gordon had been back at work again since 5th June, and much to the marketing director's disgust, instructions had been issued to steer clear of him. But enough was enough, and in Hugh's own mind an important decision had been made. He had decided that if the necessary accounting work had not been completed within the next 10 days, he would advise his chairman that his resignation was imminent if Gordon was not sacked immediately. He told himself, "This company was established with my money. He must be sacked or I pull out. I'm a man of independent means, and I don't need this job to survive like they all do. Everybody knows I've got other business interests in many different concerns in Chelmsford. Yes! It's time to take action, drastic action, if he doesn't make that fucking shirker come up with the goods. Quickly!"

The troubled fatman was lost in his mental anguish. There had been signs recently, and suspicions from his closest family and friends, but nobody really knew he was unwell, and he was doing his utmost to avoid facing the truth about his health situation. The dizzy spells and chest pains weren't happening just after Friday night sessions now, and they were getting more frequent and more distressing, and at the back of his mind he was haunted by the awful dream that he had experienced about 6 weeks ago.

Only a few feet away in an adjacent office, the boss was also pondering his problems. He was completely aware of the pressure he had put everybody under with his enthusiasm for the transformation of the company into a global player. At the same time he was pleased with the progress of his pet plan, and extremely worried and concerned that the ultimate success of the plan hung on a thread. Unbeknown to his business partner and best friend, he was helpless to resolve the dilemma created by Gordon's intransigence, and prevented from revealing the reasons why he was forced to be so lenient with the company accountant. Tiny was distressed by the situation, but he wanted to be ecstatic about the progress of his master plan. He thought about what his mate might be contemplating in his current erratic state of mind, only half believing that he would do anything stupid. Tiny had a long history of knowing that Hugh had no secrets from him. He was fully aware of his friend's other business interests, which included a share in Ahmad's taxi business, being a silent partner in Spike's decorating firm, and having an anonymous financial interest in Mike's gardening business. He also knew about the other partnerships in a hair dressing business and a sandwich shop. Unlike his friend and colleague, Tiny needed the computer games enterprise to support his lifestyle.

Although Gordon had been back at work in the last week, the accounting deadline was fast approaching, and the chairman was fretting about what would happen next in the far too long running saga. He was expecting for his long term colleague to insist that the accountant be sacked if he hasn't produced the goods soon, and he knew that if that happened he would have to stall yet again. Yes! He did have secrets, and some of those secrets were of a personal nature, and for very good reasons they couldn't be revealed yet.

Early Saturday evening the man in the Hub was showered, shaved, preened, moisturised and ready. It was no longer necessary to go commando, as his boxer shorts drawer had been generously replenished by presents from Clarisa. He awarded himself another generous splash of Erection aftershave, and he was on his way, down to Brentwood, to Sugar Hut, to try and be spotted by the scouts for The Only Way is Essex. These days the love of his life went with him, and they enjoyed being together, and being surrounded by beautiful people. Just for a change it wasn't raining, and Norman cruised the Porsche along the old A12 through the villages of Margaretting, Ingatestone and Mountnessing, and then through Shenfield, to park round the back of Brentwood High Street in William Hunter Way.

Arm in arm the lovers took the short walk to the Sugar Hut Village in the High Street, looking forward to spending an evening unburdened by the ever-present growing shadows of Duncan and Caroline. But, after enjoying the early part of the evening with their posing and preening friends, they were suddenly and abruptly interrupted by unwelcome guests.

"Hallo! We knew you two would be in here." said Caroline with a surly smirk, "And we thought we would join you."

"Hope you don't mind, shove up, and make room for us will you." she added, squeezing herself up to the table, and indicating to her boyfriend to do the same."

Norman and Clarisa remained polite and sociable despite the feeling that their personal space had been invaded. The man with a frizzy ginger barnet was hilariously out of place, but was true to type, and stayed quiet and reserved until his second drink. The Brewers barmaid with her excessively made up face, and dyed blonde hair with darker roots showing through, did what she did best, and performed bar maid duties moving empty glasses as if she were back on the job. Inevitably the Scotsman become louder and more affable as the booze flowed, and it wasn't long before Clarisa persuaded her Normie that they should beat a hasty retreat. They seized the opportunity, sneaking out quickly, when the two interlopers both went off to the toilets at the same time,

"I'm so glad that I've only got a 2 seater car." he chuckled as they walked back to the car park.

"Yes! Quick! Let's get out of here, Normie, before they follow us and try to squeeze in again." she replied laughing.

Fifteen minutes later they were back home in the Hub, with Stereophonics and Coldplay wafting through the night air. They were happy to be alone, and hoped that when Mr and Mrs Cheaplaugh returned to Chelmsford they would go directly to Navigation Road. Unfortunately, just after midnight there was a ring on the intercom entry-phone, and an insistent Caroline called for help to get a very drunk Scotsman up to the apartment. With his toes being scraped out of his cheap shoes, his frizzy hair matted, his Primark clothes stained by fancy cocktails and sweat, they dragged the barely coherent reveller to his room and threw him on the bed. Then, without hesitation, and with no sense of modesty, the barmaid stripped off and climbed in next to him saying, "I'd better stay and look after him." she said.

The man the gang now all called Doughnuts had flown south just over a week ago, but clearly Miss Bangs had her sights set on him He had been retitled "Jammy Doughnuts" after they'd all heard how he had come by his fortune. She had quickly sussed out that although he was in some respects intelligent and well read, in others he was naive, easily lead, and not at all worldly-wise. She focussed on his massive saving grace, which was that he was wallowing in wealth that he had no idea what to do with. His experience with women other than his mother was nil, and he had never had a girlfriend. He was in fact a 30 year old virgin. Due to his annoying habit of either over indulging in alcohol, or getting stoned on the stolen cannabis from Stanley's greenhouse, and despite the best efforts of his enthusiastic escort, he had so far been unable to rise to the occasion.

"So, that's what I want you to do, and no arguments about it. Do we have an understanding?" Tiny asked Hugh in no uncertain terms. It was Monday 11th June, and at Avalon House there was another football gathering. The jolly fatman just nodded a faint resignation, carrying an expression like a teenage boy who'd just left the headmaster's office after a sharp dressing down and six of the best. The Village People were expected to arrive any minute, and Tiny had popped over the road a few minutes early to circumvent any possibility of his mate having yet another go at the company accountant over the snowballing delay in the completion of his work for 1stCitySoft.

Soon they were all there, Gordon, smart and smug as usual, Spike, looking like a leather-clad refugee from Albania, and pockmarked with paint of many colours, Mike in his worst gardener gear, dungarees, desert boots, and a WWF t-shirt, and Ike, a casualty from the denim army. By contrast Norman was as finely turned out as ever, Levi jeans and Hollister shirt, accompanied by Duncan, Primark man, cheap shoes with worn toes, cheap jeans, and cheap laugh.

It was Budweisers or Speckled Hens all round then, and some, but not much discussion about the game. Mine host was being polite to everyone, on his best behaviour for now. The new Scottish recruit to the gang still hadn't got used to the idea of associating in a social gathering with an equal percentage of gay people, and despite having accounting as a common interest he and Gordon had never once discussed that area of their experience. They were just typical accountants, frugal, crafty and secretive, or should it be stingy, underhand, and sneaky? Perhaps we could now add to that unsociable until they'd had a few drinks?

Then again, despite their common ancestry Duncan didn't exactly hit it off with Spike either, and by now the man in the Hub woke up every day wishing that the cuckoo in the nest would please go home. Only the fatman had developed a real affinity with his ginger barbarian, and that was only in his "after a few beers" persona.

This football occasion, the European Championship game between France and England, was for the Ramsbottom gathering a somewhat subdued affair, especially when compared to the previous madness of the F. A. Cup Final a month or so before. This was not least of all due to the 3 hour time difference between the UK and the Ukraine.

The match took place in the Donbass Arena, in Donetsk, Ukraine, attended by 48,000 spectators, starting at 1900 local time, and on 30 minutes England went ahead with the unlikely scorer being Joleon Lescott. Sadly for England the French team equalised in the 39th minute via Samir Nasri. By half time, after several bottles of Hen and according to expectations, and much to mine host's delight, Jammy Doughnuts came alive and began to spout football.

"Do you know who invented football?" he asked with a grin.

"Well technically it wasn't invented, was it? It developed like other games over a long period of time, probably going back over centuries. Similarly to golf, which most people accept was invented by the Scots, but seems to have its origins somewhere in Holland or maybe even further back in Roman or Persian civilisations." answered Hugh.

"I can't deny that's true, and football has its origins in many games played in ancient times, just the same as golf. Many people think that football developed out of the public schools like Eton, but there is a crucial point in time that is identifiable as the first time that the modern game seems to have crystallised."

"And you, my ginger savage friend, are going to tell me that it's something to do with a Scotsman aren't you?"

"Of course, my porky friend, how did you guess?"

"Well, before you do that, let's agree that a lot of these debates are a bit like reading from and then assimilating knowledge from a holy book like the Bible. What I mean is that we all adopt and make part of our understanding those bits that appeal to us, that we have some sort of inherent consensus with."

"Can't argue with that, but unlike the Bible some things are not "The Word of God"," he said that with a slight sneer," And they're also not a collection of thoroughly contradictory riddles, which require the interpretation of a lifelong theology professor to be misunderstood."

The joker just stood there and smiled. This man was getting more like his little protégé every day. "Do continue, Jammy old son."

The Scot smiled back, while the rest of the lads focussed on the television coverage of the match so far.

"There is an early reference to a game of football where players pass the ball and attempt to score past a goalkeeper. It was written back in 1633 by a poet and teacher in Aberdeen called David Wedderburn."

"That's a great example of what I was talking about mate. If you were Welsh you'd probably have dismissed that as nonsense. It's only 'cause you're a porridge gobbler that you want that to be true."

"And it's only because you're a Sassenach that you don't."

Hugh was being verbally bounced and he loved it. This was just the sort of debate that he revelled in, a bit of history, a bit of football, a bit of bullshit, and a large dollop of potential for taking the piss if at all necessary.

"Well, I'll give you my version. As a former public schoolboy, I like the Eton bit, but I don't hold it as gospel. Football and Rugby developed together in the 19th century. But the first side to play a passing combination game was the Royal Engineers in 1869/70, and they won the F. A. Cup final playing that way in 1875 ironically against the Old Etonians."

"You don't say?"

"Yes, but there must have been more clever forms of playing around because the Royal Engineers were beaten in the first F. A. Cup Final in 1872 by Wanderers. And they were beaten again in 1874 by Oxford University, and once again by Wanderers in 1878. It makes you wonder what the actual rules were then, how they differed from each other in styles of play, and how much they learned and adapted from each other."

"Yes and there must have been a large Scottish influence in the formation of rules by the Football Association."

"What makes you say that, Ginger?"

"In the days when they were still finalising the way the game would be played Queen's Park were the only Scottish football club to have played in the FA Cup Final in 1884 and 1885."

"Yes, and they lost both games to Blackburn Rovers. Ho! Bloody Ho!"

"Never mind, they are still the oldest association football club in Scotland, founded in 1867, I believe."

"That's as may be, but the Scots are not much good at football, and never have been. Their International record is laughable. No! They're much better at oddball sports like tossing the caber."

The fatman was up to mischief, but Doughnuts was ahead of him.

"Aye, yes, but that had to be modified after the Romans gave up trying to conquer our fair land, and went to hide behind Hadrian's Wall. Before that we used to call it cabering the tosser."

They both fell about laughing.

At the bottom of all this, it was a friendly debate, and Duncan's patriotism, unlike Spike's, wasn't a bad thing in his English friend's eyes. Usually when the jolly fatman spouted his knowledge he felt it was to the ignorant or dispassionate. After all, Norman was disinterested, and Tiny was so used to him that he never responded. Usually it was only Gordon and Co who rose to the bait, and on this occasion they didn't do so. But here, just for a change Hugh felt that he had a soul-mate, who he could genuinely debate matters with. But how was that? He wondered how his new friend had managed to acquire such a wealth of knowledge, and as the second half of the match started he resolved to interrogate him sufficiently to find out. While the others all attempted to concentrate on the football while France were giving England a battering to assert their obvious superiority, the debating society were forced by shouts of "Shut Up!" and "Watch the game!" to abandon the lounge and continue their discussion in the kitchen. There the Scot explained that his mother had taught him to read when he was 4 and that when other kids were reading Rupert the Bear and other children's books he was reading Scottish authors, like Robert Louis Stevenson, Arthur Conan Doyle, and Sir Walter Scott. He reeled off all the books he had read like it was a shopping list; The Strange Case of Dr Jekyll and Mr Hyde, Treasure Island, and Kidnapped, by Stevenson, many Sherlock Holmes mysteries, of which his favourite was The Hound of the Baskervilles, and Scott's novels from Ivanhoe and Rob Roy to The Lady of the Lake, Waverley, and the Bride of Lammermoor.

Hugh was very impressed, even he wasn't that well read.

"So you only read porridge gobbling authors did you?"

"Certainly not, I also liked C S. Lewis, The Chronicles of Narnia, The Great Divorce, and The Screwtape Letters."

The joker decided to test him, since he had enjoyed a number of Lewis's books himself, "What's that about then?" he asked

"Aye, well it's Screwtape writing to his nephew Wormwood, on the best ways to tempt a particular human and secure his damnation."

Mr Ramsbottom's ginger barbarian was on a roll.

"By the time I was 10, I was reading Dickens. I loved A Tale of Two Cities. Can't help but feel that there are parallels between the French peasantry and the aristocracy in the years leading up to the revolution, and the ways in which the English aristocracy regarded their working classes, and particularly the Scottish proletariat. We could have had a similarly brutal revolution in Britain if we Scots had been brave enough to stand up for ourselves instead of being oppressed by our English landlords."

"Didn't like Dickens much myself, "offered mine host ignoring the potential for a political argument, "Nothing wrong with the stories and the morals behind them, but most of them make a bloody good doorstop."

"What about Thomas Hardy then? It takes a bit of effort to read, but it's worth the effort. I've read a few of his, and my favourite is Tess of the d'Urbervilles. It was risky stuff at the time to write about a rape."

"Agreed, but I'm a big fan of Under the Greenwood Tree, it's got an idyllic quality to it. I'm just an old romantic, see myself as Dick Dewy, to my Millicent as the school mistress Fancy Day."

"Can we find some common ground then on good old J.R. and I'm not talking about that Texan berk on Dallas, I'm referring to J. R. R. Tolkien and his Lord of the Rings trilogy, and of course The Hobbit."

"Now you're talking, Ginger!"

The match finished 1 - 1. The Book Club discussion was over. It was late, and some people had jobs to go to the next day.

Tuesday 12th June would be a pivotal day in the future of the little company that Tiny had built from virtually nothing with his business expertise and enterprise, Hugh's money, and Norman's gift in being able to write amazing and popular computer games. The chairman wasn't like a cat on a hot tin roof, because that would have suggested that he was out of control, and eager to escape any hazards, but he was perhaps like someone who was about to walk across a path of hot coals. It was exciting, exhilarating even, and perhaps a little risky, but his meticulous preparation had hopefully obviated any worries that things could go badly wrong at this important stage of the company's transition from small beer to global player. Indeed, anything that was directly under his control had been planned in the finest detail, so there were only the same two nagging possibilities for spoiling the broth. Today of all days the boss wasn't going to take any nonsense from his accountant or his marketing director.

In preparation for the arrival of business partners from Wang Wu Hoo Du Production, and Softly Softly Catchee Monkey Distribution, the old offices in Colchester had been cleaned and tidied, and smartened up with a lick of paint by Spike's decorators. Mike and Ike had spruced up the surrounding grassed area, planted flowers and trimmed bushes. There were two new signs at the office entrance displaying NerdiSoft and 1stCitySoft legends and logos. The team were all pleased with the potential first impression the company were going to make, and today wasn't really a board meeting. It was more like briefing by the chairman, who was once again in his most forthright and businesslike mode.

He began. "OK, today's the day we've all been planning for, for most of this year so far, (He was ignoring Gordon's lack of contribution, much to the fatman's annoyance), and as you know our friends from China and the U.S.A. arrive this morning, so I want everyone on their best, most professional behaviour. All joking aside, I want no mention of Chinkies. The Chinese are very, very correct in their business protocols, and I think you'll find Mr Wang and Mr Wu extremely easy to communicate with. Their company, are based in Wuxi also known as little Shanghai in Jiangsu province, and they already have contacts and contracts with other British companies. They both speak perfect English. The Chinese have a culture stretching back thousands of years, so I thought they would appreciate being put up somewhere with a bit of English history. I've booked them into The Blue Boar Inn in Maldon for the duration of their stay in England."

Hugh couldn't resist it, he had to illustrate," Yes, The Blue Boar Inn in Silver Street, the oldest bit is 14th century, but it has a Georgian facade, and it was a coaching inn in the 1750's. Great place, good choice, I love it!"

"Thank you for your support. May I continue?" the chairman asked, without waiting for an answer.

"Now, likewise I want no mention of Yanks, we will refer to them as Americans. Carlton Schumann and Bates Masters the co-founders and CEO's of Softly Softly Catchy Monkey are a very different kettle of fish. But don't be fooled by their laidback approach, they are hardnosed businessmen and are totally focussed on their company's commercial interests. They've made their own arrangements for accommodation and transport, and will be staying at the Miami Hotel in Chelmsford. We have two of Ahmad's best limousines on standby for the whole of our visitors' stay, to transport us and them everywhere."

The boss paused and asked if there were any questions. There were none, so he continued, "When they arrive, we'll show them around our operations here, and then take them over to our new offices in Chelmsford, which will obviously be far more impressive. After that, I've booked us all into Graham's on the Green in Writtle for lunch and to discuss the finer points of our contracts. Best behaviour there please, and limited alcohol consumption. Then they'll be chauffeured back to their hotels. Our guests will have had long haul flights, and they'll need some down time."

There was another pause. Only two of the three listeners were paying attention. Gordon was miles away.

"Now," the briefing resumed," Let's talk about the golf tomorrow. Originally I had wanted to take them to play golf at a championship course, but the Yanks, sorry the Americans, wanted to play at St Andrews. Typically, they don't have any concepts of distance, and they have no idea of the difficulties involved in using the British transport systems. They probably think Scotland is a suburb of London, and that St Andrews is in a place they call "Edinbro". Then, again our Chinese friends haven't actually played golf before, and would be happy to play anywhere. So to keep everybody happy, and fit in with the tight schedule, I've made what I consider to be the ideal choice, for us to play at Bunsay Downs and Badgers."

The joker couldn't hold back his amusement, there was a glimmer of a smirk as he thought, "The golf is going to be a bit of a farce then, hope I'm not playing with the rookies." but he didn't say anything.

Tiny concluded, "We'll sign contracts after the golf, and after that we'll see if there is time left, or the requirement for any socialising. Right gentlemen, now you know what's happening, I'm sure I can rely on you to do your best, and build bridges with our partners. This is an important day for our company, make it happen."

The briefing ended, the coffee machine had a busy blip, and they waited for the action to begin.

When the guests arrived, the chairman's careful planning was fully rewarded when the visits to both old and new premises went like clockwork. The Americans weren't particularly impressed with what they called "the cute little Colchester operation", but saw the forward thinking prospects of 1stCitySoft in moving to their swish new offices in the Hedgerows Business Park. The Chinese by contrast were polite and complimentary about every aspect of the company. Tiny had met them all before, and ensured as best he could that things would go smoothly by accompanying the Americans, together with Gordon in Ahmad's first limousine. Hugh and Norman were together with the Chinese in the 2nd car, and it was obvious that the jolly fatman had brushed up on his Chinese history ancient and modern. He talked at length with Messrs Wang and Wu about how Wuxi had been dubbed "Little Shanghai", and in over 3000 years of history during the Ming and Qing dynasties, was already an agricultural centre and a significant national rice market for those dynasties. Mr Wu was very keen to discuss how Wuxi was important in the origin of the Wu Culture, which had dominated the region of Yangtze River South for centuries.

By the time they all arrived at Graham's on the Green Anglo-Chinese bridges were most definitely under construction. The delicious lunch was long and leisurely, and very businesslike, and enjoyed by all present. The clear headed Americans drank no alcohol at all, sticking to freshly squeezed orange juice along with Norman. The Chinese enjoyed glasses of Chardonnay and fizzy water, and the 1stCitySoft men limited themselves to Peroni beers. Tiny noted with relief that Hugh was adhering to his limited alcohol request, in that he had for once set his dislike of lager type beers aside. The chairman held court in true head of the company style, and the development director discussed his planned visit to the States, while the fatman interjected with witty asides and interesting historical facts about Writtle, including it being the location for the first regular public broadcast radio programme in February 1922. Only the bean counter made himself an outsider, remaining aloof and uncomfortable. His one major contribution towards the proceedings being to explain that the financial information required would be available within a few days, as he had decided to coincide its formulation with the requirement for returns to Companies House.

After lunch the group enjoyed a short stroll around the village green, where the group's unelected historian imparted his knowledge about some of the larger houses like Aubyn's and Mott's, and joked with the Chinese about how unpalatable the inhabitants of the famous duck-pond were likely to be. Messrs Wang and Wu loved the olde worlde village green, but the self-appointed guide was absolutely certain that the Yanks weren't intellectually equipped to even relate to it.

At 4 pm the cars arrived and they all returned to the Hedgerows, where they finalised arrangements for the next day's golf. Then, after polite goodbyes and thank yous, the guests dispersed to their two very different hotels, and the hosts retired to very welcome and well earned refreshments in the Two Brewers.

"Well, thanks to all of you," the chairman said, taking a large gulp of Fuller's. "Today went according to plan. I'm very pleased." His face was beaming with pride and satisfaction. "Anybody got any concerns?"

"No, mate," Hugh replied chuckling, "But we should have checked Mr Wang, to see if he'd hidden any of the Writtle ducks under his jacket." Smiles all round, and he continued, "Seriously though, it went well, and the Chinkie boys are easy to get on with, but I'm not enamoured of the Yanks, especially the appropriately named Master Bates, sorry it's Bates Masters, perhaps he's a left handed wanker."

More laughter followed, the jolly fatman was in good form, and he could ease the tensions of the day without really trying. Gordon was strangely quiet, as he had been all day. He didn't want to be there, something was bothering him, and it showed.

"Strange pair, Carlton and Bates," Tiny agreed, "But we don't have to love them, just do the business with them. Just keep a lid on it tomorrow, mate, and we will be home and dry."

"Yeah, looking forward to the golf, but I'd prefer not to be paired with the beginners. Can me and Nobless pair up with our American friends? I'll bite my lip and be a good boy. Please!"

"OK, mate, but try not to antagonise them too much, just enough to upset their golf. They're both 5 handicappers the same as you. Norman's a bogie golfer, so he'll provide a good balance. Gordon and myself will look after our Chinese friends. I don't know what they're going to play like, but we'll give them 28 handicaps. We'll have to wait and see. They have learned by video, and have so far only played on driving ranges. But we will go out in the first fourball, so boys, please be patient with us."

"Mr Chairman, it'll be fine, as long as the Yanks don't cheat." concluded Hugh with a wink as he headed for the bar to get another round in, taking a quick telling glance at the company accountant on the way.

CHAPTER 21

The Rub of the Green

(Wednesday 13th June 2012)

At 9.30 the next morning the gentlemen of 1stCitySoft were drinking coffee in the clubhouse of Bunsay Downs Golf Course in Woodham Walter, waiting for their business partners to arrive. Carlton Schuman and Bates Masters would be making their own way from the Miami Hotel in the totally unnecessary, huge, gas guzzling Mitsubishi Barbarian they had hired, and Mr Wang and Mr Wu would be collected at the Blue Boar Hotel in Maldon, and dropped off by Ahmad's PAMTAX cab company.

Tiny was explaining," So, I've hired our friends the equipment they'll need. We've got Yonex clubs for our friends from Columbus, one set right-handed and one set left-handed."

"Oh, I don't believe it. It's too good to be true. Don't tell me the left-handed set is for Master Bates." the joker chuckled.

The chairman just smiled and nodded. "And I've got Callaway sets for the Chinamen."

"Made a mistake, haven't you?" asked Hugh with a playful snigger," Shouldn't it be those new Korean clubs for the Chinkies, you know, what are they called? I know, Shihtzuita!"

The chairman gave him a disdainful withering look, "Be careful what you say please."

Half an hour later there were 8 men waiting on the first tee, four Englishmen, two Americans, and two Chinamen. The weather was kind, overcast, and not too warm, but at least it wasn't raining, and despite months of rain the course looked to be in superb condition. Pairings were made, and it was time for battle to commence. At least that was the way that one particular golfer saw it.

Handicaps were agreed as:- Wu(28), Wang(28), Balls(9), Bullock(12), Schuman(5), Masters(5), Ramsbottom(5), Noble(18)

On the 1st, a 268 yard par 4 with trees both sides, narrowing to a large pond on the right, and protected by a bunker on each side of the green, the boss was relieved to see both his Chinese partners enjoy beginner's luck with perfectly reasonable shots into the middle of the fairway. When it was his turn, he hit a beautiful shot over 200 yards which trickled almost to the edge of the green. The fatman giggled behind his hand when Gordon topped his tee shot only carrying about 50 yards, and then hit his second shot in anger into the greenside left bunker. Things were pretty steady for that group for the rest of that hole, and they were all able to negotiate their way to acceptable scores, Tiny getting a par, and everybody else a 5. Once the front four-ball had scooted out of the way to the left and the 2nd tee, the 2 Americans both hit good shots up the middle of the fairway, Hugh showed his gorilla tendencies in flying a shot 250 yards right to the edge of the green, and Norman hit into the trees on the left, but then hacked out to within a yard of the hole. He managed a birdie with his short putt, and everyone else got a par.

And so the game was destined to continue, with all the usual ups and downs, mishaps and lucky breaks, oohs and aarghs, smiles and frowns. On the 2nd hole, a 326 yard uphill par 4, with a pond on the left, and bunker on the right halfway up the fairway, narrowing into trees both sides up to a large flat green, Animal Ramsbottom hit another massive shot leaving only a clip with a pitching wedge to the green, and Norman landed safely on the fairway. But both Carlton and Bates hit past the early hazards into the trees on the right. They both apparently were able to hack out to score pars, but Hugh already began to suspect that they were cheating, and resolved to pay closer attention to their activities from then on.

The chairman's group were held up by the previous 4-ball on the 170 yard 4th, a downhill par 3 with a large, slightly elevated green guarded on both sides by 2 large but relatively flat bunkers, and so their colleagues in the following group caught up with them. When the green was clear again the four-ball all reached the green with their tee shots, and a huge cheer went up from everyone when Mr Wu's shot flew in between the bunkers, landed softly and trickled slowly onto the green and into the hole for an unbelievable hole in one. The joker was very quick to explain that Mr Wu was now obliged to buy everyone in the clubhouse a celebratory drink after the game, and he replied that he would be delighted to do so.

The next hole was a long, 486 yard uphill par 5, with bunkers on both sides, a pond on the right, and again narrowing into trees left and right up to a large flat green. Only the chairman played it well, getting a par, Gordon managed a 7, but the beginner's luck for Wu and Wang ran out with a 9 and a 10. Hugh was near the green in 2, on in 3, and got a par with a 2 foot putt. Norman topped the ball on his 2nd shot and then put it in the lake to the right eventually scoring 8. Almost as a repeat of the 2nd hole, both Americans drove into the trees on the right, this time with their 2nd shots. Everybody in the four-ball then helped to look for their balls. After some searching they both apparently found their balls and played on, hacking out onto the fairway, and completing the hole with 2 bogies.

On the next hole, as both Americans drove left, and the 2 Englishmen drove to the right, they separated into 2 pairs to walk down the fairway. That was when the jolly fatman grinned, nudged his nephew and declared with a knowing look, "I thought they were a couple of cheating bastards, and I was right."

"How do you know they are cheating?" Norman whispered.

With some delight came the proof, "Look! I've got both their Srixon balls in my pocket."

After they'd finished the 8th hole, Frogs Hall, the most difficult hole on the course, with a narrow gap from the tee, sloping fairways, trees, ditches, ponds, and an enigmatic and troublesome dome shaped green, the joker's delight had turned to annoyance when Bates carded a par having forgotten to count 3 air-shots on his approach to the green.

After the first 9 holes, they all took a short break, and in the clubhouse men's changing room, having waited until the coast was clear, Hugh explained to Tiny why he was determined to beat the cheating Yankie bastards. The chairman explained to his colleague that although Wu and Wang hadn't played before they were totally honest. He added, "Never mind! Don't make an issue out of it. Keep it friendly, and complete the game without any fuss please."

The scores were totted up for the first 9, and with handicaps taken into account in the most generous way the nett scores were:- Wu 38, Wang 40, Balls 34, Bullock 38, Schuman 35, Masters 36, Ramsbottom 35, and Noble 39. Not much in it, and all to play for.

Having completed the 9 holes of the Bunsay Downs Course, they now set off to play the Badgers par 3 Course. Hugh would declare that it was probably one of the finest little golf courses in Britain, if not the World. Bearing in mind the lack of experience of the Chinese players, and the low handicaps of the American players, the Badgers was a relatively easy and pleasurable experience for all. Predictably the only hole that caused major trouble was the 6th, known as the Three Boys. This 169 yard hole leads from a flat tee, down into a small steep valley and back up to a narrow sloping green with 3 deep bunkers set in the face of the rise. It claimed 3 victims in Messrs Wang, Wu, and Schuman. On this second 9 holes Hugh watched his partners like a hawk so they were unable to cheat, and he managed to score 5 pars and a birdie. Norman proved how skilful he was at target golf and therefore scored brilliantly with 6 pars. Both Americans only managed 4 pars.

Tiny and Co had finished playing the last hole, and it was smiles and handshakes all round, as they moved from the green over to the gate leading back to the clubhouse, to watch and wait for the second 4-ball. Animal was first to tee off, and he was impatient to get his shot away thinking that the idiots in front were taking far too long to clear the area. He let loose a vicious, aggressive drive to the 146 yard green, shouting "Fore!" as it hooked over towards the gate. Everybody quickly scuttled out of the way, but Gordon tripped over his golf trolley and fell to the floor clutching his right leg. Before anyone could rush to his aid the ball struck the top of the gate rebounding 20 feet up in the air, and came down smack bang on the top of his head knocking him out, before rebounding again back onto the green. This little catastrophe took place out of sight of the 2nd four-ball, so they all took their tee shots and carried on playing, soon finishing the hole, and enjoying smiles and handshakes all round. As they moved away from the green, they saw the company accountant lying in the recovery position, and Tiny anxiously speaking to the Emergency Services to get an ambulance.

"What's wrong?" the fatman asked with genuine concern.

"Your gorilla tee shot rebounded off the gate onto his head, he's out cold, and I think he's broke his leg as a bonus." exclaimed an exasperated Tiny.

Hugh issued a genuine "Sorry! I did shout fore, and you were all well clear."

The chairman was well aware that this accident could have happened to anyone. Golf courses are dangerous places and accidents do happen. But he was also mightily relieved that neither of 1stCitySoft's Chinese partners had been the victim of this unfortunate incident. By the time the ambulance arrived, the worried fatman had totted up all the scores, and broke into a not too well disguised smile to find that his team had indeed beaten the cheating Yankie bastards.

The scores after the 18 holes were:- Wu 66, Wang 69, Balls 65, Bullock 69, Schuman 69, Masters 71, Ramsbottom 64, and Noble 63, making Norman the over all winner, and Hugh's the best team..

Now it was serious business time, on two counts. The chairman had to tie up the deal and finalise contracts with his partners, assuring them that the required financial information would be made available within a few days, while Hugh and Norman felt obliged to accompany the victim of the accident to the hospital in the ambulance. Someone was most miffed to have to accept that he would miss Mr Wu's hole in one celebration in the clubhouse.

CHAPTER 22

Tragedy and Salvation

(Thursday 14th to Wednesday 20th June 2012)

The next day before the Chinese and American delegations arrived at the 1stCitySoft offices there was a discussion about the situation. The chairman was annoyed at his marketing director's impatience resulting in an injury to their accountant, and there was a heated discussion over how they could prepare the end of year accounts now that he was in hospital. If they didn't think and act quickly it could jeopardise the whole global plan.

Tiny explained his worries.

"I know you and him have been at loggerheads for months, and I've had to be like a referee at a tag wrestling match trying to keep you apart. But what happened yesterday is beyond the pail. In the circumstances I wouldn't bet against you having done it deliberately, and now everything hangs in the balance. This could undermine our future."

The fatman was conscious of the fact that a while ago he'd considered pulling out of 1stCitySoft if Gordon couldn't come up with the goods, but he replied most indignantly," So you think that from 150 yards away I can hit a ball so skilfully that it flies off the gate, and rebounds directly onto a specific person's head, and then back onto the green? Don't be so effin daft! Not even Tiger Woods at his best could do that. It was an accident, and that's the end of it. It's just bad luck. If he hadn't fallen over breaking his leg, the ball wouldn't have hit him. So there!"

The boss thought for a minute, and then answered quietly, "Yes! Of course you're right. Sorry, mate! But I'm so wound up at the moment. We are on the verge of a huge and important deal, it's only fingertips away, and I can't have anything go wrong now."

Hugh calmed himself and replied reassuringly, "Nothing will go wrong. So, the regular bean counter is out of action for the time being. We'll get someone else to take over and do the accounts, and then the deal will be done. Stop worrying, mate."

"Who can we get in at such short notice? Got anyone in mind?"

The marketing director didn't have to think for very long.

"How's about Jammy Doughnuts? I know we treat him as a figure of fun, but that's because up till now we've only met him socially. He's available, twiddling his Caledonian thumbs doing nothing at present, and he is a fully qualified accountant. Being a stingy Scot he'll probably jump at the chance if we wave a bit of hard cash in front of him." suggested the fatman.

Tiny nodded and thought for a moment.

"If you like I'll get Nobless to give him a call, and see if he's interested." said Hugh.

After a few seconds thought the chairman agreed, "Do it! Do it now! He could save the day."

At lunch time the representatives of Wang Wu Hoo Du, and Softly Softly Catchee Monkey arrived at 1stCitySoft, and over a sumptuous buffet lunch, final discussions and the signing of contracts took place.

Hugh was now in a great mood, as he had already negotiated for Duncan to begin work on the accounts, but he hadn't told Tiny yet. But in his best form, and without consulting his colleagues he set any differences with the Americans aside, and invited everybody to Friday at the Brewers followed by a traditional "Sunday Roast" at Avalon House, and then an opportunity to watch the Euro finals football match between Sweden and England. The hardnosed Americans declined the offer saying they intended to travel to Edinburgh that Thursday evening and then tour Scotland for 2 days, before flying home to the USA on Sunday evening.

"Typical Yanks!" the joker thought, "They think they can see the whole of Scotland on a whistle-stop tour lasting two days. Fat chance to see much at all in a few days, and anything they do see will go over their dizzy, little, empty heads."

The charmed and charming Chinese accepted the kind invitation, outlining their plans to travel to London on Friday morning to see the sights, and to fly back to Shanghai on Saturday. But they were very keen to enjoy a truly English public house, were big fans of the traditional roast dinner, and idolised English football.

All that was left to do before their guests departed was to present them with their gifts. A lot of thought had gone into this, and their business partners were each given a silver-plated ornately engraved commemorative tankard celebrating their visit to 1stCitySoft and the day at Bunsay Downs and Badgers.

Once their guests had left Hugh burst into his boss's office, slapped him on the back, and exclaimed with great pleasure," Jammy Doughnuts starts here Monday. I told you everything would turn out fine."

While most of his friends were waiting in the Two Brewers much earlier than usual at about 6 pm on Friday evening, poor old Golden Bollocks was still in a coma in Broomfield Hospital. The break in his right leg had been reset and plastered, but he was still away with the fairies, and Spike had spent the best part of 2 days by his bedside without seeing any signs of recovery. So it was a slightly more subdued atmosphere than normal for a Friday night

Brewers session, but the 1stCitySoft crew wanted it that way anyway. Tiny wasn't sure that the jolly fatman in full flow was the right thing to inflict upon their guests from China, and so a quiet civilised couple of pints was exactly what he had in mind. A PAMTAX cab had been despatched to pick up Mr Wang and Mr Wu from their hotel, and shortly after 6:30 it arrived at the Brewers. The Ramsbottom charm had worked on them very well, and the fatman had become a big hit with the two Chinamen. They were greeted enthusiastically, and then plied with pints of Fuller's Pride.

"How was London? Did you see all the places you wanted?" asked Tiny.

"Yes, very good, very enjoyable," answered Mr Wu, "We visited the Tower of London, Buckingham Palace, and the Houses of Parliament, but it was a very quick tour on a sightseeing bus, and we wished that we had more time to enjoy your English culture."

"So glad you liked it," oozed the chairman, "Perhaps you should come to England again, and spend a few weeks here. Bring your wives and children."

"Yes! That would be a much better idea, but we are so busy at work at the moment, and with our new arrangements things will only get busier." smiled Mr Wang.

"I must say thank you for choosing the Blue Boar Inn for our stay in England," said Mr Wu, while Mr Wang nodded in agreement and supped from his pint," It's such a comfortable place, with lots of olde worlde charm, and last night was as you English might say, the icing on the cake. In the upstairs room over the other side of the courtyard they had a jazz band playing last night. We both love dixieland jazz, and I spoke to the gentlemen playing, and they very kindly allowed me to accompany them on the piano as they played St Louis Blues. It was the highlight of my stay there. Thank you so much."

Tiny was delighted, and Hugh added, "Well if you like to play jazz piano, you are very welcome to bash out a few tunes on my piano for us back at my house later."

Mr Wu's face was a picture.

It had been agreed that they would limit themselves to just a couple of pints before adjourning to Avalon House, and as the second round was poured, Mr Wang asked somebody to explain the game of cricket to him. "This is a most peculiar game. I understand the layout of the ground, and the bat and ball, bowler, fielder, batsman principles, but please can you describe what the point of it is for me?"

This was Ramsbottom territory, and he was gracious about his overview, which became more hilarious as the description developed.

"Cricket is a quintessentially English bat and ball game, first played in Southern England in the 16th century, which had developed into the national sport of England by the end of the 18th century, and then spread across the world via the British Empire. Real cricket lasts for 5 days, includes tea-breaks, lunch-breaks and interruptions for bad weather like rain and poor light. During the game, out of the 24 players involved, at any one time at least 11 of them will spend their time in the clubhouse drinking large quantities of warm beer and winding each other up. Everybody gets a chance to bat and to be a fielder, except for the twelfth man on each side who isn't used unless there is an injury, so he can usually get totally plastered. Some players have specialist roles like bowling and wicket-keeping, and others have to stand in dangerous positions like silly-mid-on or silly-mid-off to field the ball. When you hit the ball you score runs by running between the wickets, and you get 4 runs if your ball reaches the boundary, and 6 if it does so without touching the ground, especially satisfying if you hit somebody in the crowd. There are many different styles of bowling including a china-man and a googly. At the end of the game it's usually a draw, and everybody shakes hands and goes back to the clubhouse for more beer and cucumber sandwiches. In the final analysis, cricket isn't really a game; it's a way of passing the time in the summer sun, while drinking and talking with your mates, and taking the piss out of the opposition."

Mr Wang applauded the description but was none the wiser really. The joker's humorous view of cricket didn't pass him by, and he was clearly very amused. This was a good cue to suggest a move up the hill to Avalon House. Within minutes two taxis were waiting outside.

Millicent loved to entertain, and the table was beautifully laid out with the best cutlery, best crockery, and a magnificent feast for the guests to enjoy and remember with affection. The best beef that olde England could provide, properly hung for 28 days was expertly roasted to a medium rare succulence, and then precision carved by the expertise of someone who was king of his castle and absolutely in his element. This was complimented by a selection of organic vegetables, including carrots, cauliflower, courgettes, and green beans, lovingly prepared and exquisitely cooked to perfection. There were cartloads of roast potatoes, new potatoes and cheddar mash, and a mountain of Yorkshire puddings. There was an ocean of proper gravy made from the meat juices not gravy granules. The cheerful and charming Chinamen were feasted and feted, as Millicent and Hugh played the perfect hosts, Tiny radiated confidence and reliability, Tina flirted outrageously, and Norman and Clarisa oozed with youthful enthusiasm. The chairman was comfortable with the proceedings, and very glad that Gordon was sadly unavailable, but not in any wicked sense. Had the accountant not suffered the unfortunate accident a few days before, he would have been there perhaps accompanied by Spike, and nobody knew if the scruffbag scrubbed up well or not. The thought was that perhaps the decorator would have been out of his depth, if not an embarrassing square peg in a round hole. The Ramsbottom juniors had been fed earlier and despatched to their playroom with instructions to be seen and heard only if necessary. The 8 places at the family table were occupied by adults only, for the dinner lasting over 2 hours, and rounded off with rhubarb and apple crumble and custard, which was the Ramsbottom's favourite pudding.

There was just enough time between the end of the meal and the start of the football for Messrs Hugh and Wu to entertain the others with renditions of jazz on the family piano. Mine host rattled out "Blueberry Hill" and "Goodness Gracious, Great Balls of Fire" and Mr Wu repeated his triumphant "St Louis Blues" and an improvised Scott Joplin style ragtime number. Faces were cracking with mirth and jollity all over the household.

Then it was time for the serious business of England's Euro match against Sweden. But there was a slight hitch, a delay in the process, because the previous match between Ukraine and France that had begun at 19:00 local time was interrupted by heavy rainfall and a thunderstorm, and the referee was forced to suspend the game during the fifth minute. Play was only resumed 58 minutes later, and therefore UEFA delayed the start of the match between Sweden and England to kick off 15 minutes later than originally scheduled, instead of beginning at 22:00 local time, to avoid the matches overlapping.

The match, which took place in the Olympic Stadium in Kiev, attended by 65,000 spectators was full of incident. But by the time it was played everybody in Avalon House had had a long day, and there were many excuses for nodding off. There was great pleasure and high fives when Andy Carroll scored a brilliant headed goal from a Gerrard cross in the 23rd minute, and the score remained at 1 - 0 to England until early in the second half. Then came a sinking feeling when Sweden equalised in the 49th minute with an own goal from Glen Johnson. Ten minutes later Sweden went 2 - 1 up via Mellberg, but the situation only lasted 5 minutes until substitute Theo Walcott equalised. To crown a brilliant performance against a strong Swedish opposition Walcott turned provider for Danny Welbeck 12 minutes from the end, and England therefore won 3 - 2.

It was gone midnight when the taxi arrived to return Mr Wang and Mr Wu to their hotel in Maldon, but before they departed all smiles and good wishes they were presented with another memento of their stay in England. Mindful of the appropriate gift of the Huishan clay figurines they had presented him with on his visit to Wuxi a few months earlier, Tiny presented each of them with a Royal Doulton Toby Jug.

They left tired, elated, and pleased as Punch, and the boys from 1stCitySoft congratulated themselves on a job well done. Again, it had been a very different affair from the F. A. Cup Final, but this time they had cracked it, won the gold medal, and whooshed to the top of the tree.

The rest of the weekend passed quickly, but on Monday it was back to the grindstone. There was work to be done, loose ends to tie up, and accounts to be sorted out once and for all.

In the posh Hub apartment the clock radio alarm burst into life, and the familiar voices of Heart FM and Martin and Sue introduced another play of "Tonight's gonna be a good, good night". It was Monday at 8 am, and the usual buzz of activity was starting to well up around the centre of the first city of Essex. All things weren't by any means expected to be stirring awake. Norman Noble opened one eye and looked very briefly at the red digits on the face of the alarm. "Hmm 7.59." he muttered.

Then he realised that today he had a different responsibility other than the usual one to just turn up at work. Today he would have a passenger, the lodger who had now been living with him rent free for nearly 3 weeks, and who as far as he knew habitually didn't normally show his face until midday. However this morning strangely he could hear the water running in the bathroom. He dragged himself out of bed, ready to face the day, and found to his surprise that Duncan's bedroom was empty. He made coffee, sat down at the kitchen table to sip it, and waited for his cousin to appear.

What a surprise! There he was; Primark man, suited, booted with new shoes, white shirt, black tie, smart dark blue suit, looking very professional. Even his ginger barnet was under control.

"Ready when you are." Duncan smiled, "I'll make some toast while you're in the bathroom."

Norman scratched his head in disbelief, and just grunted, "OK, I'll be about 15 minutes."

At 8.45 am precisely the Carrera 911 engine roared, and the car slid out onto Springfield Road, making for the A12 and Colchester. Porscheman gunned it on the slip-road at the Cramphorn flyover, looked at his watch, and gave it the turbo large.

"18 minutes, to the office, easy".

Duncan popped out the one Hawkwind CD he'd brought with him, and pushed it into the player. "I've got a Silver Machine," sang the space cowboys.

"No, you haven't," thought Norman, "But, I have."

Upon arrival in Colchester, the new recruit was quickly installed in the accountant's office, and under close scrutiny from the marketing director, began on the job of sorting out the mess that Gordon had left the company in. They worked well together, and the huge pile of papers quickly receded to an easily manageable level, with Doughnuts sorting and instructing, and the fatman phoning and filing. After 3 hours and several coffees, they moved on to the computer to try and work out what exactly the position was. That was where they encountered a major obstacle towards achieving their aims.

Duncan asked, "Right, do you know Gordon's email address?"

"Yes, I've written it down for you here." said Hugh handing him a sheet of paper.

"Good, and have you got the password?"

"No, I don't know it, but maybe Tiny does."

A quick phone call and the chairman arrived, "What's the problem?"

"We don't know Gordon's email password, and of course we can't ask him, because he's still unconscious."

"And we'll also need his password to sign on, and I hope he's protected all the accounting files." added Duncan.

"Fuck! We're up shit creek without a paddle if we can't break into his files."

For several minutes they just sat there looking at each other wondering how to overcome the problem. Then a smart young man poked his head around the door, "How's it going?"

"We've hit an iceberg," said Hugh glumly, "We haven't got the effin' bean counter's passwords."

"Have a look in his diary, he might have written some clues in there." was suggested.

It took a while to find it, but a close inspection of the diary revealed nothing obvious, and it was back to scratching heads for all except the development director, who just said, "Give me 20 minutes. Have a coffee break or something. I'll come back to you."

Then he disappeared back into his own office, while the remainder of the team waited and drank more coffee as instructed. It was an anxious time for twiddling thumbs and wondering how to extricate themselves from this dilemma, and to be honest they felt a bit stupid that they had trusted their accountant and their office systems to such a degree that no arrangements had been made to deal with the contingency they now encountered. Duncan's experience at P.O.O.S. had proved invaluable up to this point, and he explained confidently that given the vital clues he could sort everything out pretty quickly.

Then the development director returned with a big smile on his face, "Cracked it!" he said, "Just as I thought."

He handed over a piece of paper with all the necessary passwords for Gordon's files; email, sign-on, and protected files.

"God! That's magic! How did you do that?" asked the chairman.

"Well, it's easier if you know how. Most people's passwords are related to something they remember easily. It's always a compromise between providing protection, and remembering what the password is, and keeping it simple. If you try birthdays, favourite holiday destinations, children's names, significant other's names, things that are close to your heart or valuable, places or events with a pleasant memory, addresses, and other things of that nature, it might take a while, but you'll get there eventually. They looked at the piece of paper, on which was written five lines,

"Email - Soldierboy,

Sign-on - Figueretas,

Files - Titaniumx2012,
Accounts - ClaryJ250559."
Finally there was a line saying "FinbarGB1976".
He sidled over to Norman and grinning madly he hugged him.
"That's wonderful! Well done!" he said," I get nearly all of it. Yes! Soldierboy is what he calls Spike. Figueretas is where they met. Titaniumx2012 is about his new car, and that one's Julian Clary and his birthday. But what's the last line."

"Oh, that's nothing, "said the computer genius with a grin, "That's the code you'll need to break into all his encrypted files."

Tiny was even more pleased, about to burst with delight, "But how do you know that?"

"Boss, you must have forgotten that I wrote all the encryption algorithms for him."

Someone had been worth his weight in gold that day, and everybody knew that without him they would be wallowing like hippopotami in a rapidly drying waterhole.

At 1:45 on Tuesday 19th June, in the Donbass Arena in Donetsk 49,000 spectators watched Wayne Rooney return for England in their final group match against the Ukraine, and score the only goal of the game in the 48th minute to put England through to the quarter finals against Italy. There was a double controversy about the result because Marko Devic was denied a goal in the second half, when his shot was hooked clear from behind the England goal-line by John Terry under the eyes of the additional assistant referee standing beside the goal (as confirmed by video replays). This incident reopened football's goal-line technology debate. UEFA and the chief refereeing officer Pierluigi Collina admitted on the following day that an error had been made and that Ukraine had possibly been denied a legitimate goal. But, video replays also showed that the match officials failed to spot that Artem Milevskiy was in an offside position in the build-up to Dević's ghost goal.

By the next day, Duncan had been charging his way through the accounts for 3 extended working days, and had news for Tiny, who on hearing the results of the investigations immediately called a meeting.

"Well, gentlemen," he began, "Our friend here has been wrestling with the tricky situation on the accounts, and I must report to you both good news and bad news."

There was silence and a steady concentrated interest. After so much tension they all wanted a quick and painless resolution. The chairman continued, "The good news is that Gordon had the accounts surprisingly close to completion, and our colleague assures me they won't take long to finalise and be ready for distribution."

That's exactly what they all wanted to hear, but then came the fly in the ointment.

"The bad news is the discovery that he's been cooking the books, and planning to line his own pockets by way of an immense scam. He had made a big play about co-ordinating the Companies House end of year returns with work for the new deal, but that was really because that's the only way his scam would work. I'm sorry to tell you that the returns were going to be falsified, and our former accountant was obviously planning to fly off into the sunset with a huge bundle of cash tucked under his arm."

"The dirty, cheating, gay bastard! I'll ring his fucking neck if he ever recovers." was perhaps an expected response from the marketing director. Norman didn't say anything, as he was only too pleased to have been so crucial and instrumental in helping to discover the attempted financial trickery in the nick of time.

There was a big, relieved pause, and then Duncan added, "Given the opportunity, and with the invaluable help of my trusty assistant, I can set everything back the way it should be, and salvage the situation in a couple of long days."

They were very pleased with their new bean counter and the way he had diligently applied himself to the daunting task of rescuing the company from financial quicksand. He would be a 1stCitySoft hero for many a fine day. The meeting finished and Tiny returned to his office with Duncan in tow. "Right! There are 2 things I want you to do for me now." he said very firmly. The new man had only worked for him for a few days, but recognised the assertive tone of the chairman's request. "What are they then, Boss?" he enquired.

"In your haste to get the job done for us please don't destroy any of the evidence of the attempted fraud. I've just spoken to an officer at Chelmsford Police Station, and they'll be sending someone round within the hour to work with you on building a case of fraud and false accounting. Make sure you retain all the records of how he was going to screw the company and embezzle all the money, so that we can hand everything over to the police. When he recovers, I'll make sure Hugh won't be anywhere near him wringing his neck, because he will be doing porridge at Her Majesty's pleasure. Oh! No pun intended. Sorry!"

Duncan smiled, "And the second thing, Boss?"

"I want everybody's passwords and entry codes changed to make sure that the swindling bastard cannot possibly get back into the system. And then I want all security records set up in a file that only myself, Hugh and Norman can get into."

"Sure thing, Boss." said a very happy Scotsman getting up and returning to his office.

CHAPTER 23

Revelation and Discovery

(Wednesday 20th June to Sunday 1st July 2012)

By Wednesday 20th June Gordon had been in Broomfield Hospital in a coma for a week, and Spike had endured the waiting game by his side for 12 hours of every one of those long and worry-filled days. On the morning of the 7th day, a Wednesday, he was there again; tired, dishevelled, distressed, and not looking forward to another empty, forlorn, desperate day. But overnight there had been a development. There had been clear signs of revival, and the specialists had decided that the patient could breathe without the aid of the ventilator. Although he was heavily sedated, his partner was pleased with a movement in the right direction, and resumed his bedside vigil. The morning passed slowly and inexorably towards another gloomy afternoon. The lunchtime drinks trolley was rattling its way along the ward, cups and saucers clinking together, and there was a subdued low chattering as patients ordered their teas and coffees. Suddenly the wounded golfer's eyes flickered open, watery and unfocussed; he groaned, took a laboured breath and came round, looked at his bedside companion, smiled painfully and croaked, "Hello, Soldierboy!"

The news of the recovery hit the 1stCitySoft team via a phone-call from Scruffbag at about 2 o'clock. At this precise moment in time this man who'd been unconscious for a week was a workmate, a friend, a human being in trouble, and whatever differences there were between him and the others were set aside. There was a collective sigh of relief. Old Golden Bollocks was 1stCitySoft's computer genius's worst nightmare but as a friend, Norman wished him no harm. The gay accountant had been the root cause of a great deal of aggravation with the marketing director, and the recent uncovering of his fraudulent plans had hardened the attitude towards him, but there was no way that the jolly fatman wanted him to be disabled or dead as a result of an accident on a golf course. The bean counter had been appointed by the chairman, and he had abused his position of trust in many ways, most of which nobody but Tiny knew about.

Initial reaction to the news was a sense of relief, but now that the full extent of the treachery had been discovered, it would be preserved in detail, and then circumvented to enable the company to move forward into its global future. This presented further problems for the boss, and he would need to tread very carefully in order to negotiate a way out of the dilemma unscathed.

During the afternoon the chairman decided that the best thing to do at the moment was to organise for him and his work colleagues to pay a visit to the hospital that evening. But before they went he insisted that they agree to say nothing about the discovery of the accountant's fiendish plans, adding that procedures were in place to gather all available evidence, confront him with it at an appropriate time, and ensure that he would then be arrested and end up in prison. Agreement was not difficult to achieve. Norman had a very strong sense of justice, and Hugh just said, "OK, I'm sure you know what you're doing, and it'll be fun to pretend we're all being nice to him. But I want to be there when the cheating, pooftah bastard gets his comeuppance."

At 7.30 that evening the 3 of them went to the hospital armed with presents. Tiny took a large box of Thornton's chocolates, Norman took a bunch of white grapes, and the joker, perverse as ever, took the latest issue of Zoo Magazine "To show him what he's been missing!"

Before they were allowed onto the ward, they were kept waiting in the dayroom while the nursing staff went off to find the consultant. After about 10 minutes of thumb twiddling and the fatman moaning about how much he hated hospitals, the neurology expert arrived and began to explain the situation. "Your friend has been very lucky," he said, "It's an odd case, but we can never be sure with this sort of accident exactly how long the patient will be unconscious. So the fact that he's now back with us is a bonus, and the first step on what may be a long road to a possible full recovery."

"How long?" asked Tiny.

"That's totally unpredictable. How long is a piece of string? Could be days, could be years."

"So, he's conscious and he knows where he is, and how he got here, does he?"

"I'm afraid that's not the case. Yes! He is conscious, and there's no indication on the scan of a long-term injury that would make it likely for him to lapse back into unconsciousness. Yes! He knows he is in hospital, and he recognises people. But, and it's a big but, he has no idea how he got here, and what happened at the golf course."

"Does he know that he's an accountant working for 1stCitySoft?"

"Definitely not! Not at this moment. And we can't tell you if that will come back to him in time or not. We will have to wait and see. He is suffering from a type of selective amnesia."

"OK, how long will he be in hospital for?" asked the chairman.

"He will be under observation for at least another 2 weeks, possibly longer. Now, I suggest you all go to see him together. It might bring parts of his memory back. But I can only give you 5 minutes at the most. He needs to rest." the consultant concluded.

He opened the dayroom door and led them to the bedside. Surprisingly the patient recognised all three of them by name, shaking hands and thanking them quietly for the presents, even the tongue in cheek gift. The 5 minutes was over in a flash.

The 3 visitors left the hospital accompanied by Spike, and Hugh already had it mind that the scruffy decorator might be spoiling for a fight and wanting to square up to him. So as soon as they were outside, he cut him off in his prime by grabbing his hand saying, "Listen, my friend, I'm very sorry for what's happened. It was an accident, and I know I played a part in it, and it makes me feel sick to think of it. Please forgive me?"

It hurt him to say that, especially in view of what secrets he guarded about Scruffbag and Tina. But the jolly fatman also knew his opportunity for justice would come. Tiny winked approval at his long term friend, knowing that his opportunity would also come. The Bohemian painter was surprised, and it cut the legs from underneath him, because he had wanted very much to punch someone's lights out. But all he answered was a quiet "OK, I understand. Least said soonest mended."

After Norman had been dropped off, the other 2 headed back to Tyrell's Close. Tina was over at Avalon House with Millicent, and so the boys talked over a coffee. For Tiny it seemed like an opportune time to take the risk that Gordon would forget about everything permanently, or at least long enough for the necessary wheels to turn, and perhaps it was the right time for a frank discussion. The two friends sat in the comfort of the lounge, and began with small talk about the hospital visit, sipping their coffee, totally comfortable in each other's company, but there was a sense that the conversation was leading up to something very significant.

"Nasty business, what he was up to," the chairman exclaimed, "Could have jeopardised our plans."

"Yes! Remember I kept on at you about his reluctance to do the necessary. I knew he was up to something, but you just kept protecting the cheating bastard."

"I know, mate, and I'm sorry, but my hands were tied, and I think it's about time I let you in on the reasons why I was powerless to do anything about it."

"I'm all ears." said Hugh with a smile.

"No, you're not. I know you, you're all heart, well beer gut actually." said Tiny smiling back, "Let me explain. It's a long story, be patient and listen carefully to what I have to say. It goes without saying that this is between me and you, and doesn't go outside this room. Agreed?"

"Agreed!"

"OK, you remember about 5 years ago we played in a charity cricket match against a team from the Brewers over at Coronation Park. It was just for fun, nothing serious?"

"Yeah, we thrashed them. I scored 35 runs, took 5 wickets for 9 runs, and we won by 87. It was a great day!"

"OK, well, I mislaid my cricket box that day, and that lanky bugger, what's-his-name, Charlie Evans, chucked a no-ball right in my nuts. Didn't half make my eyes water."

"He's an animal, can't bowl for toffee. What a wanker!"

"Well, since then I've been rendered incapable of, how shall I put it, rising to the occasion."

"No! Oh, mate! That's terrible being deprived of your pleasures, but surely you must have sought medical help. Surely they can do something, surgery, Viagra, whatever."

"No, I went private to Harley Street, had months of tests and prodding me about, and in the end it's just a fact of life. My firework is now definitely a damp squib."

"So, what's this got to do with our accountant, and his evil plans? I don't understand."

"I said it was a long story, and you'd need to be patient, so give me a chance and I'll get to the point eventually."

"OK, mate, sorry!"

Tiny took a deep breath, and continued," I'm quite a bit older than Tina, and after this stupid accident we had a serious chat. We love each other, and there's no way we would ever go our separate ways, but with me not functioning, that part of our marriage for her needed supplementing with the real thing. I had to recognise that she had needs beyond what I could do for her, and so we agreed that she could, shall we say, get her kicks elsewhere, and I would overlook her little flings. We would have what you might call an open marriage, a bit one-sided, but nevertheless that's what we decided."

Hugh was so surprised, he could say nothing, he just sat there and listened, stunned by the revelation about his closest friend's unbalanced open marriage being revealed to him.

The chairman continued." So she flirts, and has her flings, and I turn a blind eye, because I love her. I just insist that she doesn't make it too obvious."

"You say that you love her, mate, and are you sure that she loves you?"

Tiny rolled his eyes and frowned. "Yes! She loves me in her own way."

"What does that mean?"

That seemed to cause some annoyance.

"Look!" he explained, "We can't all have perfect marriages like you, with the lovely little wife, 3 great kids and a soppy lump of a dog."

That made the fatman think of just how lucky he was.

"Let's put it this way. There are many kinds of love. One man's good loving, is another man's not enough, and a third man's far too much. We're all different. Tina and I are happy together, and that's all that matters in the end. Like I say, as long as it doesn't take place under my roof......."

At that point, knowing what he knew, his colleague nearly choked on his coffee.

"You alright, mate?" asked Tiny, slapping him on the back, "Cough it up."

He still didn't want to say anything about the Spike and Tina incident, but now he also knew that what Millicent had declared about Tina's promiscuity a few weeks back was absolutely true.

"Anyway," he resumed, "That arrangement went on for a while, and we were both happy enough with it, until Gordon found out about it."

"That bastard crops up like bad apple again and again. How did that happen?"

"Well, you remember that fellow the police arrested trying to steal the goldfish after we had the garden remodelled while I was on my Phileas Fogg trip."

"Yes! Blimey! This is getting like an episode of bloody Eastenders, whatever next?"

"No! Listen! Tina doesn't know that I know he was a bloke called Simon, Simon Poole, and he had been stalking her since when we were living in East Bergholt. He was an old flame of her's from when she lived in Madrid, and worked as a model. Now, this Simon Poole bloke was known to our gay friend, because they met in Figueretas 12 years ago, round about the same time as he first ran into Spike. Unfortunately about 6 months ago Gordon bumped into him again and that's how he found out about Tina's flings."

"This is more complicated than an Agatha Christie plot; if there's any more I'll need to get Poirot in to sort it out."

"OK, so if you're with me so far, I'll get to the point."

"OK, Boss, fire away!"

"Back in February I started to have suspicions about the accounts being doctored. To me the monthly figures just didn't add up, and so I tackled him about it. That's when the shit hit the fan. He was very blatant about it. Held his hands up and admitted what he was up to. But he threatened to publicise my Tina's affairs and ridicule my name at a critical time for 1stCitySoft. If the truth had got out, it would have undermined our plans for the global project. So effectively the underhand bastard has been blackmailing me ever since I found out about his plans to cook the books. I couldn't do anything about his fiddling, or his reluctance to carry out the accounting review, or his leg swinging, staying off work when he wasn't really ill."

Now Hugh realised why the chairman had been unable to tell him about what was really going on, because if he did, Gordon had threatened to tell all. So in recent months the boss had been covering his arse trying to work out a way to make the progress towards 1stCitySoft with possibly falsified accounts, and money about to go missing into the fraudster's personal bank account. He was flabbergasted. All he could say was, "What a mess!"

Then the chairman added," Oh, and by the way, his plans were not a salami fraud, shaving bits off the system little by little. No! He was a greedy bastard; he was going for the big one. He was intent on embezzling over a million pounds in one fell swoop. That wouldn't have wiped the company out, but it would have made it look less promising to our Chinese and American partners. But in the plan that he had formulated, he needed to finalise the end of year accounting and submit falsified returns to Companies House to achieve his evil ends."

The fatman just sat there again. He couldn't believe it. What had been revealed to him was so much revelation, and so much underhand subterfuge by Golden Bollocks.

It was a few minutes before he responded. "Well I'm glad it's all out in the open now, but why didn't you just tell me? I'd have bought him off, and then found a way to have him disappear before he could get a chance to enjoy his ill gotten gains."

"You know that wasn't possible, mate. I'm glad it's out in the open too, but you must keep it under your hat."

They had been friends for a long time, and they had worked hard and played hard together, and now this conversation had brought them even closer together. Tiny was so glad he had someone like Hugh as a friend, and Hugh had even greater admiration for the man who could tolerate and survive such a difficult situation.

"That won't be a problem." was the reassuring reply, as Tiny started to boil the kettle for another coffee, and right at that moment they heard the sound of Tina opening the front door.

Then she appeared in the kitchen, Miss Iberia, looking as gorgeous as ever, perfect makeup, and not a hair out of place. It was difficult for the jolly fatman not to look at her in a slightly different way after what he had just learned, but she made it easy to carry on as normal.

"Hugo, dahling, how are you?" she smarmed

"Hola, chica," he grinned, and added "Where you beena, Tina?" with the best false smile he could manage.

"A su casa hombre, con Meelysont." she replied, kissing him on his outstretched hand.

He turned his back towards her and wiggled his immense arse, and then looked provocatively over his shoulder with a smile. "Does my boom look big in this?"

"Sure thing, hermano!" she answered, giving him a playful slap, and they both fell about laughing realising that without any hint of practice or preparation they had performed their usual greeting in reverse. Mr Balls had heard it a 100 times before, but not that way round, and he poured another coffee and chuckled as he greeted his little chica with a kiss on each cheek Mediterranean style.

"And how is Gordon?" she asked.

"Oh, much better, but he has lost part of his memory, he can't remember anything about 1stCitySoft, and the golf day is a complete blank, and it may or may not be permanent." he replied.

"Oh, poor thing!" she sympathised.

Thursday and Friday were hectic days at 1stCitySoft. The chairman cracked the whip, as he didn't want any time wasted in getting all the accounting work finished, and as a result both Duncan and Hugh worked well into both evenings to get the job done. It was gone 9 o'clock on Friday by the time they arrived at the Two Brewers well ready for a good drink. Tiny obliged with two pints of the Fuller's Pride, and Duncan, still in work mode, explained," It's all finished. We've tidied up the books, and finished the accounts review, and produced the Companies House end of year returns. As soon as we'd done that the information confirming 1stCitySoft's stable financial situation was immediately emailed to China and America. Oh, and don't worry, all the necessary evidence of the attempted fraud was preserved. The police are happy with the information that they've gathered, and are certain that they have a cast iron case against your former bean counter."

Everyone was both delighted and relieved. The joker was over the moon, and he was in danger of cracking his chubby face, he was smiling so much.

"Well done! Well done!" Tiny gushed, "Many thanks to both of you for your sterling efforts. We can all sleep easier in our beds tonight knowing that the situation has been rectified, and most important of all our plans for globalisation are now on a firm foundation."

Norman was in two minds. He was naturally pleased with the resolution of the outstanding problems at work, but not with the continuation of the cuckoo in the nest at home, especially now that Caroline was never off the scene. He suggested glumly,""Funny the way things turn out sometimes, isn't it? If my auntie Brunhilda hadn't had that unfortunate hang-gliding accident, then Duncan wouldn't have been here with his massive inheritance, and who knows where we'd have been with the accounts? He was lucky to land the job at 1stCitySoft when he did and we were lucky to get him, but now he's definitely earned the name Jammy Doughnuts, hasn't he?"

They all laughed, and Hugh ordered another round of drinks, making no exceptions for Spike, Ike and Mike who were as usual clustered around the dartboard. "See what the poofs want to drink will you, Nobless?" he requested. He wasn't going to spoil the fun of soon being able to watch his boss drop Gordon right in the shit from a great height, and so he kept up a pretence of being nice to the unaware Scruffbag. He did find it difficult to speak to him, now that he was sure of what he saw at Tina's when his colleague was away in China. His dislike for the decorator was not too obvious despite the occasional clashes. But he looked at him thinking "My God! He would roger a rabid dog. But why Tina? I thought she'd have more class than that bit of rough."

The pints flowed, and the evening progressed in its standard vein with the resident comedian holding court, ably assisted by his sidekick ginger barbarian. In the chief tellytubby's absence, the Vicarage Road mob didn't seem as easy to take the piss out of, but that wasn't going to deter their main antagonist.

"Hey, you know when we had the fancy dress night in here a few weeks ago?" enquired Hugh of the gay entourage.

"Yeah! What about it?" Mike replied.

"It was strange really, I was expecting you lot to take the opportunity to turn up dressed as the Village People; after all I spend so much time referring to you by that moniker. Then you blow it all, and surprise me by turning up as the Tellytubbies. I wasn't disappointed though. It gave me a lot of scope for pulling your legs. Brilliant night over all, but I'm intrigued as to why the switch."

Mike piped up, "There are six Village People, that's why."

"I know. There's a Policeman, a Native American who's a Red Indian, a G.I. or is it a Sailor, a Construction Worker, a Cowboy, and a Biker."

"Very good, Rambo, you passed that feat of memory, I didn't know you were so well educated regarding the gay community, "snarled Spike, "But I suppose you'd worked out who was who by then?"

"Of course, my friend, Attention to detail is my forte."

"Well, let's have it then."

The bar room comedian had been waiting for this, but he wasn't about to explain every facet of his reasoning.

"I thought Gordon would be the cowboy."

There was no explanation why, but he had his own private reasons.

"Spike, you would be the biker, as you wouldn't have to bother to change your normal mode of dress much. Ike would be dressed as a construction worker because of his muscle bound physique, and that leaves Mike as the Sailor, as I suspect 'cause he's the prettiest one, and perhaps it's nearly always his turn in the barrel."

Among the gay boys, there were smiles, as they had thought of appearing as the Village People, and the joker was spot on with his guesses, but not necessarily for the reasons he gave.

"Very good!" said Mike, "But we decided not to do the Village People because there are 6 of them, so we agreed on 4 Tellytubbies instead. Satisfied with that explanation are you? Good! Anybody want another drink?"

Scruffbag tried for the last word on the matter "Never mind, Rambo, it's all irrelevant anyway, as you said the world's going to end on 21st December whether you were pretending to be Roy Chubby Brown, or Billy Bunter, or Fatty Arbuckle, or even Giant Haystacks."

Duncan had got past his booze threshold now, and suddenly made a contribution to the discussion, "They can't schedule the end of the world for the 21st December. What about Hogmanay?"

Attention was switched from the gay entourage to the hero of the moment.

Hugh answered, "I don't think the Mayans were very likely to ask a load of porridge gobbling Caledonian Ceilidh cavorters if it would be alright to stage Armageddon 10 days before one of your pagan rituals."

"Bloody unfair if the prediction comes true," was the reply," but actually the 21st December 2012 is one of the most anticipated dates in history. Nobody knows what, if anything, will happen, but people always assume the arrival of some cataclysmic event. What we do know is that on that date the Earth crosses the middle of the Solar System, and that there may be a shift in magnetic polls from the ends of the earth. This could cause electronic devices to fail worldwide, and imagine how we'd cope if that happened. Nothing will work without electricity."

"Too heavy for me, my wee friend." screeched Hugh in a mock Billy Connolly accent.

All too soon the end of the evening's boozing was fast approaching, and the taxi to go back up Springfield Road arrived driven by Stanislav. He was by no means the favourite cabbie. There was still something sinister and dislikeable about him, and Hugh in particular seemed reluctant to communicate with him more than necessary. As they were all leaving, there was the usual last jibe at the slightly depleted gay clique, "Well you know, I expected the Village People, you turned up as the Teletubbies, and tonight you were the three stooges!"

They responded with fingers in the air as was customary, as they crammed into Spike's van as the less than adequate substitute for the nearly new Galaxy.

During the taxi ride home the passengers discussed Duncan's three personalities; normally quiet and unsociable, educated but mouthy after a few drinks, and thankfully very professional at work. They then resurrected Norman's assertion, in the way providence had intervened and begun to sort things out for them. They agreed that the accident to Gordon had resolved the financial mess, but only because of his memory loss and Duncan's mother Brunhilda's death in a hang-gliding accident in Scotland. When the taxi reached its destination and they climbed out, Stanislav spoke up, saying, "Yes! Sometimes providence plays a part in our lives. I would not be here in England now if my brother had not been deported back to Poland."

On Sunday 24th June the boys minus one assembled at the Ramsbottom mansion for another helping of European football. England had ridden their luck, and made their way through to the quarter finals against Italy. At 21:45 the Budweisers and Old Speckled Hens were ready in Avalon House, and 64,000 spectators sat with an air of expectation in the Olympic Stadium in Kiev. Hugh and Duncan were under orders from the rest of the lads to shut up and watch the football, and not repeat the distractions they had inflicted upon their mates for the previous game against France. However, when the Italians dominated from start to finish, and the England stars failed to live up to the occasion, there were oohs , arhhs and sighs of frustration, and the TV watchers felt like they may as well have been watching something more positive and exciting like "I'm a Celebrity get me out of here."

No score at half time drifted on, to no score at 90 minutes, and almost predictably to 0 - 0 after extra time. So it was penalties, and at that point in the game mine host uttered the bleedin' obvious that any England fan knows to his ultimate despair, "Oh dear! We are NOT good at penalties".

It was time to hide behind the couch and watch with a beer in one hand and the other hand half covering your eyes.

But it started well, with Gerrard equalising after bad boy Balotelli's characteristic scowling as he scored. Then Montolivo failed to net, and a miracle seemed possible as Rooney put his effort away. England were 2 - 1 up; could it be their day to win on penalties at last?

No! The joy was short-lived, because the dependable Pirlo strode up and confidently chipped in, and Ashley Young blew his shot bringing the score back to 2 - 2.

To take England's chances from looking at a victory, to staring down the barrel of a gun within a few short minutes, Nocerino then made it 3 - 2 to Italy, before another Ashley, Ashley Cole this time, took the next penalty, and bottled it, giving Italy advantage.

Mine host swore," Effin wankers! We shouldn't let players with names like Ashley represent their country at football."

Everybody knew it was a knee jerk reaction, typical Ramsbottom, spur of the moment comment. Nobody reacted; they were transfixed on the TV screen waiting for the inevitable. All it needed now was for Diamanti to put his attempt home. He did!

England had lost on penalties again. Italy on reflection had deserved to win, they were the better side, and proved it by going on to the final.

The boys left Avalon House to go their separate ways, all beset with a familiar sinking feeling, a feeling that their footie host reflected many in our small, proud country had endured repeated times since the glorious triumph of Bobby Moore's heroes back in 1966.

It was Monday morning and the clock radio alarm burst into life, and the familiar voices of Heart FM and Martin and Sue introduced another play of Rihanna singing "We found love in a hopeless place". The usual buzz of activity was starting to well up around the centre of the newly invested City of Chelmsford. In a posh flat in the Hub things were beginning to stir awake. Norman Noble opened one eye and looked very briefly at the red digits on the face of the alarm. "Hmm 7.59." he muttered.

Then he realised there was nobody lying next to him in the bed, and propped up on one arm looked at the picture of Clarisa on his bedside table.

In only a few short months she had changed his life. Now, he was a one gal guy, and she was that gal with a certainty that he had never felt before. He picked up the picture frame, and examined it, rolling back onto the mattress and holding the image above him with both arms outstretched declared, "She is beautiful! Look at those lovely green eyes, that sensuous smile, those dimples by the sides of her mouth. Oh. I wish she was here with me now."

He closed his eyes, and clasped the picture frame to his chest, and slipped into a daydream about making love with her, slowly, and ever so, ever so, deliberately.

Only a few miles away across town in her flat in Sandon, Clarisa Hinton was also waking up at about the same time, to the same radio station, and the same song. She sang along under her breath, and just like every morning when she woke up, the first thought on her mind was a wonderful, gentle, handsome, well groomed man; her Normie. There was a chill in the air, and just as it had done for months and months it was raining outside. She snuggled back under the duvet, and imagined that her Normie was there, holding her close, snoozing gently, breathing in her ear, whispering things that she longed to hear.

"He is my man; he is the one," she thought, "Oh. I wish he was here with me now." as she drifted off back for a short doze.

A few minutes later, she was gently woken up, as a furry, purring, slightly damp moggy expertly negotiated the top-light window, jumping down, and began padding her paws on the pillow next to her head. "Phyllis, you naughty girl, where have you been, it's been 3 days you've been out on the tiles. Mummy was worried about you. I suppose you'll be hungry now?"

Clarisa got up and moved slowly into the kitchen yawning. She put the kettle on, and opened two pouches of Whiskas for Phyllis. Without ceremony or gratitude, her feline friend devoured the food quickly, as her mistress prepared herself for another day at work.

She loved her little flat, it was perfect for her needs, with a big enough lounge, kitchen and bathroom, and 2 small bedrooms. It was the upstairs flat in what had formerly been the Sandon General Store and Post Office, converted into 3 maisonettes in 2000 and from the street it looked like a semi-detached house. She liked the fact that there was no garden, and she had no window boxes, or hanging baskets to tend to. That suited her because she had the opposite of green fingers, in that every plant she had ever nurtured had died. She also liked the anonymity of her home, which could only be accessed via the path around the cottage next door, and that made her feel safe and secure.

At just after 9 o'clock she patted Phyllis goodbye as the moggy settled down for another lazy day indoors. She grabbed her brolly, went down the stairs, and locked her front door. Then she walked quickly through the continuing rain past the church of St Andrews, and the Crown pub on the village green, and along Brick Kiln Road towards the Sandon Park and Ride.

She had lived in Sandon for 5 years, and it was her village, pretty, unspoiled, green, quiet, and surprisingly rural for somewhere that was only a short walk from the civilisation of the Chelmsford suburb of Great Baddow, and a 5 minute bus ride from the City centre.

Soon, the bus came to a halt outside what had once been Dukes nightclub, and she alighted ready for another working day as a legal secretary for Crooks, Watt, Sawyer, Cumming legal partnership in Duke Street.

With England out of the running for the European championships, interest in the football had waned somewhat, but Hugh was delighted to learn that on Thursday 28th June the Italian team had beaten Germany, the old football enemy, 2 - 1.

Between that game and the final on 1st July the fatman had been feeling unwell again, and had pleaded tiredness due to recent work overload in order to avoid the Friday session at the Brewers. That wasn't like him at all. He had been having further dizzy spells ever since what he was now calling the "Pork Scratchings Nightmare" at the end of April. It was in his nature to make light of it, but underneath the bravado he was becoming more worried. Every time he ate a little too much, which for him was quite often, or exerted himself, which for him wasn't very often, there would be a strange tightening sensation in his chest. When he had arrived home after each of the Friday evening sessions at the Two Brewers he had the same sensation, accompanied by a headache and breathlessness, and that occurred whether he'd indulged in pork scratchings or not. To his great despair for a man who enjoyed his food so much, he found himself frequently losing his appetite, which didn't really fit with his assumption that he was merely suffering from indigestion. Nevertheless shares in the company that manufactured Gaviscon were rocketing, as he attempted to ease his discomfort with daily dosages.

But Millicent had been watching him closely for weeks, and had noticed a change in the way her man behaved, and eventually on Sunday 1st July, as preparations for another boozy get together for the Euro final game between Spain and Italy were being made, she squeezed the unpalatable truth, and the extent of his worries, out of him. Her immediate reaction was to phone all the boys, say that Hugh wasn't well, and to cancel the gathering. He watched the game by himself, miserable and feeling isolated, closely monitored by his concerned wife, who allowed him only orange juice to slake his thirst. The Spanish team overwhelmed the Italians and demonstrated their undoubtable superiority with a very convincing 4 - 0 win.

At the beginning of that weekend the Environment Agency had declared that the period April to June was one of the wettest on record across England and Wales. The rainy weather had by then broken UK records for the previous three months of this year, and had been the wettest second quarter in the UK since records began in 1910. This was confirmed during a 2nd day of disruption after torrential rain doused parts of the country leaving thousands without power, and affecting transport and schools. Wales, the Midlands, North-East England, Northern Ireland and parts of Scotland were deluged with continuous downpours. Even without the latest storms, this had been the second wettest June since 1910, as up to 27th June, the total UK rainfall was 130.1mm - just 6mm short of the 2007 record.

CHAPTER 24

Raindrops keep falling on my Head

(Monday 2nd July 2012)

Predictably it was pouring down again on Monday morning, and Millicent wasn't taking any nonsense from Hugh this time, and now that she was fully aware of the frequency of his "indigestion", she insisted on going with him to see the doctor.

"So, did you read the leaflets I gave you?"
"Yes, of course, but I'm not sure that they're at all relevant to me."
Doctor Harriman noticed an uncomfortable shift of his subject's posture in the chair when he asked the question, and therefore was convinced that the answer was far from the truth.
He also noticed the concerned look that the patient received from the wife, before she said "What leaflets, darling?"
The G. P. leaned back in the padded leather chair, swung around 90 degrees to look away and out of the window, drew a deep breath, sighed, and suggested, "Well, what do want me to do? I can send you away with some pills, a blood test form, and some reassurance. But it won't do any good until you stop your denial, quit hiding things away, and tell me the truth, the whole truth, and nothing but the truth. I can only help you with the right diagnosis, if you first help yourself by being honest with me, and I've known you since you were in short trousers, so your body language today is like an open book to me."
Mrs Ramsbottom was giving her husband a pleading look as if to say, "Please, darling man of my life, let's get this problem out in the open now once and for all.", and then after a pregnant pause, suddenly tears rolled down his cheeks, and he broke down sobbing like a baby.
The G. P. was very correct and very patient, offering a box of tissues, and waiting for a response. Several minutes passed before Hugh brought himself back to some composure, and then still fighting back the tears he started to talk.
"I'm Hugh Ramsbottom, the jolly fatman, and people have expectations of me. I laugh off everything bad, I take the piss out of the slightest weakness, and I always have the last word. If you're in trouble you can come to me, you can depend on me, and with a quick quip and a cheery wave I'll solve all

your problems, because I'm strong, I'm tough, I'm reliable and I'm a big man who doesn't have any problems."

Doctor Harriman listened taking in every nuance, and anticipating a big shift in the mode of the assertion that he was hearing, a "but" that would change the direction and tone of the confession.

Millicent just looked at her man relieved that at long last he was revealing his heart.

"So, my friend," sighed the G. P. empathetically, and leaning forward to grasp his patient's hand he stared deep into his tearful eyes and added, "That's the foundation from which you are working. But if we are to make any progress here, you are going to have to tell me just exactly what it is health-wise that you feel is undermining your foundation. Do you understand, Hugh?"

That was it! The dam burst, and a flood of tears and information poured out of the distinctly unjolly fatman, as he explained everything from the "Pork Scratchings Nightmare" to all his recent uncomfortable symptoms. The whole story surged in a relentless tidal wave, with no holds barred. Stress at work, admissions of binge drinking, confessions of comfort eating, descriptions of mood swings, feelings of depression, it all came out, and at the end, when the doctor was completely sure that the catharsis was exhausted, he smiled and simply praised, "Well done, my friend, now we've got something to work on."

Time for tears was over. Now both the Ramsbottoms were almost giggling with relief as the petite little cashew nut quietly smiled a "Thank you, darling, I love you." and the incredibly obese marketing director nodded back a "Ditto, my little Reepicheep."

"Right!" uttered the clinician with a renewed confidence, "You're obviously not at death's door, but you may have suffered a heart problem, and we'll need to have you checked up pronto. What you're describing, that tight sensation in the chest and breathlessness is called angina, and that's caused by the narrowing of your coronary arteries. Until we know exactly what's been happening I can't prescribe anything for you, but I'm going to make you an appointment to see a cardiologist, to get an ECG and an echocardiogram done. Go out to the nurse with this blood test form, and when the pathology lab have analysed your results we may, or may not, be able to tell if you've had a recent heart attack. After the time lapse it might not be conclusive. In the meantime, I'm going to sign you off work for a month, and I want you to rest, take it easy, and here's that collection of leaflets for you to read again, or should I say read instead of binning this time. You must take your situation seriously. You are overweight, and probably don't take any real exercise other than lifting pints of beer. Frankly, it's a bonus that you don't smoke. Any questions?"

The patient and his lady wife both shook their heads, and the G.P. reached a salutary conclusion.

"Try not to worry. We will sort you out as quickly as possible, but I stress this isn't a game, this is for real. Promise me you will take all the advice seriously, otherwise I am flogging a dead horse, and to put no finer point upon it, Hugh, that dead horse could be you."

They shook hands and went out of the consulting room. The blood test was taken, and as they were about to leave Dr Harriman came out to the waiting room with a letter showing that he had made an appointment at the Cardiology Centre for 10 am the next day.

The Ramsbottoms, with their considerable wealth, were private patients, but nevertheless their G. P. had found it necessary to pull a few strings in order to arrange for such a quick consultation with the cardiologist. So when they attended the Broomfield Hospital Cardiac Centre the next morning the ground had been well prepared. Five minutes after arriving they were called to see the top man, Mr E. C .Gee. The fatman knew he couldn't tell him any lies, and his wife wasn't going to let him do so. Again, it had to be the truth, the whole truth, and nothing but the truth, and the complete episode was poured out, this time without tears. Then the specialist smiled and with a confident sincerity said "Thank you for your honesty. I can reveal now that I've been fully briefed by your G. P., and I already knew all about you. Forgive me, but I just had to double check that we hadn't missed anything."

"So what happens now?" the patient asked.

"There's no need for any alarm, but you have possibly had some sort of critical cardiac episode, and remarkably for a man of your weight, and obvious interests in food and drink you have survived, and appear to be relatively healthy. We need to carry out some tests, to establish what the true situation is. Unfortunately yesterday's blood test was, as suspected, inconclusive as to whether there has been a myocardial infarction. So we'll start with a more comprehensive blood test, take your blood pressure, and then there'll be an ECG, that's an electro-cardiogram which will illustrate the electrical activity of your heart rhythms. After that we'll do an echocardiogram which will gives us pictures of your heart in action. At the end of those tests, I will talk to you again, and we'll take it from there."

They left the consulting room, and spent the rest of the morning going through all the prescribed testing. It seemed that a weight had been lifted off Hugh's shoulders now that his problems were in the open being analysed, and he joked his way through the various investigations.

They sat in the atrium of the hospital entrance, and ate tuna and sweet-corn sandwiches for lunch, with fresh orange juice. The fatman could have eaten 3 or 4 sandwiches and a plate of chips, and would have preferred to sink a few pints of bitter, but his ever present carer had him on a tight rein, and she wasn't going to release it. At just after 2 pm they were called back into the consultant's room. He looked serious, but not excessively so. "I've got some bad news, but it's not the end of the world. We have the technology, and we know how to use it to alleviate your problems."

"OK, I can take it. Tell me what you've found." The patient insisted with a contrived grin.

"The ECG and echocardiogram indicate that you've had a myocardial infarction, a heart attack, probably around the time you describe as the Pork Scratchings Nightmare, but your heart rhythm is fairly stable, and we need to ensure that it stays that way. We need a further test to confirm it, but I would suspect that you have some atherosclerosis in one or more of your coronary arteries. Your cholesterol readings are unsatisfactory, and we'll need to address that. Your blood pressure at 150 over 100 is too high, and we need to bring that down. I will be prescribing a lot of medication to help avoid any further problems."

The cardiologist stopped and looked over the top of his glasses waiting for a response.

"There's more isn't there?" a deflated fatman questioned.

"Yes, and I think you know what's coming. Doctor Harriman tells me that in your twenties you were an athletic 12 stone. You are a tall, large, man but when we weighed you today it was frightening. You are now over 20 stone, and you didn't get that way by jogging to work, after swimming 10 lengths at Riverside, and pumping iron for 20 minutes in the Excel gym."

He paused and got no response to his scolding forthright statement other than a look of resignation. Then he continued," Hugh, you have had a serious warning. Please heed it! The cemetery is full of men, and women, who ignored the facts, and were unable to adjust to a healthier lifestyle. If you want to be one of them soon, ignore all the good advice, otherwise what I want you to do is follow it as if your life depended on it, because it does!"

Despite the rather brutal way in which Mr Gee was illustrating the situation, the fatman liked his tell it like it is approach.

"OK, what do I have to do then?"

"Take the medication I'm prescribing religiously. You must lose weight, begin an exercise regime, and cut down drastically on the booze. The leaflets you've been given outline a plan for starting an alternative lifestyle gradually and we'll discuss that with you further."

Millicent nodded at her man in agreement, "I will be with you all the way, darling." she promised.

"OK," asserted Mr Gee, "Take this prescription to the pharmacy. Start taking the pills immediately as prescribed. I've made you an appointment back at your surgery this evening to discuss this further, and I'm fast-tracking you for an angiogram, so we can have a look at your heart from the inside. He paused again, "Any questions?"

The Ramsbottoms looked at each other, and then both said, "No! Thank you."

The consultation was finished, and some time later they made their way home with a different perspective on the remainder of their lives, and with a large bag full of medication.

Later that evening they returned to see their G.P.

"I'm sorry, that you've had this bad news," he sympathised," But look at it this way. Now you know what's wrong, we can start to do something about it. First of all; have you read the leaflets?"

"Yes." replied Hugh honestly this time, while Millicent nodded again, "And we've been googling for a couple of hours to find out more."

"That's good and bad. Having some knowledge that helps you to understand the whys and wherefores is good. But the reason why they say a little knowledge is a dangerous thing could have been perfectly designed to warn you off setting too much store by Internet information. Be discerning and careful with what you read there."

"It's learning not knowledge," the jolly fatman offered with a grin. This was one that we couldn't resist whatever the gravity of the moment,

"Sorry!" replied the G. P. quizzically.

"Alexander Pope actually said that a little learning is a dangerous thing." informed the learned one.

The doctor looked at his patient and smiled, "You haven't changed have you? I stand corrected."

After a brief pause he resumed with, "Let's get back to the point then. You've had the tests and they've confirmed a problem, and when you've had the angiogram we'll have an even better understanding of the cause. The medication is routinely prescribed and we know it works, although there may be some side effects. Let's see, we've prescribed a beta-blocker to prevent arrhythmia and keep your blood pressure down, and a statin to lower cholesterol. We've got Bisoprolol, that's going to keep your heart rhythms stable, and Simvastatin because your cholesterol reading is 7.1 at the moment, and it needs to be more like 5. There's also this little bottle. It's a GTN spray, and whenever you get the angina sensation you give it a couple of puffs under your tongue. I'm sure you've read up about all of these, but are there any questions?"

Two heads shook in mutual response, so the analysis continued," Right so far we've only gone over what we can do for you. Now it's your turn to do something, or to be more precise everything, for yourself. I suggest that you regard these things as instructions instead of advice if you like."

Hugh knew that what was coming again was the expected advice about food, and beer, and exercise.

"First priority is to lose weight by cutting down on your food intake, and for the next month no booze at all. Then I want you to begin an exercise regime, very gentle at first but building up to something that will have long term benefits. You won't be on your own working out how to do those things, because I'm booking you on a Cardiac Rehabilitation Course. That'll be once a week for 6 weeks at Broomfield, and they'll deal with all the necessary aspects of caring for your heart in a controlled and monitored environment. Oh, and myself and the Cardio Team will continue to monitor you regularly."

It had been a gruelling few days for the Ramsbottoms, and they were becoming numbed by all the information flow. They sat there in silence. Hugh had been a snotty little brat in short trousers when Dr Harriman had first become the Ramsbottom seniors G. P. Although he hated bothering "the quack" about anything, there was a feeling of trust, a humanity, and a warmth between them.

"OK, I'll see you again, once you've had the angiogram, and we know then what the next steps will be."

Tiny and Tina popped over to Avalon House later that evening, with flowers and sympathy. Millicent was very pleased with the unexpected tokens of friendship and support, and Hugh made jokes about racing his mobility scooter through the High Chelmer Shopping Centre knocking over all those youngsters too busy on their mobiles to look where they're going. Behind all his bravado, he was shocked. He'd had his very large sense of immortality thrown in the dustbin. Mrs Ramsbottom was going to be the resolute and consistent one now. In a sense she would be taking over, she would guide the ship, and make sure that her man "took the medicine", all of it, at the right time. It was going to be tough for both of them, but she was sure that the only way she would fail to do the necessary to knock her husband back into shape would be if she died in the attempt, and that prompted him to fall to pieces as a consequence.

The very next day she set ground rules and they discussed them at length. The first bone of contention would be the booze, and the insistence on no alcohol for a month would be difficult, but she was determined to play tough love on that score," It's no booze at all, or myself and the boys pack our bags and go and stay at my mum's, and leave you to stew here and commit suicide on your own."

She'd never talked to him so assertively since her insistence on what she'd wanted for their wedding nearly 20 years ago, and he knew in no uncertain terms that she meant what she said. There was an equally controlled regime as far as food was concerned. Three properly balanced meals on a rigid timetable everyday, and no snacks, seconds, extras, night time fridge raids or takeaways was going to be the norm. Then, convinced she was on a roll, and as a drastic diversion from mere discussion, she suddenly said, "Right put on your most comfortable walking shoes. We are going to take your dog for a walk."

Hugh was like a scolded child, and he obeyed without question. Bimbo was very excited, and happy to be going out earlier than usual with both his masters. They strolled slowly down Stump Lane, and through the alleyway to cross Springfield Green, and then back past the Endeavour to their home in Springfield Road.

He would have given his eye teeth for a quick pint in there, but under her close supervision he was batting on a sticky wicket. They hadn't broken any records for speed on the walk, but he had an angina attack as they neared the house, and had to use his GTN spray. He was upset, and almost cried, and she showed the expected sympathy, but was also glad that the extent of his problems had been so easily demonstrated. That was a little event with big consequences. It was from that point on in their lives that the jolly fatman knew he had to make changes, and his loving wife became convinced that she could help him do everything that was necessary.

EPILOGUE

"Chelmsford - The First City of Essex"

There are many unanswered questions as we leave Norman and Hugh and the rest of the crew at the beginning of July 2012. Throughout the first six months of the year there have been many changes.

But what lies in store for boys and their nearest and dearest?

Norman's life has changed in 2012. He was an important factor in the NerdiSoft development. But he's a much bigger wheel in the 1stCitySoft plan. He used to be an incorrigible womaniser, but Clarisa has changed him into a one gal guy.

Will the path of true love continue to run ever smooth for Norman and Clarisa?

What will happen to the giant moggy Phyllis?

Hugh has always been his own man; a law unto himself. Now he's got big, big, problems, just at the time when his investment in NerdiSoft could turn into megabucks when it becomes 1stCitySoft.

Will Millicent be able to set Hugh on the right track to a healthier lifestyle?

Will Hugh live to see the fruits of his labours?

What triumphs and disasters are waiting for Hugh's beloved Clarets in the season 2012/13?

Tiny's life has changed in 2012. He was the chairman of NerdiSoft; a small UK company. Now he's on the threshold of becoming the main man in 1stCitySoft, a global player.

Will Tiny see 1stCitySoft successful in their massive venture?

Will Tina and Tiny's open marriage endure?

Gordon has never really been a mainstream NerdiSoft man, and has seriously undermined the potential transformation of the company into 1stCitySoft.

Will he make a full recovery from the unfortunate golfing accident?

What will happen to him now that his plans to embezzle a million pounds from 1stCitySoft have been uncovered?

How will Spike react to his partner's situation?

What will happen to Mike and Ike if Gordon goes to prison?

Stanley and Lisalotte have been muddling their way through the year, and there has been good news and bad news.
Will Stanley be able to start up his butcher's business again?
What unusual sources of local meat will Stanley have at his disposal if he does?
Will Chester Gannet be involved again?

Will Lisalotte allow Stanley to start up his butcher's business again?
Will she ever gain relief from her gout?

Will the truth about what happened with Chester Gannet ever come to light?

What does Cher and Helen's relationship have in store for them?

Why is "Ector Blunt such an obnoxious little prat?

Will Duncan thrive and prosper among the Sassenachs?
What does the future hold for him and Caroline?

Will Terry Smith survive the Double Trouble fruit cocktail?

The drought came to an end in April, but will it ever stop bloody raining?

Will the Olympics and the Paralympics be an overwhelming success for Britain?

All these questions may be answered in the 2nd novel in the series.
Coming soon - "First City of Essex - Many Diversions, One Destination"

Lightning Source UK Ltd.
Milton Keynes UK
UKOW04f1916110917
309009UK00001B/196/P